UNFORGETTABLE

Lindsay McKenna

Blue Turtle Publishing

Unforgettable
First edition 2023
Original Copyright © 2015, R. Eileen Nauman
ISBN: 978-1-951236-48-9, Print Edition

Excerpt from *Hostile Territory*
Original Copyright © 2015, R. Eileen Nauman

All rights reserved. Except for use in any review, the reproduction or utilization of this work in whole or in part in any form by any electronic, mechanical, or other means, now known or hereafter invented, including xerography, photocopying, and recording, or in any information storage or retrieval system, is forbidden without the written permission of the publisher, Blue Turtle Publishing, 7050 Oak Level Road, Bassett, VA 24055 USA.

This is a work of fiction. Names, characters, places, and incidents are either the product of the author's imagination or are used fictitiously, and any resemblance to actual persons, living or dead, business establishments, events or locales is entirely coincidental.

This edition is published by arrangement with Blue Turtle Publishing Company.

Dear Readers,

You've met the Shadow Team in *Last Stand*, Book 1, and Book 2, its sequel *Collateral Damage*. Readers have fallen love with the strong secondary character, Ukrainian combat medic, Alex Kazak. They clamored for his book, *No Quarter*, Book 3 of the series. Now, his best friend Nik Morozov story begins in Book 4, *Unforgettable*. Daria and Nik were strangers. They had a mission to perform. And it all seemed small in comparison to Ukrainian combat medic Nik Morozov, who went under cover and turned to illegal drug smuggling to save his brother's life. The US government insisted Nik have an undercover woman partner to help capture a Russian drug team leader, Ustin Korsak. The last thing he needed was to fall hard and fast for the woman who would pretend to be his romantic interest.

Daria Kozlof was abandoned by her mother in St. Petersburg, Russian. A kind Ukrainian couple adopted her and took her to Kiev where she found family. She had talents and real skills that the US military wanted badly, and she became a citizen of that country and became a world-class Marine Corps sniper fighting in the Middle East.

Thrown together in the Peruvian jungle, each with their brutal baggage from their pasts hanging over them, Nik and Daria had nowhere to turn but to one another. Neither of them expected the fierce passion that exploded between them. It was the wrong time and wrong place. Russian drug smugglers took no prisoners when someone crossed them. Danger spiraled into pushing Nik and Daria closer to one another. And closer to death.

Warmly,
Lindsay McKenna aka Eileen Nauman

Dedication

To all the readers who love romantic military suspense!

CHAPTER 1

Daria sat tensely in the mission briefing room, waiting for Jack Driscoll, the owner of Shield Security, to arrive. She groaned to herself, her hands damp as she opened her laptop, getting ready to discuss her forthcoming mission. Her left thigh ached and she shifted to relieve the tension in it. Three knife wounds had been sliced into it as she'd fought for her life against the Taliban soldier who had tried to kill her with his curved dagger. Daria pushed the visceral memories away. They haunted her nightly. She couldn't allow them to cloud her thoughts now. Jack was giving her a chance to retain her position as a security contractor at Shield, after she'd refused to be a sniper any longer.

Her throat closed with tension as she swept her long, thick black braid between her shoulder blades. The early May spring air was welcome to the Alexandria, Virginia region. Daria wore a bright-red long-sleeved cotton pullover, and her black leather jacket hung on the back of her chair. Her leather boots, a matching black, were wet due to the Spring rains coming and going in the area. She fiddled with opening her work laptop, moving the cursor to the mission tab on the toolbar. Was she ready for a mission after what had happened to her four months earlier?

Daria didn't know, but the psychiatrist who worked at Shield, Dr. Kate Armstrong, felt she was ready for some kind of low-level mission to get her back in the saddle once more. She hated that her fingers trembled as she pushed a few errant strands of hair off her furrowed brow. Her hands had always been steady as a rock before she'd nearly died on that Afghanistan op. Daria tried to control her breathing. Any moment now, Jack would enter. She had worked for two years with SHIELD as a sniper and had always done a good job, had always been successful on her missions. *But not that last one.* Her spotter partner, Melissa Andrews, had been stabbed to death during the botched mission, and Daria had barely survived it herself. Guilt ate at Daria. Why the hell hadn't she paid closer attention to her instincts? When Jack had told them there was perishable intel from a nearby village located by the Af-Pak, Afghanistan-Pakistan, border, and that they were to take out an HVT, high value target, there, Daria hadn't felt good about it, but hadn't spoken up. Two days after building their hide to wait for the Al-Qaeda HVT to cross the border, they'd been attacked one night by five Taliban soldiers with knives.

"No...," she whispered fiercely beneath her breath, shutting her eyes. Kate had taught her that when the memories came slamming back, when the adrenaline started to course through her veins, to start taking slow, even breaths. Kate had offered to give her anti-anxiety medication, but Daria hated the thought of being drugged up. She would handle this on her own, or else. Everything else in her life had been hard and challenging. The attack she'd survived was just one more thing she had to struggle through.

The door quietly opened.

Daria's eyes snapped open as Jack Driscoll entered the room. He gave her a slight smile of welcome, his sharpened gaze on her. He was six feet tall, as lean as his military nickname, 'Jaguar', implied, and moved with the silence that only an ex-Navy SEAL could pull off. He was dressed in a bright Hawaiian shirt and ivory Chinos and wore a pair of Merrill hiking boots, a favorite of some SEALs. Jack, as always, appeared casual. He nodded to Daria and pulled out the chair at the other end of the polished maple table that gleamed with gold highlights. His black hair was military short, emphasizing his oval face and strong chin. There was nothing soft about Driscoll and Daria had always appreciated that he ran SHIELD like the military: Well-disciplined and organized. His employees, for the most part, had been handpicked from the various branches of military service.

"Hey," Jack said, sitting down, "good to see you back here, Daria. How are you feeling?"

She wanted to tell him the truth, that she was unsure about any mission, still feeling so raw and uncertain. She'd pushed and begged and pleaded with Kate to certify her ready for some kind of low impact mission. Daria was slowly going crazy in her two story cabin outside the city, as her physical body healed from the massive damage done to her left thigh. The walls were closing in on her. She *had* to be distracted and a mission would sure as hell accomplish that. But if Kate, and especially Jack, knew this truth of why she was here, sitting in the briefing room, neither would approve her ready to return to mission status.

"I'm fine, Jack." Daria forced a smile. "Feels good to be back here, frankly. I'm ready." All lies of various colors and intensity. She saw him gauge her, open his laptop and turn it on. Jack was renowned to have an almost psychic ability to look through a person and see their real mental and emotional state, as well as their intent. Could she fool him? Would Kate's written approval be enough?

"How's the leg doing?" he asked, looking up over the top of his computer at her.

"Really good."

"I see here you've finished the physical therapy portion on it," he said, pointing to the screen, looking over her medical evaluations.

"Yes."

"Still tender? Hurt a little when you put a lot of stress on it?"

Daria wasn't going to lie about that. "Yes, but a hot bath or shower cures the stiffness afterward. No problem."

"I see Kate's released you from your psych eval, for duty."

Nodding, her mouth going dry, Daria said, "I'm more than ready to get back to work, Jack. I'm climbing the walls. I'm not used to being put out to pasture like this."

He gave her a thoughtful look and nod. "Yeah, but this is the first time you've been wounded and almost died, Daria. Sometimes, Type A operators, like ourselves, want to try and bounce back too fast from such an experience."

Stomach clenching, Daria held his incisive look. She could feel Jack's almost psychic energy piercing her mind and heart. She had one hand beneath the table, resting on her right thigh, finger curved into her palm. "I'm ready," she said abruptly, as if daring him to disagree with her. Because, if Jack smelled any weakness in her, she knew he'd take her off whatever mission he had in mind for her. And she'd be forced to pace rooms, climb walls, and want to scream, unable to stand the cascade of memories that she couldn't escape. If she had a mission, she knew the past would haunt her less. She'd be focused on something else. Distracted. And she was desperate to avoid all the emotional pain and horrifying memories of that attack. Especially the loss of Melissa, which she held herself personally responsible for. She had been the sniper and Melissa, her spotter. It had been her duty to keep her spotter alive and safe. But she hadn't. And now, Melissa was dead. Would she ever get Melissa's screams out of her head? Daria didn't think so, but would give her right arm if they would stop waking her up every night.

There was a knock on the door. Jack lifted his chin, calling out, "Come in…"

Confused, Daria stared at the opening door.

"Ah, here's Alex and Lauren…," and Jack gestured toward the married couple as they entered the room.

Alex Kazak shut the door behind him. He sat down next to his wife, Lauren Parker-Kazak, across the table from Daria.

Daria smiled, happy to see them. She was Ukrainian by birth and so was Alex. Ever since she'd come to Shield, Alex had been a guiding force, like a big teddy-bear brother to her. And Lauren, who was the chief sniper instructor at Shield, ran the program for those entering the civilian security company. Both had taken her under their wings, and she felt warmth combined with happiness spread through her chest by their mere presence. "Hey, nice to see you two here. I didn't know you were coming to this briefing."

Alex grinned and laid his arm across the back of Lauren's chair. "Jack asked us to be here." He gave Jack a curious look. "We do not know why yet. What do you have in store for Daria?" he asked his boss.

Jack gave a faint smile in their direction, waiting for both of them to open up their laptops so the briefing could begin. "Oh... something."

Snorting, Lauren said, "Beware whenever Driscoll says 'something,' Daria. It always means an off-the-wall mission."

"I'm more than ready for one," she assured Lauren.

Alex gave Daria a warm smile. "You look good this morning."

"Feeling better every day." Daria knew she could fool Alex and Lauren. It was Jack she was worried about. She saw some concern in his incisive stare every time he looked in her direction. Her heart was beginning a slow pound of desperation. Jack *had* to give her a mission! She *HAD* to get the hell out of her cabin before she went stark raving mad.

"Ready?" Driscoll asked all of them. When he saw three heads bob, he put the mission up on the huge screen hanging on the wall at the other end of the table. "Okay, Daria, here's your mission, if you want it." He clicked a couple of keys and several photos came up along with a map of Peru.

Alex groaned. "You have to be joking, Jack."

"That's why you and Lauren are here. Both of you had time and experience in Peru."

Daria stared at the map and at the photo of the bald-headed man, a Russian named Ustin Korsak, on one side of it. On the other side was a photo of another man, a rugged type, judging by his face, the name 'Nik Morozov' beneath it. Daria knew that Nik was Ukrainian, and had been Alex Kazak's best friend when they'd been on the same Russian mafia drug team together in Peru. She knew better than to ask questions. Jack would give the briefing and, afterward, he'd invite any questions that still lingered. Her heart did funny things as her gaze automatically went to Nik Morozov's image. She'd never seen a photo of Nik, but had always heard Alex speak passionately about the man, near his same age, and like a brother to him. They had been Spetsnaz soldiers in the Russian black ops Army as combat medics for years before going to Peru to join Alexandrov's Russian drug team.

Alex scowled. "You have Nik down there. What is going on?"

"Don't get protective," Jack cautioned him smoothly. He turned to Daria.

"Okay, this is a level two mission. That means it's not lethal if you play your cards right." He flicked another photo up on the wall. "This is Sergeant Mace Kilmer. He left the Army after getting bit by a Fer-de-Lance snake. And, as you know, he's working here with us, in Mission Planning as a South American expert. A month ago, I asked him to reassemble the team he had been in charge of before he left the Army. The DOD, the Department of Defense, gave its permission for him to do so. Right now, he's the leader of an Army three-man Special Forces hunter-killer team that's operating in the Highlands and jungle area near Machu Picchu. I had the Army send him and his team down there a month ago on this one, special mission that he said he'd take. The reason is this: The CIA just lost their case officer, Sam Hutchison, two months ago in Aguas Calientes. A small tourist town sitting at the base of the World Heritage site: the Machu Picchu complex. All evidence points to Korsak, or one of his men, finding out Sam was CIA, and slicing his throat.

"The Peruvian police found Hutchison dead in his apartment six days later. The stink alerted nearby neighbors, and the police were called. Up until that time, Hutchison was working with three other Spec Forces teams, trying to pinpoint where Ustin Korsak's drug team would be. Their job was to try and capture Korsak and take him out of the leadership position, bring him back to the USA and try to flip him. The Department of Justice, DOJ, wants him bad. They think if Korsak can be apprehended, that they can work with him, squeeze the intel out of him, and promise him Witness Protection here in the states for the rest of his life. If he gives up the other Russian teams in the region that is." Jack shrugged. "Sounds like a pretty cushy deal to me. The US offers Korsak ongoing protection and a much better, safer life than he'd ever get back in Mother Russia."

"Mace knows Korsak better than anyone," Alex agreed. The other three teams haven't been able to touch him, as I understand it."

Jack nodded. "There's two reasons we've pulled Mace back into the situation. First, he knew Sam Hutchinson very well and they were friends. Secondly, if Daria agrees to this mission, I want Mace down there shadowing her throughout it. Providing it's a successful mission, and everyone comes home, Mace will be coming out of the jungle and returning here, to do mission planning.

"I bet Sierra isn't happy about this," Lauren said, frowning. "They just got married and she was glad Mace was out of the Army."

Grimacing, Jack said, "Life changes. Mace wants to avenge Sam's death. And he wants Korsak and he'll find him."

Daria felt the tension in the room, but inwardly, she was relieved that Mace was going to be in the area where she was supposed to be.

With a keystroke, Jack put another photo up on the screen. "Okay, let's move on. We have a new Russian mafia leader in New York City: Rolan Pavlovich. When Yerik Alexandrov's son, Vladimir, was killed by Sergeant Mace Kilmer, the next in line, Petrov, took over. He was also killed. Rolan Pavlovich filled that vacant mafia position in New York City and took over. Pavlovich is new to the position, and the five mafia teams operating in Peru were previously under Petrov's direction. Now, Pavlovich, from the intel the FBI is picking up on, is going to fly down there shortly to meet with these teams, each of which are composed of five or six to ten ex-Spetsnaz Russian soldiers. He'll ask for a loyalty pledge from them. He's heading down there, but we don't have his exact ETA yet. When we do, you will be alerted, Daria."

"Pavlovich is filling the power vacuum left by the death of Yerik Alexandrov," Alex growled, unhappy.

"Bound to happen," Jack said. He glanced at Daria. "You're going to go undercover as a Russian. You speak the language because you're an orphaned Russian child, later adopted by Ukrainian parents, but you hold dual citizenship. My team is preparing deep-cover protection for you as we speak. You'll go in as a botanist from Kyiv National University of Culture and Arts, taking a one-year sabbatical from your teaching duties there to write a book about orchids in Peru," and he flicked a hand toward the map on the wall. "I hope you like flowers?"

Daria nodded. "I love all of Nature."

"She might have been orphaned, but I believe she was born on Ukrainian soil, but no one knows her past history," Alex said, "and we are tied to our beloved Ukraine and the Earth. We would rather be outdoors than in."

"I hope someday to know where I was born," Daria said with some hope behind her words. "I was at a St. Petersburg orphanage the first year of my life. When my Ukraine parents adopted me, they tried to find out a paper trail on me, but there was none." She smiled a little. "I hope you're right, Alex because I've always love plants, flowers and Nature."

"I'm sure of it," Alex said.

Jack nodded. "Good, because I'm sending you a file right now on orchids in that area that you'll have to commit to memory. Plus, memorize the photos of the orchids themselves. Your cover is that you're renting an apartment in Aguas Calientes. You'll be out and about, in the jungle, in the Highlands area, hunting for local orchids, taking photos, sitting and taking measurements and anything else a botanist would do to a flower. You'll be putting your 'findings' in a journal or notebook and then, later on, transfer the information and photos to a special laptop we have ready for you to carry on you."

"There are many orchids down there," Alex said, nodding. "Beautiful ones."

"I saw a lot of them," Lauren agreed. "Jack gave me a similar cover when I went down there, but I never had to use it. Should be an easy cover activity for you, Daria?"

"Well," Jack interrupted, holding up a hand, "Daria might not think this as easy. Let me lay out the rest of this op."

Daria grew tense inwardly, not liking that half-smile Jack had on his face. It warned her there was a twist coming to her mission.

"Nik Morozov, is the combat medic in Korsak's team, and it's well known he would never rape or hassle the Quechua Indian women in the villages on their circuit. He abhors rape of a woman and walks away when other men on the team do it. Later, he cares for the woman medically. Then, Petrov was killed in a firefight. Nik was wounded and brought stateside to recover. DOD and CIA wanted him to infiltrate his old team, the one that Ustin Korsak has taken over. Korsak hates him because he won't be 'one of the boys' and 'have a little fun'. But he can't do without a medic in the unit because, as Alex and Lauren well know, bacterial infections that take hold can kill a person within forty-eight hours without antibiotics or swift medical intervention. Never mind Dengue Fever, Malaria, Hanta Virus, Cholera, and a whole host of epidemic infections you can get down there for free."

Alex nodded, scowling. "All of that is true."

"Plus, Nik had agreed, via the CIA, to become a mole in Korsak's unit and feed them information. He's seen as a loner by the team, but is accepted because he's a damn good medic. He and Alex used to work together, so Alex knows how good Nik is."

"Nik is one of the best when it comes to jungle medicine."

"He saved me," Lauren told Daria. "After I got kidnapped, it was Nik who cared for me and then got me the hell out of that situation."

"I owe him," Alex said, giving Jack a glance. "I wish Nik had not agreed to return to the CIA."

"He didn't have a choice," Jack said. "His younger brother, Dan, is in need of a technique called brain entrainment, that can only be performed by one neurologist who has a clinic in Colorado Springs, USA. The CIA has promised Nik that, if he'll be a mole and help get Korsak captured, the State Department will grant Dan and himself political asylum. They'll be able to remain in the US and obtain citizenship. Plus, Dan will receive the brain therapy free of charge."

Alex's eyebrows raised. "Really?"

Jack smiled a little. "Yes. Your best friend is seeing the light at the end of the tunnel. All he has to do is hook up with Daria, and keep feeding her intel on where Korsak's team is heading next on their jungle and Highlands circuit."

"How will he do that?" Daria wondered.

"Well, you are probably not going to like this, Daria, but Nik has already been told you're coming down to Aguas Calientes and that you are his new contact. Not only that, you're going to eventually, after meeting, pose as lovers."

Her own eyebrows shot up this time. "Excuse me?" Her heart pounded once and she stared at Nik's photo in the projection on the screen. Already, she was drawn to him. But his lover? "What, exactly does that mean, Jack?"

"Nik is known to have no relationship with any woman in Korsak's team. He will meet you in Aguas Caliente at the Catholic church, noonday mass, on the main plaza, in plain sight of Korsak and/or his men when they come in for R& R for five days in that town. Nik will make overtures toward you, as if meeting you for the first time, and you'll show interest in him. While the Russian team rests up, Nik will be out and about with you. You will show that you're interested in him. We need Korsak to buy into the facade that Nik has finally found a woman that he wants a relationship with. That way, Korsak won't realize that you are Nik's contact and that you'll be the one taking any intel he can give you and sending it on by satellite phone to the CIA. You will also be in sat phone contact with that Special Forces team I mentioned, Sergeant Mace Kilmer's, so they can hopefully, at some point, corner Korsak, capture him and get him the hell out of Peru and back here to us on US soil."

Frowning, her heart skipping beats, Daria said, "Just how far does this love-interest thing go?"

"Hold hands while out in public," Jack said. "Later, maybe Nik gives you a quick kiss on the cheek or something. You two can work out the details. Nothing will be asked of you that you aren't comfortable with. Eventually, he will be living with you at an apartment during those five day R& R periods when Korsak's team comes back to Aguas Calientes to rest up."

Daria felt her heart twinge. "Live with me?"

"You have to make it look like you two have a serious, torrid affair to Korsak. Right now, when Korsak's team comes in for R& R, they hire prostitutes, and they do drugs and get drunk. Nik will spend time and nights with you. During the day, you can go with him to where he spends his time as a medic helping at an orphanage that is run by the Healing Hands charity in that town. He never participates in what the rest of the team does when on R&R."

"Nik is a man of strong morals, integrity and values," Alex told her. "Like me, he hated seeing the team rape women out in the villages. It was wrong. It will always be wrong. Nik and I would leave the team in the village. If we had tried to interfere and stop the rape, our leader would have put a gun to our heads and killed us. We were helpless to stop it, Daria. But Nik never approved of hurting anyone, especially an innocent woman or child. We are medics. We care for the sick and helpless. We do not harm people."

Daria considered the information. "So, he has to stay at my apartment?"

"Yes," Jack said smoothly, "otherwise, Korsak won't buy his cover that he's finally fallen in love with a woman. This will all make him more trustworthy to his team in general, but especially with Korsak. That way, Nik is hoping that Korsak will trust him and give him pertinent info on where he's taking his drug team next. They have a ten-village circuit and Korsak keeps mixing it up concerning the exact day when he'll go into a village to collect the cocaine the Quechua Indians have been forced to make for him. If Nik could know ahead of time, he MIGHT be able to give you the information so that Kilmer's Spec Forces team could be in place to kidnap Korsak and remove him."

"But Morozov is only coming into Aguas Calientes once a month," Daria protested.

"Well," Jack said, "that's why you have the botanist job as cover. Nik has a woman in each of these ten villages that he passes notes to. And the woman will then pass it on to his contact, which used to be Hutchison. As a botanist, you are expected to be out in the field, in the jungle, looking for orchids. You can wander into these villages, approach Nik's contact, and see if there's info for you or not. If there is, then you can alert the CIA and the Army team via the sat phone you'll have with you."

"I see."

Alex scowled. "What are the chances of Daria showing up at a village the same time Korsak and his team is visiting it? That could be dangerous to Daria. Korsak or one of his other men could rape her."

Jack shook his head. "We aren't letting Daria stick her neck out in the field until it has been well established with Korsak that Nik has claimed her as his woman. He will respect that and leave Daria alone."

Rubbing his jaw, Alex's mouth pursed. "I do not know, Jack. Korsak, if anything, is unpredictable. He has an eye for beautiful women. And Daria is very beautiful. She will attract his attention."

"He won't lay a hand on me," Daria growled.

"Let's not go there," Jack said. "We need Daria to have time to talk in-depth with Nik about all of this. I'm leaving it in his hands to decide if Daria will be safe out there or not. If he says no, then we play the cat-and-mouse game with Korsak. The best that can happen is Daria will be given intel by Nik once a month. It lengthens their time of trying to catch Korsak, but no one wants to put Daria at risk or in that situation, either." He looked at Daria. "The choice is up to you. Even if Morozov is sure Korsak will leave you alone because you are his woman, you do your own gut check on this, okay?"

Daria nodded, her heart in turmoil. She was already drawn to this Ukrainian medic! What if he honestly liked her? And she liked him? What then? Where did mission end and personal time begin? She wasn't about to admit she was drawn to Morozov to anyone. That would be disastrous, and Daria wanted out in the field more than anything. "Okay, sounds good. I can do this." She felt Jack's gaze trying to penetrate her innermost thoughts and feelings.

"I think," Alex said, "that if Nik acquired a woman in town, this would go toward Korsak trusting him more. He would be living with this woman and they would like that. He would appear to be more like them in some ways, not standing off, as he did before. I think it is a well-planned mission, Jack."

"Thanks, Alex. I think so too." His voice lowered as he looked over at Daria. "More importantly, how do *you* feel about all of this?"

Shrugging, she said, "So long as Morozov understands my ground rules, I'll lay out to him. We might have to spend time together at night in my apartment, but he'll sleep on the couch and I'll take the bed."

"Well," Jack murmured, his mouth twisting in a slight smile, "I know you will set him straight on the rules of the road regarding his behavior toward you. During the day, though, you need to be seen together, like lovers. You have a problem with him holding your hand? Putting his arm around you? Maybe a kiss? He has to convince Korsak one-hundred percent that he loves you, and that you are his woman."

"I'll deal with it," Daria grumped, avoiding Jack's penetrating stare. She knew Nik well enough from Alex's and Lauren's stories, that he was a kind man who cared deeply for people who were in pain and suffering. He was truly a medic, just like Alex. The stories Alex had shared with her about Nik had always made her wonder what it would be like to meet the man someday. Well, she was going to get her chance to find out, wasn't she? Part of her thrilled at the idea. The other part of her was wary.

"Alex? Do you know if Nik has a relationship?" Daria asked.

"No... none. Nik's only focus is on his brother, Dan, and getting him the medical help he needs. All his money he earns in the drug team, goes toward Dan's welfare in Ukraine. Dan has a traumatic brain injury and he is in need of a very specialized TBI technique. It can only be performed here in the USA. Nik is determined to get his brother here, in order to receive the treatment. It has something to do with brain syncing of electrical impulses."

"And that's why he allowed the CIA to use him," Daria said.

Alex sat up a little straighter. "Yes, that is true. But Nik and I were ready to leave the drug team because of the rapes, and the unprovoked beatings of the Indians. We could no longer stand it. I was lucky, I escaped. But Nik must bear up under this terrible situation, and he does it for Dan. No one else."

Nik was a certified hero in Daria's book. When she was invited over to

Alex and Lauren's home for a good, Ukrainian meal, Nik was always brought up in the conversation. "I see," she murmured. Giving Jack a steady look of confidence, she said, "In some ways, Jack, I already feel like I know Nik via Alex and Lauren. If I didn't, I probably wouldn't take this mission, because the man would be a complete unknown to me."

"I know that," Jack said. "Given your last mission and the fact you're still coming out of it, I felt this one was perfectly suited for you. You know Morozov in one sense. Alex has said that he's reliable and trustworthy. I wanted a soft mission for you, to bring you back onboard. I'm not convinced your leg is all that sturdy yet. You are a mission specialist, with a pretty easy assignment if you keep your cover. I believe Morozov will respect you, Daria. I don't think he'll try anything on you that you don't want."

"Nik would *NEVER* push himself on Daria," Alex agreed strongly. "*Never*. He is a man of absolute integrity, honor, and with a compassionate heart. He is sensitive to others. He is a healer." Alex gave her a steady look. "Nik is very protective of women and children, just as I am. He will respect you, Daria. You need not ever fear being in his presence."

CHAPTER 2

"DO YOU THINK she is ready?" Alex asked Jack after Daria left. His voice was heavy with doubt.

Jack shrugged. "Kate gave her approval."

Lauren turned to Alex. "In this country, a shrink has the override."

Shaking his head, Alex muttered, "Jack, she is NOT prepared for a mission yet. I do not care what anyone says. I love Kate. I think highly of her, but Daria is not ready. I see it in her eyes. I feel it around her. She is suffering greatly from that firefight where Melissa died."

"Daria is not in good shape," Lauren agreed, and she raised her hand in silent protest before Jack could speak. "I know, I know, I'm not a therapist. But dammit, Jack, she has PTSD. Anyone with a set of eyes in their head can see it. I think sending her out now is too soon."

Jack looked closely at all the tests Kate had given Daria over the past three weeks. "Look, she's passed all the mandatory tests. And who among us doesn't have PTSD? We still can operate, regardless."

Alex got to his feet, shoving the chair back. "Daria may have been born in Russia, but she is Ukrainian in her heart," he snapped, striking his chest with his hand. "I have greater connection with her, Jack. I am telling you that she is a liability to herself, to Nik, and to this mission. You should NOT send her out. She is still healing."

"She has so much grief and guilt," Lauren argued passionately, "over Melissa's death. To this day, Daria has told us she feels that Melissa died because of her. That's crazy. They were attacked by Taliban soldiers with knives. But Daria doesn't see it that way, and that worries me, Jack."

Jack eased back in his chair, studying his two contractors. Alex was breathing hard, his eyes flashing with anger and concern. Lauren looked upset, which wasn't like her because she was a cool-headed sniper that never allowed emotions to enter into her duties. "Okay," he said in a low tone, "what's the workaround?"

"You're still going to let her go down there?" Alex demanded hotly.

"Yes, and there's no more discussion about that. What I need from you two is other ideas, outside the box, on how we can support Daria during this mission?"

"Keep her here," Lauren muttered, angry at Jack. "She's still too raw. Too emotionally unstable."

"Prove that to me," Jack challenged her in a quiet tone, holding her flashing gaze.

"I had a talk with Daria two days ago," Lauren told him, getting a hold of her emotions. "Daria's hands tremble. All the time. She doesn't sleep at night. Wakes up screaming. Has flashes of Melissa bleeding out next to her while she was fighting for her own life. Never mind she'd been stabbed three times in the thigh already and was bleeding out herself. I asked Daria if she'd cried yet." Lauren's mouth tightened. "She said she hadn't cried since it happened. Jack, that's just pure craziness! I've been in firefights where my life was at stake before, too. And I can guarantee you that afterward, I cried my eyes out. I cried for days, weeks, and months more. Just ask Alex."

"We've never seen you cry, Lauren."

"That's because I hid it. I did it where no one could see or hear me."

"So," Jack said in a reasonable tone, "why couldn't Daria be doing the same thing?"

Alex paced the room, muttering curse words in Ukrainian. He jerked his gaze to Jack. "I believe she has not. She is a stubborn Ukraine woman."

"What does that mean?" Jack asked.

"That we are very strong people emotionally. That we can take a beating and never cry out. Daria might be a woman, but she is as tough as a Ukrainian bear. She will not break down. She will not show her pain to anyone."

Lauren gave her husband a softened look. "That's true," she told Jack. "I'm still learning the ins and outs of Alex. He hides his stuff and it's damned hard to access it or get him to let it go. It's VERY frustrating."

"So, Daria is doing the same thing?" Jack demanded.

"Yes," Alex growled.

"Okay, then don't you think that Nik, who is also Ukrainian, is going to sense this situation? We have no way of contacting him and bringing him up to speed on Daria or her present emotional situation with her PTSD. The CIA needs Korsak kidnapped sooner, not later. They have contacted every security contracting company, trying to find the right woman to plant in Aguas Calientes to be Nik's love interest. We're the only company who had someone who is a Russian born female: Daria. So, this isn't just something we can lightly dismiss or walk away from. Korsak knew more about Alexandrov's operation in Peru than any other drug team leader. That's *why* the CIA wants him so badly. They know that Pavlovich is going to be visiting Korsak's team sooner or later. The CIA would like to snatch Korsak as soon as possible and cut off that intel trade to Pavlovich."

Running his fingers through his hair, Alex continued to pace, his large body moving with surprising grace around the small room. "This is not good."

"Can Nik sense where Daria's at emotionally, Alex? Does he have the same intuitive gear you have in place?" Jack asked.

Halting, Alex stared hard down the table toward Jack. "Yes, of course he does."

"Then, don't you think Nik will feel her out? Know that she's emotionally fragile? He might not know what caused her to be in this state, but maybe he'll sense it and deal with her accordingly so the mission can move forward?"

Lauren rolled her eyes. "Jack, she's a human being who is hurting, big time. I know her leg has healed up enough to deal with the demands of this mission, but dammit, her heart is in shreds over Melissa's death, not to mention almost dying herself."

"Daria flatlined twice on that Medevac helo that came in to rescue them," Alex darkly reminded Jack. "She had lost so much blood enroute that she effectively died. Twice! If there had not been good combat medics on board and plenty of fresh blood available on that helicopter, Daria would be dead now and we would not be having this conversation. They saved her, brought her back."

Lauren leaned forward, clasping her hands onto the edge of the table, buttonholing Jack. "And you know damn well that when you almost die, it changes you forever. And it's even harder to work through that, never mind losing your partner in the firefight, too."

Grimly, Jack barely nodded, his gaze moving from Alex to Lauren and back. "We can't pull her off this op. That's a done deal. What can be done to support Daria through it?"

"Nothing from our end," Alex said heavily. He rubbed his eyes and then dropped his hands to his sides. "It all falls on Nik's shoulders to figure her out, to sense where she is at. He must protect her at all costs because, if Korsak decides to go after her, Daria will NOT be able to handle the stress of it, *at all.*"

"But you said Nik is a big, protective guard dog," Lauren argued, giving her husband a concerned look.

"He is." Frustration came through Alex's thickly accented voice. "I do not believe Daria will be forthcoming with Nik. I believe she will refuse to tell him anything about herself or what has just recently happened to her. She will hide her real feelings, her wounded heart."

"Well," Lauren murmured, "I got *you* to loosen up."

Alex gave his wife a patient, but loving look. "That is because I love you and you love me. You made it easy for me to open up and confide in you, Lauren. You gave me a safe place where I could finally spill everything, all my fears, my pain, my grief and guilt. You were there to hold me and listen. You never judged me. You just let me cry in your arms when I needed to do that."

Jack grimaced. "Nik is not in love with Daria or vice-versa. They're playing undercover roles."

Lauren, hands on hips, cut back, "So were Alex and I! But I still think, knowing what Alex has told me about Nik, that he's a wily Ukrainian wolf that can smell what's going on with Daria, in a manner of speaking," Lauren said. He's a combat medic. One of the best in the world because Spetsnaz has a medical program commensurate to the Army's 18 Delta program here in the USA. They are field surgeons, when needed."

"But," Alex said gently, "this is not about surgery, Lauren. This is about Daria's wounded soul and her grieving heart that was torn apart by the loss of Melissa. She carries deep guilt about it and none of us have been able to get her to release any idea of it in four months."

"Well," Lauren muttered, "she's a sniper and the lead sniper is responsible for his or her spotter. Of course, Daria is feeling guilt over it. It was trained into us in the Marine Corps sniper school we are fully responsible for our spotter at every turn."

"Okay," Jack said, "what's the consensus of opinion here, then? That Nik has the goods, the perception and sensitivity to feel out Daria and know she's hurting? To maybe be a support of sorts to her? Is he a good communicator, Alex? Can he get her to talk or fess up about personal things?"

Alex replied, "In the field, the Quechua Indian women and children love him. Nik is very kind and gentle with them. The children flock to him, they do not fear him. The mothers lean on him because they know he cares about all of them. He is a good listener."

"In other words," Lauren said, "he's got a damned good bedside manner."

"Then," Jack said, standing and closing his laptop, "that's what we all have to pin our hopes on."

"NIK, THIS IS the operator you're to meet." Sergeant Mace Kilmer said and handed the Ukrainian a small photo and a piece of paper. He studied Nik as he frowned and took the documents. They stood behind a ten-foot waterfall. The cave chamber was large enough to hide away from prying eyes and was one of the few places where they could safely meet.

Nik scowled, looking at the grainy black and white photo of a woman's head and shoulders. "Is this in response to the CIA operative, Hutchinson, being killed? She's taking his place?" he asked, looking over at Mace.

The Special Forces sergeant shrugged his broad set of shoulders. "Don't know. The agency didn't tell me. That's all we got." He poked at the paper. "This is the time and place you're to meet her in Aguas Calientes. She should already be there by now, waiting for you. When are you going there for R&R?"

"Tomorrow the Russian helo will pick us up and drop us off at that small airport just outside Aguas Calientes." Nik rubbed his beard and gave his Army friend a long look. "A woman?"

"Read the rest of the mission brief, maybe?"

Nik lifted his head. The sound of the waterfall was almost drowning out their voices. Korsak and his team were at the village of Kurmi, Quechua for 'rainbow,' on the banks of a small, unnamed river, picking up bags of cocaine for transport tomorrow morning, to be put aboard the Russian helicopter. This afternoon, Nik wasn't needed for such a task and had faded into the jungle and had hurried at a swift jog to meet Kilmer. A week earlier, at the village of Tinti Kaballu, 'dragonfly,' the wife of the chief had slipped him a written note from Kilmer to meet him here at this specific time and date.

Quickly, Nik scanned the one-page brief concerning the mission operator, and what was to be expected of him. His mouth tightened as he finished reading the orders. "Have you read this?" he demanded of his American colleague.

"Yeah." Kilmer grinned. "I was jealous. If I wasn't already married? I'd wish to hell it was me instead of you. I'd have liked the idea of shacking up with a lady for five days straight once a month. Been two months without my wife. All I want to do is go home and stay there."

Flashing Kilmer a look of teasing contempt, Morozov growled, "Suffer in silence, Kilmer." The sergeant's mouth drew into a beatific smile. He didn't smile often. Nik was always amused by the fact the black ops soldier looked like a mischievous little boy when he smiled, and not the lethal soldier he really was. Kilmer was deadly, and Nik knew it for a fact. Every man on their team was a hunter and a killer. They were a focused team out here for one reason: to keep American interests protected, and able to survive their enemies' attacks. Even Kilmer's wide, intelligent blue eyes, which now danced with mirth, didn't give away the fact he was veteran hardened in the ways of deep undercover ops like this one. He knew Mace had been recalled to this role because of this new op, and his time down here was temporary. Nik was jealous.

"I think it's a good idea. Korsak doesn't fully trust you because you won't screw around with the prostitutes or take part in the village rapes." Mace gestured toward the paper in Morozov's long, slender hands. "If you fall in love with a tourist, that makes you one of them, bedding a woman. Korsak's always questioned your sexual preferences."

"He's a bastard," Morozov hissed under his his breath, giving Kilmer a deadly look. "Women and children should be treated with respect, never used like Korsak and his men use them."

Mace patted him on the shoulder. "Nik, you're the only white knight out here in this fucking jungle. I'm sure this woman operator will be safe when you're around her."

Shaking his head, Morozov handed the papers back to Mace. He couldn't afford to be caught with anything on him that might rouse Korsak's suspicions that there was a mole in their midst. "It's a good plan, actually. I just don't feel up to it."

Kilmer's grin widened. "Up to it? Is that a pun?" and he snickered, tipping a significant glance down at the crotch of Morozov's dark green cargo pants.

"Get off," Nik growled.

"No, no, the American slang would be: 'fuck off'."

A sour grin pulled at one corner of Nik's mouth. "That too. Alex Kazak always had a bad time with American slang, too. Maybe it's a Ukrainian thing?"

"Maybe, my friend," and Mace chuckled and tucked the papers away in the knapsack that sat between his wet combat boots. He straightened up. "So, tomorrow you're outta here for five days? Then back on the circuit again?"

"Yes." Nik gave him an unhappy look. "But Korsak, as usual, isn't telling us where we'll start on that circuit."

"And that leaves us in the lurch," Mace agreed, hefting the one-hundred-and-twenty-pound ruck across his broad back. He cinched up the straps, adjusting the weight across his shoulders. "Maybe if Korsak sees you with a woman, visiting her monthly, he'll start trusting you a little more, *compadre*."

"That is the plan, isn't it?" Nik said, hauling his own heavy-enough ruck, still only half the weight of Kilmer's, onto his back. He cinched it up and then thrust his hand toward Kilmer. "Stay safe out there?"

"Right," and Mace grinned, clenching Nik's hand in a brief shake, the sweat standing out on his bearded face. "You too, hear?"

Nodding, Nik rasped, "You leave first."

Mace turned and walked toward the other escape route from the cave behind the waterfall. Nik stood there; his AK-47 rifle in a chest sling anchored across his body. After watching the Special Forces soldier disappear into the gloom, he turned, walking silently toward the waterfall. Waiting a few minutes, he moved closer to the waterfall entrance and exit point. Light spray hit his face and body as he peeked out one side of it, and then the other side, to check that no one was in the immediate vicinity. So far, in the years he'd spent here in the Peruvian jungle, none of the Russian teams had ever discovered this place. That was lucky for him and his American contacts.

Often, he would have met Sam Hutchison here and they'd exchange intel. His heart felt heavy. Sam had been a damn good CIA case officer, and hadn't deserved getting this throat slashed by Korsak. How had Korsak found Sam out? The Russian was wily, and Nik never forgot it. He was glad that Mace Kilmer was down here for this new op, and that Mace was very aware that Sam had been his good friend. He was glad that Mace had brought him in on this mission, and especially glad knowing that the CIA agent was out for Korsak's blood. He glanced down at the watch on his wrist. Five more minutes and then he'd slip out and head back to the village. Along the way, he'd grab some plant or other and Korsak would think, as usual, that his interest in Quechua herbal medicine was the reason he'd taken off and disappeared for a while. He kept a notebook, filled with drawings and scribbles, plus the Latin identification of the plants he'd found. It was part of his cover.

The mid-afternoon humidity dampened and stuck his olive-green T-shirt and camo trousers against his tall, lean body. He moved like a ghost out from behind the waterfall and into the surrounding jungle. Nik heard the nearby thunderstorms that popped up every afternoon and evening, their rumbles vibrating through the air. There was never any sunlight in this jungle. Only foggy-looking clouds that hung drunkenly just above the triple canopy and then, at night, lowered to the ground so that no one could see their hand in front of their face at times. The wet plant leaves slapped against his lower body, keeping his clothing damp as he moved swiftly away from the hiding spot.

Topping another small hill, Nik took the three-foot-wide red clay trail that would lead him back to the village of Kurmi. Loping along, his legs long and covering a lot of ground, he felt his knees start to gripe dully. He'd been out here humping around the jungle and Highlands for too many years and his joints were wearing out from carrying such a heavy medical pack. His mind turned to Dan, his brother, who was twenty-seven, two years younger than he was. His brother was six foot two inches tall, with green eyes, brown hair and a square face, taking more after their father. Nik took after his mother in looks. Last month Korsak had had the whole bunch of them flown into Cusco for seven days R&R, which was more than welcomed by the exhausted team. There, Nik called his brother in Lviv, Ukraine, to find out how he was doing.

Dan had been a member of Spetsnaz, just as he had, following in his footsteps. Dan too, had become a vaunted combat medic. And then he had incurred traumatic brain injury in a fierce fire fight with Russian rebels. Nik's heart ached as he remembered the Dan of old: dancing green eyes, his deep voice filled with laughter and good humor. Now, his brother was an introvert and rarely laughed. Even more rarely joked. He longed for his real brother back, not this stand-in who was a shadow of Dan's former self. And he prayed that this new, advanced technology created in the US, syncing brainwaves together again, could make the difference. As his boots hit the muddy red clay, puddles of water splashed around them, Nik's resolve deepened. He would continue this mole work in Korsak's murderous, brutal team of hardened Russian soldiers so his brother could get that help found nowhere outside the USA.

If he could deliver Korsak to Kilmer's stealth team, his job down here would finally be over. And he was more than ready to see it done. Nik hung on tightly to the promise of the CIA to give him and Dan political asylum. They both spoke English, which was lucky for them. He wouldn't allow himself to dream too far ahead. If he didn't keep his head in the game with Korsak, who distrusted him, he could find himself with a pistol pointed at him, and the bastard more than willing to pull the trigger and kill him for some perceived infraction. No, Nik knew how to manipulate Korsak, but never got too cocky about it. Korsak had already killed two members of his team because they'd failed to follow one of his orders fast enough. The two replacements were Neanderthals in comparison: rough, brutish and with no humanity in them at all. Korsak was never to be taken for granted. Ever.

The male Quechua Indians were loaded down with sacks of cocaine and were being ordered to the edge of the village when Nik returned. Korsak was in a good mood judging from his expression, his bald head shining with sweat. The other men were buckling up their rucks, and getting ready to move. The Indian women all had worried looks on their faces for their husbands. Their children clung, hiding behind their mother's skirts, as their husbands were herded toward the trail like mules bearing heavy loads. Nik stopped and made a noteworthy show of stuffing his handful of carefully chosen plants into his opened medical ruck. Korsak was used to him doing so, and would think nothing of it.

The Indians would be herded at a fast pace up the steep climb from the jungle to the Highlands above the village. Up there, mostly only rocks survived, with a bit of soil clinging in between them at seven thousand feet in elevation. The Indians would offload their heavy sacks from their skinny backs, stuffing them into a hiding place in a series of nearby caves. Once they'd done their duty, they would be released and told to go home, and they'd gladly do so. A Russian helicopter, manned by pilots who were KGB in disguise, would land at 0900 at that GPS location. The drug team would then load the cocaine, and then, climb on board themselves.

Nik had nothing to do but follow and remain watchful as he brought up the rear of the group. No one spoke to him, which was usual. They considered him to be an oddball, not part of the group. But no one would outright say that because what if they got infected or bit by a venomous Fer-de-Lance snake? It would be he who took care of them and saved their sorry-assed lives. And one never made an enemy of a combat corpsman. Ever. But their glances confirmed their disgust at him from his refusal to act like the rest of the team. That was all right with Nik. He'd withstood this pariah status for many years now, and the end was in sight. All he had to do was meet this new woman operator, pretend she was his new lover, and hope like hell Korsak would let down his guard and allow him in on the intel he gave to the rest of the team. It sounded easy, but Nik knew it wasn't.

As he kept watch by turning often to look down the trail that wound through the dark, green, humid jungle, he felt exhausted. Tired to his soul. And yet, as he divided his sharpened attention between the group strung out ahead of him and keeping their rear protected, his mind wandered back to the woman operator known as Daria McClusky. He was sure that wasn't her real name. But she was beautiful! Even with a lousy black and white printed-out photo of her, Nik wasn't blind. In fact, when he thought about her, his lower body stirred. That surprised him in some ways because he'd always equated sex with some kind of meaningful emotional relationship with his woman partner. He didn't even know Daria. Only that she was a Russian orphan by birth, adopted by a Ukrainian couple. She was fluent in both languages. He knew little else of her background. And he doubted she'd fill him in on anything unless it was need-to-know basis only. She was undercover like himself.

Still, his curiosity was piqued because his body seemed to know more than he did. Smiling to himself, he felt as if cooling winter air was flowing through him, refreshing and vitalizing him. He missed the winters of his home. The snow. The biting cold. And he'd loved ice skating as a child when growing up with Dan. They had done everything together. Now, they were separated half a globe away. Would this woman be a CIA agent like Sam had been? He'd never interfaced with a woman undercover agent before, only men.

It was titillating to think about getting to touch her, hold her hand and maybe, steal a kiss out in public now and then. But it would have to be where Korsak or his men could see them. Korsak might finally trust him if he had a woman he'd even fictionally bedded when they next came into Aguas Calientes. He would be one of them. *Finally.* In all their years together, his team had never seen him take a woman or even show any interest in one. In a way, Nik thought, it would be VERY interesting to see the men of this team's reaction to him finding a woman that finally suited his tastes. At least, that is what they would think. He wondered how far the team would welcome him back into their collective embrace. Especially Korsak.

There was no question he was an outsider. And what kind of woman was Daria? He had so many questions to ask of her. What part of Ukraine did she live in? Was her family still there? How did she get caught up in undercover work? What was her story? Nik found himself wanting to know everything about her. It was her eyes, he decided, that spoke most powerfully to him. What color were they? She looked exhausted in that photo. Maybe it was an old photo? Not a recent one? What had made her look so soul-deep sad?

He laughed to himself because he was a sucker for any child or woman who was hurting in any way. Alex Kazak had always roughly teased him that he couldn't stand the sight of a woman's or child's tears, that he would turn himself inside out to stop their pain and suffering. And, in the photo of Daria, it looked as if she was so close to crying. *About what?*

As Nik jogged along, the Indians keeping up their fast pace up the slanting red, muddy trail that would lead them to the harsh, rocky Highlands, his heart wanted answers, too. Which was odd. How could a grainy photo of an unknown woman touch him so profoundly? He almost felt like a lone wolf who had searched all his life for his mate and never found her. Until just now…

CHAPTER 3

THE MID-MORNING SUNLIGHT peeked through the cottony, slow-moving clouds that drifted about a thousand feet above Aguas Calientes. Tension ran through Daria as she looked around her recently rented second floor apartment. It sat halfway up the long asphalt hill in the small, but very crowded tourist town. It was on the side where the volcanic hot springs were located. She wiped her damp palms down the sides of her green cargo pants, glad to be in a place that had some heat to stave off the cool dampness outside.

She tugged at her bra, wanting to take it off from beneath her long-sleeved cream-colored top. She hated bras and never wore one when out on an op. But this one was different. She didn't want men ogling her breasts as she walked and they just naturally moved and bounced beneath the material covering them. Not that she had huge breasts, she was small there, matching the slender, model-like body she'd been born with. Still, Daria detested the tightness of the bra around her torso, lamenting the whole situation. It was just another way to control her body in one more way and she really hated the idea completely. Her body belonged to her. In the end, she got rid of the bra and said to hell with it. She'd be wearing her jacket, anyway. Her freed breasts would remain hidden from the sight of males.

Looking at the watch on her wrist, Daria saw that she had to meet Nik Morozov at the settlement's only Catholic church, at the other end of town, in thirty minutes. Not that the town was all that large. It would take her five minutes to walk down the hill and over to the plaza at the other end of it. The people who lived here were mostly Quechua Indians, with a few rich Peruvians from Lima scattered in, owners of the many shops that lined both sides of the only concrete road in the area. She wiped her brow, standing in the small living room with its rectangular coffee table set between a black leather couch and a dark-blue fabric sofa chair. The furniture had seen better days, no question, but the place was clean and she spied no cockroaches, which is what Daria cared most about. As a sniper, she lay for hours unmoving while anything and everything in the area crawled over and around her as if she were part of the natural landscape. She had a special hate for cockroaches, smart bastards that they were. They seemed to know that she hated them, and delighted in running up and down her arms or getting up her trouser cuffs, and racing up and down inside her pant legs. They knew what they were doing. They knew she would not move to crush them.

She hoped she had memorized everything that was needed for her to pose as a botanist and, frankly, was glad for the distraction. She'd even slept without screaming and waking everyone up around her on the American Airlines flight from Miami, Florida to Lima, Peru. Being on this mission was a way to shove all the horror and emotions far down inside her where she wouldn't be bothered by them. At least, not for a little while, Daria hoped. The month of May in Peru was the beginning of their winter. It was supposed to be drier, but it had rained on the trip from Cusco along the Inca railroad line to this little town two hours out from the major city. It had kept raining when she'd disembarked and had two boys carry her luggage from the station, across a violent, dangerous river channel and then up the opposite bank and into the town. Her clothes were still damp even though she'd worn a rainproof nylon jacket, her trousers getting especially soaked. Alex Kazak had warned her she'd be wet or at least damp all the time, no matter what season it was. The ancient radiator heat was warming up the equally damp rooms of the apartment, and was beginning to dry out her trousers. It was the high humidity that made Daria feel like her lungs were slightly clogged. She was used to the dry, desert climes of Afghanistan and Syria.

Her heart stuttered when she thought of Nik Morozov, and her upcoming meeting with him. Lauren and Alex had invited her over for dinner two nights before she'd left for Lima and they'd tried to give her a verbal picture of the man. He sounded really nice. A reasonable, honorable man who just happened to live and work with murderous thieves. Alex had told her many stories of he and Nik working together and how they had both delivered their fair share of babies over the years, a high for both of them. Lauren had nothing but good things to say about Nik, too. He *had* helped capture and kidnap her, but later, as she'd pleaded with him, and then, after Nik found out that she knew Alex, he had released her. Nik then risked his own life to get Lauren back to the safety of the Army Special Forces team that was trying to find and rescue her.

After having heard all the stories, and seeing the photos of him that Alex had brought out, Daria wondered how someone like Morozov managed to hang on and continue to live in such a brutal environment. She understood it was his loyalty to his brother Dan that was his motivation, but still… it was a lot to ask of any human being for that long a time. It showed that Nik, when dealt a bad hand, remained responsible and did the right things for the right reasons. He was so much like Alex in some ways and that stilled a lot of Daria's worries and anxieties about working with him.

And the truth? She was so moved by Alex and Lauren's heart-centered sincerity that frankly, Nik sounded like a dream hero concocted from their wildest imaginations. Daria honestly didn't know what to expect when they met inside the church during the noontime Mass. She supposed that Korsak and his men would never set foot inside a church, given the brutality of their dark souls. It was a safe place to meet for the first time. Daria wondered if Nik was Catholic; it would explain why he wanted to meet there. Soon, she would know.

NIK SAT IN the back-most row of pews, away from the two large, heavy wooden doors, swung open to invite people in for the Mass. Quechua Indians were silently filing in, taking blessed water from the bowl near the door and making the sign of the cross before moving up the polished cream stone aisle toward the dark wooden pews, where the priest stood nearby to greet them. Nik tried to tame his expectations and concern. Would Daria show up on time? Or not? If she was an operator, she would, unless she was dead. Just as the hand on his watch hit noon, he saw her enter.

It felt as if someone had stolen the air out of his lungs. His eyes widened slightly as she entered, hands stuffed into the pockets of her down jacket, looking for him. His heart beat rapidly in his chest as their eyes briefly met, held, and then their gazes drifted apart. She was artful, Nik decided, as she continued to look around as if she were a curious tourist. She, like all the others, dipped her fingers into the marble-cut bowl and made the sign of the cross. Trying to breathe normally, Nik watched her move with the grace of an animal. Her eyes. Even in the poor light of this church, he could see they were a golden brown, reminding him of a shade browner than a lion's large, amber eyes. His gaze missed nothing. Her nose was clean and straight, nostrils slightly flared. That mouth of hers sent his lower body into a spasm of sudden, molten desire and it surprised the hell out of him. Nik had met plenty of pretty young women but had never had this kind of reaction to any of them.

But Daria McClusky, or whoever she really was, brought back to mind for him the best of the feminine attributes a woman could have at her disposal. Her hair was set in a single, long black braid and her skin was a golden color, making him wonder how many hours she had spent out in the sun. Her face was oval, with a slightly stubborn chin. His gaze flicked back to her wide mouth and those full lips that were now a bit pursed.

Their eyes met again. Nik looked down to his right, as if to tell her to come and sit near him.

She did.

His nostrils widened and, as he caught her subtle scent of oranges, he wondered if it was from the shampoo she used on her luxurious black hair that gleamed with blue highlights among its strong, silken strands. Her long, thick lashes were incredible frames for those gold eyes of hers that held such intelligence, that missed nothing. She might look like a tourista to everyone else, but to Nik, no. He saw far deeper into Daria.

As she scooted over a bit more his way to allow two other Quechua women to come and sit in the same pew, he moved away from her an equal amount in order to give her some room and allow her to become comfortable in his presence. Nik saw her lean forward and pick up a hymnal written in Spanish, holding it between her graceful, long fingers. No matter what she did, it was like being in the presence of a ballerina. His lower body tightened. What an unexpected reaction to her!

Nik drew in a ragged breath, trying to still his rebelling body. He hadn't known what to expect when meeting this woman, but it certainly was not what was happening with his physical body right now. It wasn't her fault. If only he could stop picking up the unique, feminine scent that was her. Nik had always had an acute sense of smell. Dan had often accused him of being a Ukrainian wolf in disguise, what with his exceptional hearing, smell and vision. Daria smelled so damned good that his body was going into its own silent kind of celebration. She was less than three feet away from him and he could feel the heat of her body in the cold, damp church.

The doors closed and the sound echoed, as if in a cavern. Like a prison door shutting forever kind of sound. The church had been built sometime during the 1700's by the marauding Spanish, all out of gray stone. The pews were crowded with Indians, but the first rows were reserved for the white-skinned rich Peruvians exclusively from Lima. The priest began his litany in Latin. Nik wondered how many of the Indians, who only spoke their own Quechua language, understood anything he was saying. Most Indians knew pigeon Spanish and no English. They held on strongly to their tribal customs.

Worse, he had to sit here for forty-five minutes and say nothing to Daria and vice versa. The church was only being used as a way to meet one another. Korsak would laugh, but accept his excuse to leave the team because often, Nik *did* go to church. It gave him nearly an hour of being alone and away from them. He prayed for the women his team had raped, and the men Korsak had killed, and the children the Russians had beaten to force their fathers to carry cocaine up that godforsaken mountain to the Highlands. Nik had lost track of how many times he'd found himself kneeling, his head buried between his crossed arms, hot tears rolling down his cheeks as he sat in this church. He believed in the power of prayer for others. It was the only thing that kept him sane at times in this deadly dance with Korsak.

Just having Daria next to him was calming in another way. This shook Nik. He was always usually tense. On guard. Alert. But right now? He felt PEACE. As if… that was *possible*? The feeling of coming home? To her? He gave himself an internal shake. What the hell was going on here between them? Was this some kind of magic? Insanity? Wishful thinking on his part because he'd been so damned alone for so long? He hadn't touched a woman in five years. His life in Peru hadn't allowed him any real time to get to know a woman like he needed to in order to pursue an intimate, ongoing relationship with one.

Nik never saw women as sex objects like Korsak and his men did. They were a nameless body to be used by these men, as far as they were concerned. They did not see them as human beings. They were a set of breasts and a vagina, that's all. Women were to be used by the men to pleasure themselves, but never to receive pleasure back in return. Nik had had three meaningful relationships in his life and each stood out in his heart. Those three women had each given their heart to him as he'd given his heart to them. Each had been a fair, wonderful exchange. But this woman sitting quietly beside him, her face so incredibly serene, was unforgettable to him.

Nik closed his eyes momentarily, her profile burnt into his brain, branded into his skittering heart that was thumping like a wild, living thing in his chest. Automatically, his medic hand pressed against his jacket, above his heart. Her scent encircled him as if it were the rarest and most delicate of all the orchid fragrances he'd ever inhaled. It was HER. Not the shampoo she used on her hair, nor any perfume she'd sprayed on her skin, but that subtle scent of alluring spice that was just her. Nik swore he could feel her heart beating, the palpitations, the urgency with which it moved within her. She sat like a small buddha who was at one with the world and everything in it. Her lips parted slightly, dressed up with a soft pink glistening lipstick that merely emphasized her slightly fuller lower lip. Nik closed his eyes again, visualizing how good her mouth might feel against his. How lush her lips would be. Daria would open to him like an orchid spreading its petals to the world for the first time. She smelled like the orchids he would pass by in the jungle. That scent of heavy, sensual fragrance entering his nostrils, now moving deep into his lungs, reminded him of all the beauty that existed in this world between a man and a woman. He did not belong in the world he lived in now. Daria's scent was like a drugging heaven, and reawaken hope within him on every possible level.

Crazy! What was going on with him? Was he finally having that long-overdue nervous breakdown from all the unrelenting stress of being a CIA mole? Trying to stay one step ahead of the darkly intelligent Korsak? Or was it HER? *Daria*. He played her name over and over again in his mind, catching the nuances of all the vowels and consonants of it, a melody that kept on singing to his heart, his soul, bringing him fully to bright, burning life. He knew Daria was a Ukrainian name. Was it her real name? He hoped so, because it fit her so well. It suited her. She was a symbolic island of calm to Nik, soothing the tightness in all his muscles. She soothed his worry and the constant anxiety that haunted him, and he felt all that burden dissolving more and more with every slow, shallow breath she took. Out of the corner of his eye, Nik watched the slow rise and fall of her jacket. There was such serenity surrounding Daria. How could that be? How could an agent appear to be so relaxed and utterly trusting?

Did Daria sense him? Trust him in particular? Did she have more intel on him, perhaps knew him much more intimately than he'd realized? And that was why she could sit next to him and be the island of tranquility that he so desperately sought? The one that had always been out of reach until now. *Just now...* He wiped his mouth with the back of his hand, feeling suddenly unsure of his feelings toward her. This was an undercover operation. They were supposed to pose as lovers discovering one another for the first time. But what was real? What was not? Her breathing, slow and cadenced, flowed through him, pouring coolness on the flames of anxiety and danger that always threatened him. He had a thousand questions for her.

Halfway through the Mass, they all stood. Nik watched her unwind like a lithe jaguar awakening from a long nap. Daria clasped her lovely, long hands together in front of her, reciting the words of the priest in a breathless, hushed Latin that his wolf ears picked up, absorbed, and consumed like the beggar he really was. And never once, did she look over up at him, her eyes straight ahead, her expression focused on the ceremony echoing around the massive stone church. And yet, Nik stared down at her, helpless not to do so. He saw the tiny black strands of hair that had been crinkled by the thick, heavy humidity, saw them curling around her high cheekbones and the long, tight braid that lay over the right shoulder of her nylon jacket.

His gaze fell to her lips and his entire lower body flexed and he groaned inwardly. Surprised, Nik had never felt such lust, such a driving need for a woman as he felt right now. Her lips beckoned. Incredibly beautiful in their shape. Their fullness, and the way the corners where they met curved upward, inspired his fevered imagination. He was reminded of the Madonna, St. Mary, whose statue was to his left, holding the Christ child. He looked at Daria's classic features and saw the Madonna in her. He wondered if she already had children? Married happily to a man who appreciated her as much as he did right now? His gaze drifted downward to where her hands were relaxed and clasped across her softly rounded belly.

No, she had never been pregnant. From his years of training as a medic, he knew a woman's body quite well. He'd delivered more than enough babies down here in South America to know the difference, seen too many young bodies changed by the child growing within their bellies. After a woman had a child, her shape subtly changed. Her hips flared a little wider. Her belly grew a little more stretched and pearlescent and, even from his brief glance over at her, he could see that Daria had never carried a child. And, for a moment, Nik fantasized that she was carrying *his* child. Their baby. He'd seen the glow of pregnancy on the faces of many Quechua Indian women and it was beautiful, and yet, indescribable. To him, growing up in the Catholic religion as he had, he always thought of that glow as Madonna-like, something so sacred, so sublimely radiant and magical. And Nik saw it time and again. Pregnancy made a woman luminous from the inside out. And it was the most sacred of moments a woman would ever experience. He'd felt blessed, literally even, to help bring over fifty babies into the world over the last five years. To hold the slippery child coming out of one of those women's exhausted bodies, to be the first human to touch and welcome that child into the world, was akin to a miracle. Nik could never give adequate words to that sacred, miraculous moment. He could only feel the waves of emotions flowing strongly through him as he worked with the pregnant woman. Then see her baby crown from her straining body, and have the child slide into his awaiting, gloved hands.

Only, this time, it wasn't the birth of a child he was coaxing out into the world. No, right now, with Daria, this was a symbolic birth of a different nature, Nik dimly realized, trying to quantify it, to understand it. But he couldn't because it was birthing right now between him and this agent. Daria made him feel as if he could finally surrender his tattered soul to her after five long, hard years. He could collapse into her arms and Nik knew intuitively that she had the strength to not only hold him, but to slide her arms around him, rock him and allow him to sob out all the horrors that were alive and prowling around within him on a daily basis. Only that kind of very special rebirth could take away all that dirtiness built up inside him: the terror, the disgust and revulsion at all he'd seen. Only holding a newborn, clearing the fluid out of its tiny nostrils, cutting the cord and then cleaning the tyke off, bundling her or him into an awaiting soft, warm alpaca or llama blanket of welcome, had ever made him feel clean once more. Worthy to continue to live.

Daria was a dream-spinner. Someone who, by her mere presence, could give a dying man hope that there was something better than the life that he was quickly losing his grasp upon. Something worth fighting for. Something worth giving one's life for, if necessary. Her energy, her aura, whatever anyone wanted to call it, was touching, infusing and healing him. Ukrainians were great believers in mysticism, in the magic of life. In the mystery of the unseen that truly did exist. Nik might have grown up Catholic, but his mother had imbued him with the mysteries of the world through Ukrainian folklore, and had taught him that those too were just as sacred, as profound, and as transforming, as sitting in a church pew and praying.

Nik had no idea what to do or say as the Indians silently filed out of the church, the Mass having just concluded. If this was what heaven felt like, he didn't want to ever leave it. Or her.

CHAPTER 4

Daria watched the last of the parishioners leave the church and then her and the medic sat alone in the hallowed, partially-darkening church. The altar boys assisted the priest as they went around putting out the candles and shutting off most of the overhead lights in order to save the pricey, valuable electricity.

It was time. She lifted her chin, tilting it his way to engage him. But, just as she did, she saw Nik turn, his gaze meeting and locking onto hers.

"I'm Nik Morozov," he said, holding out his hand to her.

Relief fled through Daria that he'd taken the lead. She'd not done undercover work like this before and didn't know all the nuances and rules about it. "Daria McClusky." She tried to hide her eagerness in lifting her hand and sliding it into his. Her fingertips were cold because there was no heat in the church. His hand was large, warm and rough-feeling to her smoother flesh. Her heart amped up momentarily when she saw his eyes narrow slightly, turning a darker shade of blue. Daria felt as if he were literally burning her face into his memory. His grip was firm, but he didn't crush her hand, either. Tiny sparks leapt from her hand into her wrist, flying up her arm. And when the corners of his mouth relaxed and she saw a wry quality in his expression, her heart flew open. For whatever reason, he dropped his game face. Stunned, it took her breath away.

Releasing her hand, Nik said quietly, "Would you care to join me for a cup of tea at a local restaurant on the other side of the plaza?"

She felt bereft as his hand fell away from hers. Her flesh was doing more than tingling now. It was *itching* to continue to touch this man with the faint half smile on his wonderfully-shaped lips, his gaze intent and curious as he studied her. "I'll come if you offer me a cup of coffee, instead, Mr. Morozov. I'm not a tea drinker."

Nik unwound, standing up. "Call me Nik? And of course, Peruvian coffee is always good to drink." He offered her his hand once more.

Daria was struck by his European courtliness. Her lips lifted into a smile of her own, and she placed her fingers into his opened palm. Not only were there thick callouses dotting it, she also saw a number of old, white scars and even newer ones that were pink and shiny. Nik had beautifully-shaped hands, just as she'd imagined. As Daria rose, she reluctantly withdrew her fingers from his. She pulled the strap of her purse over her shoulder and left the pew.

Outside the church, she waited for him. The broad, white marble steps still shined from the most recent shower. Above them, the clouds churned silently and a break in them allowed a momentary ray of sun to peek through. The warm slats of light cascaded around her. Daria felt Nik approach and stand slightly behind and to the right of her, a very protective gesture on his part toward her. She twisted and looked up at him. He was half a head taller than her, and she watched his gaze move circumspectly around the crowded square plaza. That sense of his radar being on and scanning was a very real sensation to Daria. She could feel the heat of his body behind her on her back and right shoulder, and luxuriated for just a moment in what it felt like to be shielded by a warrior. Back in the church, he had dialed that energy way down. But out here? As she watched him scanning the colorful crowd of locals mingling with the tourists, there was no question he was on guard once more. Had the church given him a moment of reprieve? Daria wanted to ask him.

"Do you come often to this church?" she wondered, engaging him. His mouth had lost that half smile and was now a thinned line. It made him look hard and uncompromising. But, when she spoke, she saw the corners of his mouth soften. And so did the look in his eyes as he settled his gaze upon hers.

"I get into town once a month for five days. I like to go to the church and sit in the back."

"Does it give you peace?" Daria wasn't sure she was playing the role or if it was her curiosity eating her up alive about Nik. She saw a veiled sadness come into his eyes for a moment. His mouth twitched and then he gave her a lazy shrug.

"I'm still trying to find it. I thought it would be in there…"

That response slashed through her heart. Oh, she knew exactly what he meant. Nodding, Daria's throat tightened as she whispered, "It's like that for me, too." Instantly, she saw regret and something else in his eyes.

"Well," he teased lightly, "let's get you that cup of excellent South American coffee and it may improve how you feel?" He placed his hand lightly against the small of her back to urge her on down the fifteen wide, marble steps.

His hand felt warm and comforting against Daria's back. It was a possessive gesture, as if he were not only guarding her, but that he had claimed her as his mate and was going to make sure she was protected. She didn't protest his lingering hand. Didn't pull away from him. Rather, eased back a little more firmly into his opened palm. She could feel his fingers through the material of her jacket, her skin prickling pleasantly beneath them.

As they descended the steps, she looked around, trying to pretend she was a tourist. She felt Nik monitoring the pressure of his hand upon her back. An overwhelming sensation of being shielded by him avalanched over her as they reached the busy, crowded plaza. The pavement's white stones gleamed through the standing puddles. Nik guided her smoothly, never bumping into or halting someone in their path on the way to the small restaurant, marked by a Peruvian Flute sign out in front. Once on the wooden porch, he released his hand and opened the door for her. It struck her again that he possessed old-world charm and excellent social skills.

Inside the small restaurant, the round wooden tables were draped with red-and-white checkered tablecloths. Most of them were empty. The noon crowd was gone. She heard Nik switch to Spanish as he raised his hand to the Peruvian owner behind the counter, calling a greeting to him. He then guided Daria to a corner table diagonally opposite the door and pulled out a chair for her. She could get used to this.

Thanking him, she sat down. For the first time, she got a really good look at Nik Morozov. He wore a very old brown leather jacket, with a dark-blue long-sleeved sweatshirt beneath it, well-worn Levi's and scarred leather combat boots. There was nothing trendy about his man. He was hard- and lean-looking, and Daria would bet his muscles were ropy and powerful. Nik was deceptive upon first sight, but to her trained eye, the way his shoulders stood back with pride just shouted of military bearing along with undeniable confidence. Even more teasing was that male sensuality she'd picked up on earlier. He was not a flirt. But she could feel his maleness and how it stirred her body to life. Nik reminded her of an eagle, his gaze seemingly missing nothing. His black hair was military short, his skin darkly tanned from years of being outdoors. More than anything, the ruggedness of his face, the deep lines here and there, told her of the harshness of his life as nothing else ever would.

"Black coffee?" And then he smiled a little. "Or are you one of those who needs milk and sugar to tame the taste of it?"

Heat swept through Daria, that look he gave her was of a man wanting his woman. Was it for real? Or was this him playing his role with her? Daria found herself wishing it was real. "No, just black. Thank you."

Nodding, he turned and casually walked over to the counter where the owner stood waiting for their order.

She liked his rangy way of walking. It was a deceptively relaxed stride, but she felt tension radiating naturally off him. Daria sensed that if a crisis occurred, he'd snap into muscle memory, with a swiftness that would be nothing but a blur of reaction toward the threat. She saw no pistol carried by him, unless he had one tucked down the back of his Levi's, hidden in the waistband and cloaked by the jacket. Did the Russian crews carry weapons on them here in town? In Peru it was illegal to have any military weapons at all. Even pistols had to be registered with the government. But she was sure, since they were drug runners, that they had to have an arsenal hidden somewhere.

Her heart wouldn't settle down. To see Nik fully, in good light, made her want to stare at him even more. He had an arresting face. It wasn't a young man's face, but that of a man who had seen too much. That was part of the complexity of him, Daria decided. She looked around, her gaze moving around the plaza through the huge windows. Everything seemed normal, but what did she know? This was her first day here in Aguas Calientes.

It took every bit of control Nik had to remain calm and collected. He slid the yellow ceramic mug with fresh, steaming coffee, across the table to Daria. Having deliberately placed her so that he could see who entered and left the premises from where he sat, he sipped his own coffee, nearly burning his tongue. In the druzy sunlight shining through the carelessly-washed picture windows, he really saw how fresh and beautiful Daria truly was. Blue highlights caressed the long, thick braid that lay over her right shoulder and down across her upper chest. Her skin was a golden color. Most of all, what the grainy black-and-white photo of her had failed to show was the slight tilt to her eyes, giving her a decidedly exotic look. Her high cheekbones, and her eyes, told him that she might have Russian mixed with Scythian and possibly Mongolian heritage somewhere in her family tree. He smiled to himself and wondered if it came from the women warriors of that time in Asia, because she looked like royalty and warrior all at the same time. Daria's earthiness went far beyond just being attractive. That photo did her no justice at all.

Nik forced himself back to the present. "What are you doing here in this tiny town far away from civilization?"

"I'm an adjunct professor from a Kiev University," she said in Spanish. "I'm taking a one-year sabbatical to write about the orchids that grow in this area. I'm collecting information to write a book on them."

"A biologist?" he asked, also switching easily to Spanish.

"No, a botanist." She managed a slight smile and saw a bare nod of his head. "I love flowers. All plants, actually."

"So do I," he admitted, watching how her lips fit against the ceramic rim of the cup. She was so lush. Like a ripe fruit he wanted to peel open and eat. And he wanted to taste her, starting with those shapely lips and work his way downward, slowly, across her entire willowy body. There was a flame deep in the recesses of her gold-brown eyes. His senses were finely honed after years as an operator and, if Nik wasn't misreading Daria, that was sexual interest banked up in them. *For him.* He could feel it. Literally. Which didn't help his situation. He silently thanked the Levi's he wore. No one would realize. The zipper was wide and strong, the fabric even stronger. But it was beginning to feel a little cramped down there for him.

"To photograph them?"

"Yes, but also to measure them, and make observational notes in my journal about each one I find." She shrugged. "I have a laptop, but everyone told me, unless it was a Toughbook, to leave it in the apartment and transfer my field notes to it in the evening where it couldn't get rained on. I intend to rely on good ole ancient notebook and pen for now."

Nik was impressed with her role playing. He saw the owner, Pedro, half listening to their Spanish conversation. And he'd deliberately chosen that language so that Pedro, if questioned by Korsak or one of the other men, would tell him about their flower conversation. It was the perfect cover to not rouse Korsak's suspicion that Daria was something much more than what she'd just claimed. She spoke the language fluently and with ease. "When did you arrive here?" he asked.

"About nine a.m. I have an apartment for the duration of my stay and I need to get settled in." Daria brushed some hair away from her cheek. "I wanted to explore this town, so I came to see the church close up. I love Gothic types of cathedrals."

"It's a good place for downtime too if you're wanting to get away from that crowd out there," he agreed, slipping his long, large knuckled fingers around his bright red mug.

"What are you doing here?"

Now his lies began, but Nik knew them by heart. "I'm with an exploratory mining team. We're looking for mineral deposits between here and the Highlands. It takes us out in the jungle and we come back here for five days to rest up and get some decent sleep and food."

Nik saw her tilt her head and study him. His heart cracked open. It had been shut for the last few months, and he'd felt numbed to the world. Now? He felt a trickle of returning feelings and it felt damn good to him. Truly, Daria had magic. At least for him.

"Then, you must know the good restaurants here?"

"Yes. There's three. The rest," and he raised an eyebrow, "let's just say that there are no sanitary rules down here in this jungle outpost. No FDA around to protect people from how the food is handled."

"Food poisoning." Daria wrinkled her nose. "Definitely let me know the names of those clean restaurants."

He looked at her through his thick, short lashes. "Actually? I was wondering if I might take you to dinner tonight to one of them? I could give you a lot of information about the area. There's plenty of orchids around here, and I could suggest some trails that you might take to find a lot of them in a hurry?" Her eyes widened slightly and her lips drew into a line of relief.

"I'd love to take you up on that invitation, Nik. Thank you. You're a lifeline to me because earlier in my apartment I was wondering who I could talk to to find out about the flora and fauna around here. A local always knows where the orchids would be."

"I'm the person you want." He looked at his watch. "May I escort you back to your apartment? I could drop by, say, at seven p.m. tonight and take you to dinner?" He saw her cheeks grow pink and it made her so damn becoming to him. That wasn't a reaction an actress could force. There was eagerness shining in her eyes and he could feel her truly looking forward to seeing him alone. He was too, but for different reasons. Behind closed doors, after sweeping the place for bugs, they could shed the role playing and get down to business.

"Wonderful," she murmured, tipping the mug and swallowing the last of her coffee. She set it down and, before she could get up, Nik had stood and pulled the chair out for her.

"Chivalry is not dead," he murmured in an amused tone near her ear.

His moist breath sent a skitter of tingles across her ear and scalp. Turning, their faces only inches from one another, she found herself drowning in his stormy-looking blue eyes, and her voice went oddly husky. "I see that. Thank you…"

NIGHT FELL QUICKLY in the jungle, Daria had discovered. It was completely dark outside the venetian blinds of the window that looked down upon the busy tourista street of Aguas Calientes. Nik would arrive any moment. She felt anxious. Excited. Along with some dread. Her heart wouldn't stop skipping around, telling her how much Nik affected her as a woman. The man was, in her eyes, a certifiable hunk. Now, Daria wished that Lauren had warned her about that. Maybe it would have prepared her more, made it a little easier not to be ensnared by that slow, heated smile that sometimes shadowed his chiseled lips. Or to fall so easily into his narrowed gaze, and feel consumed by the invisible fire that throbbed organically between them. Her body was at a five-alarm-fire stage of alert, and she couldn't douse it, ignore it or stop it. The man reeked of male sensuality so thick and primal, such that Daria had no experience with. Sometimes in that cafe, as she looked at him, sensed him, she thought he might be more jaguar than human. There was a decidedly primal animal side to him that he hid well, but it was far from hidden from her. And that is when Daria realized that he was just as powerfully drawn to her as she was to him.

Rubbing her palms against her black wool slacks, she didn't know what to do or what to say. Maybe just ignore this invisible, scorching connection simmering between them? Stay focused on the assignment? Her fingers trembled slightly as she smoothed her white silk long-sleeved blouse and tucked it into her waist a bit more. She'd chosen a pale-pink alpaca wool scarf that she'd looped around her neck and shoulders, and a set of small gold Incan earrings. There was a soft knock on the door and she jumped, her heart slamming into her ribs. She was acting like a teenager full of wild, uncontrollable hormones! Gulping, she nervously threaded her fingers through her long, combed hair. Did she look all right? She wasn't sure what to expect because they hadn't had a chance yet to actually sit down and talk without being overheard.

Opening the door, she looked up and met Nik's warm, shadowed eyes.

"For you," he said, holding out a spray of white and purple orchids wrapped in silver foil encircled with a purple ribbon.

"Oh…," Daria whispered, taking them, brushing his fingers during the transfer. "They're beautiful. Thank you," and she stepped aside, allowing him in. How different he appeared tonight. Earlier in the day, Nik had looked like an adventurer of Indiana Jones origin. Tonight, he wore a pressed white long-sleeved shirt, a black blazer over it, and black chinos trousers. Over his left arm was a tan raincoat. His combat boots were gone and he wore black leather oxfords instead. The change in him was startling. He reminded her of a rogue corporate businessman, the idea making Dara smile inwardly. Nik's rugged face would never be that of the suave, elegant businessmen that graced the covers of GQ magazine, but that didn't bother her at all. She quickly shut the door. As soon as she did, her voice sounding a little breathless, she said, "Please, sit down? Do we have time to talk at all before we go eat?"

Nik nodded and casually folded the raincoat over the back of the black leather chair. "Yes, the reservation is for eight p.m. We have an hour." He placed his finger to his lips.

Dara understood he wanted to check the apartment for bugs. She already had, but another set of eyes wouldn't hurt. She'd found none, but gave him a grave nod of her head, stepping out of the way as he began his thorough search, saying, "Do you mind if I briefly use the facilities first?"

Daria, understanding his ruse to disguise the lack of talk between them while he looked around, replied, "Not at all. Go ahead. I'll be right here waiting."

Once the search was done and he hadn't found any bugs, Nik came back to the living room where she stood silent. He nodded in affirmation to her that they could drop the act now.

He opened his sports coat and sat down.

Daria placed the spray of orchids into a vase and sat it on the coffee table as she sat down on the couch across from him. "I've got to say, you're really good at undercover work."

He raised his eyebrows. "You were perfect out there this afternoon." He saw instant relief in her expression.

Giving him a rolled-eyed look, Daria admitted, "This is new for me. I'm a sniper by trade. Shield Security, who I work for, gave me the mission because I speak Russian, Ukrainian and Spanish languages. I've never done undercover work before." Dara leaned back, crossing her long legs. "I'm counting on you to help me, Nik."

He frowned and studied her. "I will take care of you."

Daria's heart took off. He'd said those words to her with great weight and she suddenly felt that armor-like energy almost visibly surrounding her. There was a look of the warrior in his eyes for a moment as he silently regarded her. It made her anxiety dissolve. This man was more than a soldier. He was a long-time operator. A hardened warrior, a fact which he masked for the most part from the world around him, putting on the combat medic facade, instead.

"Thanks for the support." she said. "First, I want to tell you that Alex Kazak said to tell you hello."

Nik straightened; his voice suddenly thick with emotion. "Alex? You know him?"

Her heart clenched at the raw, sudden emotion flooding his voice and expression. If Daria had ever doubted a genuinely warm tie between the two men, she had her proof now. Nik's eyes glistened and, for a moment, she thought she saw tears in them. Just as suddenly, they were gone. "Yes, I know him and his wife Lauren very well."

"Alex? Married? Wait… Lauren…? Lauren Parker? The woman that I helped kidnap and then helped to escape?"

She saw disbelief flare in his eyes as she nodded. "Yes, the very same woman. They were married after coming back from that mission in Peru with you." Lowering her voice, Daria became more emotional than she wanted to appear, "They told me so much about you, Nik. I came here with far more information about you, your background and life, than what is usual. And Alex loves you deeply, as you know, like a brother. Lauren is forever grateful to you for helping save her life. They both want only a good outcome for you down here in Peru." She swallowed convulsively as she saw so many feelings reflected in his suddenly readable expression. It was like a miracle, reminding her sharply of Luke and his ability to shed that operator's mask when he was alone with her. Nik was doing the same thing. It made him just that much more of a draw to Daria because he was able to expose the softer masculine side of himself to her.

Sitting up, Nik pushed his long fingers through his hair. "I-I didn't know…"

"Alex said to tell you that you'd better get your ass home to Virginia. He said they have a room at their new cabin in the woods and it's got your name on the door. They both want to help you and Dan when you're finally able to get free of this place… free of Korsak."

Grimacing, Nik stood up, his scowl deepening. "Thank you for letting me know, Daria. I love Alex with all my heart. But you know that already?"

She gave him a warm look. "Yes, I do."

He stood and paced, moving to the now closed venetian blinds. Carefully, he peeked out from one side of them, studying the hill and highway below them. Turning back to her, he said, "Slavik Brudin, second in command of our team, saw us at that restaurant this afternoon." He walked over and sat down, holding her worried gaze.

"That's what you wanted. Right? That they know you've hooked up with a woman?"

"Yes. It was a good thing. Do you have photos of the rest of the team?"

"Yes, Alex provided them to me."

"And their backgrounds?"

"Yes. Why?"

"Because Brudin saw you coming down the hill from your apartment before you made it to the church. He told me later, when I came back to the hotel we all stay at, that he didn't know you were my woman. He had set his sights on you already and was going to hunt you down."

A chill worked up her back. "Hunt me down?" Her voice sounded hollow even to herself.

Nik gave her a grim look. "I told him I'd just met you, that I had an interest in you."

"What did he say?"

"He was surprised. It's the first time I've laid claim to a woman in this town." His mouth thinned. "I know Brudin will take that info back to Korsak."

"Again, that's good. It's what we want."

"Yes," he muttered, studying her beneath the weak lamplight. "Brudin is a loose cannon. He's a predator with no human feelings."

"Where I come from? That's what we call a sociopath."

"He is, believe me," Nik rasped.

"So, your team knows we're going to dinner?"

"Yes. And I wouldn't be surprised if they shadow me. More out of curiosity than anything else. I've been with them five years and never had a relationship with a woman."

"It's been two years for me," she said wryly, giving him an understanding look.

"My job leaves me no time to develop a relationship with the right woman," he said beneath his breath. "I don't like it. I never did. But I'm not going to pay for a prostitute like they do. It's not in me, I guess."

She felt his heart open more. "I saw how lonely you are at the church, Nik."

"I am. Five years of nonstop hell."

"You're doing it for a good reason. Dan will be brought over to the US. That neurosurgeon has agreed to help him. You are courageous in my eyes," Daria admitted quietly, holding his hooded stare. "I don't know if I could last five years down here to make enough money to pay for that kind of cutting-edge medical technique for a kid brother or sister, even if I had one. But what you're doing? You're a hero in my eyes." She saw ruddiness come to his cheeks.

"I'm no hero. Don't ever call me that, Daria. I'm as far away from one as you can get."

The low snarl in his voice, the pain behind it, slammed into her. She saw the anger and years of regret in his eyes, heard the weariness and disappointment in his low, tortured voice. He sat down. "Okay," she said, "I won't repeat it." But dammit, he *was* a hero to her, whether he ever heard it from her again or not. The devastation in his expression tore at her and she knew from what Alex had said that they'd seen the rapes and murders of innocent villagers on a regular and ongoing basis. Daria couldn't imagine what that did to the combat medics. She saw, clearly, how upset he had become. Holding out her hands, she said soothingly, "Look, let's focus on *us* right now. Where are we at with Korsak's team? With Brudin? Do you think Brudin will be tailing us tonight?"

"I'm sure of it," Nik muttered.

She saw the tension in his shoulders, heard the mounting tightness in his voice. "Tell me what I need to do to make this solid and safe for you," she urged. Because Nik had to convince Korsak that he was falling in love with her. That there was a relationship burgeoning between the two of them. Daria wasn't about to put his life on the line any more than it already was.

"Just what you're doing. Tonight, we need to look like two people who are helplessly drawn to one another."

"Like, me touching your hand at the table while we eat? Smiling a lot? All my attention on you?"

"Yes, all those things." Nik gave her a flat look. "I don't imagine you ever signed up for this... I mean... us..."

"I was briefed fully on my role for this, Nik. I know I'm to be your lover. At least, in the public's perception. It's important we convince Korsak, and if Brudin is going to be watching us like a fox, then we just play the parts."

He stared moodily at her. "You've never done undercover before."

Daria gave him a patient look. "Listen, you're a very handsome man in my eyes. And I like you already because of what Alex and Lauren have shared with me about you. I'm not stressed out about it, Nik. Does that put you at ease?" Daria could see some of the shadowed worry in his eyes dissolving beneath her sincerely-spoken words. If he only knew how powerfully drawn she was to him! And yet, she didn't DARE breathe a word of the truth to him. He had enough on his plate to handle. And she wasn't completely sure *he* was drawn to *her*, even though the signs were there.

Releasing a breath, Nik sat back, slowly rubbing his palms down his long, curved thighs. "That is good to know. A relief, really. I will have to kiss you goodnight at your door tonight. Brudin will take it all back to Korsak and give him a report. Are you okay with that?"

Her heart cracked a little because now she realized Nik was a chivalrous knight of old. He lived his life within those boundaries. Alex had told her as much. But then, Alex was just like that, too. Daria could see why they were brothers in arms, and fellow combat medics, sharing so much in common as they did. Yet, the rest of Korsak's team were little more than barely-controlled predators toward all women. "I'm more than okay with that. It's just a show to convince Korsak. I'll be fine with it, Nik. Don't worry."

"I worry." He shot to his feet and began to pace, his fists opening and closing at his sides as he moved around the room. "I've seen too many Quechua women and girls harmed by Korsak and his team. I cannot get their cries of terror and pain out of my head. I live in fear of ever making any woman feel powerless and fearful of me."

Getting up, Daria stopped him mid-stride, reaching out, curving her hand around his arm. She felt his bicep, tight and lean. He halted, turning, his eyes dark with anguish as he stared down at her.

"I'm looking forward to kissing you," she whispered unsteadily. And that was all she could say to try and convince Nik that she didn't want him to angst over hurting her. Daria couldn't imagine the hellish life he lived under these ongoing circumstances. Alex had told her it had gotten so bad that he couldn't deal with it any longer, glad to be out of the team. Glad to be in the US. He worried about Nik remaining in this situation, what it was doing to him.

Now, as Daria searched his eyes, she saw the utter hopelessness, the suffering palpable in his blue gaze. She wanted, in that moment, to throw her arms around his shoulders, draw him to her, share her warmth, her ability as a woman to give him a momentary safe harbor. Daria knew she could do that for Nik. The raw, unhinging violence of seeing men hurting others had torn open a canyon of pain within him. He was, after all, a medic. A healer. He lived to help stop suffering, not watch it occur and not being able to do anything about it. The tension in him was palpable as he stood stiffly, watching her.

He was fragile, Daria slowly realized as she searched his gaze. Nik was not hiding from her in any way, and what she saw was horrifying to her. He'd carried so much anguish over so many years, helpless to stop the constant violence from happening to people who could not defend themselves. Her fingers curved more surely around his arm. "Listen, we'll get through this together. You and I. We'll convince them, no question. And you must know that I'm not disgusted or feel uneasy about pretending to fall in love with you, Nik."

Daria forced a tight smile for his benefit and gave his arm a little shake. "You're not hurting me. I personally like you. Okay?" She bit back the words that he was a good man, just as he'd requested. Nik didn't believe he was good at all because he'd allowed those predatory men to hurt others.

"Are you SURE?" Nik demanded, digging into her gaze. "Are you VERY SURE, Daria?"

To hell with it. Daria realized in those tense seconds that, of the two of them, she was the less wounded. "Let me show you how I feel about you," she breathed, sliding her arms around his tight shoulders, leaning upward. She placed her lips against the harsh line of his mouth. Instantly, she felt Nik tense. He was shocked by her boldness as her mouth moved softly against his, asking him to participate. And then, she felt him relax as the heat rapidly built between them. She was taking a terrible risk by doing this but, as his lips parted, almost shy in their exploration of her offering, she wanted to cry for all that Nik had endured. No one but another military person who had been in battles could truly understand the depth of wounding the combatant carried. She felt an explosion of surprise and disbelief shatter through him as he lifted his hands, gently framing her face.

Daria closed her eyes, her flesh reacting wantonly as he leaned into her mouth, taking hers more surely, sliding, tasting and feeling his awakening, but tightly controlled, desire. Daria had been kissed before. She knew when a man really wanted to kiss her or not. Nik was holding back. She could feel it all through him as his long fingers closed more firmly against her face and gently angled it so that he could afford full contact with her searching mouth against his. She felt his terribly fragile state, the surprise at her action, the warmth that swirled and built like a bonfire between their barely-touching mouths. Daria stood quietly, no longer the aggressor, but simply allowing Nik to explore her at his own pace, as if deciding what he wanted to do.

Her heart snagged in her chest as she felt his continued hesitation and yet felt the strength of his mouth brushing against hers, tasting her. This was one-sided. Her side. She ached for Nik, as woman to his man. But it wasn't mutual. He was sipping from her lips, as if testing her, as if to adjust to her needs and desires. She wanted to cry, but instantly shoved that reaction deep down inside her.

And then, she felt something snap and break within Nik. Not in the literal sense, but she felt a huge shift within him but was unable to define what it was or what it meant. His moist breath flowed across her nose and cheek. Then, her world tumbled into a shocking heat as he stepped closer, pressing the length of his hard, male body against her softer, curved one. His mouth was no longer hesitant or shy. In the next second, she felt him open her lips with contained strength, deepening their kiss, widening his exploration of her, his lips gliding hungrily against her own. A soft moan rose in her throat, her arms tightening around his neck as she surrendered completely to his embrace, to the gentle strength of his mouth against hers. Her lower body throbbed, hungry for his touch.

Her mind was barely functioning now as she became lost in the heat, scent and power of him as a man wanting his woman. And it was clear to her that he WANTED to kiss her now. Whatever had happened at first, whatever hurdle or wall he'd encountered within himself, was now dissolved. This man knew how to kiss. He reminded her sharply of Luke, who had taken great pleasure in slow exploration of every nook and cranny of her mouth and body. Nik was the same... only... better. *Much better.*

Her knees began to feel weak, and Daria had to lean heavily into him to remain standing. Nik sensed her quandary and eased his hands from her face and allowed them to drift across her shoulders and slide down the long length of her spine and cup her hips. When he splayed his strong fingers out across her hips and brought her firmly against his erection, she groaned, deepening the kiss between them. Her whole body went red-hot and she nestled her hips wantonly against his own. Daria didn't want to think about what was happening. It was very clear to her right now that Nik *did* want her. As his tongue slowly moved across her lower lip, tasting her, she moved sensually against him, letting him know she liked it. And, as his tongue touched hers, Daria clung to him, hungrily returning that first contact.

She was breathing raggedly as Nik reluctantly eased his mouth from hers. Lips throbbing from the power of his kiss, she dragged her lashes upward, meeting his dark, searching cobalt gaze. He was trembling. But so was she. Daria saw shock in his eyes, entwined with the sudden new realization that she liked kissing him just as much as he liked kissing her. There was raw arousal in his eyes and she absorbed the hardness of his erection against her soft belly. Her arms unlocked from around his neck and she fiercely held his searching gaze, filled as it was with a mixture of awe, arousal, surprise and pleasure.

"Now," she whispered in an unsteady voice, "don't *ever* think from here on out that I don't enjoy you touching or kissing me when we're out in public, Nik. I think you know that I like it. I WANTED to kiss you. I LIKE your touch. This isn't role playing. It's for real…"

CHAPTER 5

NIK COULD BARELY think, the taste of Daria on his lips, her scent arousing him until he wanted to continue that kiss to a blazing conclusion. The sincerity of her words pulverized his pounding heart. He kept a hand on her shoulder because she appeared dazed. So was he. He'd never expected this! Not ever! Five years not even touching a woman, and then to have this special one come boldly up to him, press her warm, willing mouth to his? His mind and body exploded with shock. For that moment, Nik had been stunned by her lips moving lightly across his. Her scent filled his nostrils, the warmth and curves of her breasts lightly pressing against his chest, her arms firm and warm around the nape of his neck, all conspired to momentarily place him in a state of paralysis. It were as if a fairytale had turned upside-down and the princess had awoken the sleeping frog-prince from a hundred years of deep, long sleep!

He saw a hint of chagrin come into her wide, glistening gold eyes, although arousal clearly pooled in them, along with what he dared hope was pleasure from the kiss he had returned. Nik knew how to please a woman. The surging starvation tunneling through him right now made him want to take her into his arms, and carry her into the bedroom. Shame paralleled those animal thoughts as he searched her innocent features, the stubborn set of her chin, her words echoing through him, through his raw heart that was suddenly so needy and hungry. His mind shouldn't go there. He was nothing like Korsak and his men. Nothing like those predators.

He treasured the act of love with a willing woman who wanted him as much as he wanted her. The drought of no sex was like a jagged edge sawing through his rock-like control. Daria's mouth lifted a little, unsureness, even a touch of shyness, coming into her expression. He sensed her worrying that she'd done something wrong. She'd done something *so* right. Her kiss, her boldness, had reminded him that he was human and had needs like any man.

"That was," he managed in a rasp, "... unexpected..."

Daria gave him a confused look. "I know... I didn't... I mean, I didn't mean to kiss you. Well, that's not true. I did," and her hands fluttered nervously as she ducked out from beneath his grasp. Wrapping her arms around herself, Daria stood there, uncertain, with heat stinging her cheeks. "I'm not making much sense."

Wryly, he murmured, "No, you aren't…" There was uncertainty in her eyes. Her cheeks were a bright red and he managed a slight smile. "But it's okay. I think I understand why you did it."

"You do?"

"Alex told you about all the stuff we've seen and been through," he said heavily, avoiding her caring gaze. "I just didn't want to enter into this with you and have you feel as if I was taking advantage of you, was all." He met her eyes, and saw them growing even more sympathetic. "Was I right? You kissed me to show me that you didn't mind if I kissed you when the situation demanded it?" And Nik wished suddenly, that Daria had *wanted* to kiss him because she was attracted to him as much as he was to her. That was his secret wish. He knew he had no right to expect that from her at all. They were strangers thrown together on an op. And yes, Daria had gone into the op knowing the part she must play. Still, in Nik's mind, it was a highly personal, intimate kind of demand being thrust upon her, this fake relationship. And it bothered him, maybe more than it should.

"You were right," Daria admitted quietly, allowing her arms to drop to her sides. She swept her thick hair across her shoulder. "I'm not apologizing, Nik. You needed to know I'm okay with all of this."

"Oh, I got your message loud and clear."

"You're not going to hurt me. I know that. But don't err on the side of caution, either because if your team is watching us, it has to look genuine between us. We have to sell to them that we're falling in love. That's all."

His heart twinged and he couldn't stop the hurt from flowing through him. Daria's kiss had been convincing. Too convincing to his sex-starved body, to his heart that yearned for the softness of a woman in his life once more. "You're right, we do. They will never see it as love, however. Only sex."

She looked incredible with her long, straight black hair laying across her shoulder like a dark cape, emphasizing the clean lines of her face and those golden eyes that he swore still had arousal in them. He had kissed her for real. It wasn't an act on his part at all. Once he'd gotten past the shock, the heat of her mouth and the press of her sweet, innocent curves against him had smashed through his rigid control, and he'd kissed her reverently, with all of his heart, through every movement of his mouth. A kiss was far more than just lips meeting. His heart was involved. His soul. And Nik had allowed himself, for that brief, exquisite moment, to kiss Daria with all the need and beauty he had to share with her. Only… she was such a good actress.

If he believed her explanation, it had all been just an act on her part to convince him that she was okay with him being intimate with her up to a point. As he pushed his fingers through his hair, his heart, which had never led him wrong, whispered to him that she'd meant every last bit of that kiss. That it *wasn't* a game. Or a cover. Or a convincing lie to fool Korsak's team. Daria had kissed him because she was drawn powerfully to him. His instincts, the same ones that had kept him alive so many times when he should have died, knew he was correct. His head warred with his heart. To believe Daria's offered explanation or not?

He didn't want to, dammit. His body was on fire. His erection throbbed. Not having had a woman for five years, after living like a monk all that time, like the man in prison that he was, her kiss and the innocent movement of her body against his, was like the key that had unlocked a dungeon door, flung it wide open, and released all his imprisoned needs. All those urges, the ones that he ignored up until just now, came roaring to the surface. What a hot mess!

"We need to go," he said, his voice thick with hunger, desperately trying to once again wrestle all those needs back down into a dark, hidden corner of himself.

"Yes… of course…," and Daria turned, picking up her light, wool camel-colored coat. It turned cool and damp in the evening around here.

Nik moved over to her, taking the coat and helping her slip it on. He watched her arrange her black hair and pink scarf with such feminine movements that he felt like a slavering, half-insane wolf wanting his mate. And honestly? That is how he felt toward Daria. She was his mate. She just didn't know it. *Yet.* Nik found that he had to willfully force his fingers to release Daria's coat to be able to break away from her and walk over to the chair across which his raincoat hung, and pull it on. His hands weren't steady. Hell, *he* wasn't steady, his body for a start, not to mention his head spinning with heat, arousal and desire for her. And, judging from the look in Daria's wide, flawless eyes, she was just as dazed by their coming together as he was. She wasn't a good liar. He still saw arousal in her eyes. That couldn't be faked.

He opened the door for her, and the cool dampness hit them. Daria started down the exterior stairs, hands on the wet metal railings and Nik followed. Below, there was the noise of rasping, throaty flutes, drums pounding a rhythmic beat, and tourists in front of the many brightly-lit stores dancing in the street. Nik swiftly scanned the area. He knew Brudin was down there somewhere in the shadows. Watching.

Daria pulled her pink scarf tighter around her neck and then turned and waited for him at the bottom of the stairs, her hands in the pockets of her coat. The street lights were glaring and bright on both sides of the wide, asphalt concourse. Colorful flags hung everywhere outside shops to attract customers.

Nik halted just behind and to the left of her, his hand naturally caressing the small of her back. He could smell the spices and the meat cooking, the air filled with their odors. Dinner started between eight to eleven p.m. in South America. He leaned over, his mouth almost brushing the hair covering her ear. "I'm sure Brudin has been ordered to be Korsak's eyes and ears."

Daria turned, their faces inches apart. "Did you run into them earlier?" She saw his eyes flicker with anger and then it was gone.

"We're all at that hostel outside of town. When I came back after escorting you to your apartment, Brudin jumped me about you." Nik didn't want to go into all the lurid details of the man's cruel remarks nor mention his small, mean brown eyes dancing with deviltry as the usual teasing commenced.

"They hassled you."

He placed his hand on her shoulder, smoothing her coat's golden wool, feeling the strength of her beneath its fabric. "It's their nature. But," and he became grim, "Korsak took instant interest. Brudin always does his dirty work for him. You have a photo of him?"

"Yes."

He could smell her scent and it was driving him crazy, "If you spot him? Pretend not to see him. Just tell me? I'll probably see him, anyway. I know their tactics."

She smiled a little and leaned in against his tall body. "Then, let's make them *really* think we're falling in love with one another."

The huskiness in her voice, that smoky look in her shadowed eyes that gleamed with mirth, made him relax a little. "You remind me of a female jaguar, you're a *kotya*, a little cat." he whispered, deliberately dropping the low, rasping endearment right by her ear.

Laughing a little, Daria slipped her hand around his arm and remained close to Nik as he guided them into the busy street, heading up the hill. "I've been called a lot of things in my life, but never that." She gave him a teasing look.

How badly Nik wanted this to be real. The urge to see even a single look in her eyes to fully persuade him that it was, made him long for a real relationship with an intelligent woman like her. "*Moya kotya*," he said, giving her a heated look she couldn't misinterpret. *My little kitten.* It was the term of a lover whispered, and as he murmured it by her ear, strands of her hair tickled his nose and mouth for a moment. Nik felt and saw her react to his deeply meaningful words. "And yes, it is my sweet words for you. Ever since I met you, you reminded me of a lithe, beautiful female jaguar. You know," he said, lifting his hand toward the darkness where Machu Picchu rose high above them, "there are jaguars in this area?"

Daria raised her eyebrows, and said, "I read that there were. Have you ever seen one?"

One corner of his mouth lifted slightly. "I have one on my arm right now." He saw her eyes flare slightly, saw them soften, and knew without a doubt that Daria liked the endearment he'd chosen for her. *Kotya* was a kitten, but in his eyes and heart, she was a fully-matured, dangerous and sensual female jaguar. There was a solid confidence that radiated from Daria and it intrigued him. He wanted desperately to have the time to find out more about her on personal terms when they were alone and away from prying eyes.

He guided her to the top of the hill and lead her into Hotel Machu Picchu, the newest one the small town had to offer, boasting a full four stars. Nik saw that only well-heeled patrons, those with a lot of money, were going inside. There were two bellmen in gray-and-black uniforms at the crystal-cut double doors. Beggars had been driven off, not allowed anywhere near the entrance, he saw. Normally, he would never eat here, preferring instead a local eatery down near the church that served good, clean, solid food at a low price. All his money was going into a bank account for Dan's medical help. But tonight… just this one time, Nik was going to loosen up those purse strings. He wanted to give Daria only the best and, from the look of awe on her face at the hand-carved quartz crystal doors that reflected Machu Picchu rising above, she was impressed. He couldn't wrap his head around the fact that he had this beautiful, sensual woman on his arm. She was smart and quick and he loved being around a woman like that.

Daria managed a whispered, "ohhhh…" as they walked into the huge rotunda-like foyer. The tiles were gold-veined white marble interspaced with black ones in designs that honored ancient Incan designs and symbols. Above them hung a thousand-piece quartz crystal chandelier, sending out sparks of lights in all directions.

Nik enjoyed her reaction to the elegance and richness of the hotel. The staff, all Quechua Indians, were in gray-and-black uniforms. "Your beauty outshines anything you see in here," he told her as he eased the coat off her. He saw her lips twist, her eyes flashing with warmth up at him over his whispered words.

"You are a romantic, Nik. More from the Victorian Age than a modern-day twenty-first century man. How did you get that way?"

"I don't really know. Perhaps I need you to discover those things in me?" He led her over to the coat room and the young woman with long, black braids took their coats, giving the check stub to Nik. He slid it into the pocket of his blazer. Turning, his hand on her upper arm as he led her toward the sumptuous restaurant, he said lightly, "We have all night. I'll tell you many tales, *Moya kotya*, if you want to hear them."

She gave him a merry look. "Oh, I'm all ears, *Moya prekrasnyy yaguar*, my beautiful jaguar, believe me."

He managed a sliver of a grin. "I like your endearment. It slips like music off your tongue. Thank you…" He walked up to the tuxedoed maître d who was clearly from Lima, Peru, and not from around here. The middle-aged man with his thin pencil mustache and arrogant-looking face waited for them. He looked them up and down critically, sniffed and then nodded, as if giving his blessing that they were dressed well enough to be allowed entrance into the dining room. Nik maintained his hardened expression, speaking not only in Spanish, but in *Castilian* Spanish, which only the upper-crust Lima residents spoke, not the bastardized, common Spanish that the masses spoke. The maître d's eyes popped. And then he quickly cleared his throat and looked nervously down at his reservations book.

"Yes, of course Señor Morozov, you are right here."

"I want that booth over there," and Nik pointed to one in the darkened corner.

"Of course, sir," he said, nodding and with a flourish, said, "I will take you there myself, Señor and Señorita?"

Daria looked up at Nik and withheld a smile. When he wanted to be, he was pure alpha male. Around her, he was not. Protective, yes. But nothing like the unearned arrogance of this maître d who was putting on so many airs that she wanted to laugh outright. But that wouldn't have been a good idea, so Daria kept her game face on, pretending to be looking around utterly bored. Inwardly, her heart was starting to turn to mush. Every time Nik leaned close to her, she inhaled the male scent that made her lower body shimmer with possibility. She wished she could control her body, but she couldn't. It clearly had a damned mind of its own. His softly-spoken endearment for her made her want him even more. She liked that he saw her as a deadly female jaguar. Indeed, she was.

The maître d made a huge, grand celebration, gesticulating with his arm, of pulling out the gold-colored mahogany chair for her. It was upholstered with a rich tapestry of blue, gold and soothing green tones. In fact, the pale green of the ceiling along with the equally pale blue of the walls did help her relax a little. She sat down and got comfortable, glad to see the maître d leave and a young Indian woman in a crisp long-sleeved white blouse and long black ankle-length skirt come over. She smiled at them and it was genuine.

"Welcome," she greeted in flawless Spanish. "I am Maria." She handed each of them a huge leather-bound menu. "May I get you something to drink?"

Nik looked at Daria who sat at his left arm. "What interests you?"

"I like wine. Do you?"

"I was weaned on wine at our local Catholic church, so yes, I like red wine. What kind do you prefer? Red or white? Or, perhaps champagne?" Nik opened the wine menu for her. He was going to spare no expense this night. He knew Korsak and the team would laugh themselves silly because he was well-known as 'The Penny Pincher' among them. They spent hundreds of US dollars on prostitutes. He saved his money. But there was no expense he would spare to make Daria happy. And that came from his heart, not from some act they were supposed to perform. He noticed, as he covertly slid his gaze around the room, that Brudin was not yet present, but he hadn't expected the coarse Russian to be here right on time. He'd never get past the inspection of that haughty maître d. He'd be outside, hidden in the brush and trees, watching through a window. Nik hoped it started to rain and it soaked the bastard. That, or a poisonous centipede could maybe crawl up inside his pant leg and sting the hell out of him.

"Are you a white or red guy?" Daria asked.

"Either. I like all wine. Pick something you want to drink. We'll order a bottle."

Daria gave him a warm look and nodded. She showed their server the name of the wine, pointing it out on the menu.

Maria nodded and replied, "A very good white, Señorita. If you like a citrus finish? It is semi-sweet."

"Sounds wonderful," Daria said, thanking her.

Another waiter, an eager younger man, came over with a basket of freshly-baked bread and a silver bowl of butter accompanying it.

Daria sighed and looked around and said in Ukrainian, "This is truly a beautiful restaurant, Nik. Hard to imagine something this fancy out in the middle of the Peruvian jungle," her expression softening even more.

"My eyes are only on you," he murmured. He liked the fact that Daria knew Ukrainian as well. Brudin would go out of his mind when he found out she spoke that language. The other patrons nearby were from many countries, but he was betting that no one knew their shared mother tongue, so it was safer to talk in Ukrainian, instead. He saw Daria's cheeks grow pink over his rasped compliment. His words stirred Daria and, to his surprise, she gave him a sweet smile that melted his heart.

"I think there are many sides to you, Nik Morozov."

"I am complicated because of the life I chose."

"Aren't we all?" She sipped her iced water. "But, you honestly intrigue me. I feel there's so much to you, and all I'm seeing is just the tip of the iceberg."

"That is American slang?"

She grinned. "Yes. We're great at slang, aren't we? Do you know what I meant?"

He nodded his head. "I took an advanced immersion course in English when I was in the military. My friend, Alex Kazak, did not. He never could grasp contractions. And he's awful at slang. But," and he gave her an amused glance, "I don't pretend to be a complete expert on American slang, either."

Daria laughed outright.

Her laughter riffled through him like a lover's caressing hands. It was a rich, full-bodied sound, husky, straight from Daria's heart. His chest expanded with so many emotions that Nik couldn't process them all. But among them was happiness. It had been such a foreign feeling to him. Until *she* walked into his life. The sparkle in Daria's eyes whispered through him. There was real joy radiating from her to him. And that delicious mouth of hers that he'd tasted earlier, and instantly become addicted to, was his undoing.

CHAPTER 6

Daria could feel the tension in Nik as they ate their dinner. It was nothing obvious, but it was there. They sat close enough together so as not to be overheard because of the booth he'd chosen.

"Are you concerned about Brudin watching us?" and she saw him hesitate fractionally as he lifted the fork to his mouth. The change in Nik, just from a clothes standpoint, was amazing. They were out in a jungle where sweat and high humidity were the norm. Yet, tonight, he looked like a self-assured corporate lion. His confidence was rock solid and she knew he'd become that way through his life as a black ops soldier.

"Yes. Korsak always sends Brudin to do his bidding."

"Do you think you'll be hit with a lot of questions when you get back to the hotel tonight?" She cut some of the carrots on her plate with her knife and fork. They'd been drizzled with local Peruvian honey and were amazing. She saw the corner of his mouth draw in fractionally in place of a verbal reply, and then she continued, "I take it that's a 'yes'?"

He met and held her gaze. "Brudin is a bully. He lives to hurt others."

"Do you think they'll buy our burgeoning relationship?"

"Yes. Tomorrow? I want to pick you up around ten a.m. There's a lot of different trails around Aguas Calientes. The Pachamama trail, which winds around her base south of town, along the railroad tracks. I'd like to take you there. We need to verify your cover as a Kiev university botanist in hunt of local orchids." He gave her a slight smile. "That particular trail is loaded with orchids hanging off the branches of the trees all along either side of it."

"Mmm, sounds nice. Away from prying eyes too?"

"Can't assume it. Brudin knows how to hide and trail with the best of them. We're going to assume they have eyes on us any time we're together, unless I tell you different."

She felt her lower body twinging with need again as he gave her that dark, heated look of his. How she wished she could kiss Nik again. It wouldn't even be to show Korsak's team. It would be because she wanted to. The memory of his strong mouth cherishing hers was… *unforgettable!*

"Have you given any thought to staying overnight with me in my apartment?" she asked.

"Yes." He wiped his mouth with his white linen napkin before putting it back across his lap. "They've never seen me have a woman in my life until now. But they know I'm a cautious person, a conservative one." He frowned and cut into his beef steak. "I've given a lot of thought to this, Daria. I think by the third night, I can stay with you all night, and the team will expect it. If I do it too soon, it may come off looking fake and raise their suspicions. On the second night, I'd like to spend about an hour with you on the plans when we go back to your apartment. I can get you up to speed on the villages we frequent. There's pictures I can draw for you that will help everyone, including the Army Special Forces team that is trying to shadow Korsak. Staying over will have to wait for a few more days."

She thought about Nik being in that apartment with her. "You know them, so I'll trust whatever you say."

He studied her for a moment. "Trust me, I would like to go home with you and stay all night."

Daria wasn't sure how he meant it. To love her? To finish that kiss in the bedroom? Or to give her the information she was seeking that would help the Army teams shadowing Korsak? It wasn't something she could ask lightly about out in public. "Whatever you think will work best to convince them is fine by me." She saw the look in his shadowed blue eyes and felt a powerful longing within him. It was sweet, sharp and poignant. Nik opened his mouth, but then frowned and shut it. What was it that he'd wanted to say to her?

Nik walked Daria up the flight of wooden stairs to the door of her apartment. Overhead, going on ten p.m. now, the white, gauzy clouds had lowered to just above the town still rocking with drums, flutes and wandering tourists crowded on either side of the street. He followed Daria up the stairs. It was chilly, and the dampness ate into his clothes. He enjoyed the view of her hips swaying in front of him, his fingers itching to cover those shapely cheeks and feel her warmth and her mouth upon his once more. It was impossible to wipe that kiss from his mind and heart.

The nape of his neck prickled in warning and Nik knew Brudin was nearby. Probably invisible somewhere in the crowd below, watching. Always watching. Reaching the platform in front of the brightly-painted red wooden door, he took the keys Daria had in hand and opened it for her. The humidity had made the tendrils of dark hair around her face soft, and his heart took off.

"I need to kiss you goodnight," he said in a low, gritty voice, slipping the keys into her awaiting hand. He saw her give him a playful smile as she placed them into her purse.

"Yes, Brudin would expect that." She slid the strap of her purse over her left shoulder and lifted her arms, sliding them around his shoulders. "I'm looking forward to it…," and she leaned upward as his hands cupped her shoulders, gently drawing her against him. There was a hint of confusion in Nik's eyes for a split second. Did he not want to kiss her? If she had any question about that, he expunged it by leaning over, his mouth brushing hers gently 'hello', as if asking permission. Daria felt the tension within him as his fingers curved around her back, drawing her closer until her breasts lightly came up against his jacket and chest. His breath was warm and she opened her lips, wanting more contact with him. Daria thought she heard him groan, but wasn't sure. His mouth slid across hers, capturing her, and Daria felt heat flood her lower body. This was a man who wanted to kiss her. If he was unsure, it didn't feel like it now as he coaxed open her lips more, sipping from her like a bee gathering nectar from a flower.

Daria felt cherished, and sensed his wanting to take her along with him. This was no raw, sexual kiss. This was a man exploring the woman he held in his arms, almost worshipfully, as he caressed her lips, deepening their sacred connection. A small sound of pleasure vibrated in her throat as he brought her fully against him, his mouth masterful, stirring her to bright, aching life. She was lost in him, in his scent, in his strength that he monitored as he claimed her mouth more surely. Daria wanted so much more. Nik felt solid and trustworthy against her. She knew without proof that he would protect her, that impression swirling around her. She could feel him guarding her and she knew obliquely, through the heat and fire flaring to life within her, that he would give his life for her without hesitation.

That jolted her. Daria felt as if they were in telepathic connection with one another, feeling his intense, consuming hunger wrapping around her own, his mouth taking hers to a level where she could no longer think, only feel. Only *need*.

As their mouths reluctantly parted, her breath was shallow, and as fast as his. She lifted her lashes, staring up into his stormy, blue gaze. He held her solidly against him and she could feel his erection pressing insistently into her belly, flares of heat throbbing down through her.

"Wow," she murmured, her own voice sounding dreamlike to her, "you really know how to kiss a woman."

Nik slowly released her and she swayed. He kept one hand on her upper arm, seeing the heat in her half-closed eyes, seeing it in the richness of her parted lips, and in the flush creeping up into her cheeks. "You make a jaguar hungry, Daria," was all he could force out, the throbbing in his erection clear proof that he wanted this woman: body, heart and soul. She fueled the yearning in him, whether she knew it or not. She was a soldier, a strong woman with confidence to burn, and he'd tasted all of that in her bold, arousing kiss. Daria didn't seem at all afraid to commit to him. The only real question was: was it real between them? Or only part of her undercover act?

It hadn't been from his end. Not at all. Nik wanted to lead her through the open door, shut and lock it behind them, lift Daria into his arms and carry her into the bedroom where he wouldn't allow her to leave his arms until he'd pleasured her, and then she would never want to leave his side again. It was all a fevered dream, but one that had sprung to life within his chest and lower body until he couldn't think coherently any longer. He felt as if a wild, primal animal was howling within him. One that wanted to be released.

He saw Daria's faint smile, saw the arousal clearly in her eyes this time. No woman could fake that look, and he knew it. Joy flowed through him as this realization hit him. Nik reached up, caressing her cheek, pushing a few strands of hair back behind her ear.

He said, "I'll see you tomorrow at ten a.m.? Wear your jungle hiking clothes? Boots? And bring a knapsack with water. I'll bring us something to eat for lunch."

She gave him a heated look, her hand moving down his other arm. "That sounds wonderful. Thank you for a lovely day and night, Nik. Please stay safe?" and her gaze dug into his.

Nik heard the concern in her husky voice and released her arm, allowing her to stand on her own. "I'll be fine, *moya Kotza*." He nodded toward the open door. "Go inside? Lock the door behind you." He saw the regret in her eyes, the way her mouth closed, that lower lip in a slight pout, enticing him all over again.

"Yes," she said in low voice. She let her hand fall from his arm. "Goodnight... *Moy prekrasnyy yaguar*, my beautiful jaguar..."

Nik gave her a slight smile and touched her cheek one last time. The last thing he wanted to do was leave Daria. The invitation was there in her eyes. Was it real? How he wanted it to be! But she was a consummate actress and it might well be for Brudin's benefit. Waiting until she slipped inside and quietly closed the door, Nik stood there until he heard the lock slide into place. Turning, he walked slowly down the steps, the round metal pipes of the railings beaded with the dampness of the high humidity hovering over the town.

As he walked into the now thinning crowds and the music blaring out from the restaurants at the top of the hill, Nik felt the nape of his neck prickle in warning again.

A sleazy shape he recognized slid out from under the shadows of an eave.

"Well," Brudin growled, giving him a leering look as he caught up to Nik in the center of the street where they started dodging clumps of tourists, "that was a sweet kiss you gave her, Morozov. Why didn't you follow her inside? She looked like she wanted you to do just that."

"Because I'm not like you." Nik reined in his irritation at the bald-headed soldier who was dressed in a dark green t-shirt and cammos and muddy, wet hiking boots. Nik smiled inwardly. Brudin had spent quite some time in the mud, hiding among the plants near the window, while himself and Daria had eaten their meal in warmth and comfort inside. He knew Spetsnaz-trained soldiers were tough and that physical discomfort was something they had learned to ignore. Still, it gave him a considerable sense of satisfaction that Brudin had spent two hours in the damp chill and rain watching them.

Brudin chuckled darkly, matching Nik's stride down the street toward their hotel at the base of the hill. "She's a fine piece of tail."

"Shut your mouth, Brudin."

Brudin grinned, showing two lower teeth missing in the front of his mouth. "Touchy, are we?"

Anger soared through Nik, but he instantly clamped down on it. "I will NEVER treat a woman like any of you do."

Crowing, Brudin delighted in his prickly reaction. "Why, Morozov, I don't know what to think. Ever since I joined the team, you've been a monk. Now, suddenly, this new woman coming into town has turned your head. It's rather fascinating to me. We've never seen you around a woman before. Maybe you can teach us something, Comrade."

Grimly, Nik flashed him a glare. Brudin was thicker and heavier than he was, but a good three inches shorter. "None of you treat a woman with respect. I always will."

Chuckling, Brudin gave him a merry look. "Right. I saw that erection of yours. You're no better than we are, Morozov. And you're a liar. You want to fuck her, pure and simple. No question about that. And just because we don't wine and dine a woman, it doesn't mean our objective isn't the same. We need a good fuck. That's what women are good for."

Ignoring the laughing Russian, Nik said nothing. He'd learned a long time ago that Brudin was a bully who delighted in torturing anyone else, man or woman.

"So," Brudin said, "tell me about her."

Nik gave Brudin her cover story. The idiot's thick brown eyebrows rose. "She's from Kiev, Ukraine?"

"You know every nation on Earth comes to Machu Picchu. Why not Ukraine? Do you know what a botanist is?" Nik goaded him.

Shrugging his meaty shoulder, Brudin shrugged. "A biologist."

"Close. She is an expert on plants and South American orchids."

"So?"

"She's here to write a book about them." Nik was going to drip-feed as little information about Daria to this piece of shit—even about her cover identity—as he could, feeling aggressively protective of her. He saw the interest in Brudin's eyes for Daria and that wasn't a good thing. The Russian soldier got this same feral look in his face whenever he was going to run a woman down and rape her. The nape of Nik's neck tightened. His hands curled into fists but he forced himself to relax.

"So," Brudin muttered, sliding him a sly glance, "that means she's going to be around here for a while, eh?"

Scowling, Nik said, "I didn't ask her."

"I imagine you're maneuvering her so that she yearns for your body when you are gone and you just conveniently show up once a month and can spend five days in her bed."

Nik shook his head. "Unlike you, Brudin, I respect women. I don't know where this is leading with Daria. But I want to find out."

"Looks like you'll have the time to plot, plan, and then get her to be pining for you when you're out with us in that green hell."

Nik remained silent as they reached the bottom of the hill. Their hotel, one that was used by prostitutes, was always busy with men coming and going. It suited Korsak and his team perfectly, but Nik hated it. He wished he was back in Daria's clean, quiet apartment instead of going to his room on the third floor with too thin of walls. And by tomorrow morning, Nik expected Brudin to have filled Korsak in on his burgeoning relationship with Daria.

Desayuno, brunch to an American, would not be a pleasant meal with his leader tomorrow morning, either. He worried that Brudin was showing far too much interest in Daria. The two men reached the porch of the hotel and then split up upon entering the foyer. Nik went to the stairs to go to his room. As he walked through the lobby, to his left he saw Korsak and his men with women on their laps, drinking vodka and singing bawdy Russian songs. Their voices were deep and hoarse and he wanted to crush his hands against his ears and blot all of it out.

"So," Ustin Korsak said slyly to Nik over their brunch of *desayuno* at the restaurant the next morning, "Brudin tells me you have finally found a bitch in heat."

Nik cut into his steak and glanced across the table. Everyone else was hungover, their eyes red-rimmed and blurry-looking, their faces unshaven, their bodies unshowered, and their hair uncombed where they sat around the table in the otherwise empty restaurant. "I've met a very nice young woman," he snapped back, glaring at Korsak whose thin mouth lifted at its corners into a parody of a grin.

"He's a gentleman," Brudin stage-whispered to Korsak. "You should have seen how sweetly he kissed her last night at her apartment door."

The other men hooted and grinned wickedly at Nik.

"I didn't know you had it in you, Morozov," Ustin said mildly, smiling. "Here, we thought you had taken a vow of chastity. A Catholic monk among us, without the robes."

"Unlike you," Nik muttered, "to me women aren't animals to be manhandled."

All the men snickered, the clink of cutlery against plates the only other sound.

Ustin's brow rose slightly. "So, she's a Ukrainian botanist? Here on assignment?"

"Yes." Nik knew Ustin wasn't stupid. Unlike Brudin, who had no idea what a botanist was, he never assumed such ignorance of Korsak. He might be hungover this morning, but that steel-trap mind of his worked flawlessly. Nik forced himself to chew his food and pretend he wasn't tense and worried.

"Where did you meet her?"

"At the Catholic church yesterday at the noon Mass."

Brudin snorted, "Imagine that? Meeting a woman in church. This union has to be blessed by Heaven itself."

The group snickered and laughed.

"Well," Ustin told his second-in-command mildly, "you would never meet one there because you never go to church, Brudin. Maybe you are missing something, eh? A much classier type of woman?"

The table of soldiers chortled, well entertained.

"Morozov, on the other hand, is in that church two or three times in a week when we come here for R&R," Korsak pointed out, stabbing his fork in Nik's direction. And then his smile grew as he pinned his gaze on his men. "He prays for our depraved souls. Don't you, Nik?"

"You're all going to Hell. I don't ever pray for any of you bastards. You're all a lost cause."

The table erupted into rolling, rollicking laughter. Korsak gave Nik a thoughtful, amused glance.

"Ahhh," Korsak said, "our mild-mannered do-gooder combat corpsman has his hackles raised this morning." He cast a look to Brudin who sat on his right. "I wonder? Is the good doctor falling in love with that black-haired beauty? Head over heels? What do you think?"

Brudin sneered. "He's got a set of balls on him after all."

Nik ignored them, taking a sip of his coffee, giving Korsak a calm look. He knew not to break and become emotional. The tension at the table was strung taut and he could feel it.

Korsak had put a pistol to his head one time when he'd tried to rescue a screaming, frightened fourteen-year-old girl they'd chosen. He hadn't been about to let them harm her. Alex Kazak was already gone from the team by that point, and might have made a difference. But Nik, even on his own, had been desperate to protect that screaming, terrified child. And that's all she was really: a child. Her parents had sobbed and pleaded with Korsak to not hurt their virginal daughter.

Korsak had jammed his pistol against Nik's temple and cocked the trigger. It was the darkest moment of Nik's life and he'd had to leave, scramble away from under the threat of the gun, away from the shrieks of the helpless girl's cries. He had hidden in the jungle, blindly taking a trail, losing himself, crying for the girl, for her family. And the overriding sense of shame and anger that he hadn't been able to do anything about it haunted him to this day. Alex Kazak had come within a hair's breadth of being shot by Alexandrov when he'd tried to stop another woman from being raped by the team a year earlier.

Bitterness thrummed through Nik, his mouth tightening. The tension in his shoulders was daunting and yet he had to look relaxed among his team, as if nothing were wrong. He felt Korsak's digging stare, but he did not raise his head to respond to it. He could feel Ustin trying to figure out what was going on between him and Daria. He'd started inwardly when the bastard had called her a 'black-haired beauty.' Nik was sure Brudin had given Korsak every last damn detail about her.

It sent dread flowing through him. These men used prostitutes while in town. None had any kind of decent relationship with any woman. It was all about sex. Again, he was the anomaly standing out among the team members. He prayed that Korsak didn't get too interested in Daria. Would he try to rape her? Every protective gene in his body reacted to that question. Nik had no experience with Korsak when a team member had one steady woman in their life. He had no idea what his boss would do. But he certainly knew what the monster was capable of.

One thing that helped tamp down his sheer terror for Daria's sake was that, when the team came to a larger town, they left women and girls alone. They didn't just grab one of them off the street, drag her into a house, and rape her as they would out in the smaller villages. Korsak had a standing order that none of his team was to touch any woman or girl here in this tourista town. This was their safe place. They couldn't afford to bring the *policia* into it, cause a stir, and then have the Peruvian government become involved. So, maybe based upon Korsak's directive, Brudin would leave Daria alone too, because she lived in the town. He dragged in a long, ragged breath, praying his logic was correct.

"What are you doing today, Nik?" Ustin asked casually, cutting into the steamed vegetables on his plate.

Nik lifted his head. "I'm taking Daria down a trail where there's a lot of local orchids. I'll be seeing her from ten a.m. onward."

Nodding, Korsak said, "You like this woman?"

Did he? *God yes.* But he played it differently. "We have just met. I like her. But I don't know where this will lead."

"The way she kissed you last night," Brudin said with a grin, "I'd have dragged her into that house and we'd still be in bed fucking through the night and into the morning. I wouldn't be taking her anywhere this morning. Tie her up to the bed. Keep her my prisoner."

Nik was well aware of Brudin's sadistic streak. He liked cuffing the prostitute of his choice to the headboard and having his way with her. Every morning, the men bragged of what they'd done the night before. Nik left early, and never returned to the hotel until after dark. That way, he avoided the whole sordid affair. Lifting his chin, he said, "That's the difference between us. I respect women. You would be the last people I'd ask for suggestions on how to treat one."

More guffaws.

Brudin scowled deeply, his lip lifting to reveal his yellow-coated teeth.

Korsak chewed his food thoughtfully, not joining in with the laughter. "You've been with the team five years, Nik. What is it about this woman that suddenly draws you out of your monk's cave?"

Nik reflexed inwardly, feeling Korsak wanting to know more. "I don't know. I wasn't looking for a woman, like all of you always do."

Korsak considered Nik's reply. "How long will she be in this area?"

Shrugging, Nik said, "I don't know. How long does it take to write a book on orchids? I have no ruler to measure that by."

"Sounds boring as hell to me," Brudin growled.

"There's a lot of orchids in this area," Korsak said conversationally, finishing off his vegetables and cutting into his beef steak. "So, Nik? If things go well? You will have something to look forward to once a month coming back here to Aguas Calientes?"

"I will," he said.

"Instead of sleeping, eating and hiking around here, and playing doctor to that orphanage at the other end of town to fill your hours," Brudin said sarcastically.

Nik leveled a glare at Brudin. He hated the man to his very soul. Hated what he'd done to the villagers. "Mind your own damned business."

More snickers and humored looks between the men.

Nik didn't take any guff from these men. Just because he was a combat medic didn't mean he was worth less than any other trained Spetsnaz soldier. He was just as good as any of them. And, although Brudin pushed him at times, the idiot circled him warily because Nik was not one to be pushed too far. He'd already broken Brudin's nose two years ago and the soldier remembered that event. He'd stopped bullying Nik at that time because the medic had refused to just lie down and take his shit. And, although Brudin was pissed at him to this day and still made petty riposte attempts to gig him, he knew if he pushed Nik too far, he'd react. And he didn't want his nose broken again. Or worse. Nik was a CQC expert, close quarters combat, and that meant he knew how to kill. His hands were literal lethal weapons and Brudin kept that in mind.

"Well," Korsak said lightly, "perhaps, if things go your way, you will introduce me to her at some point?"

Nik snorted. "In a pig's eye."

Brudin grinned.

Korsak gave Nik a steady, assessing look for a moment, nodded, said nothing and popped a slice of meat into his mouth, biting down on it hard.

Nik could feel Korsak wanting to know a hell of a lot more about Daria, felt a tinge of curiosity from the man, but more along the lines of trying to see if she was legit or not, rather than anything more sinister. Today should seal that for Korsak. Nik intended to spend a lot of time out on the trails with Daria doing whatever she did for the book she was supposed to be writing. It was important to get her cover solidly in place and this was the way to do it.

Nik pushed back from the table, his plate clean.

Korsak looked up. "When we see you? Fill us in on what your hike was like today."

Nik hesitated and gave his boss a hard look. "What? You're not sending Brudin out to follow us today?"

Shrugging, Korsak said, "We'll see... He didn't like sitting for two hours out in the rain and mud last night watching you two eat."

This time, it was Nik's turn to laugh.

CHAPTER 7

"Do you think Brudin will follow us this morning?" Daria asked, shifting the straps of her knapsack across her shoulders. She walked with Nik down the always noisy and crowded tourist area of the town. Overhead, the clouds had parted and she saw rifts of blue sky here and there between them. Machu Picchu rose like a loaf of French bread sat up on one end. Its massive black lava sides were covered with thousands of orchids and bromeliads, making it green, hiding the sharp, cutting basalt it was made from. She cast Nik a concerned look. He had been quiet and she could feel him digesting something but didn't know what. She tried to keep her emotions out of this op, having given herself a stern talking to last night before she fell asleep, all the while her body aching for this complex soldier.

"There's a good chance." His mouth lifted a little. "But I lied to them at *desayuno* earlier this morning. I told them I was going to take a certain trail but we're taking another one. If Brudin thinks he can get ahead of us and hide on the trail we aren't going to use, I don't care."

"Aren't you the sly fox," she teased. Daria wore a rainproof jacket with a hood because the weather was still coolish and one never knew when it was going to rain again in the jungle. She wore her dark-green cammo pants, waterproof hiking boots, and a short-sleeved gray pullover with her jacket over it. Nik was dressed in nearly the same colors and style except for a black t-shirt that showed off the expanse of his deep chest beneath his waterproof black jacket. Like her, he had a knapsack or what he referred to as a ruck, on his back. She'd made sure she'd brought all her tools and orchid identification books with her. If they were going to be watched, she had to turn into a botanist for a while.

Nik shrugged. He kept his voice low, so that only she could hear him as they turned onto the plaza, made a left turn and headed for the railroad tracks just outside of town. "I have to be."

"How is your team handling your new romance?" she wondered aloud to him.

His face hardened. "They tease me, but that's nothing new. I feel they are buying it, but Korsak isn't sure yet." He gestured down the tracks and stepped over them. "We need to continue to validate that you're a botanist."

"Well, I've got everything in my knapsack to prove it, plus a degree in it," and Daria gave him a wry smile. He wore a black baseball cap and he hadn't shaved this morning. The dark stubble did nothing but emphasize the rugged, harsh lines of his face. Yet, Daria was constantly surprised because he usually spoke in a low, softened tone exactly like she would expect of a military medic. No one knew better the power of a calm voice during the chaos of combat when a fallen team mate was bleeding out than the wounded. She would never forget the combat medic, Pascal, who was the first on scene after the Black Hawk medevac had landed to rescue her and Melissa. The carnage, the bodies, her continued bleeding out as he knelt next to her, his hands incredibly gentle, his voice low and soothing. That was when Daria knew she would survive.

Stealing a look at Nik as he walked down the middle of the railroad tracks, the gravel crunching beneath their boots, she felt that same sense of protectiveness radiating out from him toward her. There was more than care burning in his blue eyes when he'd knocked at her apartment door earlier. There had been desire in their depths. Daria had tossed and turned all night, her body achy with the memory of what good sex felt like. Having had none for such a long time made her edgy. And the look in Nik's eyes confirmed that he wanted her as much as she wanted him.

As they followed the tracks out of town between the huge, rising monolith of Machu Picchu on their left, Mama Putukusi, the equally loaf-like lava mountain on their right and between the two, further down, Huynu Picchu, Daria felt the size of an ant in comparison to these mighty giants thrusting up out of the green jungle that surrounded them on all sides. To her left she could hear the roar of the Urubamba River which snaked and slid between these three massive mountains. The river almost sounded angry. Looking around, Daria saw they were alone, now that they'd left the town behind them. Only a swath that had been carved out to allow the trains to come and go through the massive, thick triple-canopy jungle, embraced them now.

"Is it safe to talk right now?" she asked.

"Yes." Nik cut her a look, his gaze never still, always alert. "What do you want to ask?"

"I've got hundreds of questions," she assured him in a droll tone, watching the corner of his mouth hook upwards for a moment. Nik was tense and on guard this morning, although to any observer he would look relaxed and casual. He was not.

"Korsak suspects something about us?" she asked him.

"I think he's being very careful, which is normal for him." Nik replied.

"What do we have to do to convince him?" She saw Nik grimace.

"Probably, by tomorrow night, I need to stay at your apartment. They will think we're making love, of course. We want him to think that. I believe if I spend the nights with you from now on, it will convince Korsak about us."

"Okay," she murmured, her body suddenly taking off with possibilities. The way Nik had kissed her, had cherished her, left Daria wanting to explore this man intimately and thoroughly. But would he go that far? Daria wasn't sure about anything right now.

"It's just a cover," he reassured her, giving her a concerned look. "I'll sleep out on the couch. They'll never know otherwise."

Nodding, Daria said nothing, afraid to broach how she really felt. "What trail are we taking?" because she saw two branching off and Nik was slowing down.

"The one on the left." He stopped and turned, looking back down the railroad tracks toward Aguas Calientes. There was no one following them. He shifted his attention back to Daria. "From this point on, you must expect we are being watched and monitored. Only when we get back here to the tracks, can we speak more honestly."

"Got it." She followed him up the narrow, winding path that would take them to the slope of Mama Putukusi. Everything was muddy, wet drops would fall off and strike her hat and shoulders from the canopy of leaves above. By the time they had climbed about five hundred feet around the base of the lava mountain, the bill of her cap dripped with the water coming off it. The jungle was dark, hiding the druzy light from above. It was a depressing place to Daria.

Nik halted at a wide spot in the trail and pointed up at some trees. "See the orchids up there?"

Narrowing her eyes, about ten feet above them on an overhanging limb, she saw two flowering orchids growing where the branch forked out from the trunk of the tree. "Yes."

"How do you want to do this? I can climb the tree and pull them out of that notch and bring them down to you?"

"Sounds good to me. But can you put them back up there when we're done?"

"Yes." Nik shed his knapsack, laying it over some damp branches that had fallen near the trail. Better to keep it out of mud if he could.

Daria found several limbs on the ground and laid them in a grid so they would keep her own knapsack off the wet earth. She opened it, pulling out a square oilcloth, and then finding her notebook, pen and a small Canon camera. She spread the oilcloth across the limbs, creating a waterproof table of sorts. She remembered all the things that a botanist would do on the hunt for an orchid. Pulling a cloth measuring tape from her pocket, she set it down with her other items. Nik came over to take a look at her equipment. She felt his body heat as he neared. The temperature was lower within the jungle, she'd discovered, and was glad for the jacket she wore.

"You are out in this for thirty days at a time?"

"Yes. They call it the green hell. But I call it a virus-laden Petrie dish."

"No kidding," she said. "I've done a lot of work in the Amazon, but nothing like this. It has a dry and rainy season. When its dry? There is no mud and easy going walking-wise."

"Not in this kind of jungle. It's miserable. You never get dry. You never warm up. Everything is always damp. Mold, bacteria and fungus are everywhere."

She knelt by her knapsack; her voice low. "I don't know how you've done it, Nik. I know I couldn't," and she risked a look up at him. He stood with his hands on his hips, mouth set, staring up at the tree where the orchids were nestled. When she whispered those words, he cocked his head in her direction and she saw the raw pain in his eyes for a moment.

"We all do what we must," he rasped, placing his hand against the damp bark of the tree, testing the strength of the trunk.

The heaviness in his voice, his utter exhaustion from dealing with the Russian drug team, weighed on Daria. She wanted to rise to her feet and simply walk up to Nik, slide her arms around his waist, lay her head on his chest and hold him. It wasn't about sex this time. It was about human compassion and caring for someone carrying deep pain. She was discovering that her heart was wide open of its own accord toward him. He was a tragic figure to her, having gone through so much and having lost so much. All of that stress was multiplied on him right now with her thrown into the mix. He knew this was her first undercover assignment, a newbie that could easily get them killed if she screwed up by accident.

Looking around, having picked up her camera and coming over to stand by Nik, she said, "I don't see how anyone could get around in this jungle without being heard. It's so thick. You'd hear them coming a mile away."

He rested his hand on the tree, studying her. "In this area the jungle is very dense. Further up, near the Highlands, there are wooden vines twisting and turning so that only small animals can negotiate and get through them. Even if Brudin is here, he's on the wrong trail unless he followed us and saw we took a different trail. Besides, none of them are good at tracking. I am. That is why I made some tracks up the wrong trail that were obvious, so he'd follow it." Shaking his head, he gave her a warning look. "Let's stick to our script."

Right. Daria nodded and stepped away as he hooked his hand around a lower limb and quickly hefted his lean body up into the tree. In no time, he had gently pried loose the first orchid and carefully handed it down to her. There, on the trail, she would measure the longest leaves, then the full orchid itself and then photograph it, write her notes and hand it back to him. The plop, plop, plop of rain gathering on the leaves far above them and then dropping earthward and the monkeys screaming off in the distance were the only sounds. Daria felt as if she had cotton in her ears, all the sounds muted. She wondered how close Brudin was, if he was here at all. Still, she stuck to the business at hand and this was how the hours passed for the two of them before they packed up and headed back to town.

"Why don't you come inside?" Daria invited to Nik on the porch of her apartment. It was late afternoon and the cloud cover had cleared further, showing even more light blue sky through above them. The cliffs of the sun-bathed Machu Picchu towering above was washed with strong, swift moving shafts of light, and the town itself was as bustling, busy and noisy as always. She tilted her head and pleaded with him silently as she saw him considering her request.

Nik's heart lurched over at her invitation, seeing the pleading in her eyes. It would give them a chance to talk without being overheard. And to not be potentially followed or listened in on. He looked down at his muddy boots, his cammies as soaked as the shirt he wore. They had long ago taken off their jackets as the temperature rose and combined with the high humidity. His hair was damp and shining in the sunlight. "I could. It wouldn't be out of the norm for our growing relationship," and he gave her a slight smile. Not once had she caught sight of any of the Russians along the railroad tracks as they'd returned to Aguas Calientes.

Daria gripped Nik's hand. "Good, come on in. And don't worry about the boots. We'll stand on the rug inside and take them off."

She had such long, beautiful fingers, and when they curled around his hand Nik needed no further urging. He stepped inside. Daria took her half of the dark-green rug and set her knapsack down on it as well. Everything she wore or carried was muddy. Nik's throat felt dry as he watched her bend down to ease each boot off her feet. There was nothing but grace with her movements. Nik shut the door behind him and locked it. The blinds were open, allowing a lot of sunlight into the apartment, lifting his spirits. At last, he was alone with her again. They'd played their parts, kept their banter within the boundaries of her being a botanist. He took off his boots across from Daria on the rug. Then he did another quick sweep of the place in case any bugs had been planted in their absence. He gave her a thumb's up, indicating that the apartment was still clean and they could relax and speak freely.

"I'm going to take a quick shower," Daria told him, holding her damp socks in her hand, her feet bare on the wooden floor. "Would you like one, too?"

"Yes. You go ahead. I'll try to wash some of the mud off my arms and hands," and he gave her a warm look. How badly Nik wanted to follow her into that bathroom and get into the shower stall with her. He'd seen Daria's face relax once they were inside the apartment, and felt so much of the tension she carried slough away. "I could make us a good cup of coffee?"

"Great idea," she said, walking across the living room toward the hall.

The sway of her hips made his lower body tighten with need. Her hair was mussed, curled thickly from the humidity, her clothes sticking to her like a second skin. Daria was in top athletic shape, but he'd noticed today, after climbing several thousand feet up and down the trail, that she had a slight limp. Why? He decided to ask her after she'd taken her shower and they had sat down over coffee together.

Nik was in the kitchen when Daria emerged later from the bathroom. His eyes narrowed as she padded on bare feet around the corner. She'd washed her hair and combed it out, the sleek black cape of it with its blue highlights pouring over her shoulders. It was the white terrycloth towel she wore around her body, the edges of it barely brushing mid-thigh, that anchored him. It was then that, as her legs and the towel moved, he saw several recent, pink scars just above her knee on her left thigh. Before he could say anything, she halted at the entrance to the kitchen.

"Your turn. Have you made the coffee yet?"

"No. I was gathering things." Did Daria realize she was turning him inside out with need? That towel hinted that she had small but full breasts beneath its material. And she was long in the torso, the fabric hanging over her rounded hips. He already knew she had a fine butt.

"I'm going to pull on a set of clean clothes. When I come out, I'll start the coffee?"

Swallowing, Nik nodded. There was a scent of oranges as he passed by her, wanting to reach out, touch her bare shoulders, thread his fingers through her shining hair. Forcing himself to do nothing of the sort, Nik murmured, "Sounds good. I won't be long." He hesitated fractionally. "You need to automatically sweep your apartment first thing each time after you enter from now on."

"I forgot all about that. Thanks for remembering to do it right after we entered."

"Don't worry," Nik soothed, reaching out, unable to help himself as he barely brushed the crown of her head with his fingers. "Undercover work is new to you. I don't expect you to remember everything." He saw the guilt and apology in her eyes. "You're doing fine," he added, understanding that she was probably feeling pretty bad about missing the sweep for bugs. Nik had given her the time enough to think about doing it on her own, and she hadn't.

"Not really," Daria muttered, shaking her head. Her hand tightened on the front of the towel between her breasts.

He gave her a patient look. "*Moya kotya*, this is a joint effort. We're a team. We each bring strengths and weaknesses to this mission. Don't be hard on yourself. If I'm fine with your performance, you should relax, eh?" and he grazed her cheek with his thumb, forcing himself to back away from her before he did anything else. Nik was so close to taking her and yet, he knew that would be wrong. Daria hadn't given him THAT signal. But he did see a melting look in her eyes when he touched her cheek. She LIKED his touch. They no longer had to play act. Whatever was going on now, was between them as far as he was concerned. And it was real.

"If you say so," she said, apologetically.

"Look at it this way. If Korsak hasn't ordered bugs to be put in your apartment, it means he's buying that we're a couple. That's a good thing. Besides, he would know I would look for them. And then that would put him into an uncomfortable position with me. I'm the only medic they have and they can't risk me walking out on them." Nik forced himself to break away from her and walk down the hall to the bathroom.

By the time he'd showered and put on his scruffy, humidly damp clothes, he still felt a hundred percent cleaner. Sweating was an expected part of the tropics and it was always refreshing to feel clean, if only for a little while. He'd washed his hair and used her comb to tame it into place. He wished now that he'd shaved. His beard had only darkened his lower face, giving him, he thought, a more lethal look. Nik knew he was already not pretty-boy handsome in the least. There was Latin music on a radio, low but cheery, coming out from the kitchen. Inhaling, he smelled the fresh coffee in the air. He quickly rolled his long sleeves up to just below the elbow and padded in bare feet out into the kitchen. For a moment, he just stood there watching Daria. She was focused completely on opening up a box of cookies and placing each of them one by one on a small white saucer. Her hands were delicate and long, and he wanted so badly to feel them exploring him. Her back was partially turned toward him and he knew how to walk silently so that she'd never hear him coming. Daria wore a bright-yellow capped sleeve top that outlined her trim, tight body. The white cotton shorts that hung mid-thigh outlined her long, long legs. He smiled a little as he saw that she remained barefoot. It brought back the wild woman image he had of her once again.

It was Daria's hair, now slowly drying in the humidity, the strands of it glinting reddish and bluish-black beneath the fluorescent light above her, that drew his gaze back up from her legs. She had left her hair down and it enticed him, made his hands itch to explore its strands, run them through his fingers, feel their strength and their silky quality. He knew she had been a Marine, saw it in the sleek muscling of her upper arms and the latent strength hidden in her lower arms. There were many, many old scars, white and shiny, along both her arms and he knew she'd probably collected them as a sniper lying on hard, unforgiving rocks, lying in wait for her next HVT, high value target.

For just this moment before she discovered him, Nik hungrily absorbed Daria. Yes, he saw the Marine in her, each of her movements precise and smooth. The feminine side of her, however, was equally strong, from the curve of her breasts beneath the yellow material of her blouse, to the flare of her womanly hips astride those long legs he wanted to explore inch by inch. He absorbed her profile, clean, soft and nonthreatening. He wondered what the toll on her in the military had really been all those years. Nik knew there was always heavy payment for jobs like hers and his. Daria hid it well. Where did it spill out? What would trigger all those emotions she kept from public scrutiny? He was desperate to know her on a much more intimate level.

"The coffee smells good," he said quietly, not wanting to startle her.

Daria lifted her head and turned, smiling over at him. "It does, doesn't it? It's almost ready." She picked up the plates. "Here, put these on the table? I thought you might like a few cookies. We worked hard out there today. A little reward."

He took the plates, their fingers briefly touching. Agony of another type raked his lower body. Right now, he was seeing Daria relaxed. She was no longer as tense or as on guard as she had been earlier. Understanding that she felt safe in this apartment, Nik knew she shouldn't feel safe around him. He was a starving wolf without a mate, lacking the warmth of his woman. As he walked to the table and set the plates down, he heard her open a cupboard and take down two mugs.

"Cream? Sugar?" he asked, ambling into the kitchen proper.

"Yes," and she pointed to the small refrigerator. "Thank you. How about you?"

"Depends if the coffee is good or not," he said, opening the fridge and taking out the small bottle of cream. "If the coffee is good, I like it black. If it's made weak or the beans are burnt-tasting, then I will smother it with cream and sugar." He grinned over at her as she poured their coffee. For a split second, Nik dreamed that they were married, having coffee as a couple, simply enjoying one another's company and thoughts. He sadly pushed those dreams away. His was a life destined to be about suffering loss, heavy responsibility, and nonstop service. Daria allowed him to dream. And the dream was so beautiful that Nik almost wanted to cry inwardly, knowing she would never be within his reach. His life was at risk all the time. One wrong move with Korsak, and he'd have a bullet through his head.

He took the bowl of sugar and carried it to the table. As Daria brought the mugs over, he pulled back the chair for her.

"Thanks," she said, placing a mug to her right.

Nik sat down, their elbows nearly touching. Their knees brushed against each other and he reluctantly shifted away so that it gave her room. Above all, he didn't want Daria feeling as if he were stalking her. She didn't seem to mind, but Nik wanted no mixed signals between them. He tasted the coffee and made a sound in his throat. "This is good coffee."

"It is," she agreed.

"Are you feeling better now that we're indoors and away from Brudin's prying eyes?"

She sighed and gave him a look of concern. "Yes, more than you know. I've decided that I never want to do undercover work again. I'm so used to being myself. It's hard for me to play a part. I've always been an upfront kind of woman. I keep having to self-censor my thoughts, what I was about to say, and then splice in what I need to say as a botanist." Her mouth curved down. "I really hate it, Nik. I'd much rather be myself."

"Tell me more? I saw that you were slightly favoring your left leg of the trail. And earlier, when the towel was wrapped around you, I saw what looked like fresh new scars on your left thigh?" He saw her eyes grow hooded and felt an instant shield suddenly rise between them. What was that all about? What had he said?

Daria sat her coffee down, her hands sliding around the mug, staring at it for a long moment. "It's a pretty gruesome episode in my life, Nik. I don't know if I'm ready to tell anyone about it yet," and she gave him a look of apology.

"No worries," he soothed, nodding. So, it had happened in combat. His senses were well-honed and sometimes, Nik thought he was almost psychic. The anguish that suddenly came to her eyes slammed into him like a rogue wave. He heard an almost imperceptible tremor in her low, strained voice. Even more, he felt the terror, the grief and trauma that still lived, alive and well, within Daria. Nik understood how that all worked because he also held so much of it within him as a soldier and medic. He reached out, moving his fingers down her lower arm in a gesture to try and calm some of the sudden storm he felt swirling invisibly within her. "I'm sorry," he said, "I didn't mean to make you feel bad. What would you like to talk about?"

Daria mustered a weak grimace. "You're right about my legs. You're pretty observant. The docs gave me an okay to go back into the field, but today out on that steep trail, I guess it's not as fully healed as I'd wished."

"Are you in pain, Daria? I can give you something for it." He wasn't a medic for nothing. It was his job to not allow her to suffer, if he could help it.

"No… it's just stiff… ouchy. I've got aspirin if I need it, but I think I'll be fine now. The hot water of the shower really helped and sitting down, resting, I'll be okay."

"If you would allow me?" He lifted his hands. "They looked to me to be knife wounds. I know what that does to muscle tissue. I could massage that area very gently and I guarantee you that your leg will feel so much better than before. Let me at least do that for you? I'm in medic mode now," and he gave her a faint smile, never wanting anything more than to do this for Daria. He could see the pain in her eyes now, and he'd noticed it before out on the trail, but he hadn't put both together until just now.

Daria sighed and rolled her eyes. "A massage? I'd *love* one! It's the first thing I do when I get back off an op! Head for my favorite masseuse that lives near our HQ. Are you sure? We could do it after we finish our coffee?"

"Yes, whatever you are comfortable with." The idea of getting to touch her even in a healing way, thundered through Nik. His lower body flexed with possibility. No, this wasn't about sex. It was about helping Daria relieve some of the stiffness that he knew always occurred from a knife wound. They were the worst injuries to heal through because the muscles were usually sliced and then having to sew them together once more only added to the physical trauma. He'd seen his fair share of them because Russian terrorists were knife wielders like the Taliban. He saw Daria yearning to get that massage, but also hesitant about it. "I will be very careful. I promise, this is about healing, nothing else." Because Nik didn't want her to think it was a way to get his hands on her. His offer had been pure of heart. And he would keep it that way. The longing in her expression made him warm, his heart opening. "Even the Quechua villagers allow me to work on them with massage. Some of the older men and women have very bad arthritis in their joints, in their hands. I'm able to soothe their pain, get the muscles to move, and coax the painful parts to relax."

Daria regarded him from beneath her lashes. "I'll bet they love to see you coming into their village, then."

It was his turn to wince. "They love to see me. They fear the rest of the team I'm with, for good reason," was all he'd say. Just as Daria didn't want to discuss her combat wounds, he did not want to get into Korsak's brutality towards the Indians.

Drawing in a breath he said, "Are you game?" and he held up his hands. "See what I can do to maybe get some blood and circulation into that area? One massage can last for days and it's very helpful to the entire healing process."

"You've sold me, Nik. Let's do it."

CHAPTER 8

DARIA LAID DOWN on one side of the bed so that Nik could easily work with her left thigh. She hadn't thought about the towel she'd worn earlier showing those wounds until he'd mentioned it. He had brought a bottle of massage oil from his medical pack into the bedroom. The light was dim, the venetian blinds pulled. How she looked forward to his touch as she settled onto her back. Already, her body was anticipating his hands upon her.

Nik set the bottle on the bed stand. He walked around to the other side of the bed and took the second pillow, bringing it back around to where she lay. "We need to put this beneath your knees. It takes the stress off your lower back." As she lifted her knees, he slid it in under them. Daria had left him ample room on one side of the bed to sit down facing her. He opened the bottle, pouring some of the oil onto the palm of one hand.

"My hands are rough-feeling," he warned her as he rubbed the oil between them.

"That's okay. In our line of work, our hands are always like that."

He smiled a little, sitting down and closely observing the knife scars. "Do you mind if I do a little examination on them? It will help me understand the best way to manipulate the muscles in each area."

Daria shook her head. "No… go ahead."

"I will be very gentle but, if it hurts, let me know?"

"Yes, because that whole area is really tender."

Nodding, he moved his fingers lightly across the three pink scars. The flesh was shiny, indicating early-stage scar tissue. He felt the solid firmness of her thigh, once again reminding himself she had been a sniper for a long time and was used to hard, physical punishment, hiking through some of the worst possible terrain in order to gain the high ground for her hide. "Relax," he urged her quietly as his fingers grazed each of the scars.

"Sorry, it's just sore."

"Am I hurting you?"

"No… just my reaction. When I was doing physical therapy, which was brutal and painful, my leg was always bruised-feeling afterward…. it's just an old knee-jerk reaction... excuse the pun." She saw Nik's eyes grow hooded as he nodded and continued to gently palpate the skin around each wound. His contact was amazing to Daria and she found herself sighing, relaxing and enjoying the skimming of his long fingers as they began to slowly probe around each of the old knife wounds.

"It's all right. I understand." Nik frowned, beginning to move the muscles lightly below the first wound, the one highest above her knee. "From the looks of this one, I'd say a curved blade was used. Do you know?"

Mouth flattening, Daria placed her arm across her eyes. "Taliban always use a curved blade." She saw his mouth thin a little as he began to investigate around the scar. Grunting, she stiffened.

"Sorry," he murmured, lightening his touch. "Just a little more? I need to know how many layers of muscles are involved."

"Now you sound like my PT gal. She was always saying the same thing." She saw a corner of his mouth lift momentarily. There was utter intent in his face as he leaned over, looking and feeling around that first wound.

"Yes, we all say 'just a little more,' knowing full well it's hurting you, but it's for a good reason." Nik moved his thumb in a caressing motion downward from the scar.

"Owwww," Daria muttered, scowling.

"I'm done." Nik smoothed his hand across the shiny welt. "You've still got healing to do, Daria. At least on this one," and he gestured to it. "It's not fully restored. I'm perplexed why your doctor would release you for duty."

Shrugging, Daria muttered, "I had nothing to do with it."

"But did you tell your doctor how tender your leg was? How much it stiffened up on you after use?"

"Yes," she muttered. Daria saw Nik give a slight shake of his head, absorbing his light, soothing stroke. Instantly, the pain went away and in its place was warmth. And care. She was privy to his compassionate medic side right now. "Honestly? Alex Kazak checked it out and argued passionately that my muscles weren't fully healed like they needed to be. He argued with Jack Driscoll, my boss, that I should be given another two months of rest before being put out in the field again."

Smiling faintly, Nik held her gaze. "My dear friend Alex was right. He's a good medic."

"So are you."

"How does it feel now? Is the pain less?"

Just the slow, gentle strokes around her wound made her sigh. "Yes. It feels so good right now. Don't stop, Nik..."

"I won't. I can feel the muscles begin to trust my touch. They are sagging with relief. They were very tight and hard before. I'll do more serious massage, but first, I want to check out the other wounds. The muscling and ligaments are different the closer you get to your knee."

"Sure, go ahead." Daria didn't want Nik to ever stop laying his roughened fingers upon her flesh.

The second scar was in the middle, the worst-looking one. As he manipulated her thigh carefully, he saw her mouth flex. "Pain?"

"Stiffness more than anything else."

"This knife wound went in at an angle opposite of the upper wound."

She was blown away by his knowledge. "I wasn't exactly watching what was going on when it happened." Daria saw his mouth flex.

"I understand, *moya kotya*," and he followed the damage done to the muscles beneath. She stiffened and he murmured, "Just a little more…"

Daria tried to relax, but his fingers probed. "I swear, you have x-ray vision. How could you know the direction of the blade?"

"I can feel the disturbance to your muscles that were torn open by it."

She blew out a breath of air when he began the soothing strokes after the examination. "Glad you're done poking around."

"This one is very deep," he said, concern in his voice. "Much deeper than the upper one." He saw the pain in her eyes, the memories.

"The PT gal said the wound closest to my knee is the worst one."

"Well," he said lightly, "let's find out."

Daria was used to his examination routine now and she tried to relax. She saw Nik's straight eyebrows draw down as he followed the entry of the knife into her leg. His mouth pursed more as he slowly and thoroughly examined the old wound.

"The trajectory of the blade tells me the knife must have sliced near your femoral artery. Did it?"

She managed a grimace, arm resting across her brow. "Pascal, the combat medic who was first on scene, said it had nicked my femoral artery." She closed her eyes, not wanting to go back there, but knowing she must. "My leg was filling with blood, swollen, distended and he tied a tourniquet above the knife wounds. God, that hurt. I passed out from the pain." She felt Nik's hands move protectively across her wounds, as if to try and sooth her experience. It nearly broke Daria because he was excruciatingly nurturing and gentle with her. More than anyone had been since she'd been wounded. Tears jammed up behind her closed eyes and she was surprised by the reaction. Instantly, she fought them away.

"Yes," Nik said in a low, rasping tone, "the blade tip just barely nicked your femoral artery." He closed his hands protectively around her lower thigh.

"You could have easily bled out, Daria."

"When I came to in the Black Hawk, Pascal was there, watching over me like a guard dog. He told me much the same. He'd given me enough morphine to stop the worst of the pain, but I could feel that tourniquet biting into my thigh, but good."

"He had some fine lines to walk with you, medication-wise." Nik agreed, stroking her leg, beginning to massage it from mid-thigh down to, and just below, her knee. "And he saved your life. Pascal is a good man. I wish I could meet him sometime. He sounds a lot like Alex and I."

"You three are clearly good at your job," Daria whispered, feeling the lightness of his fingers moving and coaxing her muscles to acquiesce to the manipulation.

"And your partner? How did she fare?" he asked.

Daria tensed. She didn't want to look at Nik, so close to tears once again. "S-she didn't make it."

"I'm sorry, Daria. So very sorry..."

His roughened words started to dissolve the shield she'd put up to stop from remembering, stop seeing the flashes of the attack, hearing Melissa's scream, hearing her own scream of rage as the assault came. The flashes of the curved blades coming in all directions at them made her wince internally. The first blade struck her level four Kevlar vest, the point breaking and snapping off, flying away somewhere into the black night. She remembered the snarl of the Taliban soldier, saw the hatred gleaming in his eyes as he suddenly realized his knife was broken and his chest blow hadn't penetrated.

With each sliding movement of Nik's hands across her flesh, Daria felt her muscles truly beginning to sag with utter relief. His hands were calloused and rough, but that only made her skin prickle with silent enjoyment. She groaned.

"Too deep?"

"No," she whispered, "just... feels so good..." She heard him make a softened growl of appreciation in his throat.

"I'll get more circulation into those areas. It will help them heal more quickly. Massage should have been a part of your healing protocol after you arrived home."

Nik was healing *her*. Daria almost blurted it out. With each glide of his hands, she felt herself melting a little more beneath his careful, sensitive ministrations. At no time did he cause her pain. He only gave her leg relaxation. And, if but for a moment, the relief from the darkness when the nightmares came, haunting her of the attack, was a blessing to Daria. The sense of safety Nik accorded her was dissolving all her boundaries with him. She had never felt as protected as when she was with him.

Lauren Parker-Kazak had told her how Nik had saved her life, how he'd cared for her when she'd been injured. Well, now *she* was at the receiving end of Nik Morozov's remarkable healing abilities. And it was dismantling the walls she'd placed around that horrific night. With each stroke of his hand, she felt an upwelling of emotions pushing from deep within her, heading toward the surface. It scared her. Daria didn't want to deal with all the feelings about the attack that she'd buried. How could Nik massaging her leg do all that? Panic hit her and she lay there, mouth taut, arm tight across her eyes, feeling tears stinging the backs of their lids, fighting to stave off everything.

His questions had sliced through and opened up a dam of terror, trauma and grief. Daria knew he hadn't meant to do that. It was just him being a caring medic, trying to understand the extent and depth of each of her wounds. Each time his calloused hands moved, coaxed and soothed those battered, bruised muscles that had absorbed such violence, Daria wanted to let a scream tear out of her. Nik was giving her a safe place to let go, and somewhere in her shorting-out mind, she knew that. *Oh, God...*

"Stop!" she cried out, suddenly sitting up, pushing his hands away. Daria saw the shock in his face, the sudden confusion in his eyes. Her throat tightened. She sat tensely, hunched over, breathing raggedly. Nik wouldn't understand. She hadn't meant to yell at him.

"Did I hurt you?"

"N-no... it's just that...," and Daria struggled and scooted across the bed to the other side. She slid her legs down, the coolness of the tiles hitting her bare feet. Struggling to stop the fist jamming up through her, she gripped the sides of the bed, her knuckles whitening as she fought to shove all of that horror back down into that dark place deep within herself. She was only minimally aware of the bed shifting as Nik stood, and of sensing him coming around to her side of it. She had her eyes scrunched shut, head bowed, fighting to not cry.

Nik crouched down on her right side, one hand on her arm, the other coming to rest on her right knee. "What is it?" he intoned, digging into her opening eyes with his intense stare. "Speak to me, Daria?"

Her chest heaved sharply and rapidly. She lifted her head, holding his concerned, warm gaze. Daria wanted to burst into tears, throw herself into his arms and be held. She knew Nik would do that for her. Knew that he would take care of her. How long had it been since she'd had that feeling? Nik stroked her arm and held her gaze. His face blurred.

With a muffled sound, Daria tore away from him, hurrying out of the bedroom, down the hall, and into the living room. Wrapping her arms around herself, she stood wavering in the middle of the living room, wanting to run.

But to where? There was no place to go. She was trapped. She felt, more than heard, Nik approach her from behind. Automatically, she tensed, not wanting him to touch her because, if he did, she was going to break.

Nik halted inches from Daria. She was shaking, her arms tight around her torso as if to gird herself against something unseen. Something terrible. He raised his hands and they hovered momentarily over her hunched shoulders. The need to help her was overriding. Something had happened in the bedroom. And he thought he had some idea of what it was, but wasn't sure. He allowed his hands to rest lightly on her shoulders. She stiffened. He heard her gasp. Did Daria want his help or not? Nik was unsure, but wasn't going to back off from her unless she told him to. And then, he would.

"Daria," he whispered, gently pulling her against his body, his lips near her ear. "I'm here. I know I can help you. Please?" Nik felt her shudder, heard a choking sound in her throat, her hands flying to her face.

She didn't pull away from him.

Gently, Nik turned her around, keeping her close, allowing *her* to decide how near or not she wanted to be, his hands back on her shoulders. He saw the steaks of tears running down her cheeks, her eyes tightly shut, her hands against the sides of her face. He saw how hard she was fighting to stop the tears. She was battling so much, all on her own. It didn't need to be that way. They had one another. He felt so on a visceral level. Daria was entrusting her vulnerable self to him right now and Nik felt the monumental decision she'd just made to allow herself to do so. He felt her struggling with so much that was invisible to him. He understood intuitively that his massaging of her knife wounds had ripped the door open on that whole, sordid moment of her life. Gently, he threaded his fingers through her hair.

"Talk to me?" he urged her quietly, watching her eyes open barely, awash with tears, agony within them.

Daria reached out, placing her hands against Nik's chest. He continued to stroke her hair as if she were a lost, hurting child so badly in need of just that. Just his healing touch. Hot tears streamed down her drawn cheeks, and an explosive sob burst its way unwillingly up and out of her.

"Come here," he rasped, drawing her deeply into his arms, holding her tight against him. Cupping her head, he held her, feeling her trembling as if an earthquake was about to erupt from deep within her. How many times had he seen this reaction before? Nik closed his eyes, his head resting gently against hers, allowing Daria to sag fully against him, holding her safe, holding her while that terrible storm overcame the massive control needed to contain it. "It's all right, Daria. Let it go? I'm here. I'll hold you through it, *moya kotya…*"

He felt another giant sob wrack like a tsunami wave up through her, and

Daria slid her arms around his waist, leaning into him, burying her face deeply against his shirt, trying to hide as the sounds unwillingly kept ripping out of her. Nik knew he needed to remain quiet and strong for her as she shook and sobbed in his arms. He couldn't fix what was wrong within her. But he could stroke her hair, move his hand caressingly up and down her back. He knew the value of touch, of holding. The agony he felt in his heart for her, not wanting to see her so damaged and anguished, lacerated him. Nik wished he could absorb Daria's pain and loss and grief, but he knew he couldn't. All he could do was give her safe harbor to release that toxic brew that lived like a prowling monster within her. *Better out, than in.*

Time dissolved, and all Nik was aware of was the warm, brave woman he held tenderly within his embrace. His shirt quickly became damp with her tears and she clung to him as if he were the last anchor in the world for her to grasp before she was forever lost. He understood. How many times had he wished he'd had a pair of loving arms to welcome and hold him when he was hurting so deeply? The scent of oranges from the shampoo she used in her hair complimented the sweeter, spicier scent of her flesh, calmed him, fed him in ways he couldn't describe. Just getting to hold Daria, to know she trusted him with her worst fears and emotions, rocked his world in the best of ways.

If Nik had any questions about their mutual attraction, they were laid to rest right now. She was a Marine, as tough as they came from the US military. Nik knew that Daria had probably not cried since that horrific incident. It was just the way military personnel were taught and trained: keep your emotions boxed. Don't cry. Don't feel. Focus on your job. Nothing else matters because, if you get emotional, you can get distracted and get killed. Yes, he knew this verbatim. Had heard it a thousand times during boot camp in Spetsnaz so many years ago. They were right, of course. It worked for the unit, but the terrible price paid by the individual, by one who had seen and experienced accumulated traumas, terrible human atrocities that no one should ever see, always came up owing.

He pressed a chaste kiss to her hair, the strands tickling his lips, his nostrils flaring as he dragged in her scent, as if breathing life into himself for the first time in so many years. Daria's sobs gradually lessened, her trembling slowly ebbed, and he could feel a slight loosening of her arms around his waist. The initial storm had expended itself and now, he knew she was going to feel exhausted in the aftermath of its passing. Easing her away just enough to see her face, he saw that it was pale and drawn. Her eyes were marred with anguish.

"Come with me? I want to lay next to you on the bed and just hold you, Daria. Nothing more. Sometimes," and he nudged the strands of her hair sticking to her wet cheek away with his fingertips, "the best healing is simply to be held afterward."

She lifted her hand, trying to wipe away some of the tears. "Y-yes…"

He smiled softly down at her, giving her a look of praise, and nodded. Opening his arms, Nik allowed her to lean against his side, an arm wrapped around her shoulders as he slowly guided her down the hall to the bedroom. He had no thought of sex in his head right now. Only to continue to give Daria that supporting enclosure she needed most to start healing internally from the trauma. She was wobbly on her feet and he held her firmly, letting her know silently that he had her. That she could trust him, continue to lean on him.

Daria felt as if someone had scrubbed the inside of her out with a wire bottle brush. She felt nothing but raw hurt piled upon endless grief as Nik helped her climb onto the bed. All she wanted right now was him. And when he came and laid his long body next to hers, sliding his arm beneath her neck, his other hand on her hip, drawing her next to him, Daria acquiesced without hesitation. Laying her head in the crook of his shoulder, nestling her face against Nik's neck and jaw, her arm going around his torso, she felt him monitoring the strength with which he held her.

Closing her eyes, Daria released a ragged sigh, feeling safe. Feeling loved and deeply cared for. All those emotions flittered over the top of the grief and loss still roiling through her like a savage storm. She placed one leg over his, wanting his solidity, the quiet strength and heat he offered. Care radiated out of him like sunlight, enclosing her, holding her safe. Holding her forever. And that was the last thing Daria remembered thinking before the exhaustion, the toll of the months since the trauma, overwhelmed her. In Nik's arms, Daria felt utterly protected. She could finally relax as never before, because he held her. And somewhere in the tumult of all the sharp-edged emotions raging through her, she felt his undeniable love and loyalty for her as she wafted into peaceful sleep.

Nik closed his eyes, his chin resting against her hair, feeling Daria completely surrender into his arms, her body sinking trustingly against his. His heart stirred with such deep feelings for her that it shook his soul. He'd never felt this way about a woman before. Daria was not a helpless woman, no bird with a broken wing floundering around. He'd pieced together enough to understand that four months ago she'd been attacked on an unnamed ridge while setting up a sniper op. Her spotter and her had been attacked by an undetected enemy and knives had been used. Most likely as to not alert anyone else in the area by firing off AK-47's against their foe. It was a Taliban tactic. Stealth. Knives were their favorite weapon and they knew how to wield them. He had so many questions about her op. Did they get bad perishable intel?

Had a Taliban mole pretending to be pro-US set them up? Similar cases had happened in Nik's own experience with Russian separatists way too many times.

Sliding his arm gently against her back, fingers splayed out across her hips, keeping her close, Nik felt her soft, moist breath as it shallowed out, indicating to him that Daria had fallen asleep. Yes, after a storm like that, he'd be exhausted too. Something deep and hurting rose in him as his mind ran through all the grief that had occurred in his life. It felt like an endless string of such, and he wondered if it would ever end. If it ever did, it probably meant he was dead. Nik wanted to keep his focus on Dan, on getting his brother the medical help he needed. Nothing else had mattered. Not until Daria had stepped unexpectedly into his life. She mattered just as much now.

Nik slid his fingers through her drying hair, felt it sift and slide like the silk it was. Daria trusted him. And that stopped him from doing anything inappropriate. His lower body had flared to aching life as she had sunk against him, her hips lightly meeting his. They were only scant inches apart in height and he marveled at how Daria fit against him, as if they had always been meant to be together. She was soft in his arms, luscious, curved and feminine. He still had to shake himself sometimes because he knew she was military. The two concepts seemed juxtaposed. Her softness against his toughened body was the polar opposite of a hardened soldier. And nothing had ever felt so right to him as this moment did. Five years through a desert of no emotions had abruptly come to an end, and he felt nearly overwhelmed by the unexpected mission, need and hunger filtering through him.

Nik closed his eyes, allowing himself to truly relax. It wasn't something he was able to do very often. Oh, he knew Brudin was probably still on watch detail outside the apartment, but that bastard wasn't going to come busting in anytime soon either. No, they were as safe as they could hope to be and his body sagged deeply into the mattress as he absorbed Daria's form against his. One of her hands was pillowed between them, its slender fingers slightly curled in sleep. Delicate, beautiful fingers. His heart ached for her, for the load she carried from that broken and devastating op. It would never be gone from her, and Nik knew that. All he could do is be an island where Daria could forget it for just a little while, round the vicious emotional edges off it, and give her a healing harbor of reprieve.

His heart and body sung about making love with her. It would be beautiful, he knew. Rich and lavish, because he knew how highly-tuned she was. A sniper lived on the edges of his or her senses. It was something no one spoke about but, sure as hell, that highly evolved intuition kept that sniper alive.

Nik visualized his fingers skimming across Daria's naked body, feeling her respond, watching the look in her sultry eyes change, watching the heat and arousal rise to a crescendo as he explored her inside and out. He would worship every inch of her, absorb her sweetness, her womanliness, and luxuriate in the sighs and sounds that he would coax out of her. Nik wanted to hear her cry out as he stroked her. Wanted to ask her body to share those rare gifts to him. He knew a woman would not orgasm unless she truly trusted her partner. There had to be some kind of powerful emotional connection. And, more than anything, that invisible, yet unsaid, connection was alive and well between them. He felt it every time they were together. And now, it throbbed brilliantly with a life of its own, palpable, breathing, wanting, yearning within him.

Sleep claimed Nik gently as he held the woman in his arms that he knew he was falling in love with. Only, he knew he could never speak those words to Daria under these circumstances. But, if he had his way about it, he was going to get this woman not only into his arms as she was now, but love her until she fainted with pleasure. There were so many ways to express love to a woman and Nik wasn't above using all of his experience to do just that for Daria. If anyone deserved love, it was her. It was true, he didn't know her full story but, over time, he would coax it out of her. Being black ops, she wasn't one to give up information about herself easily.

Daria trusted him with her most vulnerable self. She'd shown that to him just now. He would gently shield her, keep that small flame that had just sparked to life between them lit, and continue to give her this sense of safety. A fierceness rose in his heart. It was a mix of euphoria combined with terror. They lived on the edge of a scimitar every hour of every day. He'd just found a woman who endlessly and magically mesmerized him. And, more than anything, Nik was desperate to keep her safe and make the most of their time together.

CHAPTER 9

NIK SLOWLY PULLED himself awake, Daria tucked against him, his arms still enfolding her. Strands of her hair grazed his nose and chin. He savored the quiet in the room, alone with her sleeping form, even though he *could* faintly hear the muted pulse of drums and flutes down the hill below the apartment building. Celebration went on day and night in this tourist town, as if people were free of their inhibitions out here in the middle of nowhere in this godforsaken jungle. He noticed a birthmark, shaped like a quarter moon phase, behind her delicate left ear, something that had been partially hidden just beneath her hairline until now. Nik recalled glimpsing something there before but, because her hair had hidden it, he'd never fully seen it until now. Moving his fingers lightly across the tiny crimson crescent, he wanted to ask Daria about it. Birthmarks were DNA signatures passed on from parent to child. He had so many questions to ply her with. His soul ached to know her so much better than he currently did. He hungered like a starving man for that food she would share with him about herself.

Patience was the answer. Nik knew this could not be rushed, but for once, his patience was shortened considerably. Daria had reached down deep within him, unplugging that reservoir of restraint, artlessly holding his heart, skimming his weary soul with her strength, bravery and determination. She was a strong woman, no question, but at the same time, she could be vulnerable with him. That shook him more than anything else. What did she see in him that he didn't see in himself? What had made Daria trust him from the gitgo? Did she have some insight into him that he himself did not? No other woman had grazed and awakened his heart as she had.

Nik had no explanation for it, but was grateful she'd stepped unexpectedly into his life. Now, she slept deeply. He had no wish to disturb her, and luxuriated in this moment that he had dreamed about but had never thought would happen. His five years of monk-like existence had finally come to an end. Just the feel of her soft, warm body next to his made his heart sing and his lower body flare and flood scaldingly to breathless life.

He had no idea what time it was until he lifted his arm and squinted at his wrist, looking at the dials on his military watch. It was 2100, nine p.m. He eased his hand down across her shoulder, feeling the inherent strength of her beneath the fabric, wanting badly to disrobe Daria and feel her velvet skin against his. Yet, Nik knew, because of his age and maturity, that that would be a foolish move on his part. If Daria did not come to him of her own accord, then there was nothing for them to explore. Perhaps all she needed was someone to feel safe with after that brutal op? Nik knew how a busted mission could play hell on one's psyche. He'd experienced them himself. He'd been through the emotional and mental carnage that had destroyed him for months, even years, afterward. He understood all too clearly why so many soldiers returning from Iraq and Afghanistan were committing suicide. They'd seen too much, obliterating chunks of their souls, unable to be held, to be heard, to entrust themselves to someone who understood the carnage they'd managed to survive up until the point where they'd made that final, terrible choice.

His fingers slid comfortingly down across Daria's long back to her womanly hips. She was tall, medium-boned, and he knew she could easily carry a baby should she want motherhood. Wondering about that, what had pulled her into the Marine Corps? He couldn't stop his curiosity that need to know so much more about her.

Daria stirred. She pulled her hand from between them, barely awake. She made a snuffling noise in her throat, fingers resting against her face.

Nik's heart bounded as he took in the sight of Daria awakening in his arms. It was a stolen moment, and like the lone wolf he was, he absorbed her on every level. Her cheeks were pink, tendrils of hair against her wrinkling brow as she yawned and stretched, her hips meeting his momentarily. He remained quiet, allowing her those cherished waking moments, opening his arms so that she could fully move as she desired. And when her lashes barely opened, revealing those cloudy golden eyes of hers with their exotic tilt, Nik fell helplessly into their molten depths. Her pupils were huge and black and he saw the vulnerability in them. Again, that sense of trust lingered sweetly between them. There was nothing sexual coming from her; merely a beautiful young woman awakening from a long, healing sleep, looking refreshed. And even more lovely.

"How are you feeling now?" he asked, turning onto his side, resting on one elbow, his other arm still beneath her neck. He watched her lips part, a vague smile pulling at the delicious corners of her mouth.

"Mmmm, like I died and went to heaven…"

You are heaven. The words had nearly leaped out of his mouth. Instead, Nik caressed her cheek with his fingers, pushing strands of stuck hair away here and there, watching the reaction in her opening eyes. Instead of cloudiness, there was now pleasure in them as he grazed her warm flesh gently with his knuckles, outlining the slope of her high cheekbones. Daria slid her arm across his ribs, fingers moving slowly up and down his torso. It was an intimate gesture. Nik soaked it up, starving for each touch she would bestow upon him. As if... as if in this heated exchange, she was getting to know him, getting to feel his body beneath her fingertips. How he wished they were naked.

"You slept deeply," he said, cupping her cheek, holding her clearing gaze. Her lips remained parted and so close that he knew he could lean down and kiss them. Is that what Daria really wanted? His intuition flagged him and he anchored himself, waiting. Sensing. Right now, Daria was trustful in her just-awakening state and he wanted to do nothing to destroy this fragile connection growing between them.

"I needed it," she admitted, turning, pressing her face into his neck, giving him a hug. As she eased back, she whispered, "Thank you, Nik. You have no idea how good it felt to just be held like that..." and Daria searched his gaze, her voice still husky and slightly hoarse from having cried so much earlier.

Nodding, he moved his hand lightly across her hair. "Did you ever cry after that op, Daria? Or did you hold it all inside?" Instantly, Nik saw pain return to her eyes. He hadn't meant to bring it up, but the medic in him, the one who was trained to find infection and root it out, had spoken for him. The moment was broken, and he already missed it acutely.

"N-no... I cried on that ridge... holding Melissa. But she was dead." Her lips tightened and she looked away for a moment.

"You need not go there right now. I'm sorry I brought it up."

Shaking her head, her hand growing still on his torso, Daria moved her gaze up to his. "It's all right. The shrink at Shield Security where I work tried to get me to let it go but I just couldn't."

"Do you feel it's because of your sniper training? Being in the military?"

"Yes... in part..." She wiped her eyes with her fingers, yawning again. "You have a way of making me feel safe, Nik. I don't know why, but you do." She lifted her hand, skimming his stubbled cheek with the back of it. "You started to massage my leg and, all of a sudden, I felt this upwelling of grief that was so powerful that, no matter what I did, I couldn't stop it this time." Her mouth slashed. "I don't cry."

"Sometimes," he said quietly, moving his thumb across her scrunched brow, smoothing out those furrows, "we all need someone. I just happened to be here when you were ready to release that pain and grief, is all."

Daria shook her head, closing her eyes as his thumb skimmed her brow. "No," she managed in a low, broken tone, "that's not true, Nik." As he lifted his hand away, she opened her eyes. "There's something about you that I trust with my life. I know you meant well about massaging my leg." She stretched it a bit. "And it feels so much better now. Usually, even after sleeping all night, it's stiff in the morning and I have to get up and get moving around before it loosens up." She gave him a warm look. "It's you. It's not about being a person at the right place and time, at all."

"Wasn't Alex able to help you? He was there when you came home, wasn't he?"

"Yes, both he and Lauren took me under their wings." Daria slowly sat up. Nik followed suit, placing several pillows behind him, then leaning back against the headboard. When he opened his arms in invitation to her, Daria came to him. Curving into him, resting across his body, feeling his arms loose around her, holding her gently, Daria laid her head on his broad shoulder, one hand across his heart.

Euphoria flowed through Nik. He couldn't believe it, but laying with her against him, the intimacy strong and unbroken, was building even more trust between them. He pressed his lips to her mussed hair. "Alex has a way of pulling a person's tooth and they never feel the pain at the time," he told her in an amused tone. Nik wanted to do so much more than just hold Daria. He wanted to shower her with soft, meaningful kisses from the top of her head down to her small delicate toes. He felt her laugh, her face pressed against his shoulder, the sound muted as she nodded her head.

"You've got that right," Daria murmured, turning, meeting his hooded stare. "Alex tried, but I wasn't ready, Nik."

"Then we will celebrate the first step in healing your heart and soul from that event," he told her in a roughened tone. He smoothed black hair away from her cheek, tucking it across her shoulder. "Tell me about yourself. Where were you born? I've got hundreds of questions to ask you." He saw her gaze turn introspective. Had he accidentally stepped into another painful part of her life? Automatically for a moment, before Nik realized what he was doing, his arms closed protectively around her, as if to shield her from any unhappy memories.

"I was adopted at six months from a Russian orphanage and taken to Lviv, Ukraine. My new family said, when I was thirteen, they felt I had the blood of ancient Scythian women warriors. Looking back on my life? I believed them, that I inherited that gene, no doubt. Even my eyes are slightly slanted and my skin is not white, but an in-between color, bringing my unknown central Asian heritage with me. The women of my adopted family have always kept records of our family history. I remember being shown a very old parchment by my adopted mother and she was telling me about her two women ancestors, on the maternal side historically speaking, who rode with Kubla Kahn. That was in

1350, and that is how far back our history goes. I was mesmerized by that history even though it wasn't my own, and I grew up wanting to be just like them. They were fierce and brave and protected the innocent."

"And so, you became a Marine Corps sniper."

"For many years in the Sand Box, yes." She frowned. "I'm glad that's over, though. I guess I used up that gene. I'm done with my sniper career."

"A busted op like you had is enough to make anyone think twice about going back into the trade," he said. "I'm glad you're out of that MOS career track."

"I like the way you and Alex see the world," Daria admitted softly, her fingers smoothing the coarse dry shirt fabric across his chest.

"What do you mean?"

Her hand stilled on his chest. Daria studied him in the lulling silence. "That you both see a person's heart, their soul. I think it's very Ukrainian to move deeply into a person, to really want to see them, who they are." One corner of her mouth lifted a little. "Warts and all."

His mouth curved a bit. "You have no warts, Daria."

She snorted. "Oh, yes I do, Nik. You just haven't seen them come out yet."

"No, my Kitten, whatever warts you hide? They would never scare me away. You must know that." His hand rested on her arm. "Nothing you could say or do would make me run the other way. Ever."

She closed her eyes, languishing in his arms, absorbing his strength, his steadiness and open vulnerability. "I've never met a man like you before, Nik."

"How so?"

"You're able to be who you are. You can let your game face drop."

"Are you aware of this birthmark you carry? The quarter moon?" and he brushed the hair away from her ear.

"Yes. My Mom said it was moon-shaped. I can barely see it myself, but I can hold a mirror just so and spy it." Her voice turned soft. "Secretly? I dreamed it was the sign of a woman warrior within our family, too. I wanted badly to be like my Ukrainian family's wonderful history."

Nik nodded. "You have been a fierce warrior even to this day. Do you feel the Scythian blood is running through you?"

"In my childhood's wild imaginings, I always pictured myself as a young woman riding this black stallion, clothed in armor, swinging my sword, riding with the rest of my horse-mounted women warriors into battle." Shaking her head, "Dreams of a child, Nik. Reality is a lot harsher and unforgiving if you're in the military."

He heard the heaviness in Daria's words, and understood as few ever would. "Yes," he mouthed against her hair, squeezing her a little, "a child doesn't realize the brutality, the pain or grief of war. Playing any war scene, whether daydreaming it, or on a game app, is nothing like it is in real time or real life."

"We're both older and wiser." She lifted her leg a bit. "Wounded by it. Permanently."

He leaned down, moving his hand gently across her wounded thigh. "But wounds can be cleansed, Daria, just as you are allowing that to happen within yourself, right now, to start releasing that grief and horror. It's part of the necessary cleansing and healing process and you have bravely walked toward it, not run away from it."

She studied him as the quiet eddied around them. "Because you gave me a safe place to let it go, Nik. You're a medic, but in truth, you're a healer. Somehow... and I don't know how, you reached down inside me, released my pain and everything I was holding at bay. I couldn't hold on to it as you massaged my thigh. It was as if you had some secret key and unlocked me, and it was like a volcano erupting. It caught me by surprise. I couldn't control it any longer." Daria turned her gaze over to where her hand rested on his chest. "I opened up to you, trusted you and you held me. You actually encouraged me to cry, to get it out, and I did."

"Tears are always cleansing, Kitten. Always," Nik murmured, giving her a tender look. "You should cry often. It will help you heal faster." He saw her mouth turn down, as if to reject his words.

"It hurts so much to cry, Nik. I've had enough pain. I don't want to feel it again when it comes back up. That's why I try to sit on it. Ignore it."

He shook his head. "You must trust me as a medic, Daria, when I tell you 'better out, than in'. Any emotion that we have that is negative and dark, that cuts into us, causing us constant pain, needs to be released. Sometimes people cannot do it by themselves, but need another person or event to catalyze it within them."

"Like you did with me," she said, thoughtful.

"We shared a very important moment together," he agreed, his voice suddenly roughened with emotion. "It is a compliment to both of us that we trusted one another enough to allow it to surface within you and be released."

"I know I caught you off guard," Daria said, apologetic. "I sat up, pushing your hand away from me."

He gave her a wry look. "At first, yes, but I got it, Daria. You aren't the first person I have touched and then have them break down in tears later." Nik slid his fingers through her hair, watching the pleasure come to her half-closed eyes, seeing her lips part. It would be so easy to lean in those few inches and take her mouth gently beneath his own. Resisting, knowing she was open to him, fully immersed within him, Nik wasn't going to break her trust. "I have had many women and children cry in my arms over the years."

"You have seen so much trauma," Daria agreed, her voice filled with concern, searching his eyes.

"It is the load that a medic carries, Kitten," and he forced a slight smile for her benefit. Nik didn't want her to worry about *him*. *He* was worried about *her*. And he wanted to keep the focus on Daria. "I have broad shoulders. I've learned to carry all loads very well," he teased her. "Tell me more about your growing-up years with your adopted family?"

"My Dad is a professor of Archeology at the Ivan Franko National University of Lviv. My mother is an adjunct professor of archeology at the same university. I grew up at archeological digs in Ukraine and their focus has always been on Neolithic sites. I grew up surrounded with artifacts, read many books on history, and I loved it."

"So? Were you thinking about a life being a historian?"

"Archeology is history," she said, "and my mother and I were very interested in the matriarchal world of Neolithic sites in Ukraine, as well as other surrounding countries that once were part of Scythia. Marija Gambutas, a woman archeologist and anthropologist from Lithuania, was famous for finding the matriarchal society of the Neolithic people in our area of the world. I was entranced with my family genetics going back to the central Asian people. I told them I wanted to be a warrior, not carry on the family archeology as they had."

"Then," he said, "our backgrounds are very different." He saw her eyes widen a little in interest, and Nik couldn't help but give her a pleased look. "My family grew up on a farm collective in the center of Ukraine where wheat is grown for export. Alex's family lived close to us, and we were the best of friends growing up. Dan, my younger brother by two years, always followed us around. Alex and I would ride the family plow horses. We had a tractor, of course, but my father always kept a good team of draft horses on hand in case it broke down, which it did. Alex and I used to steal out to the barn, put bridles on them, leap upon their backs. Dan always rode behind me. The three of us would go cantering off along the pathways around the fields and into the woods. We'd find all kinds of things to explore and get into," and he laughed softly, warmth stealing through his chest. "Those were good days," he told her thickly.

"They sound wonderful. But I hear sadness in your voice, Nik."

"It's my turn to want to run and hide," he admitted, irony in his tone. "Russian separatists destroyed Alex's family farm. He and his sister, Kira, were the only survivors." His mouth turned down, his voice growing dim. "At that time, Alex was in the Russian army with me and he came home to his family farm and it was no more. A year later, Kira, who was also in the Russian Army as a nurse, had their field hospital overrun by the separatists. Everyone was killed except the nurses, who were repeatedly raped. Kira was sent to Moscow for a while to be rehabilitated, but that did not work and she left the Army. She moved to Kyiv to try and start to live her life again. Dan joined Spetsnaz two years later and he also became a medic. It was then that our farm was raided by Separatists. They killed our entire family."

Daria gasped, sitting up. "I'm so sorry, Nik. For you and Alex. He never told me any of this." She laid her hand on his arm, searching his pained expression.

"It's not something you bring up in social conversation, is it?" Nik took her hand in his, curling his fingers around hers.

"No… you're right…"

"Alex and I waged war against the Separatists with our Spetznaz teams. We gave no quarter. It was bloody and it was brutal. I lost part of my soul during that time. I was torn open by the loss of my entire family, three generations, Daria. I couldn't come to terms with it, with the murder of all of them at their hands. They'd done nothing to deserve that kind of fate. They loved the land; they loved their animals and all they wanted was to be able to find peace by working the land."

"That's so heart-breaking," she whispered, rubbing her brow. "I-I don't know how you got through it, Nik."

He gave her a gentle look. "And I sat here wondering how you survived that broken op." He brought her hand to his lips, kissing the back of it, and then watching pleasure come to her gold eyes once more. Knowing that she'd liked it, Nik was content in that moment to take things no further. Time wasn't necessarily on their side. He had only a few more days here in Aguas Calientes before he returned to the green hell. Nik silently promised Daria that he was going to make sure they spent as much time together as possible.

He was content to let Daria decide what was appropriate between them. But, if he were any judge of her and their growing closeness, the closeness between them that was molten, burning and hungry, he was certain that, in the future, they would become more intimate. Giving her a serious look, he said, "I feel like I've waited my entire life for this moment to occur, Daria. You're easy to talk to." He held her hand a little more firmly, looking deep into her eyes. "I've only got a few more days here. I know we have our parts to play. But, in truth? I want to spend every minute I can with you, starting tomorrow morning. It will be time for Korsak and his men to think I'm staying overnight to bed you."

"I want the same thing, Nik," Daria admitted quietly, holding his somber look. "I feel as if I've been waiting for you all my life. I can't explain it. It just feels so good to be around you, to be with you. You make me feel a happiness I've never felt before and I'm so afraid of losing it… losing you…"

"Let's take this one step at a time? Let's play our parts for Korsak. It's true that it will be another four weeks before we can see one another again, but you have much to fill your time with between now and then."

Daria nodded. As soon as Korsak's team left for the jungle again, she already had a time and place set up to meet Sergeant Mace Kilmer and his three-man army Special Forces team. Nik had already given her drawings and info to pass on to Kilmer that he couldn't otherwise get to the team. She was an important go-between on this mission to capture Korsak.

"You're right, I do." she replied.

He eased his hand from hers and looked at his watch. "It's nearly 2200. I need to go to keep my cover in place. I have to get back to the hotel whether I want to or not."

Daria nodded and slowly edged off the bed and stood. She pushed the hem of her shorts down into place over her scars once more, threading her fingers through her mussed hair, taming it. She watched as Nik stood, unwinding with that male grace of his. His shoulders were broad and strong, unlike hers. "Do you have any plans for us tomorrow?"

"Yes. Tomorrow morning, I'm taking you up to the orphanage with me. When I come into town, I always spend a day up there as a medic. Korsak would expect that of me and I don't want to break my normal patterns and rouse his suspicion. Would you like to go with me?"

"Sure, I'd love too," she said, coming around the bed. Daria slipped into his arms, resting her head against his chest for a moment, feeling his arms come around her. "I'm going to miss you tonight…"

He snorted. "I'll miss you more, Kitten." He kissed her hair and leaned back enough to catch her flawless golden eyes that held so much more in them. There was need in them. For him. It made him feel incredibly powerful and heady. His heart was wide open to Daria. He would do anything to make her smile and help her release her painful past. "To go back to that seedy hotel, to thin walls, to noises going on all night long, is not conducive to sleep, believe me."

She gave him a stricken look. "It's that bad?"

It was worse, but Nik didn't want to stress or burden Daria with anything more tonight. "I've been putting up with it for five years, and it hasn't killed me yet," he teased her lightly, placing a kiss on her nose. There was such openness between them that Nik found it tough not to dream of a future with

Daria. He squeezed her. "I have to go..."

"Do you want me to follow you out? Kiss you on the porch for them?"

He shook his head. "No, not tonight." He gestured to her shorts. "Don't wear those outside. If any of the team sees your wounded leg, they'll immediately know you were knifed and then they'll start asking a lot of questions about you."

Glumly, Daria said, "I hadn't even thought of that. I'm a lousy undercover agent, Nik."

He smiled and kissed her cheek, inhaling her special, spicy scent. "I will be your big, bad guard dog," he promised. Easing away, he wanted to kiss her, but knew he'd be lost if he did so. Nik was so close to lifting Daria into his arms and carrying her to the bed. And he knew, if he didn't leave right now, he'd end up doing just that. His lower body was on fire. Burning with hunger for her. Yet, he saw no arousal in Daria's eyes and knew she was content with where they stood with one another right now. They had touched, they had shared a few chaste kisses. It was enough. He could hope for more later, but didn't expect it. Daria had to set the pace.

"Guard dog," she teased, easing away from him.

"Every woman needs a man in her life who will protect her from time to time," he told her, walking down the hall with her. "It doesn't mean you aren't capable of defending yourself at all. It's a human thing to want to protect those you care about."

"Then," Daria said, touching his lower arm as he walked over to pick up his ruck, "let me be your guard dog, too. It works both ways, Nik."

He smiled fully, brushed her hair away over her ear and kissed her cheek. "I will come by for you at 0800. I'll take you to our restaurant down on the plaza to have *desayuno* early and then we'll walk up to the orphanage. Does that sound like a good day for you?"

Daria lost her smile, sliding her fingers along the line of his jaw.

With suddenly sad and serious eyes she said, "I can hardly wait, Nik..."

CHAPTER 10

"I WAS SURPRISED you left that woman's apartment last night," Brudin sneered as Nik made his way down the stairs to the lobby of their hotel the next morning. The idiot was standing there in a dark green t-shirt and cammos, unshaven, his eyes red-rimmed, reeking of cigarettes and alcohol.

Nik ignored him. He owed this bastard nothing, and walked on by him, hefting his medical pack over his shoulder.

"Where are you going?"

"Why don't you follow me and find out?"

Brudin glared at him.

Nik walked out of the delipidated hotel that was a cloying mix of stale cigarette smoke, marijuana, vodka and sour smelling male sweat. It was a place he hated, never spending one more moment in it than he had to with the team. Pushing out through the doors, the gray skies greeted him through their falling mist of light rain. He lifted his face, allowing the drizzle to cleanse him and remove the noxious odors he knew already clung to his freshly-cleaned clothes. Nothing stayed fresh or smelled very good in a jungle for very long. Dampness infused everything. He'd had to shake out his black t-shirt, dark green cammos, and black waterproof boots to ensure there were no venomous creatures within them who might have taken up residence while he'd slept. Not that the sleep hadn't been great. He'd slept like a dead man with Daria in his arms. Nik had forgotten what real sleep was like, and hungered for more. He walked quickly across the empty plaza. The first train from Cusco would come in at ten a.m., disgorging hundreds of tourists into Aguas Calientes. Most would climb into the red buses that would then chug up the switchbacks of a muddy road to the top of Machu Picchu for half a day.

His stride picked up, the asphalt gleaming wetly beneath his boots. The air was fresher now, cleansed by the rain, taking away the odors from last night's parties. None of the tourist shops were open at this hour, all were shuttered, their owners probably still sleeping. All was quiet and he absorbed the silence readily, trying to get the yells, screams and moans out of his head from the prostitutes working their johns over, a wall away from where he slept. He hated this life. He was so close to getting out of here. It was just a matter of time until he could alert the A-team as to where Korsak would go next. Or so he hoped.

Halfway up the hill, Nik's heart quickened. In just moments, he'd see Daria. Was she all right? How had she fared after he'd left? It was important that Brudin had seen him leave the hotel this morning. He took the wooden stairs to Daria's place briskly and, at the top, he knocked on the red door.

Daria opened it and smiled up at him. "Hey, look what the jaguar dragged in. You're wet!"

He grinned sheepishly, gave her a nod of hello, and eased past her, putting down his heavy medical ruck on the rug. "You look beautiful," he murmured, straightening, moving his fingers through the strands of his dampened hair. Daria wore a set of loose jeans, but they couldn't hide the length of her gorgeous legs or that fine butt of hers. The pale-peach alpaca sweater she had bought earlier, with its feminine cowl neck, only enhanced her natural beauty. Her golden eyes were warm and welcoming. He needed this. He needed her.

"I don't know about beautiful," she murmured, closing the door, "but I'm starving this morning. This is the first time in a long time I've actually been hungry."

Nik itched to take her into his arms. She stood before him and he felt and saw her happiness. "Your eyes are more clear this morning. A good cry will do that. It cleanses you in the best of ways."

Daria wrinkled her nose and went to retrieve her nylon jacket. "I don't know about that either, but I can tell you I slept so soundly and that I didn't wake up until an hour ago."

He inhaled her sweet scent as she moved close, pulling on her jacket. "I wish I could say the same. That hotel is noisy."

"Well, tonight you're staying here. Right?"

"Yes. If nothing else, I'll sleep well," he said, giving her a half grin. He gestured to his ruck. "I'm going to leave my medical gear here. We have to go down to the plaza for *desayuno*. And then we need to go up and over the hill. The orphanage is down the slope on the other side of it. The charity won't open until 0900, so we have a good hour to eat and be seen by Korsak's men if they happen to be up and about."

"Are they usually asleep at this time of day?" she asked, picking up her black baseball cap and settling it on her head.

"Drunk. Hung over. Drugs. Take your pick. I did run into Brudin, so he's going to tell Korsak I didn't stay with you last night."

"Good. I'm ready. Don't you want a coat, Nik?"

"No, I'm fine." He opened the door for her. "I'm used to this place."

"I don't think I'd ever get used to it at all. At least, during the Amazon's dry season, it might be humid, but it's not raining every day like it does here."

They stepped out and Nik shut the door behind them. Daria locked it with the key, depositing it into her pocket. She turned, sliding her arms around his shoulders.

"For those who spy on us," she whispered as she leaned up, closing her lips across his mouth.

Nik was jolted by her unexpected action, but at the same time, felt the heat and warmth of her mouth sliding across his. There wasn't any play-acting on his part as his arms naturally slid around Daria, hauling her up against him, kissing her hard and hungrily. She smelled faintly of oranges, and he felt her mouth blossom beneath his own, her hips moving suggestively against his. Fire shot through him at her unexpected sensuality, her femaleness shaking him to his core and making him want to take her right here and now. As the kiss deepened, his breathing became more ragged, as did hers. Daria pressed wantonly against him, her breasts firm and lush against his straining chest. Daria was all woman. And he'd named her rightly: she was like a sensual feline, a female jaguar on the hunt for her mate. She wasn't wearing a bra. That stunned him, and he damn near brought his hands up instinctively to cup her breasts. Luckily, what little was left of his functioning brain flagged that instinct down before he actually followed through on it.

Dazed by the passion of her kiss as Daria withdrew from it, her eyes drowsy, telling him so much, Nik kept his hands around her waist. He gripped her firmly, staring intently down at her. A playful glint came to her eyes and he wanted to drag her back into the apartment and follow through on what she'd just ignited in him. His voice was barely a growl. "Tell me you were doing this for show?"

"I didn't do it for show. It's what I wanted to do last night, but I knew if I kissed you, then you wouldn't leave and we couldn't continue this charade of ours." A playful smile came to Daria's lips. "I didn't want you to leave, Nik…"

"And I don't want you doing this because you think you owe me something," he rasped, his gaze digging into her widening eyes. Their irises were gold and he could see sienna specks deep within them, making them almost shimmer. Daria felt so alive beneath his hands. He could feel her pulsing, yearning and wanting him just as much as he desired her.

"What you did for me last night is something I'll never be able to thank you for enough," she said slowly, fearlessly holding his gaze. "And I would never use sex as a 'thank you'. I value myself way too much for that."

His lips twitched. "You're sure?" and he caressed her hips.

"There's a difference between love, sex and thanks. Don't you think?"

An unwilling grin spread across his mouth. "Where did *this* Daria come from?"

Shrugging, she slipped out of his grip. "Maybe you released her last night," she called over her shoulder, laughing, as she headed down the stairs.

Still stunned, Nik gave himself an internal shake. This woman knew how to kiss. Not only that, she had moves that made his lower body scalded by such starvation that he could barely think. If Brudin was watching, and he was sure the bastard was, there would be no doubt in the errand boy's tiny brain about why he was staying over tonight with Daria.

Kicking himself back into gear mentally, Nik took the stairs quickly, catching up with her, scooping her hand up into his and leading her up the hill to a nearby restaurant. The soft rain had stopped and the asphalt shined in the low light of the morning, the gray clouds thick and crawling silently above the town. First, breakfast, and then they'd go to the orphanage.

"Tell me more about the orphanage?" Daria urged as they crested the empty hill. They'd had a wonderful breakfast, and then gone back to her apartment afterward so Nik could pick up his medical ruck.

Before her lay the green expanse of the jungle, the railroad track carved through it and, center stage, a squat two-story gray concrete building with a ten-foot-high cyclone fence surrounding it. Along the top of the fence coiled concertina wire, with sharpened blades all along to discourage anyone breaking into the place. It was set off to the left side of the compound, near the hot spring pools. The whole area, Daria had read, was sitting on top of volcanic activity. The hot springs were divided into five long, rectangular swimming-pool-lengths filled with murky green, opaque water. Furthermore, they looked far from hot. More like tepid, going on cool. They didn't look appealing to Daria at all, but she'd heard that many tourists swam in their lukewarm depths, thinking the water had healing properties. She'd never go into what looked like green slime to her. Not willingly.

"Healing Hands is a modest charity in South America," Nik told her, gesturing toward the fenced-in orphanage. "Liz Standsworth, Senator Jacob Standworth's daughter, runs it. She cares very much about third world countries. Up in the Highlands, she and her volunteer diggers are drilling wells for ten villages in this region... ones that have no clean water available to them. There's a forty-percent infant mortality rate because the young children drink the dirty water that is filled with parasites, fecal matter, bacteria or dead animal debris that causes Hepatitis A. In the States, if you get Hepatitis A, you can get medication for it and are quarantined for six weeks. Out here, if a child drinks polluted water, he or she will die. There are no medications available. Liz does what she can, where she can. She's got a lot going on in Peru, essentially in this area for right now. She hires women who are widows or volunteers from the U.S., and they run these orphanages in Peru. There is an American here, Megan Cantrell, who is the volunteer who manages this one orphanage. You'll like her a lot. As a matter of fact, when I'm gone for this next month, I know Megan would love to have your help. Do you like young children?"

"I love babies and children." Daria smiled a little, squeezing his hand. Nik was a man who wore his heart on his sleeve, no question. She could see the excitement in his eyes as they drew closer to the gray compound.

He shrugged. "Some women don't for various reasons. I never assume, nor do I judge them."

"I do love kids."

"These children will love you."

They walked down the well-trodden muddy path that led off the asphalt hill road toward the orphanage. Daria could see that the jungle growth continually encroaching around the compound was being held at bay, presumably by a lot of regularly-swung machetes. Everything grew at a swift and alarming rate around here due to the constant rain. She saw the concertina on top of the ten-foot-high fence. "Why the wire, Nik?"

Frowning, he said, "There is a handful of very poor, desperate drug-addicted Quechua Indians around here. They have resorted to stealing. Liz had to put up the fence with the razor wire. The orphanage was getting broken into all the time and the children were at risk by the constant robberies. She didn't want anyone getting hurt." He slowed his pace as they came to the main gate. There was a huge rusty padlock on it. Lowering his voice, he said, "Two years ago, Megan was jumped from behind, blindfolded and then raped by a band of men. I'm not so sure it wasn't the other Russian team who is in this area. Word is, it was by the people who live here, but they are cautious about talking about it. No one can prove anything. They tied her up and Megan couldn't identify any of them. It was a brutal attack upon her."

"Oh, no," Daria whispered, struck by the tragedy. "I wouldn't think Quechua would do that. They're a very peaceful people."

"They are, and yet Korsak keeps telling us it was them, not the other Russian team who had come in for R&R. I didn't believe him for a second. The other team near where we work are nothing but sick, predatory Russians. They sometimes visit Aguas Calientes, and the people who live here run and hide when they enter the village. They should," he muttered, his mouth thinning.

"And Megan stayed on after that?" The worst thing Daria could think that could happen to any woman was rape. It was a violent assault upon her being, pure and simple, meant to disempower her, to control her and put her in her place. It sickened her and she touched her stomach, feeling regret over Megan's plight.

"Yes." His voice lowered as he opened the padlock with a key from his pocket. "Megan is a strong, good woman. She comes from a military family, the Trayhern's, and she served in the Air Force, and was a transport pilot for six years. When it happened, one of the women came and found her unconscious on the floor in her small room where she sleeps. It took hours to get a helicopter in here from Cusco to pick her up." He opened the padlock, which creaked in his hands. "A lesser woman would have left this green hell, but she didn't."

"Why not?"

"Because Megan is a woman who commits her passion to her work. She's always loved children." He turned to Daria; his eyes sad. "Now, she can't have any because of the brutality of the gang rapes. She went through extensive surgery and nearly died on the table. She had to have a hysterectomy in order to save her life, it was that bad."

"No," Daria breathed. She pressed her hand against her mouth, fighting back tears for Megan.

Nik shook his head, pushing open the cranky gate that needed some oil and attention. "They cut her face, too, so don't stare at Megan. She's gone through hell and has redoubled her work efforts here at the orphanage. It's her sanctuary of sorts, I think. I don't know. She's a complex, caring woman."

"My heart aches for her," Daria breathed. "Would Russians do that to a woman?"

He grimaced, shutting the gate but leaving the padlock open. "That's why I know it was the other Russian team. Spetsnaz is handy with knives. We're taught how to carve up a person to get them to tell us what we want to know. When I was able to get into Aguas Calientes after it happened, I took a farm train up to Cusco and visited her in the hospital. By the cut on her face, on her upper chest, I could tell it was Spetsnaz work. Quechua Indians don't work with knives. It's not a tool they use."

Rubbing her brow, Daria stood near him, if nothing else but for the sense of protection he radiated. "I-I didn't realize this…"

Grimly, Nik cupped her shoulders, giving her a small shake. "Listen to me. This is a very dangerous game we play. I'm surprised Alex didn't tell you about this."

"Jack, during the briefing, said the Russian teams were cruel. He didn't go any further into explanation. Alex did say that Korsak and his team routinely raped women at each village. Sometimes… young girls…," and she frowned.

"And if the woman doesn't do what they want, they use a knife to control her. They will cut her, bleed her, until she gives in and stops fighting back. They have their methods." He brushed some hair away from her taut brow.

"Don't worry, okay? I'm here. Korsak and his men will leave you alone. They know better than to tangle with me. I might be a medic, but I'm just as highly trained as they are, and I won't take anything off them. Especially when it comes to you."

She felt a chill. "Do you think they would come after me?"

"No. Not unless they suspected you, Daria. And we're not giving them any reason to go in that direction." He tried to smile, but failed. "Just treat Megan like you would anyone else. All right?"

"Of course," Daria answered faintly, nausea rising in her throat over Megan's horrific assault.

Nik patted her shoulder, his hand sliding down and coming to rest in the small of her back, guiding her down the concrete walk to a dark-green wooden door that said 'Welcome' on it.

Inside, Daria heard squalling babies, children laughing, and saw the back of a woman with long red hair, in a denim skirt to her ankles, brown leather sandals and a white peasant blouse, getting all of the kids to sit at a long wooden table for breakfast. Daria inhaled the scent of quinoa cereal, one of the few grains in the world that contains thirty-percent protein. Despite another two, older Quechua Indian women in colorful skirts and blouses, Daria still couldn't tear her gaze away from the American woman who had her back to them.

Nik halted at the door and waited. Daria watched his expression and she saw affection for Megan in his eyes. When the woman turned, she had to stop herself from gasping. A long scar ran from the top of her right cheekbone and down that entire side of her face to her jawline and it made Daria want to cry. It was a faint scar, but there, forever. A mark of her courage to survive such a terrible assault, as far as Daria was concerned.

"Nik!" Megan called, throwing open her arms, rushing toward him.

Daria stood back, watching the tall, willowy woman grab Nik and hug the hell out of him. She had pale blue eyes that had suddenly sparkled with so much warmth and happiness once she'd spotted him. Daria couldn't help but smile in response, watching the woman hug Nik until he blushed. He was a big man, and Megan probably weighed around a hundred and forty pounds, but there was such an encompassing joy vibrating in her alto voice for him that it diminished their size difference. He patted her shoulder and pulled back, grinning sheepishly.

"It's good to see you again, Megan." Nik turned and held out his hand in Daria's direction. "I want you to meet Daria McClusky. She's a botanist on sabbatical to write a book about local orchids. I thought you two might like to meet. Daria, meet Megan Cantrell."

"Welcome," Megan said warmly, stepping toward Daria.

Daria held out her hands. Megan had an oval face, high cheekbones, and wide-spaced eyes that spoke of her intelligence. There was such a fierce energy surrounding this woman that Daria was stunned by it. No question, she was a tour-de-force. "Hi," she said, smiling, "it's nice to meet you, Megan. Nik said you might like some volunteer help?" Daria released the woman's hand. "I'm not a licensed child care specialist, but I love children. He thought I might be helpful to you when I need a break from writing my book."

"Oh," she bubbled, "I'd LOVE to have you help us, Daria! We need all the help we can get around here. I'm missing Maria today. She's home sick," and Megan looked to her left toward the table where the Indian women were serving the hot cereal to the noisy, impatient children.

"Well," Nik murmured, giving Daria a significant look, "why don't I perform my medical duties around here, and perhaps Megan can sort of fold you into her working day? Get a feel for what it's like around here, Daria?"

"I'd like that," Daria murmured to the red-haired woman. Megan was either in her late twenties or early thirties. It was hard to tell because she was so energetic, her face, even with the scar, youthful looking and reminding Daria of a young college-aged woman. Still, Daria saw oldness and tiredness banked up in Megan's eyes, too. Her hands were red and chaffed, telling Daria that the woman didn't take care of herself. Either that, or she was doing a lot of hard handwork all on her own. "How can I help?"

"Well," Megan said, giving her a worried look, "you are probably going to faint, but I need someone to wash the children's clothes. My washer died on me and I'm trying to get a replacement from Lima down here, which is next to impossible. Liz has it in Cusco, but the train owner wants to charge us an arm and leg to transport it down here." She pulled Daria along to another room, a smaller one. "And until this situation can be resolved, I've been using a washboard and washing all the kids' clothes by hand."

Daria saw the washer and dryer. There were two huge service sinks nearby. Megan walked over to them and picked up a washboard.

"I need you to wet the clothes down, soap them up and scrub them on the board. Then, put water in this sink and rinse them out. My dryer still works, thank God. Nothing dries down here, but it will with this dryer." She pointed to a pile of children's clothing piled up in a mound nearly four feet tall. "Are you still game?"

Daria grinned and pushed up her sleeves. It was chilly in the structure as it was naked gray concrete and little else. "You bet."

Megan held up her reddened hands. "See these? I've been doing this four hours a night, every night, for the last two weeks." She smiled and flexed an arm, pointing to its bicep. "And I'm going to look like Arnold Schwarzenegger pretty soon if Liz doesn't get that washer down here to us ASAP."

Daria nodded. "You do know there's a laundry place in town?"

Megan's full mouth twisted. "Yes, I know the owner. He's an unmentionable word in my world. I can't afford it, anyway. He won't give me a discount. We're on a very tight budget and getting the kids three square meals a day is my priority."

"Okay, I'll go to work."

"Don't over do," Megan pleaded, touching her shoulder. "And if you need me? I'll be somewhere around here. It's not that big of a place. You'll find me."

Daria smiled and watched Megan hurry away, her denim skirt flapping around her thin ankles. Sadness moved through her. How could Megan be this cheery after what had happened to her? She was only four months out of her trauma and it was obvious that it still affected her heavily whether she wanted to admit it or not. Daria's admiration and respect for Megan increased exponentially. Obviously, the woman was made of tougher stuff than she herself was.

Nik was just wrapping up his last examination of the day on a tiny six-month-old baby girl when Daria moved quietly to the small, cozy nursery room. It was the warmest room in the place and she closed the door behind her, watching him gently handle the infant. If he was aware of her, he made no indication, bending over the cooing baby in his arms, her tiny arms and legs moving energetically, gurgling and smiling. The cloth diaper made Daria wince a little. The old-fashioned way, with cotton fabric, made for good diapers. No first-world amenities down here. She watched as Nik rubbed the stethoscope between his hands to warm the metal up before placing it on the baby's chest. How he cared for the infant made her melt inwardly. There was exquisite tenderness in this man as he listened to the infant's lungs and heart. He picked the baby up, holding her on his knee, bracing the infant with his free arm and hand, listening to her lungs some more.

It was the soft words in Spanish that he spoke to the baby, smiling and tickling her, that made Daria's smile widen. The baby gurgled happily, her large brown eyes glistening and pinned on Nik, whose face was only inches away. He put his stethoscope away and took the baby's temperature with an ear monitor. Taking each of her tiny hands, he let the child grasp his own long index finger. Nik was testing her strength and coordination. And when he was done with the examination, he hoisted the child up into his arms, pulled a pink alpaca blanket across her tiny body, laying her against his shoulder, gently patting her back. There was a loud burp.

Daria laughed a little.

Nik turned, smiling over at her. "You caught me."

She ambled over to the table and she held out her hands. "Can I hold her? Would she want to come to me?"

"I don't see why not. Meet Gabriela. Megan found her shortly after her birth, dropped off at the front gate to the orphanage, wrapped in a Quechua blanket. Let's get her dressed in her onesie? You can then sit in that rocker over there and I'll get her a warm bottle of llama milk and feed her. Sound like fun?"

It did. Daria found the clean pink onesie and brought it over to the table. Nik was a breeze at putting it on the baby.

"You've done this a few times."

He smiled and nodded, brushing his fingers across the baby's mussed black hair, patting it down into place. "I come over here every month. There's a lot of sick children who are dropped off here. All malnourished, needing a lot of TLC, vitamin and mineral packs, and medical intervention of one sort or another."

"Who pays for your supplies to help them?" Daria wondered, taking Gabriela from him.

"I do," he said, stuffing everything into his ruck and velcroing it shut. "It's the only allowance I give myself: to buy the medicine these children need at a Cusco pharmacy."

"Korsak wouldn't buy it out of his millions of dollars of drug money?" Daria asked, sitting down in the rocker, smiling into Gabriela's huge, wide eyes as the baby gazed up at her.

Snorting, Nik said, "No. Stay here and just rock her. She loves to be rocked. I'll get her bottle warmed from the kitchen…"

There was such peace in rocking back and forth with a baby in her arms. Gabriela's angelic little face was precious to Daria. She watched as the baby's eyes closed, nearly asleep by the time Nik quietly returned with a bottle in his hand.

"Cute little thing," he murmured, handing the bottle to Daria.

"She's beautiful. So sad her mother gave her up," she said as she fitted the nipple gently between Gabriela's tiny bow-shaped lips.

Nik crouched down in front of Daria, his hands light on her knees, searching her eyes. "There's much love around here," Nik murmured, looking around. "The building is old. It used to be a miner's home, built of heavy concrete. It was abandoned and left to be eaten up and covered by the jungle until Liz came down here and reclaimed it. The Peruvian government gave it to her so she could open up the orphanage. It serves the entire area around Machu Picchu, plus the Highlands area."

"That's a lot of square miles."

"There's a lot of abandoned babies and children here," Nik said sadly, shaking his head.

"Why so many, Nik? What's going on around here?"

"Nothing that isn't going on in every third world country," he told her quietly. He rose and brought a chair over, turning it to face her. Sitting down, he crossed his legs, his hands resting in his lap. "How did you do in the laundry room today?"

Daria grimaced. "I've got red, chapped hands to prove I worked in there, but I'm not complaining. At least it's one day's worth of clothes cleaned that Megan won't have to do tonight."

"You did her a great service today," he praised, giving her a look of pride. "She's been without a washer for weeks."

"That's awful. She's so busy, Nik. Does the woman ever get any rest?"

Shaking his head, he looked over his shoulder to ensure the door was closed. Turning, he said in a low tone, "Ever since being gang raped, she barely sleeps two or three hours a night. It's pretty bad and it's PTSD. But I can understand why…"

"Why doesn't she go home to the States and get therapy and help?"

"It's not that simple, Daria. If Megan left here, all these children have no place to go. The orphanages in Cusco are overflowing. I know that because sometimes, when I want to get out of here and clear my mind, I take the train into Cusco and go to those orphanages, offering my medical services for three days at a time."

"So awful," she whispered, gazing lovingly at Gabriela who was sucking hard on the bottle's nipple, her eyes closed, her little hands waving constantly. "This is horrible."

"I've pleaded with Megan to go home, get the help she needs, but she won't leave these children in the lurch. I've talked to Liz about it and she agrees Megan should go home, but she refuses to go."

Frowning, Daria whispered, "But… why?"

He shrugged a shoulder. "Humans are all built differently, Kitten. If you have ten people face the same crisis, there will be ten different responses to it."

Making an unhappy noise in her throat, Daria nodded. She took the soft diaper Nik had provided her and wiped the bubbles gathering like little pearls from the sides of Gabriela's mouth. "You're right. I know you are. Megan was so bright and cheerful this morning."

"It's a game face," he warned her heavily. "She's combatting depression. I'm treating her medically, but she needs therapy, preferably from a warm, nurturing mother type of woman therapist. It has to be a woman because it was males that harmed her. Women did not break her trust. Men did."

"But you're a man, Nik. And she was genuinely glad to see you. She just about hugged you to death."

He smiled shyly. "I don't know why Megan trusts me so much. Maybe she senses my Ukrainian heart...," and his dark eyebrows drifted downward.

"What does that mean? You said Megan didn't know who her attackers were."

"They spoke Russian to one another during the raping of Megan," he told her wearily. "That's how I know it was the other team. Megan heard a name. Boris."

"Do you know him?" she demanded quietly, rocking Gabriela.

"Unfortunately, yes. He makes Korsak look like a saint in comparison. Boris Golub was a captain in Spetsnaz. He was in some of the most brutal fighting. He took no prisoners. Ever. They called him 'The Butcher.'" Nik pushed his fingers through his hair in an aggravated motion. "He's a monster. I'm sure it was he and his team who broke in here and gang raped Megan."

"Does she know that?"

Nik grew grim. "No... not yet..."

Daria pursed her lips, staring at him. "Why not?"

"No one in the Peruvian *policía* is going after Golub. They don't have rape kits down here in this country, Daria. The police here in Aguas Calientes know this Russian predator's reputation and they quake in fear of him. They would never try to apprehend him."

"This is unbelievable," she whispered, frustrated. "Then, maybe it's just as well Megan doesn't know?"

Mouth twisting, Nik said in a low voice, "I worry about that. It's taken Megan a year to come out of the surgery and recover to where she has her old strength returning. She's street smart. She knows there are other Russian mafia drug teams around. I don't think, given she's been here for two years, and has the good will of these people in this town, that she couldn't make some inquiries and find out about more regarding Boris Golub."

"And then what?"

He gave her a cool stare. "Megan was in the military, like you, Daria. She's trained, armed and lethal. I wouldn't put it past her, once she figures it all out, to go after Boris herself. She'll take the bastard down, including all his men." He flexed his fist, frustration in his tone. "Liz is worried about that, too. The last I heard, she was calling Megan's cousin, Morgan Trayhern. He's got a security company, Perseus, in Montana. I think he knows about all this and promised Liz he'd do something about it."

"How long ago was that?"

"Two weeks ago."

"Wow, this is a really unsettling situation." She chewed on her lip. "Do you think Megan would just arbitrarily leave her kids here to go hunt down Golub?"

"That's the dicey question, isn't it? Does she turn vigilante or does she stay here and care for her children? No one can do what she does here, Daria. She's a one-woman show. The Indian women come and help. She pays them what she can, but basically, it's all on her shoulders."

Shaking her head, Daria choked softly, "I feel so sorry for her. How tortured she must be…"

CHAPTER 11

THE SKY WAS a druzy blue as Daria emerged with Nik from the orphanage at 1600, four p.m.

Sunlight struck the western side of Machu Picchu, the bustling streets of the community below alive with wandering tourists, all the noise across the hill the town sat upon rising into the jungle that surrounded it. She felt a mix of emotions. At their forefront, heart-rending grief for Megan who appeared cheery, patient and seemed to have herself together, despite her trauma. As Nik and her walked up and over the hill, she asked him, "You said you were helping Megan medically?"

Nik cut his stride in half, taking her hand to ensure, in case Brudin watched them, they looked like a couple falling in love. "Yes, a sleep medication. I wanted to give her an anti-anxiety med as well, but she refused. She thinks she can work through this without such. I understand her reasoning, but she is here alone, without any real emotional support system. And when we go through terrible things in our life, we all need someone."

Daria heard the heaviness, the heartbreak, in his low tone, clearly moved and worried about Megan Cantrell. She squeezed his hand a little more and he glanced her way. "Did you ever get support after your family was murdered, Nik?" she asked softly. Instantly, Daria knew the answer as serrating anguish rose in his face for a moment before he quickly masked that real, raw reaction. Daria had to stop herself from pulling Nik to a halt, throwing her arms around him and just holding him. Because, as never before, she saw what lay beneath Nik's everyday demeanor. And it was as she was beginning to suspect: the man did wear his compassionate nature daily with those he cared for medically.

"No… You are an unexpected joy in my life, Daria," he said, giving her a partial smile. "More than you know."

"I'd like to be there for you, Nik." She saw him nod, give her a warm look. It was enough.

He slowed at the top of the hill. To the left was a vegetable vendor. "Tonight," he said, "I want to make dinner for you. Allow me?"

She raised her eyebrows. "You cook, do you?" and her lips curved in a teasing line.

"I'm not half bad. I end up doing most of the cooking out in the jungle for my team. They can't stand their own poor attempts. My mother had me in the kitchen ever since my head was level with the kitchen counter. She taught me everything she knew, and I liked working with her in the kitchen. It was fun. I see cooking as a form of chemistry."

Her heart broke. Daria could imagine a dark-haired little Nik next to his mother, curious, eager, holding her full attention, care and love. And it had all been ripped away from him. "Sounds wonderful. To tell you the truth," and she held up her reddened hands, "I could use some downtime on these."

Nik slowed to a stop, taking one of her hands in his, and examining it. "Red and chapped. When we get home, I'll put some special lotion that I carry on them? I always give Megan a bottle when I see her monthly."

Her body began to melt as he held her hand gently between his own. For all of his size and strength, Daria was always shocked by how tender Nik could be. At the same time, it was juxtaposed because she knew Spetsnaz operators were black ops like herself. There was no tougher breed of men or women in the world than them. The roughness of the thick calluses on his hands and fingers attested to such, her skin arcing with tiny tingles of pleasure as he skimmed his fingers across her chapped skin. "Yes, that would be great... thank you."

He smiled warmly at her. "Now, come with me. Juanita, the old woman who runs this vegetable stand, is a good person. I always buy my fruits and vegetables from her when I get into town. She will love meeting you. And this is where you should come to buy vegetables in this town when I leave."

Nik led her over to the small wooden stall that canted somewhat to one side, poorly constructed and sagging with age as it was. It had a bright-yellow, dilapidated rainproof tarp over the top of it. Under the tarp, Daria spotted a gray-haired, plump Quechua woman with a brown bowler hat perched jauntily on her head. Her steel-gray braids hung tight and shining over her ample breasts. Daria loved that the Indian women all wore bright, colorful, hand-woven tops, and matching skirts that brushed around the ankles of their brown, bare feet.

Juanita rose slowly as she saw Nik approach. When she smiled, half her front teeth were missing. She waddled slowly around the edge of her crates of vegetables, her arms wide open.

Nik rushed forward, cutting the distance quickly, leaning down, gently enfolding the old woman in his arms. She patted him heartily on his back, returning his huge hug of welcome. They spoke in Quechua with one another.

Daria smiled, feeling more and more yearning for this man, who was so unlike the other men he was forced to be with. She decided, as Nik released Juanita, that he was hurting equally, if not more than herself. Probably suffering as deeply as Megan Cantrell. Life wasn't easy down here and she knew that in spades now.

Megan pushed on, idealistic, believing in the good in life, helping the destitute innocent children who had no one else to protect them. But she could at least protect them, even if no one had come to *her* aid when Golub and his men had raped her.

Nik pushed on because of his fierce love and loyalty for his brother, his focus on getting Dan the latest medical expertise that might help him recover from his TBI.

And what was she doing? Mouth flexing, Daria didn't want to look closely at that answer. She needed to start the healing process. No one had ever said it didn't take guts to do so, as she was beginning to fully realize.

"Come meet Juanita," Nik urged, holding out his hand toward Daria.

She met the brown-eyed woman whose toothless smile infected her with happiness. Daria knew this woman had probably suffered horribly with no dental care, through the aching pain of infected teeth. Then someone, probably a fellow villager, pulled out the tooth with a pair of pliars to relieve her of her suffering, without any pain killers available. Juanita's hands were large, calloused, her fingers delicate as they held the alpaca sweater she was knitting. Daria smiled warmly and gave her a gentle hug of hello.

Juanita waddled back to her old, dilapidated metal chair, setting her latest knitting project down on the seat of it. Then she turned and came back over by the boxes of fresh produce, excitedly chattering away in broken Spanish peppered liberally with the Quechua language, talking about each of them. Daria stood back, listening and watching Nik politely chatting with the native woman. Juanita wasn't surprised at all when the Ukrainian spoke her language, and so they switched away from Spanish and into pure Quechua. As they conversed, Juanita picked up an ear of corn and peeled back the green leaves, showing Nik huge kernels, each the size of nickels, all down the length of it, telling him this was good corn that had just come from Sacred Valley, two thousand feet above their current location. And then she brought out long, healthy-looking green beans, breaking off one, giving it to him to eat. Daria had no defense against Nik at this point. He was fully invested in the moment with the charismatic Juanita who was more like the ringmaster of a circus than a simple villager, who patted and pinched his cheek like he was a much-beloved son of hers who had come for a visit. Daria watched him chew the green bean thoughtfully and nod and praise Juanita for the flavor and juiciness of the vegetable. And then he bought a pound of them from her.

This process went on for at least ten minutes until Daria was standing there with a number of brown paper sacks of fresh produce gathered in her arms. She saw Nik give Juanita many more Peruvian Soles than what she asked for and saw the old woman's eyes tear up as she saw how much money she held. Nik was generous, no question. He cared deeply for the babies and the elders of this world. Earlier, she had seen him give Megan a huge wad of US dollars wrapped in a rubber band right in her hand just before they had left the orphanage. There had been tears of gratitude in her eyes.

Juanita pinched his cheek one last time and hugged him when they had enough for their meal. She came over to Daria, pinched her cheek and patted her shoulder, saying something in Quechua to her that she didn't understand. She saw Nik grin broadly as he came up to place his hand against her back, guiding her down the hill.

"What did Juanita just say?"

"Oh," he murmured, "that you and I looked more like a husband and wife than just friends. I told her I had just met you."

Feeling heat rush up from her neck and into her face, Daria stared over at him. Nik had pulled a large cloth bag out of his medical ruck and put all the sacks of food into it, carrying it easily in his other hand as he walked beside her. "Oh…"

"Does that upset you?"

She cleared her throat and smiled a little. "No… not really. It's just a little soon?"

He chuckled indulgently and took her across the street to the local butcher shop. "Didn't I tell you? Juanita is a medicine woman? She has visions and sees things in the future."

"How accurate is she?" Daria asked warily, halting at the open-air butcher shop.

"Very," Nik said with assuredness. "Stay here, I'll get us a very nice fat chicken for dinner…"

Unsettled, Daria looked up the street toward the vendor booth. Juanita was sitting down again, knitting intently on her colorful alpaca sweater. Daria turned her attention back down the street, looking for any Russian from Korsak's team who might be watching them. Seeing no one, and yet never trusting that someone wasn't watching, she looked over at Nik haggling over a freshly-killed chicken that had just been plucked and gutted. The smell of fresh blood cloyed her nostrils. Daria was a meat eater, but didn't like the smell of blood or carcasses. All kinds of parts of slaughtered cows, chickens and hogs hung down from the ceiling of the shop like bulbs hanging off a Christmas tree. The smell and sight of blood bothered her, and she turned away, frowning. It reminded her starkly of that fateful night, and Daria moved out to the center of the street, allowing the thick, heavy crowds of tourists to flow around her.

Nik came and found her minutes later, the chicken wrapped in brown paper and string in his shopping bag. He gave her a concerned look, touching her shoulder, running his hand across it.

"Too much?"

"Yes," she choked, shaking her head. "I-I couldn't stand the sight and smell of the blood…"

"I understand, *moya kotya*. I'm sorry we had to get it there. It's the only butcher shop in town." He gave her a sharpened look. "You're pale."

"I'll be okay," she said rallying beneath his care, glad that he enfolded her beneath his left arm as they walked toward the apartment halfway down the hill.

"That's what they always say," Nik said grimly. "We all say that because we have no place to offload the terrible feelings or images that come with it, that we carry." He squeezed her and gave her a tender look. "I will cook for you tonight. You can just rest. It has been a long and emotionally stressful day for you, Daria."

"And yet," she muttered defiantly, "it's been the same for you. And you take it with such grace, Nik. What's your secret? Because I'm not doing as well as I wished I could."

He laughed a little as they halted at the bottom of the steps to her apartment. "That's easy. I ignore it. Come," he said, urging her up the stairs, "let's leave the world of suffering behind us? Let's get to your home and close the door and make our world better? Maybe a little laughter? A sense of home when there is no more home anywhere for people like us? We can enjoy the evening, enjoy the company of one another?"

"Sounds great to me," Daria agreed fervently, taking the stairs, one hand on the damp, rusting metal rail. Her heart and body responded to his low, guttural voice, that yearning for her once more in his eyes as he searched her gaze. He was a man on a tightrope that could break at any moment, Daria realized as she reached the door. Nik came and stood behind her as she fished out the key from her pocket.

"When we get inside, let me sweep for bugs again," he told her quietly.

"Okay," she said, pushing the door open. To Daria the place looked untouched. She closed the door behind Nik as he came in and made a beeline for the small kitchen, setting the sack of goods on the counter. The change in him startled her. His face, a moment ago so relaxed and open, was now shut. The emotions, just before so clearly visible on it, were gone. Now, he was in black ops mode as he quickly and efficiently swept every room of the house. He found a bug placed in the lamp that hung over one end of the couch, held it up to her and then placed it on the floor, smashing it with the heel of his combat boot. The angry, dark look in his face as he straightened told Daria that, more than anything, he was a warrior, not just any soldier. The glint coming to his darkening blue eyes put her on notice. She was privileged to see the softer side of Nik, not his hardened Spetsnaz side.

He made a second sweep, intensity in his gaze, his mouth pursed as his lean hands skimmed every surface along every window sill, running his fingers under the lights set beneath the cupboards over the kitchen counter, looking up behind the opened blinds. Daria watched him work and learned. She would have to do this every time she returned to her apartment. No one could be trusted now. Her home had been breached.

NIK HEARD DARIA groan with pleasure after finishing the meal he'd fixed for them. The sun was setting, near 1800, six p.m., the day gone, growing darker as night silently crept across this jungle town. He smiled at her, sipping his coffee after clearing the plates and placing them in the sink. Her hands were still red, but less so since he'd given her the lotion to sooth their hard-worked flesh. Her hands were toughened by years of being a sniper in some of the worst climate conditions in the world, but they had no defense against six hours in soapy, hot water scrubbing children's clothes on a washboard the old fashion way.

"Satisfied, Little Cat?" he teased. He saw the gold in her eyes grow amused.

Running her hand lightly across her stomach, she said, "I feel like a stuffed turkey. I was actually hungry tonight. This is the most food I've eaten in a long time."

Nodding, Nik asked, "Since four months ago? Your appetite has not returned? Yes?"

"Yes." Daria shrugged. "Alex was always inviting me over for his homemade borscht and other Ukrainian food, trying to get me to put back the lost weight. Lauren makes terrific desserts and she was always tempting me, too. I just couldn't eat..."

"But if you ate, you became nauseous?"

"Yes." She studied him intently. "Is that why you're so lean, Nik?" She saw his mouth curve ruefully as he held the mug between his hands, close to his lips.

"You're a very astute observer of the human condition, my Kitten."

"Like you aren't?"

"Oh," he said lightly, "I feel we complement one another very well. You're highly intelligent, but anyone who is a sniper is far beyond the normal human being in some very unique ways. You miss nothing because you know it's the details that can either make or break the op." He sipped his coffee and then placed the mug on the table. "And, you care, Daria. That is something you can't train into a person. They either have a heart or they don't. You have a very large, giving one."

She eyed him. "And you don't? Isn't this the pot calling the kettle black?" She saw his lips lift away from his teeth; his gaze bemused.

"Caught. Once again. Remind me not to play chess with you?"

Daria loved chess and had the game on her computer tablet she'd brought with her. She'd been goading Nik into playing it with her because he said he loved chess, also, but kept resisting her. "People interest me. They're like chess pieces. You never know what moves they will make, sometimes."

He leaned back in his chair, pushing it away from the table and standing. "Yes, like this morning when you suddenly kissed me out on the front porch."

"Caught you off guard, did I?" and Daria chuckled, standing.

"Yes, but I liked it."

Becoming serious, she said, "Do you think Korsak has bought us as a couple getting to know one another?"

"Up to a point." He pushed the chair back in against the table. "Brudin probably placed that bug in here. He can pick any lock. That bothers me."

"That Korsak's not buying us?" She went to one corner of the couch and sat down, slipping off her sandals, tucking one leg beneath her and leaning back against the leather.

"He's wily. He's a Russian fox. Always alert. Always thinking. This is why," he said, sitting down in the center of the couch, hands clasped between his opened legs, "that we must carefully cultivate our image and relationship. Plus, he has never fully trusted me. Why would he now? I'm nothing like them. I've never been," and his mouth turned into a slash, his brow drawing downward as he stared at the door in front of them.

Daria reached out, her hand smoothing down the dark hair sprinkling his forearm. "I'm so glad you're not."

He twisted a look in her direction. "Me too. I'd never have met you." And Nik stopped himself from saying any more. It would be inappropriate and it was a secret dream of his. That's all this was: a beautiful dream in the insane world he lived and survived within. Daria was like a bright, shining symbol of what he'd always wanted: a woman who was strong, intelligent, caring and loving. And he wouldn't take a prostitute when what he desired was a real, honest relationship with a woman. He craved Daria with his heart and soul. The look in her half-closed eyes, that gold and sienna gaze of hers filled with such care and concern for him. And understanding. She had the incredible capacity to realize the depth of the pressures upon him. It felt good to be cared for. To be understood and appreciated.

"You've been the nicest surprise of this whole op, Nik." Daria allowed her hand to fall away, tucking it back into her lap, studying him in the silence.

"I've done nothing out of the ordinary since coming here," Nik said darkly. He wasn't about to go where Daria had. She was more than a surprise to him. She was a dream come into reality, and that grabbed his heart, never letting go of it, feeding his yearning, aching dreams. How he wanted to pursue a relationship with her. A real one, where there was no life-and-death dance around them. But an honest, genuine partnership. The kind of exploration and deep, wonderful intimacy he intuitively knew could happen between the two of them. He ached for it. The depth of his losses, the stresses and yearning for something purely uplifting and beautiful, gnawed at Nik.

"Have you seen Korsak much since arriving?"

"A few times. I had *desayuno* with the team a few days ago to take their pulse."

She frowned. "Why would Korsak order a bug *NOW*, Nik?" She searched his pensive features as he thought through her question.

"Fedor said something at *desayuno*, in their abbreviated double speak to keep me out of their conversation," he muttered, rubbing his face. "He said something like that things were going to get interesting toward the end of our time here in Aguas Calientes."

"What do you think that meant?" Daria asked, worried.

Shrugging, he sat up, rolling his shoulders to get rid of the accumulated tension in them. "I have *NO* idea. Korsak doesn't trust me. He won't ever tell me his plans ahead of time. Obviously, something is up and they all know what it is, but as usual, I don't."

"Maybe we should rethink our pattern? Would it be helpful if you went back to the hotel instead? Maybe nose around? You said the walls were thin over there. Maybe you could pick up some intel?"

"No," and he cut her a glance. "It's better I stay here tonight." He rubbed his hands down his hard thighs. "Sometimes, we receive shipments of arms beneath crates of vegetables that are being sent to us by train. Fedor Goncharov and Brudin go to the train station and pick them up. They do the heavy lifting on things like this. We're always needing resupply. The Russian helicopter at the local airport is flown by undercover KGB and Spetsnaz trained pilots. They usually fly in what we need. But sometimes, the winds are bad and they can't take off and transport us or our supplies to and from Cusco. We're constantly in need of food resupply. And my medicines that I order in."

"So Rolan Pavlovich, the latest Russian mafia boss from New York, is working with active Russian Spetsnaz spies presently? And the Russian government knows this?" She saw the wry look he gave her.

"Of course. It's Russia wanting her piece of the pie in the world drug trade, too. He was in Spetsnaz at one time. He was the hero. He has close, high government ties."

"I didn't realize any of this," Daria whispered, sitting up, scowling. "This is so much more complicated and twisted than I first thought."

"That is why," Nik said wearily, rubbing his face, "that the CIA wants to capture Korsak and take him to the US. He had very strong ties with Alexandrov, Petrov and now, Pavlovich. The CIA knows he has a lot of information that can help them because they were all together as Spetsnaz soldiers or officers. That's why those three Army Special Forces three-man hunter-killer teams are hanging around this area. Pavlovich is a treasure chest just waiting to be opened."

She wiped her mouth and gave Nik a concerned look. "I wasn't briefed on the larger picture."

He snorted. "I'm sure you weren't. This is need-to-know basis only, Daria. But you need to know, and I don't give a damn what your CIA or Jack Driscoll at Shield Security thinks about it. I'm not leaving you in the lurch. You need to understand the commitment Russia has to South America. To them, it is a lush continent with third world countries that are hungry for money, power and opportunity. Russia is slowly infiltrating all of them. They have control of Venezuela. They are at war in Columbia through local militias who want a piece of the drug cartels, and the child sex trade, also."

"And now they have five ex-Spetsnaz teams operating here in Peru."

"Yes, all in this region." He gestured around with his hand. "This is the cradle of the cocaine-growing area. That, and the area the north of us. And that's why the new Russian Mafia leader, Rolan Pavolvich, is getting up to speed to learn everything he can about the operations down here. He was elevated to that position, I believe, by the Russian government, although I can't prove it, after Yerik Alexandrov was killed."

Daria gave him a dark look. "It was Sergeant Mace Kilmer who killed that sick bastard," she whispered harshly. "He kidnapped Cal's fiancée, Sky Lambert, and Shield Security created a mission and went and tracked him down in South America, to northern Costa Rica, to rescue her. She was pregnant with Cal's child at the time, Nik. He worked for Shield when it happened."

Drawing air between his teeth, Nik rasped, "That is tragic. Is she okay? Was the baby miscarried?"

"No, thank goodness. It had a happy ending. Someday I hope you can meet Cal and Sky. They live in a cabin just outside Alexandria, Virginia. Cal is home for good. He's a father and husband now. He is one of the mission planners at Shield."

"He's a brave man going into the lion's den of Alexandrov's drug world," Nik said.

"Cal didn't have a choice. I'd have gone on that op if my fiancée had been kidnapped, too."

Nik sat back on the couch, pinching the bridge of his nose. "I need to think this through. I can't make rash decisions based upon my emotions, Daria. I want to stay with you tonight, more than anything." He dropped his hand, reaching out, stroking her left thigh lightly. "You know that?"

"Yes, I know that." She swallowed hard. "But something is going to happen tonight, Nik, and we don't know what it is? Is that what you're sensing?"

"It could be ammo or weapons shipments coming in by train, is all."

"My gut says it's more than that. Doesn't yours?" and she dug into his hooded stare.

"Unfortunately, you are right, *moya kotya*."

"Could you be receiving a new member to your team?"

"Korsak likes what we have. The men are healthy. They do their job. I see no reason for a replacement or addition to the team right now."

"What if he's getting rid of you?" Daria saw the shock come to his eyes and his mouth tighten. "Wouldn't that explain the secretiveness of Fedor's comment? If they had a combat medic coming in to replace you—"

"Then," he said thickly, his voice lined with steel, "it would mean that Korsak is going to get rid of me in the jungle. He'll find a time and place to shoot me in the head, leave my body where it lays, and let the local jaguar find it and carry it off."

Daria shivered, wrapping her arms around herself, staring blankly at him. "Wouldn't he just say you're fired and let you walk away?"

Grimacing, Nik said, "I know too much. They'd never let me walk away, Daria." He saw something raw, something startling, come to her eyes. He felt her reaction and it rocked him. What was going on between them? There was a sense of shattering terror washing across him from Daria. And something else that he dared not ever hope for: a feeling of love. It was there in her eyes, in her facial expression, unspoken, but damn, it was *there*.

Nik sat very still, digesting what he felt and saw. Was it possible he was misreading Daria? Oh, yes, because he wanted her so very damn much? The glistening look in her eyes, the worry, terror and fear for him, were overriding. He watched her as she fought the tears that suddenly threatened to jam into her eyes and as she swallowed convulsively several times before winning the battle. His heart beat harder in his chest, and the love he felt for her tripled in those stolen, silent moments as they stared at one another.

Not only was he falling in love with Daria. Was *she* falling in love with him? Was that possible? It was the wrong time.

CHAPTER 12

A LOUD, HARSH banging at the door made Daria tense up. Instantly, Nik was on his feet, his gaze focused on the door.

"Stay where you are," he said to Daria under his breath. Moving over to the door quickly, he opened it.

"Korsak wants you now," Brudin snarled. He made a quick, cutting gesture with his hand.

Nik nodded. He turned and gave Daria a meaningful glance as he went for his medical ruck. "I'll see you later." Something was very wrong. The blackness in Brudin's eyes made him go on full internal guard. He saw the look of terror in Daria's eyes as he held out his spread hand, indicating for her to remain on the couch. Under no circumstance did he want to give Brudin any choice of action from her even starting to stand up or say something. The Russian would lose it. Nik saw her quickly nod, her eyes growing hard as she stared at the door. She couldn't see Brudin standing on the porch from her angle and he was glad. He didn't want the bastard anywhere near her.

Moving out the door, Nik shut it behind him. He heard the last train of the day pulling into the station beyond the town, its whistle blowing sharply, announcing its arrival. Brudin glared at him.

"Korsak wants us all at the train station," he growled, dashing down the stairs quickly. "Right now!"

"Okay, why?" Nik demanded, catching up with him. Brudin was trotting quickly down the hill, cutting across the crowded roadway, pushing tourists out of his way.

Once they were out of the main part of Aguas Calientes, Nik caught up with him on the red, muddy soil underfoot there. He looked up and saw that the train had already pulled into the station, its bright red and yellow length stark against the green tin roof high above it. "Why?" Nik demanded again, easily keeping up with Brudin, who reeked of alcohol.

"Korsak just got word that the New York Russian Mafia leader, Rolan Pavlovich, is making a surprise visit to our team."

So, that was what this was all about! Nik nodded, remaining grim, following Brudin down the hill to the small bridge that crossed the violent, rushing tributary that cut through between the town and the station, feeding downstream into the mighty Urubamba River. The bridge route took them out of their way but it was better than to try and cross the river via the other option. If anyone tried to get across those cold, icy glacier waters from the Andes and slipped off one of the wet rocks the local children often chain-hauled tourists' luggage across, they'd be hurled down over the cataracts below and fed into the mighty Urubamba River which was at least four times more violent. Most who fell into it, drowned. Pretty much no one had ever been saved, Nik had heard, except for an American woman a long time ago, who had been rescued and made it out alive. She had been damned lucky.

His mind spun with questions. His boots thunking hollowly across the wooden bridge. There was another steep hill after the bridge, leading up to the station. The evening light was upon the area of cleared jungle in which the town huddled. Nik saw the clouds begin to close in, blot out the pale blue sky, and begin to descend as they did every twilight in the wintertime. Brudin looked upset. Maybe Korsak had known Pavlovich was coming? But said nothing until he was sure he'd arrive? If that was the case, then Korsak trusted no one on his team. Not really. But then, Pavlovich was their new boss. Was he coming to meet them? Give them new rules and regulations? Demand more cocaine be made and transported? Test their loyalty to him, now that Alexandrov was out of the picture? Nik had never heard of this new Russian, so he knew as little about him as Brudin did.

They reached the station, and Nik wasn't at all surprised as the train cars began to disgorge around fifty people each, all of many, many nationalities. Korsak was waiting by the expensive parlor car in which the rich traveled. He saw the rest of Korsak's team, Kravec and Duboff, standing off to one side. They had dressed in their cleanest clothes, were shaven and clean-cut-looking. Hmmm… so only Brudin and he hadn't known? Brudin was in a sweaty green t-shirt, soiled cammies, was unshaven and bleary-eyed, half drunk. Nik was glad that he looked halfway decent in comparison. His hand tightened on the strap of his ruck as they slowed to a stop. Korsak turned and nodded to them, his face expressionless. He looked away again; his gaze focused on the opening train door in front of him.

Nik was breathing easily, but Brudin was huffing, leaning over, his hands on his knees, head down. He was probably going to vomit. Would serve the bastard right. Nik moved around to stand on the other side of Korsak, out of the way of any potential spraying.

There wasn't a long wait. Only four couples left that rich car. The last man that stepped off behind them was dressed in a cream-colored silk shirt and dark brown slacks with a matching corduroy blazer. He was at least six feet tall, well-built like a swimmer, with an oval face and high cheekbones. Nik saw the man had light-browneyes, with an amber cast in their depths and sported a fashionably-short cut for his black hair. He spotted a gold Rolex on the man's thick wrist and several gold rings on the fingers across both his hands. The collar of his silk shirt was open, revealing the top of a white t-shirt, also of silk, beneath it. His leather loafers looked expensive to Nik, probably from Italy. The aura of the man was all about power. Rolan Pavlovich traveled alone, but the energy around him hit Nik palpably. He was surprised at first that such a man had no bodyguards with him, until two emerged from another train car further down. Both were hard-looking men, most likely ex-Spetsnaz, or maybe even Russian GRU security itself. Who knew?

Korsak instantly moved forward, extending his hand, a jovial smile on his face. Nik watched the introductions carefully. Ustin did not know Rolan, and vice-versa. It felt as if they were two male jaguars circling, sizing one another up. For once, Nik was glad to be only a soldier in the team, not the leader. The two security guards kept sharp watch. Although Nik couldn't see any weapons on them, he would bet they both had Glocks slid into the back of their belts, hidden beneath the black nylon jackets they wore.

After introductions were over with, Korsak turned. He gave a snapping order to Kravec and Duboff to pick up Pavlovich's luggage from the baggage car halfway down the long train.

"I've got a splitting headache, Ustin," Pavlovich said. "Which man is your medic?"

"That would be him, Morozov," Korsak pointed toward Nik. "Get up here!"

Nik ignored the violent gesture by Korsak, stepping calmly forward at his own pace. He held out his hand toward Pavlovich.

"Nik Morozov, sir. How may I be of help?" he asked him in Russian.

Pavlovich gave him an amused look and shook his hand. "Maybe some Ibuprofen? My maid forgot to pack my medications."

Nik shrugged out of his pack and set it on the ground, opening it quickly. He pulled a small bottle of 800 mg. Ibuprofen from a pocket and stood, handing it to the man with the soft, manicured fingers. "I have some water, sir…"

Pavlovich halted and nodded, giving him a look of praise. "Yes."

As Nik found a small bottle of water, he heard Korsak say, "He's a good medic. Damned trouble, otherwise. Too righteous. I keep him around because he saves our lives."

Mouth thinning, Nik said nothing, opening the bottle of pills for Pavlovich and placing it into his outstretched hand. The Mafia leader nodded his thanks, a curious glint in his eyes as he met Nik's own, and studied him for a moment, sizing him up like he had Korsak.

The light was low, and Nik stood waiting, knowing if he didn't think on his feet and give Korsak what he wanted, that, like yesterday, the man would try to beat the shit out of him. He could try, but Nik knew without a doubt, he would best him. They'd never come to blows, but that didn't mean someday that they wouldn't. Korsak had already broken Kravec's large nose, busted up Brudin's left cheekbone and broken Duboff's hard jaw. So far, he'd avoided Korsak's fists. Squinting a little, Nik's heart suddenly stuttered. As Pavlovich tipped his head back, swallowing water to wash the Ibuprofen down, he saw a birthmark exactly like Daria's! Stunned, he gawked for a moment. Catching himself, he saw Pavlovich notice his reaction. *Damn.*

As he brought the bottle away from his mouth Pavlovich smiled a little and capped it. "You see my birthmark, Morozov? You're pretty alert." He tossed the bottle to one of his security men, who easily caught it.

"I thought," Nik stumbled, "it might be an old wound or something, sir. I was wondering if it was causing the headache." It was a complete lie, but he couldn't get caught like this.

Pavlovich grew thoughtful, rubbed the area where the quarter-moon crescent lay on the left side of his neck, behind his ear. "Very astute observation, Morozov." He smiled. "I like you. I'm going to need more medications once we get to the hotel. Follow me and my men up? If you have the meds I need, that will be good. If not, I can have Korsak call Cusco and they'll be on the next train tomorrow morning."

"Yes, sir," Nik said, relief washing through him. That had been so close. *Too close.* Korsak glared out at him from behind Pavlovich.

"But you said you wanted to talk to *me*," Korsak protested, stepping up to Pavlovich.

Waving his manicured hand at the team leader, he said, "I'm tired, Ustin. Get me to the hotel. I want my medications and I want to rest. I'll see you tomorrow morning. We'll have our meeting then. Morozov? Are you coming?" and he took off down the hill, leaving the team to scramble in his wake.

Nik saw Korsak grow livid, saying nothing, but his eyes flashed murderously with the rage he kept to himself. Brudin hung back. Korsak hadn't even bothered introducing the slovenly Russian who was drunk and smelled sour from not bathing for the last couple of days. Nik had no idea which hotel to head for, but there was a very nice one at the top of the town's hill. Knowing better than to ask Korsak anything for fear of making him embarrassed, Nik saw him walk quickly across the bridge to get abreast of Pavlovich.

"You'll be at the finest hotel, Don Pavlovich."

"Five star?"

"Er... I don't know... they say it's the best."

Pavlovich snapped him a disappointed look. "And where are you at?"

"Oh, at the other end of the town. Down at the bottom of the hill. On the plaza."

Nik was content to remain behind them, not wanting to get on anyone's radar. The look that Pavlovich shot Korsak interested him. Unlike Yerik Alexandrov, whom he had met, this man conducted himself as if he were in the military. What was Pavlovich's background? An ex-Spetsnaz officer? Someone who had been of high rank? Maybe he could get Daria to make contact later with Shield Security and get the goods on him. In the meantime, Nik felt as if he were stepping on fragile eggs with the unknown, new mafia leader from New York City. He was brisk, a man of few words, but Nik sensed he wasn't brutal like Korsak. Maybe he was, but showed it only when necessary? Nik was unsure. Korsak was floundering. He'd showed his lack of polish already, and that didn't seem to sit well with Pavlovich. He'd better be careful himself. With Korsak not trusting him, and already badmouthing him in front of Pavlovich, he desperately needed to make a good impression on the new don.

As they made it into town, Pavlovich halted abruptly. They stood on the busy square, the Catholic church at the other end of it.

"Korsak, meet me in the lobby of my hotel at 0900 tomorrow morning. Sharp."

"Of course, Don Pavlovich. Is there anything else—"

"No." Pavlovich turned to Nik. "Do you know where this hotel is?"

"Yes sir, I do."

Pavlovich looked relieved. "At least one of you knows something. Come with us."

Kravec and Duboff brought up the rear, suitcases in both hands, out of earshot, staying well out of the don's way.

"Yes, sir," Nik murmured, falling in behind them. He felt glee, but kept his face carefully arranged as Korsak's mouth fell open. So, it seemed that Pavlovich rewarded those who were intelligent. If that was the case, he was the smartest of the five of them. It could bode well in his favor. Korsak looked confused and angry, but said nothing.

As they moved up the street, Pavlovich snapped his fingers, ordering Nik to walk at his side. "Do YOU know what star rating this hotel is, Morozov?"

"Yes, sir. It's a four star."

Pavlovich gave him a long, appraising look. "I thought you might know. You have intelligence, Morozov. I like men who think and are educated."

"Yes, sir." He saw the man's expression beginning to ease. "Is the headache receding, Don Pavlovich?" It was a bold move on Nik's part, but he felt the Russian respected his medical expertise.

"You're astute, too." Smiling a little, Pavlovich murmured, "Yes, it's going away. Does anyone else on your team have your brains?"

"No, sir."

Pavlovich burst out laughing. His guards laughed along.

Nik didn't know what to think of their reaction.

"Well, at least I can rely on you for an honest answer, Morozov. That's *very* refreshing."

They entered the hotel and Nik guided Don Pavlovich to the registration desk where he was quickly taken care of. He had the penthouse suite. Pavlovich gestured for Nik to follow him into the same elevator, not the baggage elevator that Kravec and Duboff were ordered to take. One of the don's guards went with them and another guard remained with the baggage men.

"I'm in need of some Vicodin. Do you have any in your ruck, Morozov?"

"Yes, sir, I always carry it."

Pavlovich gave him an amused look as the elevator zoomed upward. "Not to sell as a drug, I hope?"

"No, sir. Never. It's for pain relief only."

"I have a touchy back. Just got out of an operation six months ago and my doctor is slowly weaning me off the damned stuff but, if I don't get it soon, I'm going to be screaming with pain."

"You won't," Nik assured him. "I have enough to tide you over."

Pavlovich looked him slowly up and down. "How long you been with Korsak?"

"Two years, sir. Before that, three years with Yerik Alexandrov's son, Vlad."

"You've been down here for a long time."

Nik nodded, saying nothing. He didn't know where Pavlovich was going with this conversation. The doors opened and they walked directly into the sumptuous suite. Nik didn't gawk, having been in rich places before, but this one was palatial and thoughtfully designed. Pavlovich looked around and pleasure came to his face.

"Very nice. Tell Korsak he did good, will you, Morozov?"

"Yes, sir, I will."

The guard gestured for Nik to move to the kitchen table and did so. Moments later, Kravec and Duboff arrived with the suitcases. They gave Nik an odd look, not knowing why he was being preferentially treated by the Don. He ignored them, and heard the guard snarl at them to leave immediately. The guard came over to the table where he opened his ruck. He pulled out a list and handed it to Nik.

"My name is Oleg Laskin. I'm the head of Don Pavlovich's security detail. This is a list of all the medications he needs. If you don't have them, don't cross them off the list. I'll make the call myself to the Cusco hospital if we need replacements."

"Of course," Nik said, taking the list. There was a hardness to Laskin. He had dark green eyes, a square face and short black hair. He was easily over two-hundred pounds, heavily muscled, with a face marred by scars. Nik knew he had to be ex-Spetsnaz. The guard left him alone to attend the Don who was taking off his blazer. In no time, Nik had set out the medications on the table. Laskin came back.

"Only two I don't have," Nik said, handing the list back to the guard.

Giving a brisk nod, Laskin said gruffly, "The Don wants to talk to you. Say nothing. Speak when spoken to. Don't ask questions unless he urges you to do so."

Nik nodded, closing up his medical pack and hefting it across his shoulder. The Don was standing by the huge window six stories above the hill that overlooked the small town. He had a finely-cut glass in hand and Nik thought that might be whiskey in it.

"Morozov reporting, sir," he said, coming to a halt, at attention, in front of Don Pavlovich.

"Relax," he murmured, taking a sip of his drink. He turned, looking Nik in the eye. "I want you to join me for dinner in two hours. Up here, in the penthouse."

Shock rooted him. Nik nodded. "Of course, sir."

"I'll see you then."

Nik nodded and turned on his heels, reeling and stunned. What was going on here? He was only a drug soldier, not the leader of this team. His mind churned as he left the penthouse. First, he'd best tell Korsak what was going on or the man would be furious with him, feeling left out of the process. And then, go see Daria. He wanted to do the reverse, but knew better under the circumstances. Don Pavlovich had invited him up for dinner, not Korsak. His stomach tightened. The last thing Nik needed right now was to be put in the spotlight. He wanted to stay a shadow like always, seen, but never heard from. Hurrying out of the hotel, he strode down the street, urgent to get to Daria who, he was sure, was worried. After dinner, he would drop by and see her.

DARIA WAITED, BUT not well. As a sniper, she was patient, but this was way different. Pacing, it was nearly 2300, eleven p.m., when there was a soft knock at her apartment door. She hurried over, opening it. Nik gave her a tired smile and stepped in. He took off his medical pack, setting it down by the door as she closed and locked it.

"What a night," Daria murmured, going over to him, her hand on his arm, worriedly assessing him. There were slight shadows beneath his eyes and he looked worn. "What can I do to help you, Nik?"

He turned, sliding his arm around her waist, drawing her to him, burying his face in her hair, their cheeks touching one another. "Nothing but this," he growled, inhaling the fragrance of her hair, the scent of her.

Daria relaxed in his arm, folding against him, overjoyed he was home once again. "I couldn't sit still all night. My mind was jumping around over one bad scenario to another."

"Did you contact Shield Security?" he asked, drawing away, sliding his fingers across her hair, smoothing it back into place.

Nodding, she eased out of his arms. "I got intel. Jack is going crazy up in Virginia. I used my sniper scope and got photos of the men coming off the train. Don Pavlovich showing up here unannounced has thrown a wrench into everyone's plans, the CIA's, ours, and the Army Special Forces A-teams'. Everyone is scrambling. I guess they knew nothing that he was going to come down here."

Reluctantly, he released Daria. "We didn't either. Good that you got photos and sent them. I need a lot of intel on him. I smell coffee. Is there some?" and he looked hopefully toward the kitchen.

"Sure, come on. I just made a new pot. I've been drinking and pacing."

A thin smile stretched his mouth. "And worrying. You are a worrywart, Daria, there's no question."

"Guilty as charged," she agreed, moving into the kitchen. "Did you eat?"

Nik took down the mugs and she poured the coffee. "Yes. I was invited to dinner with Rolan Pavlovich. It was a nice meal but my stomach was tied in knots and I didn't eat much," he admitted.

Daria gave him a worried look. "What did he want?"

"Information about the team, how much cocaine was being picked, processed, how many pounds were yielded, and anything doing with that stuff," he said, sitting down at the table.

Daria sat at his left elbow. She stirred cream and sugar into her mug. "Anything else?"

Rubbing his brow, he muttered, "No, but I felt him fishing. I think he's trying to get a fix on Korsak. I don't think Pavlovich is impressed with him."

"Did he ask you directly?"

"No. I was sweating that. Because, top on my list is that Korsak allows those other men to rape women and young girls. I know nothing of Pavlovich's sexual needs and, for all I know, he may do the same thing. I was praying he wouldn't ask because I didn't want to go there."

Daria drew in a deep breath. "That would have marked you with Korsak for sure."

"Yes." Grimly, Nik looked away and shook his head. "This is blowing our op away, Daria. We can't continue like we did before. I don't know how long Pavlovich will be down here. Or what he really wants."

"Don't you think he needs to touch base with Alexandrov's teams, get them to know he's the boss now, and to know his men leading these groups? Make peace with them of a sort? Make sure they will be loyal to him?"

"Sure, I thought so, too. I also thought that he's down here to evaluate each team and, if he doesn't like some or all of them, to dispatch them and bring in his own teams and leaders who will be completely loyal to him."

Daria grew quiet, eyes lowered.

Nik drank the coffee. He set the mug down and reached out, brushing her fingers. "How are you doing? I was worried for you."

"Oh, I'm fine. Right now, frankly, I'm no longer center stage. Pavlovich is, and that's good for us and our cover."

"I wonder how long he'll be around here?"

"Yes, that's what has me going. Can we capture Korsak under his nose or not? That's what Jack is talking to the CIA about tonight. He's put the mission on hold until we can clear channels up and down the line."

"Wise move," Nik muttered, sliding his fingers wearily through his hair.

"What about Korsak?"

"A loose cannon. He's pissed that Pavlovich asked me to dinner instead of him. Korsak peppered me with questions." Mouth turning to a slash, he added darkly, "I didn't have answers for most of them. There's no way I'm putting myself between him and Pavlovich. I just want to fade back into the shadows again. Right now, I'm a golden boy to Pavlovich. He respects intelligence. It's the last position I want to be in, Daria."

She reached out, tangling her fingers among his. "I understand. I'm sorry it went down like this."

Nik lifted his head. "I want to stay here tonight. With you. I can take the couch. I just don't want any more of the noise, the smells of that hotel. I'm maxed-out."

Daria studied him as the silence strung out between them. "Do you think that's a good move under the circumstances?"

"I don't know," Nik said irritably. Getting up, he walked slowly around the living room. "Our mission, as we knew it, is gone. Pavlovich is who we thank for that. Korsak's no longer focused on me and you. He's worried that the new Don is going to demote him."

"Closer to the truth," Daria said, watching him pace, "is he's probably worried about a bullet in the head."

"I'd volunteer to do it."

She tucked her lower lip between her teeth because there was nothing to say. "You're pushed to your limit, Nik."

Her quiet words were like a salve across his screaming nerves. "Yes, I guess I am. I feel stretched, as if I'm being skinned alive, Daria. I had a tightrope to walk before. Now, that rope has not only gotten thinner, it's more fragile. All I wanted, my only focus, was to give Korsak to the A-team, collect the promise from the CIA to provide Dan, both of us, political asylum in your country. Now," and he opened his hands, his voice flooded with exhaustion, "we have Pavlovich to contend with. Another chess game. Another big player who could change up everything. It's become three-dimensional chess…"

She stood and walked over to him. Sliding her arms around his waist, she brought her hips against his and stood quietly. "Look at me?"

Nik slid his arms around her shoulders. "Daria, I'm beyond sex tonight if that's what you want. I'm stressed out."

Giving him a soft look, she whispered, "So am I. But that doesn't mean we can't hold one another Nik. Give each other comfort. It will keep our cover solid, anyway." She saw the anguish in his eyes as he lifted his head.

"I have no condoms, Daria. I never thought… well, you know. I never thought we'd be really going to bed with one another." Nik gave her an apologetic look. "And all I've thought of since meeting you was to do just that: make love to you all night long." The corners of his mouth turned inward. He caressed her hair. "I can offer you so little, *moya kotya*."

"Well," she murmured, skimming his shoulder, "I'm old enough to be a big girl about this, Nik. I want you beside me. I want to hold you like you held me the other night when I fell apart. It's your turn now." Lifting her chin, Daria met and held his dark eyes. "Okay?"

"Yes," he rasped, cupping her cheek, "It's more than enough. More than I ever dreamed of having with you…"

CHAPTER 13

Daria waited patiently as Nik left the bathroom after his shower and padded barefoot down the hall to the bedroom where she sat. His eyes were nearly closed with exhaustion. She understood the toll the day had taken on him. Nik was driven like no one she'd ever met, even more so than herself. He was naked except for the white towel wrapped around his hips. His skin gleamed in the low light from the hall, his hair mussed and only partially dried. There was exhaustion in his soul tonight, she thought, as she moved around the bed, pulling back the sheet and light cover for him as she went.

Nik gave her a grateful look and lay on his stomach, stretching out his long, lean frame. He gripped the pillow with both hands, closing his eyes.

"I left you some hot water," he said.

She heard the slur in his voice as she drew the sheet up over his waist. It was impossible to ignore his utter maleness, the lean, ropy muscles taut and moving across his back. "Thanks. Are you okay?" and she leaned over, moving her hand lightly across his shoulder, still moist from his recent shower. She felt his muscles tense slightly beneath the tracing of her fingertips. Just getting to touch him like this, to see him without clothes, excited her. Daria felt a little guilty, the pleasure of seeing Nik like this was overwhelming to her feminine senses. Even in the low light, she saw so many small scars across his shoulders and scattered across his long, broad back.

"Fine," he mumbled.

"Go to sleep. I'll be back in a bit." She saw his short, spiky lashes close, his tightened mouth begin to relax. Nik was already asleep. Daria stood back, wanting to touch him, wanting to give him some care. The man was beautiful, his clothes had hid so much of him. Her heart twinged with worry because, even in sleep, she saw the tension around his eyes and the corners of his mouth. They were in a changing op and it could spell disaster… even death… for either or both of them. Wanting to placate his worry, she slid her palm across his shoulders, trying to sooth away some of that awful load he silently carried on them.

Then she went and showered. By the time she came back to the bedroom, it was midnight. The revelry and merry-makers down below had decreased greatly, but she could still hear the drums being banged further down the hill. It wouldn't stop until two or so in the morning and she was grateful that the sounds were mostly muted. Only a small nightlight in the bedroom shed some grayness into it. She had washed her hair, and it lay around her shoulders, still slightly damp. Wearing a flannel, knee-length nightgown, because there was no heat at night in the apartment and it got chilly, she padded quietly back into the bedroom.

Nik was still on his stomach, face partially buried in the pillow, snoring softly. He was sleeping deeply and Daria knew he needed it. Today must have been a special hell. Standing over him, she saw that he'd pushed the sheet and blanket off his body. Only the towel was still partly clinging to his waist. He had long legs with knotted calves, telling her how much he'd walked out in the jungle. Right now, the stubble of his beard darkened his rugged looks, calling to her, making her desire amp up. Nik looked like a young boy in his sleep, so much of the tension he carried dissolving and leaving him vulnerable.

The lotion he had massaged her with was still on the bedstand. Driven to do something to help him, she decided to massage his shoulders and back. She wasn't trained in massage, but Daria had been under the hands of so many over the years that she felt she could do a reasonable enough job on Nik's back. Knowing he was Spetsnaz trained, she knew of his muscle-memory reactions. To suddenly start to massage him could startle him out of sleep, and he'd react without thinking, possibly injuring her. This was something Daria took seriously.

Taking the bottle in her hand, she carefully sat down on the edge of the bed, placing her hand gently on his left shoulder. She leaned close to his ear.

"Nik? I want to massage your back. Are you all right with that?" His mouth moved and his brow wrinkled. "Nik? It's Daria. May I massage your back for you?" She watched him slowly come up from deep sleep beneath her husky voice. His fingers flexed on the pillow and he made a low noise in his throat.

Daria took that as a yes. Some part of his mind was aware of her presence now. Most importantly, his mind registered that she was not a threat. She stood, hiked her nightgown up, and straddled the backs of his thighs, taking care not to put weight on them. The folds of her nightgown settled around her knees as she put the lotion in her palms and then rubbed them together. This was something she was looking forward to: touching Nik. And right now, her heart beating a little in anticipation, Daria spread her hands wide across his shoulders, slathering the unscented oil across his magnificent body.

His back gleamed in the low light as she followed Nik's long, powerful spine. She heard him groan softly. His eyes remained shut and he was utterly relaxed. Her lower body flexed and heated up as she thought about making love to this man who provided care, with his life on the line, for so many others. Fingers digging in just enough to make those tight muscles begin to release along his vertebrae, she watched his sleeping features. A soft smile pulled at her lips as she continued her ministrations, following the lines and curves of the powerful muscles across his back. Her hands were not soft, rather calloused and strong. With each stroke of them, however, she felt and saw Nik's body begin to truly relax. The amount of stress he carried within him had not been obvious until just now. He was a man caught between two worlds, and one of them was deadly to him.

The moments melted away as Daria focused her sniper intensity upon her hands gliding across his back. Here and there, her fingers ran into ridges of flesh she knew were from old injuries. The oil gleamed and she saw the white scars in stark relief beneath it. His back told so many stories, and Daria wanted to hear every one of them. Nik intrigued her, and they hadn't had the time to plumb the depths of one another hardly at all.

But her body wanted him without reservation. She could feel the dampness between her thighs as she leaned her weight downward, guiding the heels of her hands across his muscles. This was like making love to him without the act itself, but he'd helped her in much the same way last night. Nik's compassion ran his heart, his life. Daria couldn't even conceive the thought of him not being in the medical world in some capacity. She ached to have some quality time with him, but knew it wouldn't happen anytime soon. Probably never, what with Pavlovich here. Their op was broken. They were on their own, scrambling, unsure what direction their lives were taking. Oddly, Daria didn't feel the danger. Maybe because Nik's fierce protectiveness was shielding her. She didn't know. There was a trust she'd given this man who smiled and played with babies. Who had so gently cared for her. Who had understood the impact of the knife wounds she'd garnered. Who had held her while the storm that had built inside her for the four months since that attack had raged on, and who had scoured her clean of its trauma. Nik was healing to anyone he touched, especially her. She saw the dried strands of his black hair across his brow, giving him a boyish look. The urge to sift her fingers through his hair, to ease it back into place, was real. Daria resisted, absorbing the warmth of his flesh, the relaxation of his muscles, as she coaxed the stress out of him.

She had lost track of time until she looked at the clock on the bedstand. It was one a.m. Leaning down, she placed a kiss against the nape of his exposed neck. Nik snored off and on, telling her he was deep in his sleep, telling her how badly he'd needed this healing downtime. His skin had a wonderful fragrance to it and, as her lips lifted away, she dragged his male scent deep into her body. Straightening, she lifted her gown and eased off him as quietly as she could, not wanting to disturb him.

Nik mumbled something she couldn't make out as she pulled the sheet and blanket across his body, tucking him in. The room was damp and chilly now. She went and washed her hands off in the bathroom, dried them, and came back to the bedroom. He had moved to his right side, face still buried in the pillow.

She climbed in her side of the bed. Her body was throbbing. It couldn't happen. He had no condoms and she didn't want to accidentally get pregnant. Being a mother wasn't part of her world-view right now. As Daria slid beneath the covers, bringing them up, she couldn't stop herself. She curved the front of her body against his back, settling into it like well-matched parts that had long missed one another. She was almost as tall as he was and that helped Daria curl herself against Nik. He didn't even move, his exhaustion clearly making him unaware of her nearness. It didn't matter. She felt his warmth, his quiet strength, the slow, shallow in-and-out of his breath. Her breasts rested lightly against his back, her hips nestled against his buttocks, her legs lay parallel to his.

Closing her eyes, contentment Daria had never known before washed through her like a new, pink dawn appearing on the darkened horizon of herself. The scent of Nik made her relax, his bulk and size made her feel safe while their situation was anything but. She eased her hand up along his ribcage, her fingers flowing across it, coming to rest above his slowly-beating heart. The sprinkling of dark hair across his massive chest tickled her slightly-curved fingers as she utterly surrendered herself over to Nik.

The last thought Daria had was that she wished she could wake up in the morning with him, make slow, exploratory love with this man, and give him the pleasure he so richly deserved for all the sacrifices he'd made for so many. He was the most selfless man Daria had ever met. The desire to give back to him was fierce within her. She ordered herself to sleep. Tomorrow would come all too quickly, and it was going to be an explosive day. Daria didn't know how she knew that. She just did.

NIK SLOWLY AWOKE, the drowsiness bone-deep within him. He felt like a swimmer who was far below the surface, struggling to rise upward, but finding each effort almost impossible to make. His mind was offline, but his senses were fully open and he inhaled the subtle scent of woman, of a spicy fragrance, and she was in his arms, her body curved against his own. It had to be a dream, a torrid one. He'd had so many over the years just like this. And this time, it seemed so damned real that, as he slowly moved his head, he felt the silken strands of her hair against his cheek and nose. What was real? What was not? There was a languidness that invaded his slowly-awakening body, a sense of calm as he savored her warm curves resting against him. Where they met, his lower body eagerly consumed her contact. She was soft, rounded and, as he moved his hand down her long back, feeling fleecy softness of the flannel material beneath his calloused fingertips, his mind sluggishly came back online.

Nik barely opened his eyes. Gray light was invading the room from around the closed blinds. It was quiet on the street. No sounds. *Thank God.* His vision was blurred and he fought waking up because this dream would dissolve like the others always did. Only… she sighed and he felt her moist breath against his bare chest, her head tucked beneath his jaw. And then his senses enlarged and he felt sleep being torn from him fully as he realized this was real. It wasn't a dream.

For a moment, Nik was groggy with confusion. Daria's hair was soft against his jaw and chin. She was trustingly curled against him, her arm around his waist, holding him even in sleep. He knew now that the fleece-like softness he'd felt in his half-dream had been the material of her nightgown as he lightly moved his fingers down her spine. She stirred. He stopped moving his hand. Realizing he'd awaken Daria if he moved too much, Nik groaned softly and closed his eyes, saturated with her fragrance, her slender, firm form against his, her breath moist and slow against his chest. Slowly, he remembered yesterday, the pressures and stress, and then, coming home to Daria. He'd gotten a shower and stumbled into bed. She had covered him, and that was the last he remembered.

Or was it? His brow furrowed as he lay there absorbing her against him. One of Daria's legs was laying across his, almost in a possessive way, and he liked that about her. She was, after all, military. She had courage and confidence and he liked that she boldly asked from him what she needed. He was more than willing to give her everything. His mind gyrated as he lay there with her sleeping innocently in his arms. Never mind that his erection was far more awake than he was presently. He'd awakened with it, the throbbing becoming insistent, sending fire up through him, fueling his hunger for her, wanting her body and soul.

Was it his imagination? Had Daria massaged his back last night? Nik couldn't remember exactly, only as fragments that had drifted down into his drowsy senses. He vaguely recalled she had said something close to his ear. He acutely recalled her breath flowing across his ear, the moisture, and how sparks of heat radiated powerfully from his ear straight down to his lower body. What had she said? With no clear memory of it, Nik still recalled that he'd been so damned relaxed, that he'd groaned. Or had he? He squinted open his eyes, the grayness of the ceiling staring back at him. He ached for Daria. He had no condoms. He wouldn't put her at risk. Not in this kind of fluid, changing situation. Above where her hips met his, his erection was nestled sweetly against her rounded belly. It made him feel potent. Strong. Hungry.

A pounding knock rattled through the apartment.

Instantly, Nik jerked up, releasing Daria. He threw off the covers, grabbing the towel that had come undone, wrapping it around his waist. The pounding at the door didn't stop. He heard Daria moan and move.

"Stay here," he told her thickly, jerking open the bedroom door and just as quickly closing it behind him.

Nik answered the front door. Brudin was standing there, glaring at him.

"Korsak wants us to meet in fifteen minutes. Get your ass down to the hotel."

"All right." Nik slammed the door in his face and locked it. Anger warred with terror. He turned and saw Daria coming down the hallway, her face drowsy, her hair mussed, making her look incredibly fetching. She looked like a young, innocent college-aged woman and his erection twitched beneath the towel he held together with his hand.

"It was Brudin," he told her roughly, meeting her halfway across the living room. He grazed her cheek. "I have to be down at the hotel in fifteen minutes. Korsak's calling a meeting."

Daria groaned, wiping the sleep from her eyes. "What does it mean, Nik?"

Grimly, he answered, "I have no idea. I have to go, and I don't want to." He kissed her brow and released her, heading to the bedroom to quickly dress.

Daria made an unhappy noise, wrinkled her nose, and followed him down the hall. She stood in the bedroom doorway, hand against the jamb, watching him swiftly dress. "What can I do to help, Nik?"

"Nothing," he told her tightly, pulling a black t-shirt over his head. "Just stay here. The meeting can't last too long. Pavlovich wants all of us to meet him at the penthouse at 0900." He sat on the bed, hauling on his socks and then his combat boots. "Stay out of sight, Daria. Stay here until I can put this all together? I'll come back and see you as soon as I can." He rose, running his fingers through his dark hair, trying to tame the strands into some semblance of order.

"Okay," she said, moving aside as he stood. "I need groceries today, but I'll wait until I see you, first. I'll stay out of sight."

Nik halted at the door, sliding his hands around her face, looking deep into her eyes. "I want you safe, Kitten. Korsak's going crazy thinking he's being demoted by Pavlovich. He sees me as a direct threat to his leadership. It's a tense situation."

She reached up, sliding her palm along his stubbled jaw. "Just go. Stay safe. I'll wait here for you," she promised gravely, holding his worried gaze.

Nik leaned down, taking her mouth, taking her hotly and without preamble. He slid his mouth against her lips, feeling her open to him, feeling her body move sensually against his, her arms going around his shoulders, drawing him tightly against her. There was no time. He had to get to the hotel. Tearing his mouth from her wet, lush lips filled with such promise, he caressed her hair. "There's so much I need to say to you, Kitten. And I can't. Not yet…"

Daria gave him a sad look of understanding. "It will wait. Get going…"

IT WAS 0830 when Nik entered the apartment once more. Daria had showered, climbed into twill hiking pants and boots, and a warm alpaca sweater of many colors that complemented the rest of her outfit. She was sitting at the table eating breakfast when he entered.

Daria saw the tension in his face as he shut and locked the door behind him. "There's coffee in the kitchen," she said.

"Good, I need a cup."

She watched him stride across the living room. "What happened, Nik?"

He poured the coffee, sitting with her. "Korsak is ordering us to get ready to leave. He's rabid and angry. He doesn't know what to think of the new Don." Nik gratefully sipped the coffee.

"Did he take it out on you?"

"No. But now, the team is wary of me. I was worried that would happen. They call me the 'Golden Boy', now. They know Pavlovich favors me." His mouth quirked. "Hell of a position to be put in. I've lost my shadow position in the team."

Daria reached out and took his hand, her fingers enclosing his. "They didn't beat you up."

"They don't dare. Korsak knows Pavlovich favors what I say, now. He asked me what the Don wanted at dinner last night and I told him. Now, Korsak is ranting that the Don is trying to see if he's skimming money off the top of this operation."

"Is he?"

"I don't know for sure. It wouldn't surprise me if he was, but he'll never admit it to the rest of the team," Nik growled. He picked up a piece of bacon from her plate. "May I?"

"Sure. You haven't eaten?"

He shook his head. "No. It was like stepping into a room of angry hornets. No coffee. No food. Just a lot of confusion, anger and distrust."

"Damn," she muttered, pushing her plate toward him. "Eat this, Nik. I can make myself more after you leave for that other meeting."

He glanced at his watch and then gave her a grateful look. "Thank you," and he sat down and hungrily dug into her fluffy scrambled eggs, ate the six pieces of bacon and two pieces of nearby toast slathered with strawberry jam.

Daria stood and walked away, into the kitchen. She saw Nik was starved. Stress made a person extra hungry, and she quickly whipped up four more eggs in a bowl and put them into the skillet for him. Dropping two more pieces of bread into the toaster, she felt his worry in the very air around him. "What else can I do?"

"Report this to Jack and the CIA. Keep them in the loop. It's not much, but this is an ongoing train wreck as far as I'm concerned. I don't know what the Don has up his sleeve, or what his real objectives are. Those two security guards with him are a lot more than just security. They run different branches of the Don's operations from what I understand. And they both worked for Yerik Alexandrov before that. They are high-up in the chain-of-command."

Daria stirred the cooking eggs in the skillet. "I need to go out for food, Nik. What's a good time?"

"After the meeting gets started. I don't want you seen by any of them. I want to keep you out of sight as much as possible."

"A little late for that," Daria teased, one corner of her mouth moving upward. She brought the skillet over, ladling out the steaming eggs on his cleaned plate. Nik was starved, and her heart went out to him. She heard the toast pop up on the counter. Turning, she went to butter the browned slices.

"Probably, but I don't want the Don to see you, either." Because Daria bore the same birth mark Pavlovich did. Nik had tried to find a space to tell her what he'd see on the man's neck but things were moving so fast that he couldn't. And Nik didn't want to just blurt it out. He wanted quality time with Daria, to prepare her emotionally for it. He knew it would come as a jarring, life-changing shock. She had been a Russian orphan, later adopted by a loving Ukrainian couple. Two people would never have the exact same birthmark, but in a family, as he knew from his extensive training in genetics, a birthmark could go from one generation to another. Sometimes in the same shape, and same area of the body. But he'd never seen one like this. It was damn near identical to the one Daria bore on her neck. Nik grimly promised her silently that he would pick the time, have the time, to tell her the upsetting news. And then, Nik would hold her afterward because he knew it was a twisted conundrum.

That information was going to shake Daria's world apart.

And his, too. *What a mess.* He quickly ate the eggs and the extra toast she put on his plate. Thanking her between bites, he glanced at his watch. It was

0845. He had fifteen minutes. Jamming the food down, he gave her a look of regret.

"I'm sorry I have to leave you." Because he didn't want to.

"Don't worry about it. I'll take care of things around here while you're at the meeting. *YOU* just be safe, all right?" and she reached out, touching his hand curled around the mug of coffee.

"I'll be fine."

"What does it mean when Korsak calls you 'Golden Boy'?"

"It means I'm favored. It's status. Power."

"Then he's afraid you'll usurp him and his position as leader of the team?"

"That's what he thinks, but I don't have a clue as to what the Don thinks."

Shaking her head, she gave him a longing look. "Last night... it was wonderful sleeping beside you, Nik."

"Yes," he rasped gruffly, pushing the emptied plate aside. "I woke up with you in my arms." He traded an intent look with her. "You are my heaven. This," and he gestured all around himself, "is my hell."

"I know," Daria said gently, seeing the stress and regret in his eyes. "I have your back. You know that."

"I do." He stood, leaned over and kissed the top of her head. "I will be back here as soon as I can."

The apartment became silent and empty after Nik hurriedly left. Daria sat there sipping her cold coffee, frowning. Hell, she'd rather have a sniper rifle in her hand than do this damned undercover work. She wasn't good at it, didn't know the rules and conventions of it. That left Nik carrying her as a responsibility, too. The man's shoulders were going to break. She saw so much in his turbulent blue eyes as he left. He desired her. Wanted her. Yet, the activity level around them had shot through the roof, and there was no time for anything else right now.

Getting up, Daria went to the kitchen and cleaned up. She would retrieve her sat phone in a few minutes and check in with Jack Driscoll at Shield Security. There was no use bitching about being undercover. It was a done deal. Maybe he had some information for her. She had the sat phone number of Sergeant Mace Kilmer, but wouldn't contact him unless ordered by Jack. Everything ran through her boss to her.

Chewing on her lower lip, Daria washed the dishes and put them in the drainer in the other sink to air dry after rinsing them off. What was Don Pavlovich going to tell Korsak's team? How brutal a murderer was he? Pavlovich hadn't risen to the top of the Mafia to become boss unless he was just as ruthless as Korsak. He might be more polished, smoother, but a monster lurked beneath his skin, too.

CHAPTER 14

DARIA'S BREATH CAUGHT as Nik opened the apartment door mid-afternoon without knocking first. She met his dark, hard gaze as he nodded hello in her direction, shutting and locking the door behind him. Standing in the kitchen, she said, "What's going on?"

Nik laid his medical ruck on the floor near the door and came into the kitchen, rolling his shoulders. Leaning his hips against the counter, he watched her peel purple-skinned potatoes over the sink. "Bottom line? Pavlovich and his two security guards who are actually much more than that, grilled the hell out of Korsak on the drug numbers. He was sweating. I've never seen him so subservient before." Pushing strands of hair off his brow, Nik lowered his voice. "I don't think Pavlovich likes him personally very much, but as long as Korsak gets the numbers he's wanting, he'll let him continue to run the team." He gave her an apologetic look. "And tomorrow morning, we're taking off for the jungle. Korsak didn't mention which village we're going to, dammit."

She put the potatoes aside, rinsed her hands and dried them on a nearby towel. Turning, Daria crossed her arms. "You're still trying to get Korsak kidnapped?"

Grimly, he nodded. "Unless the CIA or Sergeant Kilmer tell me to back off, yes. Pavlovich changes nothing as far as I'm concerned. Kilmer and his marauders, as they call themselves, are ghosts. They're good at snatching people."

"But under Pavlovich's nose?"

He heard the rising concern in her husky voice. "Yes."

Rubbing her brow, she said, "We need to sit down, Nik. Tell me everything? I had a sat phone call with Jack earlier today and I need to share that Intel."

They moved to the couch, sitting down close to one another. Daria curled up in one corner, a leg beneath her. "Langley thinks Pavlovich is asserting his rights to the territory, making sure the five teams in this area remain loyal to him. They still want Korsak to be taken. They don't want Pavlovich because he's too high on the food chain and it would alert those above him, which they don't want to happen."

"Makes sense," Nik muttered, leaning his elbows on his thighs, frowning. "These two guards, Oleg Laskin and Pyotr Lukin, are Pavlovich's right and left hands. They hide their power, what they do, and how much they know. But it became very clear to me, during the interrogation of Korsak, that they knew everything about the operation down here."

"What does Pavlovich want?"

He snorted. "More production of coke, of course."

"Can Korsak pull it off?"

Shrugging, he muttered, "It's complicated, Daria. Korsak was sweating bullets, telling them that, to raise the production to that new level, more coca plants had to be planted by local farmers. It would take at least five years for those bushes to get big enough to start picking enough leaves off them to fulfill the kind of quota Pavlovich wants to achieve."

"What did Pavlovich say to that?"

"He said 'fine'... that Rome wasn't built in a day." Rubbing his jaw, Nik said, "But I think Pavlovich is testing him. I'll give him this: he asked about how the Quechua Indians who are doing the work raising the coca plants are being treated."

"That must have gone well," Daria said drily.

"Korsak lied," he snarled under his breath, his fists curling for a moment. "I kept quiet. There's no sense in bringing up any of this in that meeting. I wanted to be a fly on the wall, not the center of attention."

"Still, he's inquiring about the Indians? Does that mean he cares how they're treated?"

"I don't know, Daria. In my heart, I pray it's so. Pavlovich seems to be more a manager of people than a brutal despot like Yerik Alexandrov and his son were with the team's operating procedures down here. I don't know if that went over Korsak's head or not."

"And what about you? Are you still Pavlovich's Golden Boy?" and she smiled a little, holding his worried gaze.

Nik groaned. "I have no idea. He said nothing to me. His whole focus was on Korsak, the logistics issues with the team, getting supplies in, things we need in the field, equipment, and armory issues. We are continuing to also fight the two other Latino drug lords for the same territory. Korsak knew his stuff, and I think Pavlovich was impressed with that part of him."

"Pavlovich isn't a brute, then?"

He straightened. "That remains to be seen." He gave her a sad look. "I need to talk to Jack Driscoll, and fill him in on all the details."

Daria rose. "Yes, I think they're all a little uptight over this new development. Hold on, my sat phone's in the bedroom. I'll go get it."

And she went and did so, and then came back.

Daria puttered around the kitchen, putting a roast chicken together with the potatoes while she kept one ear on Nik's end of the long, detailed conversation with her boss, Jack. She felt unsettled, but didn't know why. Nik seemed consumed with some other issue that he wasn't talking about. Every once in a while, she'd see him lift his head and look over at her, deep concern in his gaze. She felt as if a scimitar were hanging over her head, invisible, but dangling by a thread just the same. She turned on the oven, placing the meat and vegetables into the roaster. They would eat at five p.m. At least they had tonight together and she wasn't sure what would happen between them, if anything.

It was nearly an hour before Nik ended the sat phone call. He set it down between them on the couch. "You heard everything?" she asked.

"Yes." He looked distracted. She'd known him for only a short time, but there was clearly an invisible line strung between them. Daria reached out, allowing her fingers to trail down his arm. "What else, Nik? You look, well... harried? Distracted? Something's bothering you. What is it?" He didn't need to be lambasted with more issues right now. She saw him give her a stressed look, his mouth tucked in at the corners.

He moved the sat phone over onto the coffee table. "Come over here," he urged, moving to the opposite corner of the couch from her and opening his arms. "Come sit with me?"

Perplexed, hearing veiled torment in his low tone, she unwound and scooted over to him. It was so easy to fold herself up against Nik, just like she had last night. His arm came around her and she rested her head on his shoulder, studying him, seeing the play of emotions alive and turbulent in his blue eyes. "Tell me?" she urged huskily, resting her hand over his heart. It was pounding harder than usual. "What can I do to help you, Nik?"

He brushed his hand across her jaw, looking deeply into her eyes. "You are the most unselfish woman I've ever known." He slid his other hand across hers that rested over his heart, the living connection between them. "I'm about to cause you great pain, Daria," he warned her, his voice taut, filled with regret.

"What do you mean?"

Nik took a deep, roughened breath. "When I saw Rolan Pavlovich come off the train, the light wasn't very good. But I noticed something dark on the left side of his neck. When we got to the hotel... Under better light... I couldn't believe what I saw." Tensing, he held her uplifted gaze. Daria looked so damned innocent. So undeserving of what he was about to tell her. Nik knew it would shake her world and everything would change forever as a result. He rasped, "It was a birthmark, Daria. Exactly like yours, but with just a slight change." He saw her eyes widen as the information sunk in.

"You're kidding!" she said, suddenly sitting up, staring at him in disbelief. "No way, Nik. Are you *SURE?*"

Miserably, he lowered his head and nodded. "I'm *VERY* sure, Kitten. I looked at it all morning and into the early afternoon today." He saw confusion in her face. Shock. As if a bombshell had just gone off. He saw her mind moving at the speed of light. "I'm a combat corpsman. I took courses in genomics, as well," he began heavily. "Birthmarks are a genetic marker in some families," and his hand tightened around hers, not allowing her to pull it away from him. He saw the denial come to her expression. "Birthmarks usually occur from one generation to another in a family. And usually, they aren't exactly alike, but often, they appear on the same side of the body, sometimes on the same part of the anatomy. I've seen many birthmarks over my career as a corpsman."

His heart ached for Daria as he saw the denial fade and a lost look of horror replace it. "Pavlovich has black hair, the same shade as yours. His eyes are gold and brown, too, but yours are more gold than his. He has an oval face and, honestly, Daria? I could see the stamp of him in you. It was very apparent." Wincing internally, Nik saw her lips part, her eyes widen enormously. Releasing his hand, she slipped off the couch, her arms wrapped around herself, staring down at him.

Hollowly, he said, "I'm sorry, Daria. I didn't want to tell you this, but I knew I must. If Pavlovich ever sees you in town while you're here, he'd know without a doubt that you're somehow related to him. His birthmark is nearly exactly like yours. And what then?"

"No...," Daria whispered unsteadily, "I don't want to believe this, Nik! Are you *SURE?*"

A wall of pain hit him. Daria's pain. "Yes. There is no doubt in my mind. I know what I see. If I could have taken a photo of him, I would have. But he allows no pictures of himself."

Daria shook her head, desperate, looking around the room, as if to run away from the conversation. "This is crazy! *Crazy*, Nik! What the hell are the odds I'd meet an unknown relative out here in this green hell?" and she glared at him. Spinning around, she paced the room, head down, one hand against her mouth, the ramifications closing in on her.

Nik allowed her the time to adjust. "I worry, Daria. If he sees you, sees that birthmark, I wonder what he'll do? Does he even know you exist?" He stood and stopped her from pacing, enfolding her into his arms to give her some kind of comfort. Nik knew it was too little, but he couldn't stand the anguish in her eyes. Holding Daria gently against him, his arms around her waist, he said, "You heard me on the sat phone ask Driscoll for photos of Pavlovich's two sons?"

"Well," she stumbled, "yes, but I didn't know why."

"Because Jack was able to get into the computer system at Langley and access them. I asked him if there was any identifying marks on either of them." His voice grew weary. "Both sons, now dead, had that identical birthmark on the left side of their necks. I asked Driscoll to describe it and he said it looked like a quarter moon."

"No," Daria whispered, choking, wanting to deny all of it. "What else?"

"Jack will get permission from Langley to send those photos to your computer, which is encrypted. You need to see them for yourself. I want to look at them, too."

"And if the two sons had this birthmark?"

"Then it tells me it's a predominant genetic marker of the Pavlovich family."

"But... what happens, then?" she asked in a strained tone.

"Driscoll said Pavlovich has only two children on record being born in Moscow by his wife. His two sons. No daughters."

Daria sank against Nik, pressing her face against his chest, holding him tightly. "Then, how are we possibly related?"

"I have no idea, Kitten, I'm not into genetics to that degree," and he kissed her hair, massaging her tight shoulders, feeling a subtle tremor run through her. She was shaking. He would be too, given such devastating news. He continued to stroke her shoulders and back. "My gut? I remember my genomics professor telling the class that birthmarks could skip generations for whatever reason, and then return. Not everyone gets them, and it could be that some far-off cousin in your family is related to a far-off cousin in his family." He sighed heavily, sliding his arms tightly around her. "None of this is your fault, *moya kotya*. You are the innocent in this sordid dance that's hard to keep up with."

Tears squeezed out of her tightly-shut eyes, a shudder working through her. Nik's arms felt incredibly comforting and Daria desperately needed all the kindness and love he was feeding her right now. "This is awful, Nik. If he really *is* my relative, he's a global drug lord." She buried her face against him, struggling to grasp it all.

"You're the light to his dark," Nik said unsteadily, battling to hold his emotions in check. His natural protectiveness rose up in him. He wanted desperately to shield Daria from the Don. He could feel Daria fighting not to cry, and he wished she'd just let it go, but she was strong. And there was so much for her to think through. Her arms were tight around him, as if she were clinging to him during a wild storm that might yank her away from him and she would drown.

"Come? I want to go to the bedroom and lay down with you. Hold you for a little while? It might help?" Because it was all he knew to do at the moment. There was no intent of sex. She was hurting deeply. This information was going to change her life forever. Daria had discovered, possibly, a long-lost relative who was also a drug lord. And not just any drug lord. Pavlovich was high up on the global ladder of the Russian trafficking world. He was a king in his own right, power-wise. Nik shook his head, wondering why some people like he and Daria were given so much to bear. Others bore so very few loads in life. Life itself wasn't fair, and he knew that firsthand.

"Yes, I'd like that," Daria choked out in a small voice. She sniffed and pulled out of his arms, quickly wiping her eyes.

She wasn't going to cry. Nik could see that resolve in the way she held her chin. But he could feel her mind racing, feel the agony radiating from her heart, could feel her wanting to deny all of it. Who wouldn't? He wanted so badly to insulate her, but there was no way he could. Pavlovich hadn't said how long he'd be in Aguas Calientes. Daria was here for the duration until they could capture Korsak. He caught her hand, giving it a gentle tug, and walked her down the hall to the bedroom.

Nik laid down in the middle of the bed and gestured for her to come to him. Daria sat down on its edge, nudged off her sandals, and slid over. Groaning as she fit so well against him, Nik slid his arm beneath her neck, curling it around her shoulders, holding her close, but not too tight. When her head came to rest in the crook of his shoulder, Nik sighed and closed his eyes. "Last night, I dreamed I was holding you. And then, when I awoke early this morning in the grayness of dawn, you really were in my arms." His mouth drew into a faint smile. "You have no idea how good it felt to hold you, Daria." Perhaps distracting her was the better choice? She needed time to absorb the deep shock from the revelations of their talk. Besides, this way, he could protect her, give her a sense of safety, and care for her while she dealt with the deep shock of this unwanted discovery.

She slid her arm across his belly, absorbing his strength and calm. "I massaged your back last night. Do you remember that?"

"No... I fell off a cliff. I was gone." Nik raised his head, meeting her gaze. "I'm sorry I missed that."

"You were exhausted from yesterday, Nik."

"So were you, Kitten." He threaded his fingers through her loose hair, feeling the beat of her heart against his chest. The rounded firmness of her breasts teased his senses and he stopped his mind from going there. His plan was to get her to talk, maybe cry. Nik wanted to do so much more for her.

"I wish there was a way to get a DNA test down here," she muttered against his chest.

"There is," he said. "Pavlovich sneezed and threw the tissues into a waste basket. One time, when we took a break from the meeting for bathroom breaks and such, I was able to rescue the soiled tissues and hid them in my pocket."

Daria lifted away, surprise in her expression. "Seriously? You did?"

"Yes, I put them in a small plastic baggie in my pocket. Then I transferred them to a sterile bottle when I left the hotel, and it's now in my medical ruck. I'm going to need you to take the train into Cusco tomorrow and get the sample analyzed by the hospital. I'm sure they at least have a gene services unit down in Lima. It could be overnighted by courier from Cusco to Lima, if needed. It's not the best quality specimen, but I believe there's enough of his DNA on those tissues to find out what we need to know."

"Oh, Nik!" Daria cried, throwing herself into his arms, hugging him with her woman's strength.

He smiled brokenly. "It was the least I could do, Kitten."

"Don't let there be a match…"

"We must get that evidence from either the Cusco or Lima hospital. We need to buy you a roundtrip ticket by tonight. There is an agricultural train coming into the station at 0800 and you'll be on it."

Nodding, Daria gave him a grateful look. "You are incredible, Nik. Thank you for doing this for me. I'll be on that train."

He frowned, brushing strands of hair away from her cheek. "I don't like leaving you alone in Cusco, Daria. A lone woman, especially an American one, is vulnerable. There are gangs who kidnap and ransom Americans for money."

"I can take care of myself," she said firmly, sliding her fingers across his jaw. "You just focus on what's going on with your team, okay? I'll worry a lot more about *you*. I won't have contact…"

"You'll have the paper notes I pass to my Indian women friends as we move through that particular village, though."

Shaking her head, she closed her eyes, absorbing Nik's strength and calm. "So much is going on for both of us in different ways. It's upsetting."

"I know," he soothed. Nik looked at his watch. "How long before we eat dinner?"

"Around 5:00 p.m. tonight," Daria said against his black t-shirt, smoothing some of the wrinkles away across it. "Why?"

Nik eased Daria onto her back. He lay above her, stroking her cheek with his thumb, looking deep into her eyes. "I don't want to leave here without making love to you, Daria. But it has to be mutual. And if you say no, I'll understand and respect your wishes. You touched my heart, *moya kotya*, from the moment I met you. I can't explain what happened at Mass between us, but something good and wonderful did." His voice grew low with emotion as he searched her widening gaze. "I've only known you less than a week, but I've been looking for you all my life. And I know you're upset over what I just told you right now. And loving me is probably the last thing you want..." He saw her eyes grow soft, saw yearning in them and he knew... he knew without her saying a word.

Daria felt heat flow through her, dissolving her shock. She felt it engulf her from her opening heart and pool languidly with promise into her lower body. He was offering her a distraction, but it was just the one she'd been wanting from him. She absorbed his tender look, saw his arousal, saw his need. But her need matched his own. "I have a confession to make," she said, amusement in her tone. Daria had the ability to suppress anything. As a sniper, she did it all the time. Until that DNA sample came back to prove she was Pavlovich's relative, she wasn't going to allow it to color her life. She had wanted to love Nik for so long that it was easy to put this other issue aside. At least, for the time being.

"What?"

"After I bought my vegetables and fruit from Juanita, I went next door to the Pharmacia and picked up some condoms." She didn't know how Nik was going to react to her boldness. She felt her face flush. This wasn't something she'd ever done before in her life. There was nothing straightforward or common about her relationship with Nik. It was a whole new playing field. So, she took the risk because she felt he was worth it, felt he wanted to love her as much as she needed to love him. Daria saw sudden amusement dance in his eyes, a half-grin tugging at his mouth as he considered her confession.

"You're not a kitten. You're a sleek, assertive female jaguar," he rasped.

Daria matched his grin, losing herself in the powerful look of his that warmed her heart. "I've never done something like this before, Nik."

"I'm glad you did." He lifted his chin and looked over at the bed stand. "In the drawer over there?"

"Yes. There's quite a few of them. Ready to use, if you want?" she said, and heard a chuckle rise in his throat.

"I like a woman with expectations." Nik leaned over, trailing small kisses along her hairline, feeling her relax and enjoy his ministrations. "You are a very brave and resourceful." He studied her in the lulling silence. "I haven't had sex in five years. You need to know that."

"Because of your commitment here, to help your brother?"

"Yes." Nik looked past her for a moment, brows dipping. He caressed her cheek. "I'm not the kind of man who lays with prostitutes like the rest of my team, Daria. I couldn't develop a decent, ongoing relationship with any woman here in Peru under the circumstances. Sometimes, sacrifices are made for the greater good." His mouth curved a little. "There's nothing more in this world that I want, Daria, than to make love with you. I'll try to control myself with you, but…"

"I understand," she whispered, leaning up, taking his mouth, sliding her arm around his neck, drawing Nik down upon her. Daria knew how much that admission had cost him. He was worried about coming too soon, not being able to fully please her first. They had all night. And she was sure he would be more than ready to make love more than once with her. She heard Nik groan as she nudged open his lips with her own, grazing his lower lip with her tongue, teasing him, getting his mind off his worries and focused on their mutual pleasure instead.

Nik pulled away, giving her a feral look. "I'm not going to last long the first time. Let me get undressed, and get that condom pack open. Actually, open two."

Laughing and nodding, Daria released him and sat up. In minutes, they were undressed and she felt the scorching intensity of his gaze sweeping up her naked body, hungrily absorbing her. She felt her breasts tighten beneath his predatory look, regaled in it, felt her entire lower body clench and respond with possibility. As he stood naked before her, her gaze fell to his erection. He was not a small man at all. Heat pooled in her, anticipating, wanting. She saw his need for her, but saw his worry, too. There was such tension in him, reflected in his erection as he rolled on the condom.

"Come here," she coaxed, taking his hand, guiding him onto the bed beside her. She was going to be the assertive one right now. Daria sensed he was almost afraid to touch her out of fear of coming too soon. He would come, but she would ensure he'd be within her when it happened. "Trust me?" she asked as he lay on his back and she spanned his hips, her thighs coming to rest on either side of his. Her body was a bare inch away from that powerful erection and she felt her juices flowing, felt the neediness arc upward within her as she settled her hands in a frame on either side of his head.

"With my life, Kitten."

"Then, let me love you first. Let's break the ice, get through this together, and then you can relax and we can take our time and enjoy one another on the second, or perhaps even on a third session?" She brushed her body against his erection in one, slow pass.

Instantly, he gritted his teeth, his hands closing hard and gripping her hips. "Daria…"

"Shhhhh," she whispered against his lips, rubbing against him, feeling his warm, steel-hard erection rise, stroking it lightly with her wet, weeping entrance. "Let me take you into myself... I'm more than ready for you, Nik..." and she closed her eyes, skimming against his taut, thick length. His mouth hungrily took hers and she grazed her breasts along the broad expanse of his chest. Every glide, every contact, sent wild flames licking from her hardening nipples, cascading down through her, pooling in her core that began to ache as she fitted him fully against her entrance, allowing him to feel her warmth, her coaxing, sensuous movements. A deep growl rolled up through his chest, his hips thrusting upward, wanting her. All of her. She smiled against his mouth, holding him right where he was, not allowing him to do anything but savor her, feel her, and allow that heat that had always been between them to explode.

His large, calloused hands were not still. He gripped her hips, bringing her close to the tip of his erection, and she relaxed, allowing him to guide her. His breathing was ragged. She became enflamed as he slowly moved into her, testing her, seeing if she was wet enough. Oh, yes, she was. No worries there, and Daria played her tongue boldly against his, emulating the ancient rhythm, urging him to move deeper into her. Nik was a medic. He never wanted to give anyone pain, rather to relieve it, and Daria knew his mindset. She felt his fractional hesitation and she settled down on him, swallowing him into herself, feeling her channel swelling along his width and length, moaning with pleasure over the exquisite, unfolding sensations. There was nothing like wonderful sex and she knew they would be good together.

With slow, rocking movements, in and out, Daria felt Nik tense, his fingers digging sporadically into her hips. She lifted her mouth away from his, seeing his eyes tightly shut, his teeth clenched as he thrust deeply into her several times before a guttural growl rolled through him. She felt the power of his release, urging him on with a smooth, unbroken flow of her undulating hips. She was nowhere near orgasm level herself, but that didn't matter. What mattered was Nik needed this more than she did this first time around. Just the way he held onto her, how long the release throbbed throughout her, told her everything. Sometimes, a man needed to come first, and this was one of those times.

Nik suddenly collapsed, breathing hard, sweat beading his deeply-furrowed brow as he flew on the singed wings of pleasure still throbbing through his lean, hard frame. Daria felt like her entire body was a sacred cup surrounding him, supporting him, holding him, and loving him as he floated in that beautiful netherworld of scalding, releasing climax. His fingers eventually began to ease from her flesh and Daria smiled, kissed his damp brow, his nose and finally, worshipping his mouth, letting him know she was equally satisfied, be it in a different way. Love had many angles and turns. Daria wasn't some ingénue who was guileless or innocent about sex. She had loved deeply and well with Luke. He'd taught her love had many levels and many different expressions. Daria used that knowledge to help heal Nik. Gathering him up in the aftermath, her arms curving around his shoulders, she lay there stretched out across his torso, head resting on his shoulder, brow against his jaw, holding him. Just holding him... Because that is what this man had needed for so long and hadn't received. With her in his life, Daria silently promised Nik that was going to change.

CHAPTER 15

"YOU ARE A generous woman," Nik told Daria in a roughened voice. He'd removed the condom and come back to bed, laying with her tucked against his body.

Daria lay with her eyes closed, her fingers moving slowly across his damp-haired chest. "So are you, Nik. But I don't think you see that."

He made a sound of disagreement, wiping the sweat off his brow. His whole body was still vibrating from the powerful, climatic release. It was one thing to relieve himself when needed, but it was instead wholly another to loose himself after five years inside a woman's body. The difference was night and day. Now, with Daria, he felt emotionally satisfied, desired, loved and fulfilled. Nik couldn't ever recall feeling like he felt right now. "No… I don't, Kitten. I'm not much on introspection." He heard her laugh and then caress his chest with her lips.

"Men aren't known for it."

He grinned a little, savoring Daria. "No argument. But you are deeply introspective. I've seen you go there often. It's in your eyes."

"I'm a sniper by trade," she agreed, her hand stilling over his heart. "Details make a life-and-death difference to me, and I can take that skill and apply it to anything. Even you. People interest me, Nik. I'm forever curious about why they do or say the things they do. I always wonder what is behind their actions and decisions. What sent them in that direction?"

"You would be a good police detective," he grumped good-naturedly, opening his eyes, sliding his hand through her hair, feeling its silkiness slip like a whisper between his fingers.

"Maybe…" Daria looked up, folding her hands on his chest and settling her chin on them, holding his hooded stare. "But you fascinate me. You have from the moment I saw you."

"A bug under your microscope?" he teased, his lips lifting wryly.

Her smile blossomed. "Not hardly, Morozov. When I saw you in the church, I knew you were my contact because I'd been given a photo of you. But the difference between the photo and seeing you in person? My breath caught in my throat."

"Now, that's an American slang I haven't heard before. What does it mean?" He liked the sparkle in her eyes. Nik saw the desire pent up in them. As soon as he recovered, he would take her, love her, and make her fully his, the way he'd dreamed of doing. His five-year drought had ended and he was positive he could control himself the next time around to give Daria the pleasure she deserved. The gift she'd just given him earlier had shattered him emotionally in a new way. She'd selflessly given herself to him with no expectation of reward. He would never forget her generosity. It told him how powerful the connection that was alive and growing between them every day truly was.

"It means you rock my world," Daria whispered, smiling into his eyes.

"And so, you felt this connection between us, too?"

"Did I ever. I felt euphoric, Nik. I couldn't control my body, my desire for you. It was the craziest response I've ever had to a man. It was as if I were in animal mating heat."

"Confession time," he admitted, smoothing her hair aside, running his fingers lightly across the sensitive nape of her neck. "I was having the very same reaction to you. It surprised the hell out of me. I didn't know what to think. I didn't know what was going on."

"Amazing," Daria agreed in a confused tone. She shook her head, still baffled by the reaction they'd initially had with one another in that church.

There was so much Nik couldn't put into words. He enjoyed dropping into Ukrainian, his first language, with Daria. His heart swelled as he moved his fingers slowly across her long, firm back. Nik didn't want to think about the future beyond kidnapping Korsak. But he dreamed of so much more since meeting Daria. His hand drew to a halt on her back. "I don't know what we have, except that it was strong from the beginning. I'm paralyzed by it in some ways because I have no experience with how I feel toward you, Daria."

"It's the same for me," she admitted softly, caressing his chest, feeling his skin tighten wherever her fingertips traced his flesh.

"I wish," he said thickly, "that I had met you at any other time than right now, Kitten. We live in chaos. Neither of us has control over anything."

She pressed her hips against him suggestively. "We have control over ourselves and that has to be enough, Nik. At least, for now." Daria lifted her head and looked at the clock on the bedstand. "It's nearly five p.m. The chicken should be done. Are you ready to eat? Get your strength back?" and she gave him a wicked, teasing look.

There was no sense in diving down the rabbit hole of uncertainty about where their lives were at right now. Wisely, Nik nodded. "Yes, let me get a quick shower? Would you join me?" He saw her eyes light up.

"If I did, I'm afraid we'd get otherwise engaged and that chicken would catch fire in the oven." Daria rose to her knees, sweeping her hand outward in a lingering movement from his neck, down his torso, her fingers wrapping around his semi-erection. "Let's eat. Then we have energy to last through the night?"

Her warm fingers wrapping around him instantly made him tense up with pleasure, his breath a sharp intake. He liked what he saw in her gold eyes, the heat simmering in them, and knew she was more than ready. "Keep that up," he growled, gently easing her fingers away from himself, "and we aren't leaving this room."

She laughed lightly and climbed off the bed. Holding out her hand, Daria smiled and coaxed, "Come on, let's go get some fuel?"

AS THEY ATE the chicken, the sweet green beans and tasty potatoes, Daria wanted to imagine that she and Nik were in their own home, enjoying a meal together. Her military experience hovered in the halls of her mind. There were all kinds of danger surrounding them. Her heart, however, was centered on Nik. He ate voraciously, complimenting her cooking. The man sat naked except for a towel wrapped around his waist and his lean, hard body was dessert for her eyes whether he knew it or not. Everything about him shouted relaxation. Daria couldn't imagine a five-year drought of no sex.

Did she dare to dream of a time when they were past this point in their lives, beyond their random crashing together on this op? The last two years of her life had been a desert. She'd felt herself dying little by little throughout them. Humans weren't meant to live alone as solitary monks. Daria stole a look through her lashes at Nik as he ate with relish. That ache centered again in her lower body, a promise of things to come.

"I hope Brudin doesn't come knocking at our door later," she grumped.

"Doubtful," Nik murmured, pushing the empty plate away and wiping his mouth with a paper napkin. "Korsak has all of them getting whipped into shape at the hotel. He's ordered them all to stop drinking and whoring. To get cleaned up, showered, shaved and look presentable." He thumbed toward his medical ruck near the door. "I have everything I need right here."

"So? That means Brudin won't be around to harass us tonight?"

"No. I'm to meet them at the hotel at 0600 tomorrow morning." Nik met and held her gaze. "Tonight is just for us, Daria."

She rose from the table. "I need to get a shower first."

"Go. I'll clean up here in the kitchen."

"You're easily house-trained, Morozov," she teased, grinning down at him.

Her heart mushroomed as Nik gave her a heated look, his gaze turning predatory upon her.

"My mother trained us early on to help out," he assured her, rising. "You can't come from a farm family and not start working shortly after you've learned how to walk." Picking up the plates, he said, "I'll meet you in the bedroom when you're done."

Daria didn't waste their precious time to wash her hair. She fixed it up on top of her head to keep it dry, scrubbing the rest of herself clean, unable to calm the clamoring heat that rested within her. Twenty minutes later, she wrapped herself in a pink towel and left the bathroom. The rest of the apartment was in the dark except for a bare light shining in the hall opposite the opened bedroom door. Her heart sped up. Daria wanted this so badly, wanted to love Nik, to give back to him in so many large and small ways. Already, as she padded barefoot on the cool tiles, she felt anticipation singing through her veins. Rounding the doorframe, she saw him lying naked on the bed, waiting for her. Nik reminded her of a male jaguar at languid rest, but she knew better. There was an air of dangerous arousal exuding off of him and she smiled a little, seeing he was powerfully erect once more. For her. For them. He held out his hand in her direction.

The room was dark except for the night light in the hall. Daria opened the towel and hung it over a nearby chair. Slipping across the cool sheet, she tangled her fingers with his, allowing him to draw her in beside him. He maneuvered her onto her back so she lay parallel to him. Drowning in his intense, turbulent blue gaze, she shivered beneath it as he brought her hand to his lips, slowly kissing each of her fingers, then opening her palm. The moment his tongue brushed that sensitive area, she sighed and closed her eyes, her lips parting.

There was no need for words. Nik communicated wonderfully without them as he licked her palm, sending tingles of delight all across her hand. He lay propped above her, and brought her arm up behind where her head rested on the pillow, the long fingers of his other hand capturing her wrist. There was something primal about his imprisoning of her, leaving her bare under his burning inspection. Her breasts grew firm, pleading for his touch, her nipples tightening with eager expectancy. As he slid his long, muscular leg across hers, gently opening her thighs, she shuddered with need. His calloused hand slipped around her breast, her skin on fire from the contact. A moan came from within her as he leaned over, his lips teasing the point, sipping upon it, lingering, driving her into a frenzy. As she lifted her hips in response, his hand left her breast, gliding downward, caressing her abdomen, fingers closing across her mound of soft curls, lingering once more, allowing Daria to feel the heat of his connection with her.

She felt her whole lower body turn wet and crampy as he slowly explored her, fingers sliding through her damp folds. A cry jammed into her throat and she thrust her hips toward the pleasure he was giving her. She heard a rumble of satisfaction in his chest as his mouth trailed a series of slow, soft kisses from her breast upward to find her mouth.

"You are a fiery woman, *moya kotya*," he breathed against her lips, caressing them, opening her more to him. "Wild, untamed, and I like how sleek and wet you are for me..."

Mind shorting out, she cried out as his fingers sought and found her dripping entrance, teasing that swollen knot just inside her. His mouth plundered her lips and she felt the full force of his maleness, a hot brand claiming her, and wanting her. As his tongue played with hers, emulating a slow, seductive rhythm, she arched against his fingers, a cry in her throat as she felt her entire lower body explode inwardly. The intensity of the orgasm caught her by total surprise, roaring through her in an undulating rhythm. She fell into a vat of molten, scalding fire as she felt the gush of fluids and the near-violent set of contractions within her tunnel as he milked her, not allowing her any escape from his skills, lavishing that knot, stroking her, urging her body to continue flowing powerfully beneath his command.

As he lifted his mouth from hers, Daria gasped, her eyes flying open, clinging to his slitted blue gaze as he continued to give her excruciating pleasure. She'd never had such a long, hard orgasm in her life and yet, beneath Nik's talented fingers, her body was receptive and giving him everything he was asking from her. And how her heart flew open! She panted, her heart racing, her body quivering from the unexpected explosiveness of her release. And yet, nothing... nothing, had ever felt so right, so good, to Daria. She saw a very pleased male smile shadow Nik's well shaped lips, saw the glitter of satisfaction in his narrowed eyes as he watched her come for him, gifting him in the most intimate of ways.

Her body suddenly collapsed and he eased his fingers from her depths, gliding his hands upward, fingers spreading out across her damp belly as they went. She closed her eyes, sinking into that wonderful radiant light that consumed and embraced her as the orgasm continued to ripple like molten waves throughout her. Nik allowed her time to absorb it all, kissing her hairline, nibbling on her earlobe, and then moving his tongue to the nape of her neck, nipping lightly, teasing her, reminding her she had so much more left to give him. She felt as if her whole body were suddenly his to own and play with. She felt his erection pressing insistently against her hip, felt him controlling himself for her sake as she languished in the aftermath of the ground-zero blast, a satisfied smile pulling at her lips.

And, just as she came down off that delicious precipice, he moved his body over hers, his knee opening her thighs wider to him, settling between them, his hands smoothing her flanks, skating upward, enclosing her breasts, teasing her nipples and sending her to another level of pleasure. Daria arched into his hands, felt his erection pressing against her entrance and she made a low sound of need, inviting him into her. This time... this time was going to be so good for both of them. He rolled on a condom. Nik took his time building her up with him, stroking slowly near that knot, engaging it once more, teasing it, and then he leaned forward, pushing deeper, and the heat flared to life once more within Daria.

She brought her hands to his hips, sliding her legs around his, capturing him so she could rise and drink him fully into her welcoming body. Nik growled and the sound reverberated through her. He gripped her hair, holding her in place, kissing her hungrily, allowing her to know the depths of his need for her. She smiled beneath his searching mouth, lifting, creating rhythm, letting him know how close she was to coming once more. She felt her walls contracting, tight and wet around his girth and length as he plunged as far as he could into her. The scalding sensation, the building of her next orgasm tripled, and in moments, as he thrust quickly and deeply into her, her fingers drug into his bunched, damp shoulders as it swept through her. It wasn't as explosive as the last had been, but the utter pleasure it left in its wake tore her mind from its moorings, hurling her, held deep within Nik's arms, out into a bright, bursting universe filled with her wild cries of satiation.

She was lost, tumbling, and she heard Nik call her name, felt him stiffen, felt him paralyzed with his own climax so deep within her. The world was composed of light, fire, and floating and she smiled as he suddenly collapsed on top of her, holding her tightly to him, their sweaty bodies entangled. More than anything for Daria, this was the most beautiful moment for her as she slid her arms around Nik's trembling shoulders, holding him, loving him with all of her body, heart and soul.

NIK SLEPT WITH Daria snuggled deep in his arms, her body warm and soft against him. He awoke at some point during the night, thin moonlight peeking around the blinds, so as to ease away just enough to study her sleeping face on the pillow beside him. Her hair was mussed, loose, and it framed her face. Her lashes lay long and thick against her cheeks. Following the clean line of her nose, his gaze lingered on those lush lips of hers that his own had worshipped against earlier. The lips that had sent him into a cauldron of pleasurable oblivion. In sleep, she looked like an innocent angel and a fierce protectiveness for her rose again within him. He knew Daria was fully capable of taking care of herself, far more than most women, but that didn't matter any longer to Nik. She was his woman. That made him want to safeguard her and always shield her from any menace. They had threat all around them. Worse, it wasn't going to go away anytime soon.

Nik reached out, carefully extending his index finger to slip a few errant strands of hair away from her face. Her cheeks were flushed and the corners of her soft mouth were relaxed. Being able to please this woman made his chest expand with euphoria. Her cries had been so sweet and filled with satisfaction. His own body hummed at the low frequency of the pleasure still continuing to thrum through him. To be able to love Daria, to slide into her welcoming body, was more than he'd even dreamed could ever happen. Nik studied her shadowed face in the silence of the world around them. The bedstand clock read 0300. He had three more hours with her. Despite wanting to slowly awaken her with an onslaught of kisses and touches, Nik hesitated. He wasn't a small man and Daria hadn't had sex in two years. She had to be feeling tenderness physically because they hadn't exactly gone at it slowly. More like two animals in mating heat. Nik felt his body stir with the want of her, just thinking about it, his mind replaying those first two times they'd been with one another.

His fingers smoothed more of her mussed hair, lightly, not wanting to disturb her sleep. He saw the shallow curve of her breasts rise and fall, indicating deep slumber. Exhaustion of another type flowed through him as he absorbed her relaxed features. The light revealed the curve of her strong shoulders, and he could see the firmness of her biceps and the tight muscling throughout her forearms. She was in top athletic condition, even from a military standpoint. Even after four months of downtime due to the knife wounds in her left thigh, she was athletically trim. He wanted to do more to help Daria get past her trauma and knew that he could, but time was against them right now. Leaning over, Nik allowed his lips to linger lightly against her smooth, warm, velvet cheek for just a moment, and flared his nostrils to inhale her spicy, feminine scent.

"Sleep the sleep of angels, beloved," he whispered to her.

Nik eased himself back down, sliding his arm beneath her neck, his other hand coming to rest across her blanketed hip. Daria stirred momentarily, but then sank back into that sweet abyss of healing sleep. He laid there, eyes closed, hungrily imprinting her breath, her warmth, and the way her body melted against his, into his mind. Nik had no idea where he and the rest of the team were heading out to at dawn, nor how long they would be out on patrol from village to village. With Pavlovich in the mix, all bets were off. When would he see Daria again? The only relief he felt was that she would now be safe in Aguas Calientes with the Russians gone and no longer a threat to her.

His heart desperately wanted to leap ahead to his future with Daria. To unanswered dreams, but Nik wouldn't allow it to. And yet, as he slowly moved his hand across Daria's hip, his heart cried out for some personal needs. Was it selfish to dream of her in his life after this op? Had five years of loneliness made him illogical, wanting and idealistic? His fingers lingered on the curve of her hip and then moved lightly down across her outer thigh. So much stood in the way of him reaching out to bring her into his arms and into his life. There was no assurance that would ever even happen.

And what did Daria dream of? Nik felt pain zigzag through his chest and he frowned. His roaming hand paused once more on her hip. *Time.* They had to have time. Time together. Time to explore and talk with one another. Nik had never rushed into any relationship. He'd seen so many young women and men fall in love and yet, within a few months, they were walking away from one another, after finding the other's many faults. His relationships, while few, had each been meaningful and fulfilling. He'd taken his time, he'd learned, listened and communicated with each of the women in his life because he cared deeply for them.

Death had taken his first love, and then him leaving to go into Spetsnaz had scared the second woman in his life away. She'd tearfully admitted that she feared so much for his life, that she would lose him to death, that she couldn't handle the stress of it. Nik had understood and he'd sadly walked away, his heart torn in half. That had been seven years ago. It seemed a lifetime away to him.

The corners of his mouth flexed inward. Only Daria's soft, shallow breathing soothed the serrated emotions that clamored brightly across the surface of his mind. How badly he wanted the freedom to pursue her. Is this all that they would ever be able to share? Nik took nothing for granted. Death was always a bullet's whisper away. Even if Korsak didn't shoot him in the head, he knew Pavlovich and his guards could do so, too. Nothing was ever certain for him. How could he promise Daria anything? He couldn't, and a bitterness flowed through his heart. But, as soon as that feeling left, his heart filled throbbingly with hope of a future with her. What was her favorite ice cream? What made her sigh? Laugh? What brought her to tears? What creative skills did she possess? What kind of house did she live in? Were certain colors her favorite? He had thousands of questions for her and very few answers up to this point.

Sleep stole in upon Nik and he surrendered to it, the woman he loved more than his own life in his arms, where she should be.

DARIA WATCHED NIK get dressed, shave and prepare to leave. It was 0530, the gray dawn chasing away the night through the kitchen window. She'd gotten up at 0500 and made him coffee, along with several thick chicken sandwiches and tucked them into Zip Lock baggies so he would have some decent food to eat out on the trail today. He was internalized, his brows knitted, eyes dark, mouth a slash, as if he were holding back a lot of things he wanted to say to her. She sat at the kitchen table, watching him open his ruck across from her, rapidly assessing all the bottles of medication and anchoring the more vital of them down securely into small canvas pockets. She kept her hands around her warm mug of coffee.

"I'm going to miss you," she whispered, meeting his hooded stare.

"I'm going to miss you more, Kitten." He pressed the Velcro closed, making sure it was tightly sealed so that medications could not fall out along the trail. "You look beautiful when you're just waking up."

Her lips pulled faintly upward. Daria knew he was gearing up mentally and emotionally to be with that hard, predatory team of his. Now, she understood, more than ever, the psychological cost to him of remaining with that savage group. "I'll be looking for those notes," she offered. His gaze lightened momentarily. Nik wore jungle-green cammos, Russian-made for Spetsnaz. His weapons were stowed in a compartment in his ruck. The rifles these men carried, all AK-47's, were in a weapons bag at the hotel, hidden from Peru *policia's* eyes. Her heart yearned for him to stay, but that wasn't reality.

"I'll have to be extra careful now," he muttered, his hands sliding to a halt on his huge ruck, studying her. "Now, I have three more sets of eyes along with us and they are all very observant."

"I know." Daria frowned. "I wish there was an easier way we could stay in contact, Nik. It's going to be hell not knowing where you are, not knowing when you might come back here to Aguas Calientes."

He gave her an understanding look, moving his fingers along one seam of his ruck. "Welcome to my world. That's why it's been so hard trying to coordinate with Kilmer and his men."

"Understood." She roused herself, wanting time to slow down. Pushing out of her chair, she walked over to him. Nik turned toward her. His arms came around her waist and he gazed down at her. Daria leaned upward, moving her mouth against his, feeling him start to melt, beginning to relax, some of the tension within him dissolving. She hungered to make love a fourth time with him before he left. Her body was still glowing from their third session at 0400 this morning.

She'd awoken and begun a slow, sensual assault upon him as he slept. It hadn't taken much to awaken and arouse him. The third time had been gentler, more intimate and caring, making her want Nik one more time all the more before he left.

His hands lifted, cupping her breasts beneath the nightgown she wore, his thumbs caressing her tightened nipples. She moaned into his mouth and he kissed her hungrily, unable to get enough of her.

Daria wanted that kiss to go on forever, wanting his large hands to continue their slow, teasing exploration of her as they stood together. She heard Nik groan as he reluctantly eased them apart, a fierce, burning look in his raptor-like eyes. She was breathing raggedly, her breasts begging for his expert touch to continue. Her lower body glowed and throbbed, hungry to satiate itself again with Nik. She rubbed her hips against his suggestively, his erection once more hard and thick, straining against his cammos. "We have fifteen minutes," she said breathily, smiling at him.

"You tempt me," he growled, settling his hands on her hips, pulling her away from him. "You've had enough of me. You have to be very tender and sore, Kitten."

Shrugging, she said, "I don't care. There's other parts of my body, my heart, that need you even more, Nik. In time, the soreness will go away. It's not a big deal." But she could see it bothered him. Nik didn't like creating pain in another person. Not ever. It wasn't in his DNA to do so. Pouting, she murmured, "At least you know what is waiting for you when you get home."

He caressed her cheeks with his thumbs. "Home. You know that sounds so good?"

"Well," she murmured, placing her hands on the backs of his as he framed her face, "consider me your new home?" and she gave him a serious look, meaning it. There was a flare of hope in his blue eyes, and she felt her words land with powerful meaning on Nik,

"I would like nothing more than to create a home with you, Kitten. A *real* home."

"Then, let's hold that dream together, Nik?" Longing to say so much more, Daria knew it was too soon. She wanted to leave Nik with something positive. Something filled with hope. "I live in a two-story cabin outside of town. Why don't you think about what kind of house you would like? I'll think about it, too. We'll build the rooms in our minds? Each room's color, the kind of furniture we'd like to see in it? That will be something for us to look forward to when you return? It will be something wonderful we can share with one another."

He dragged in a ragged breath. "Dream for us, Daria. I can't dream right now. I don't dare, Kitten," and he gave her an apologetic look.

Her heart broke a little more, understanding why he couldn't. Stepping back out of his arms, she took his hands in her own. "Okay, I'll dream for both of us. Stay safe out there for me, Nik?"

He squeezed her fingers. "That's a promise I can give you," he said thickly. Reluctantly, he released her fingers and shrugged on the massive ruck across his shoulders. He picked up his black baseball cap, settling it on his head. "I'll see you as soon as possible," he said. The words, *I love you*, wanted to tear out of his mouth. Deep sadness coursed through Nik's chest. He knew it was too soon to say those words. Not to mention that they were both on a slippery slope, and there was no guarantee either of them would manage to come out alive at the bottom of it. He swallowed hard and gave her a fierce, tender look of the love he held for her in his heart. He saw her eyes glisten with love in return. Unspoken. But there. It was enough.

Daria nodded, watching him turn and leave the apartment. Silence fell all around her after he left. The room was barren of his larger-than-life presence and her heart shattered. She knew she had fallen helplessly in love with this brave, self-sacrificing soldier. And it hurt that she couldn't gift Nik with the words she held tightly in her heart for him and him alone. There wasn't any time, space, or anything else left for them now. Daria turned and walked down the hall to their bedroom. She would worry about Nik, but he'd survived out here for five years on his wits and intelligence alone. What she had to do was pull together her own life and her part in this mission. Jack had ordered her to continue the mission, despite the unexpected drug kingpin showing up. Looking at the clock on the bedstand, Daria knew her clandestine meeting with the Special Forces A-Team outside of town at 1100 was rapidly approaching. The meeting that had been scheduled ever since she'd arrived here in Aguas Calientes. She'd find out a lot more from Sergeant Kilmer then.

CHAPTER 16

AT ELEVEN A.M., the low-hanging clouds were beginning to shred and show through a light blue sky above the tranquil area as Daria moved to a spot near a small clearing deep within in the jungle. She wore her knapsack and baseball cap and retained her cover as a botanist. Glancing at her watch, crouched partially behind a huge old tree, she had a clear view of the narrow clearing. With the photos from the Army Special Forces A-team in the front of her mind, she waited patiently. She'd worked with A-teams before and, in particular, hunter-killer three-man teams, in Afghanistan. She shifted slightly, her hearing keyed, her focus on the coming meeting.

Eyes narrowed; she spotted movement across the ten-foot-wide meadow. It was nothing obvious, but a trained sniper like herself would only be expected to see such subtle movements. For anyone else, they'd have thought the wind had ruffled that leaf, or turned those blades of grass, but there was no wind right now to do either such thing.

Slowly rising to her feet, hand on the bark of the tree, Daria turned to her right, well back within the line of scrub, and waited for the men's silent appearance. It wasn't long in coming. She first saw Sergeant Mace Kilmer, thirty-two years old, intelligent with shaggy black hair and a half-kempt beard lining his face, melt out of the surrounding greenery, his light gray eyes narrowed. He wore jungle-patterned cammos and carried an AK-47 across his chest, its silencer-fitted muzzle pointed down. The floppy hat on his head was dark with dampness. It was the lethal look in his narrowed eyes that told Daria this man knew his business. She saw two more men, all around Kilmer's six-foot height, following without a sound. This team was good, but Daria expected that from them. She knew they'd probably had six or seven years to perfect their shadowy movement through this green hell. She wondered what drove them, but it wasn't a topic to be brought up right now.

Kilmer's gaze never left hers as he eased into the thick foliage among which she stood. He smiled a little, thrusting out his hand. "Mace Kilmer. Daria McClusky?"

She gripped his gloved hand. "Yes." Releasing his firm grip, she nodded greetings to the two other bearded soldiers who stood casually alert on either side of Kilmer. "How do you want to handle this briefing?" she asked him in a quiet voice, her gaze never still, always watching the jungle surrounding them. She was an operator on equal standing with them.

"This way," Kilmer said, flicking his hand toward the small trail she'd come in on. "Follow me."

Man of few words. But then again, Daria mused, as she fell into step behind him with the other two soldiers bringing up the rear, living in a jungle for God knew how long, wouldn't exactly make one chatty. Besides, their whole demeanor was stealth, and silence was their greatest asset. They moved onto a wild pig feeder trail about a quarter of a mile from the meadow. It twisted and wound for another mile before it opened up into another tiny clearing. Kilmer came to a halt within the tree line and turned to her.

"Welcome to Camp Alpha," he said with a slight grin.

Looking around with her sniper's eye, Daria saw a few hints that this was a sleeping place for the team. She could read that they slept here in hammocks above the ground. merely from the nicks here and there in a few of the surrounding trees. A casual hiker would never recognize what they were looking at.

She saw Kilmer lean down and pull over a wooden box.

"Have a seat," he grunted, pointing at a partially-rotted log that had fallen a long time ago. "We'll have coffee and talk."

Sitting, Daria watched the three men go to work quietly, no talking between them. She saw their earpieces, and the mics they wore near their lips. They were each armed with a knife sheath on one leg, a drop holster with a .45 pistol in it, and their AK-47s. Each man wore a ruck that was probably their mobile home and, by the looks of them, weighed close to one-hundred and twenty pounds. She knew a hunter-killer team never remained still or in any given area for long, unless they were setting up an op to kidnap or kill an HVT: a high value target.

She slipped out of her own ruck, itself around forty pounds. Opening it, she pulled out a bunch of items and sat them at her feet. She saw Kilmer's straight brown eyebrows rise.

"Seriously?" he grunted, rising and coming over to where she sat. "Fritos?"

Daria grinned. "I found out from Nik that you guys have junk food cravings." She'd bought Fritos, potato chips and Cheetos for the three of them. And three jars; one with salsa and twos others of jalapeno bean dip. Nik knew their habits well from their many, many meetings over the past two years. He'd taken her to several stores in Aguas Calientes to acquire for them packages of the junk food that they loved, but never got out in this jungle. She saw delight dissolve Kilmer's hard features as he crouched, picking up a bag, a grin widening his thinned lips. He grabbed one of the bean dip jars, pleasure wreathing his face.

"Morozov is one hell of a man," he muttered, lifting the packages, nodding to her. "He's one righteous dude. Thank him for this. And thank *you* for bringing it to us. We appreciate it."

Daria smiled and saw the other two men come over, eagerly looking through the goodies she'd laid out for them.

Mace turned as they crouched beside him, eyeing the snack foods. "This is Nate Cunningham," he said, introducing the man to Daria. "He's our 18 Delta medic."

"Hi," Daria murmured, shaking the twenty-nine-year-old man's offered hand. "I got Cheetos for you and that other jar of bean dip. Nik said you really like them."

Nate grinned widely and released her hand. "Yes, ma'am, there's nothing like 'em out here. Resupplies the salt I sweat out by the hour around here." He took the package from Daria, holding it like a rare prize he'd just won along with the bean dip.

"And this dude," Mace said dryly, "is our communications sergeant Cale Merrill."

Daria met the other man's large, intelligent blue gaze as Cale offered his big hand to her. Merrill was at least six foot tall. He had a hard, deeply lined, tanned face. There was a chilling energy about the soldier, as if he'd witnessed atrocities. Daria saw the tiredness deep in his eyes. It came with time and the wear on a soldier's soul in this kind of work, and she knew it well. Daria released his hand and gave him the bag of Lay's potato chips along with the jar of hot Salsa. She saw sudden warmth and gratitude come to his eyes, but he never smiled. Of the three, he felt the most wounded to Daria. The one who had seen too much, and it was laying heavily on his heart and soul. She understood, as few others ever could.

"Nik said you guys have a love of candy," and she swept her hand over the choices at her feet. "Mars Bars for Kilmer, Butterfingers for Cunningham, and Kit-Kats for you, Sergeant Merrill."

"Man," Nate murmured, grabbing his stash, "this *is* unexpected. Thanks, ma'am."

"Call me Daria," she insisted, looking around at all of them. She knew that, in the military, people were called by their surname rather than their first name. But this was not exactly the military.

"Daria's a pretty name," Mace drawled, getting up and placing his stash into his opened ruck. He went back to fixing the coffee in a beat-up percolator over a wire grate, the blinding light and heat of a magnesium tablet under it heating the water to boiling point.

Daria watched each man go back to his ruck to stow Nik's thoughtful and priceless gifts in them. Her heart expanded with a fierce love of him. He'd bought these men the snacks out of his own pocket. It spoke to her of his regard and respect for them. She understood they were more like friends than mere fellow black ops partners. She missed Nik, feeling that blade of loneliness score her heart. She worried about him, out as he was with Korsak and, now, Pavlovich, the man who might be her as-of-yet unknown relative. Not wanting to focus on all that now, she shoved it deep down within herself.

In no time, Kilmer had the coffee made. Daria was given a rusted, beat-up tin cup with the steaming brew in it. The three men sat on other logs, set in a semi-triangular formation, across from her. Although they never honestly relaxed, they did get rid of their bucket hats and set their AKs aside, but within reach. Daria could tell they really appreciated the hot coffee. Nik had also bought them a large pack of Oreo cookies which she opened and placed between them to have with their coffee. The mirrored appreciation in these men's faces melted her heart. Daria knew what it was like to not have familiar comfort food from back home for months on end.

"What do you have for us?" Kilmer asked finally, in a gap between Fritos and bean dip.

Daria told them everything, leaving nothing out. The three listened attentively, never taking notes. Hunter-killer teams consisted of those with the highest intelligence and skills of anyone in the US Army, with the possible exceptions of CAG or Delta Force. They focused especially hard when she told them about Nik's info on Pavlovich. The only thing she left out was her birthmark, the one matching the drug lord's own. She'd gone to Cusco yesterday and delivered the evidence to the hospital. The bottle of tissues was then overnighted to Lima for analysis at the large hospital there in their DNA testing lab. She'd also supplied a small vial of her own blood along with the package, praying that there was no match. She'd not yet had time to sift through her violent reactions and terror over possibly being the unknown Russian relative of Pavlovich.

Mace finished his coffee, munching thoughtfully on his sixth Oreo cookie, two more ready in his hand. "Pavlovich showing up unexpectedly throws a grenade into this kidnapping op of ours," he grumbled, scratching his beard in thought.

"He's an unknown," she agreed.

"Morozov got along with him," Merrill said, giving his teammates a glance. "I don't think that's bad news. It sounds more like he's gunning to demote

Korsak."

"Yeah," Nate said, munching with delight over his eighth Oreo, "so long as Pavlovich focuses on Korsak, Nik can remain the shadow he is."

Mouth quirking, Daria studied Kilmer across from her. "How bad is this going to screw up a possible kidnapping of Korsak?"

Shrugging, finishing off the last cookie and rubbing his hands down his hard, curved thighs, Mace muttered, "Depends. First, we have to know which village they're at. That's been the one, single biggest FUBAR in all of this. Korsak doesn't trust Nik any further than he can throw him. But maybe, just maybe, with Pavlovich in the mix, Nik can get more intel out of him sooner."

"Do you have a fix on where they went?" she wondered. Because no satellites could penetrate the triple canopy with any reasonable degree of accuracy, or precisely identify body heat signatures via infrared. Any of those red blobs could be Quechua Indians, wild pigs, or even a jaguar family out for a stroll on those trails winding deep through the thick jungle, and not a Russian team at all. A satellite wouldn't be able tell the difference due to the dispersion of frequencies through the triple canopy leaves.

"They're headed in the direction of Flor," Mace provided. He shrugged his broad shoulders, adding, "But the trail they're on presently forks in three different directions and there's three village choice possibilities from that point on."

"Needle in a haystack," Daria agreed grimly, seeing the men's eyes reflect her own frustration.

"We never tail them too closely," Nate told her, wiping off his hands.

"Good, because Nik wanted to warn you about those two so-called guards with Pavlovich. They're ex-Spetsnaz, and they're a lot smarter than the average bodyguard types," Daria told them.

"Means we really go into stealth mode," Mace said unhappily.

"It means," Merrill growled, "that we're going to rely even more heavily on those notes Morozov passes to us."

"It's not going to be easy," Daria agreed, giving them all a sympathetic look.

The mood shifted and Nate gathered up the empty Oreo pack, stuffing it into one of his cargo pockets. "How are you doing down here, Daria? Does Peru suit you?" he teased.

She warmed to the 18 Delta medic. In many ways, Nate was the most open and vulnerable of the three men. But he was a medic, too, and it came with the territory. She liked his moss-green eyes that always held a sparkle in them, like he was an elf in disguise. Especially because he was the shortest of the three, leaner, but wiry. He had a more readable face, but maybe that was due to his brownish-red hair and the boyish freckles across his nose making him look younger. Maybe more approachable than Kilmer and Merrill. "I've done a lot of ops in Brazil, but the jungle's different in the Amazon than here in Peru," she told him.

"Your voice changes when you speak about Nik," he noted. "He kind of grows on everyone over time," and Nate grinned mischievously.

She felt heat flood her face. Daria didn't want these men to know about their budding relationship. It didn't have a place here at the table. "He's a nice guy, but you all know that," she said lightly, smiling over at Nate. There was care in this man's eyes, just like she'd seen in Nik's. "Are you close to him?" she asked, putting the conversation back on them, away from herself.

Nate's smile widened. "Yeah, he's almost like a brother to me. Teases the hell out of me whenever we get to meet up, which isn't too often. He's got a good heart, and it's in the right place. Did you find that out about him?"

Daria about choked but kept a poker face. "I found him to be very caring. He took me over to the Healing Hands Charity orphanage for a day."

"Yeah," Nate murmured, "Morozov does a lot of work over there. And really? He's the only lifeline for these ten villages. There is no medical help out here for any of those poor Indians."

"Well," Daria said, changing topics and pinning Kilmer with her gaze, "To continue to build my cover as a botanist, I'm going to be ranging out to all those villages Korsak holds sway over. I'll gather orchid specimens at each of them. I know Nik's contact in each one, as well. We have comms with one another and I wanted to give you my schedule for the next month." She pulled out a piece of paper, handing it to Mace.

He studied it. "Nik made this out for you?"

"Yes. He's guessing, of course, where Korsak might go, but he created this based upon past patterns. It's a bit of a shot in the dark."

"Always is," Kilmer grunted, folding the paper and placing it in his cammo pocket. "You need to be careful out there, Daria."

"Oh, the jaguars?"

Merrill snorted. "No. If you happen to walk into a village without knowing that Korsak and his team are there, that could prove to be a problem for you." His eyes grew to slits as he studied Daria. "Korsak rapes any young girls and women he wants. You need to be real cautious because he could go after you."

Her mouth flexed. "They know I'm Nik's woman. At least, it appears that way and Nik is banking on that to make his team accept me as off-limits."

Nate grunted, "Don't bet on it, Daria. You need to keep your guard up."

"I don't think, with Pavlovich along," Merrill said, "that Korsak is stupid enough to go after an American woman. That would bring all kinds of attention their way they don't want. An American woman who is raped would bring the US embassy ambassador from Lima up into the area, the Marines' diplomat guards, and the CIA. Korsak knows that."

"I don't think he's that bright," Mace muttered, shaking his head. He peered at Daria. "Let's hope, for your sake, that your visits to these villages do NOT coincide with Korsak and his team coming into them. I don't like it."

"Understood," Daria said. "But Nik will be there, and we've had five days to cement our cover. The team thinks he's in a relationship for the first time in five years and they've bought it from what Nik could see. Besides," and she opened her hands, "with Pavlovich showing up out of the blue, Korsak's entire focus is on his new boss now, no longer on us."

"All of the Alexandrov old teams," Mace told her, "are little more than sociopaths. Nik is one of the few who isn't like them."

"Him and Alex Kazak," Nate reminded him. "Alex was a medic with Alexandrov's team for years. He and Nik worked together there."

"I know Alex well," Daria said, her voice growing warm. "He's safe, married and happy up in Alexandria, Virginia."

"Lucky bastard," Mace said, grinning around at his cohorts. "We met Lauren Parker when she and Alex Kazak were down here on a mission. She was a good, strong woman and Alex is a damn fine soldier," Mace said, getting serious. "Nice to know Alex and Lauren got a happy ending."

"Unlike us," Nate said cheerfully, standing and brushing off the damp seat of his pants. "We're going to be just like Kilmer: not fit for society anymore, covered with fungus and mold, and no happy endings. We're part of the Petrie dish down here," and all three of the other soldiers laughed quietly, nodding their heads almost simultaneously.

Daria's heart went out to this team. She knew their sacrifices, knew that none of them had any real, lasting relationship with a woman. They spent three month stretches out in the jungle, with a few weeks in Cusco to catch up on badly needed downtime, before going back in to hunt their current HVT, high value target. "I always hold out hope for the hopeless," she told them gently, giving them all a caring look. "I know you lose a lot of your social veneer out here, but from where I'm sitting, you're all great guys. Heroes, in my eyes." She saw all of them suddenly perk up, turn shy, and avoid her gaze, eyes downcast and mouths pursed to hold back all the sudden, unspoken emotions. They all needed a little TLC, just as Nik did. They were human. And Daria knew the aching loneliness out on an op for month with little or no human contact. It was a brutal existence, hard on anyone, whether they admitted it or not. She was silently grateful Nik had walked into her life, never regretting any of this. Not ever.

"Where are you off to now?" Nate asked.

"Back to Aguas Calientes, after I find a few orchids to put in my sack," she said drily.

"Bet you're learning more about orchids than you ever wanted to know," he chuckled, peeling open a packet of Butterfingers.

Daria figured all the junk food would be gone by the end of this day, the guys stuffing themselves with it. She made a mental note to try and always bring them more whenever she had a chance to meet up with them again. Teams tended to stay away from civilization in general, operating unseen in the jungle during those three-month stints. This meeting was a rare one. "You could say that, but I love flowers, so it's not too much of a stretch."

Merrill unwound his tall, hard body. "Watch for snakes. Fer-de-lance are deadly and, in this area, in big-time abundance. They are one big, mean, aggressive snake."

"Oh," Daria replied, standing, "I've seen photos of the damage they can do." She lifted one of her legs. "These are Gortex snake guards."

"Fer-de-Lance go for the boot you're wearing, first," Nate warned, "and your guards have the tops of your boots protected. That's a good thing."

"Where are your snake guards, then?" she asked them. None of them were wearing any.

Kilmer shook his head, taking the now cool grate and stowing back in its old, dilapidated wooden box. It was a fruit and vegetable box with Spanish writing nearly faded away on one end. "We wear 'em out and order them again, and they never come. The jungle rot is hard on them. I put another request for them in three months ago and they still aren't here.

Nate, said, "Hey, maybe we'll get lucky in Lima. You never know, we might find some women who'll fall hopelessly in love with one of us dudes."

Mace snorted. "You're a damned idealist and a certified fool of a romantic. It ain't gonna happen for any of us sorry sons-of-bitches. Quit reading those romance books."

Daria smiled a little, hefting her ruck up over her shoulders, untwisting the straps that had bunched up across them. This was normal military trash talk. "Well, when you finally leave the Army, there's some very nice-looking, single women at Shield security, all ex-military," she suggested lightly. "Maybe you guys ought to check it out, and the three of you might meet someone nice."

"Lauren Parker was one of them," Nate informed them archly with an I-told-you-so look in his expression. "She and Alex fell in love. If they can? Why can't we?"

"Yeah, and Kilmer wanted her around our team like the black plague," Cale reminded him darkly. "He wanted nothing to do with her early on into that mission."

"Mace is a Neanderthal throwback, just like all of us down here," Merrill groused, hefting on his own ruck. And then he gave Daria an apologetic glance. "Present company excluded."

"No insult taken," she murmured, tightening the belt around her waist. She picked up her cloth sack that held two orchids she'd found along the trail on her way to this meeting spot.

"Well," Nate said, belting up, "Nik got a helluva deal with you being in the mix. He's got to be in heaven because you're intelligent and, militarily, you bring a lot to our table. Lucky bastard."

Daria's lips twitched as she settled the baseball cap on her head. Earlier, she'd braided her long, dark hair to keep it out of the way while traversing the jungle. "I wouldn't know. You'd have to ask him."

Kilmer chuckled darkly, throwing on his own hat and snapping his AK-47 into the chest sling position across the front of his body. "You'd pass in a heartbeat for a pretty Quechua Indian girl, Daria. Good cover. We'll be in touch."

"Right," she murmured.

Nate said, "Come here. You need a hug."

Surprised, Daria was suddenly enclosed within the medic's long arms as he gently embraced and then released her. How much like Nik he was, and it brought tears to her eyes that she quickly forced back. Smiling, she reached out, touching Nate's arm. "Thanks. But if anyone needs a hug, it's you guys, not me." She saw Nate give her an intense look, as if he had x-ray vision and could look right through her and know that she was already in a relationship with Nik. That look shook her. She knew 18 Delta medics were the best in the world, renowned for their high intuition and remarkable bravery and compassion out on the field of battle. Nate was like that and, uneasily, Daria wondered if he sensed something between her and Nik. From the look in his dancing green eyes, she bet he suspected something, but she wasn't going to add fuel to that particular fire.

Kilmer came up, towering over her. "Take care of yourself, okay? Don't ever get cornered by Korsak. He means business."

"I'll do that," Daria promised him somberly, seeing the care burning deep in his eyes. This man was badly wounded, like herself. It took one to know one, and she saw herself reflected in hardcore Mace. The shields he placed around himself were insurmountable. She doubted he would ever let down his guard, nor let go of all of the horror he carried alive and well within himself. He would never be vulnerable. To her, he seemed a tragic figure. "Thanks," she whispered, reaching out, only grazing his sleeve as she saw him gird himself against her full touch. As if to physically connect with him would shatter him in some way. He was in a worse place than she was and her heart ached for this brave, hardened soldier.

Kilmer looked her dead in the eyes. "Don't screw with Korsak. If you happen to end up at the same vill with him, get the hell out as soon as you can. Dump your plans. Run. Okay?" he gritted out, heavy warning in his low voice.

"I read you loud and clear, Mace." She saw concern in his eyes, his mouth going soft for a moment.

"If Korsak goes after you, Nik has to protect you. You know that, don't you? He's putting himself at risk at that point. Korsak has already put a gun to the head of two of his other soldiers who defied his authority in the past. And they aren't alive anymore." His mouth tightened as he intently studied her. "He won't hesitate to kill Nik. You're going to have to protect him, too, if that situation arises."

"I'll try very hard to ensure that never happens," Daria promised him huskily. "I have no reason to put Nik in the crosshairs."

CHAPTER 17

DARIA STARED AT the results of the DNA comparison between herself and Rolan Pavlovich. Two weeks had passed since she'd turned in his "tissue sample" and her own blood. Every day, she'd felt the tension creeping higher as she worried over her lineage. She stood in the lobby of the Cusco hospital. The results had been given by a doctor in a private meeting in his office. Now, she knew for sure.

She WAS Pavlovich's distant relative on the Mongol side of the family. It wasn't completely unknown for Russians and Mongols to intermarry, but it was at least a century ago that such a bonding was an even semi-common practice. The doctor had said that a birthmark would show up now and then, but not on every descendant. The best news was that she was not closely related to the mob boss. Leaning against the white wall in the hall of the busy hospital, nurses and doctors hurrying by her, Daria closed her eyes, the results gripped tightly in her hand. A multitude of dark, different emotions sifted through her. How badly she wanted Nik here beside her, to give her comfort, to say something… anything… that would take this monumental pain away from her chest. She felt ashamed deep down inside herself. If Pavlovich was the dark side of her family tree, then she was the light. What a crazy genetic mess this was. One thing for sure, she had to ensure her birthmark was hidden while he was down here in Peru. She couldn't risk him or one of his goons, seeing it. No telling what would happen next if it was spotted, and she didn't want to go there—at all.

She touched the birthmark on the base of her neck beneath the hair that she'd worn down loose to cover it for the train ride here into Cusco. Opening her eyes, Daria stared down through blurred vision at the paper trembling in her hand. The geneticist had told her that her distant relative had been part Mongolian and part Russian. That would explain the color of her skin, as if she were white, but with a heavy suntan. It also explained the slight tilt to her eyes and their gold-brown color; both traits strongly associated with Mongolian heritage. Nik had made more than one comment about her being able to pass as a Quechua Indian woman. He was closer than anyone before had been to the truth of her genes.

She was related to a major global drug dealer. And she was sure he still had ties to the Russian government, including the black ops branch he had been part of for nearly twenty years. Dragging in a deep breath, smelling the antiseptic combined with a faint odor of bleach lingering in the hospital lobby, she pushed away from the wall.

Nik... How she wished he was here for her! She knew he would be if he could. Every day without him, without word from him, worried her. Daria couldn't help it. As she slowly walked toward the glass exit doors, she felt like her whole life had been torn apart. The only constancy in it was Nik. In her shoulder bag she carried the sat phone. She dreaded making the call to Jack Driscoll to let him know about the DNA results. What would he do? Yank her off the op? Was she a liability to Shield now? To everyone who worked there? Daria knew she was in a compromised position, but she hadn't asked for this. She was a victim in this whole unexpected situation, too.

Mouth quirking as she pushed through the doors and out into the bright noontime sunlight, she wasn't in any kind of mood to appreciate the blue sky above Cusco. She took a taxi to the station, wanting to catch the next train down to Aguas Calientes. Once she arrived, she walked away from the crowds to make the sat phone call. She stood by the corner of the white stone building, overlooking the ceaseless car and bicycle traffic teaming along the ancient Incan cobblestoned streets surrounding the large square plaza below.

"Jack here. Daria?"

"Yeah, it's me, Jack. I got the results on the DNA." She took a deep breath and told him what the test had revealed. Her fingers tightened around the phone as a strung-out silence met her ear.

"How are you feeling about this?" he finally asked her quietly.

"I don't honestly know, Jack. It's too early to tell. I'm not happy about it, that's for sure."

"I can't even begin to imagine," he agreed. "So? Does this compromise the op you're on? Do you want to be taken off it and have someone replace you or what?"

Her heart leaped. "You're not ordering me back?"

"No. Why should I? Only if you want to. You're developing a good cover down there. I got a call from Sergeant Kilmer last week. He's pleased with your professionalism. They feel you're very good at your job."

Relief simmered through her. Daria almost didn't dare believe her ears. "Then... you're not taking me off this op unless I want off it?"

"Yes. Look, you're a known quantity to us, Daria. You had no idea about this development. It's a genetic FUBAR and not your fault. If anything, you're the real victim in all of this mess. What I'm more concerned about is that, if Pavlovich ever lays eyes on that birthmark of yours, all hell could break loose. He's astute enough to put all the pieces together."

She tucked her lower lip between her teeth for a moment, staring out over Cusco. "I can hide it with a neckerchief, Jack. No one will see it. I'm due to go out into the village of Orilla tomorrow and I'll routinely wear it anytime I go out into the jungle. If I ever run into Pavlovich out there, he won't know I have the birthmark."

"Okay, that sounds workable. Kilmer said they're setting up an op to get Korsak. Has Nik been able to find out the name of the next village yet?"

"Yes. Orilla. I'm going out there tomorrow to meet with Señora Elisa Vega. She's the wife of the chief of that village. Korsak and his team are supposed to show up there the next day."

"You need to egress out of there before they arrive," Jack warned her.

"I will," Daria promised. She had a Glock and she carried a knife as well. She had been provided the legal permit to carry a firearm in Peru, although it was concealed so that and no one could see it was on her person. In this country, if she was found with a military firearm, she could be thrown into prison. Only the *policia* was allowed to carry weapons, as well as their SWAT teams. The coolness of a sudden breeze lifted strands of hair across her face and she pulled them away. Keeping alert, wanting no passersby to overhear the call, Daria ended it, feeling more than a little relieved that Driscoll would allow her to see this mission through. And that meant she wasn't a detriment to Shield, which gave her all the relief she so desperately needed right now.

How much she missed Nik! Tucking the phone into a plastic baggie and sealing it, she wandered down the long portico filled with tourists waiting for the next train to the jungle area at the base of Machu Picchu. Above her, the sun shone down brightly and she had on her sunglasses and baseball cap to shield herself against its heat. She stopped at a vendor, a Quechua woman with a brown felt bowler hat set jauntily on her head, and bought two dark-green neckerchiefs. Paying a lot more Peruvian soles than the asked-for price, Daria slipped one of the scarves around her neck. She made her way through the ticketed gate of the train station, found the bathroom and went in. Studying herself critically in a mirror, she saw the neckerchief did indeed hide her birthmark. Patting the soft cotton material, Daria could see it would remain in place even if it shifted around on her neck. The birthmark would remain hidden to the world at large. She couldn't even allow herself to think about Pavlovich's reaction if he ever found out about it.

Daria boarded ten minutes later and sat in the first-class car. During the ride up, the gentle rocking motion of the train soothed some of the wild emotions loose and howling within her. She sat alone at her table, a cup of freshly-brewed coffee in front of her. The train was climbing up and out of the dark-brown bowl of the valley in which Cusco sat, and heading up toward the twelve-thousand-foot point where it crested the mountains before dropping down again to sixty-five hundred feet below into Aguas Calientes, an hour ahead. She rested her head back against the dark-green leather of the seat and closed her eyes. *Nik...* Daria knew he would hold her. Give her a sense that her world was going to be all right, even if it lay shattered all around her feet right now. Never before had she felt that kind of warmth: that living protection that he invisibly bestowed upon her. If only she could see Nik, hear his voice once more, feel his strong, cherishing mouth upon hers... At some point during that thought, Daria dozed off.

NIK'S HEART LEAPED in his chest as his team walked into Orilla in the late morning and he saw her.

The clouds were lifting over the jungle, the birds singing, monkeys howling and hooting. There, near Chief Vega's hut, was Daria, sitting on a small tarp with several samples of orchids lying around her, an opened notebook in her hands. What was she doing here? His heart thudded with terror as he looked over his shoulder to see Pavlovich suddenly alert, focused on her as well. Daria was dressed in her normal jungle attire, her hair hanging in one long braid between her shoulder blades. What was new was the green neckerchief around her neck as she sorted through the orchids. Many curious children also crowded around her, watching intently what she was doing.

He saw the sudden fear in the faces of the village's Indians as he and his team appeared from out of the jungle trail. Orilla was the largest village on Korsak's circuit. It had around two-hundred inhabitants, and sat about five hundred feet above the banks of the small river flowing by it. The long oval-shaped village was smooth and flat. A number of metal tripods dotted the clearing with blackened kettles hung suspended over fires below them. Nik could smell the Quinoa cereal on the air. The nutlike flavor always had a sweet fragrance to it. It hurt him to see the children suddenly start running as his team moved into the village proper, dashing behind their mothers' long, colorful skirts. Dogs didn't even bark. They ran and hid, too.

What was Daria doing here? She'd known they were arriving soon, but they were a day early. Korsak had decided to push on and get to the village to rest up overnight in comfort instead of camping out and coming in tomorrow morning. He saw Daria lift her head, her eyes widening with surprise. When her gaze locked on his, he could do or say nothing. His team knew she was his woman, and that should protect her. But Pavlovich and his men were another question mark. If only Daria weren't here! She was at risk! His hand tightened around the shoulder straps of his ruck. He saw so much in her expression for that fleeting second. This was a hot mess.

Turning, he looked at Korsak behind him. "My woman is here. Unless you have other things for me to do right now, I'm going to see her." He couldn't just peel off and leave without an explanation. Korsak made all the final decisions.

Ustin grinned. "Well, well, this is new, Morozov." He shrugged. "You know where your hut is at. Invite her in with you. I'm sure we won't be seeing much of either of you."

Relief tunneled through Nik. He nodded and walked to the right, heading to where Daria was standing, her gaze never leaving his. He heard Brudin snickering and ignored the bastard. Korsak had his hands full with Pavlovich and his men, and was probably glad to be rid of him for a while, anyway. As he strode toward Daria, he saw questions in her widening gold-brown eyes, saw welcome and wariness in them, as she looked past him at the troop of Russians entering the village.

She wiped her hands down the sides of her green trousers as he approached.

Nik knew his team was watching. He halted a foot away from her, keeping his boots off the tarp where the orchids sat. "Why are you here?" he demanded in low voice, speaking Ukrainian. The children were not afraid of him, and came running to his side, touching his pants, his hands, tugging on him, pleading for him to give them the candy that he always carried in his pockets.

"I didn't know you were coming in today," she said, frowning. "I thought you were supposed to arrive tomorrow morning?"

"Korsak changed his mind." He looked over his shoulder and saw the men heading down one side of the village. They had huts at the other end, empty and waiting for them. Turning, he reached out, sliding his hand along her jaw. "Make this look good?" and he stepped forward, leaning down, taking her mouth before she could reply. The moment his mouth met her warm, lush lips, all the terror dissolved and his world anchored hotly around Daria. He felt her arms go around his neck, drawing him close, eagerly kissing him in return. This wasn't play-acting, this was real, and he groaned in pleasure as she hungrily returned his kiss. For just this stolen moment, Nik inhaled the fragrance of the orchids she'd gathered, and the scents clinging to her black, shining hair. Her fingers caressed the nape of his neck, his flesh tingling wildly there, recalling its memory of her scalding, teasing touch. Finally, he eased back from her wet lips, studying her from beneath his short, thick lashes. The love he saw shining in her eyes was real.

"The last two weeks have been a special hell," he growled, caressing her hair, her shoulder, and finally sliding his fingers down her arm to her hand, holding it. He glanced toward the team. Nik saw the women hurrying their young daughters inside their thatched huts, afraid that one of Korsak's men would grab one and rape her. He saw Pavlovich standing, hands on hips, looking imperiously around, as if he owned this village and its innocent inhabitants.

"I know," she whispered unsteadily, placing her free hand on his chest, searching his eyes. "I'm sorry I'm here. I didn't know. Should I leave?"

He shook his head. "No. That will rouse their suspicions." He slid his arm around her waist, bringing her against him as he pointed to a lone hut at the other end of the village from where the team stayed. "Señora Vega has a special hut for me over there. I hold a medical clinic there when I'm in town, and it's larger than the others. That's where we'll stay." He gave her a heated look. "Tonight, you're mine."

Daria leaned into Nik, absorbing the feel of his arm around her shoulders drawing her against him. She felt his worry, felt his protectiveness, as they stood together. "What should I do in the meantime?"

"I'll take you to meet Pavlovich to dispel any issues that might come up later regarding you. I'm sure Korsak has told him you're my woman." His mouth thinned as he studied her. "What's wrong?" He saw sudden pain in her eyes and her soft mouth pursing up.

"Nik," she choked out quietly, holding his gaze, "the DNA test results came back. I'm a long-lost relative of his."

Feeling as if someone had slammed him in the chest, Nik's arm tightened around her. "God… I'm so sorry, Kitten…," and he leaned over, pressing a kiss to her hair, wanting somehow to take away the anguish and shame he saw in her face.

"That's why I'm wearing this neckerchief. It hides my birthmark."

"Good plan," he said, relieved. He turned and smiled weakly at the children surrounding him, begging him in Quechua for sweets. "Listen, just stay here for a moment? I want to give the children their candy." He saw her eyes grow tender and she nodded.

It gave Nik time to think as he dug into his cargo pants' thigh pocket and drew out a handful of hard candy all wrapped in bright, colorful foil. He knew the children were deathly afraid of their team and with good reason. But these five boys and two little girls were braving the situation, their tiny hands held upward toward him, their faces smiling because he was the only one they trusted out of the team.

Daria stood back, collecting her orchids and putting them delicately into paper sacks. Picking up the tarp, she shook it out and carefully folded and packed it into her open ruck. After he gave the kids their candy, they ran to their respective huts, their treasures clenched in their tiny fists.

"Come," he urged Daria, picking up her ruck and shouldering it for her. He slid his arm around her waist and brought her in step with him, heading in the opposite direction from the Russian team.

Daria moved out with him, her legs long and almost able to keep up with his stride. She saw the tension in Nik's face, the worry deep in his eyes as they walked. "Listen, Kilmer and his men are here, around the village and in place, in case they can nab Korsak."

"That's good," Nik said, taking in a ragged breath. "Do you know where?"

"Yes, near where the Russians stay. That end of the village. When I received the note you left at Flor last week with Señora Chavez, I called Kilmer's team on the sat phone. They've been scouting out this village and the surrounding area since then. They need egress routes because, if they're able to snatch Korsak, they're gonna have to get the hell out of Dodge. I don't know how Pavlovich will react. Or what his guards will do."

Eyes hardening, Nik drew her to the left where a large thatched hut sat apart from the rest of the village. He slowed, releasing her. "Let's get inside. Korsak isn't going to expect me to introduce you immediately. We'll talk quietly inside."

They slipped into the airy hut. There were three large windows with their lids propped open to allow sluggish jungle breezes entry. Removing her black baseball cap, Daria saw that the interior of the rough structure consisted of three large rooms. The largest one had a rusted gurney in one corner. That was where Nik probably saw his patients.

"In here," Nik murmured, motioning down the short hall to a room on the right. He pushed the door open, revealing a room where fresh leaves had been brought in, and a blanket thrown over them, to create a makeshift bed. He slipped in, dropping her ruck on one side of the doorway, and setting down his own right up against it.

Daria stood, looking around for egress points. The windows were large enough to slip out of, if necessary. She saw the grimness in Nik's face. "I'm sure Mace Kilmer is probably stressing out over this FUBAR too."

"More than likely," he muttered. "What is their plan?"

"They're going to wait to see which hut Korsak is in. If he goes out to do his business in the jungle, they'll be waiting for him. They're going to have to hope for a break, Nik."

"With Pavlovich here, he's a good distraction." He rubbed his jaw, thinking. "It's going to be dicey, Daria. No matter what happens."

"What do you think Pavlovich and his men will do if Korsak suddenly disappears?"

"I don't know. They know nothing of this area. They are unfamiliar with it."

"Who's second in command of the team? Brudin?"

Making a sour face, Nik nodded. "Yes. He's a loose cannon. He doesn't think clearly when things go wrong. He starts screaming and shouting."

"That's good for Mace and his team."

"Precisely. Brudin *is* a distraction."

"Do we need to go make introductions?" She saw his face go hard, his eyes flash with concern. Reaching out, she slid her fingers down his arm. He'd rolled up the sleeves of his dark-green shirt to just below his elbows. His lean forearms gleamed with the sweat that highlighted their ropy muscles, hinting at the strength he possessed.

"Yes, unfortunately." He peered intently at her. Nik touched her cheek with his thumb. "Are you SURE you can handle meeting your relative?"

"I have to," she said. "Let's just get it over with? I want to get as far away from that sick bastard as I can."

A slight smile tugged at one corner of his mouth. "Tonight, we are here, alone. With one another. That is the gift I am waiting for, *moya kotya.*"

She stepped up to Nik, framing his face with her hands, feeling the stubble of beard against her palms. She knew, when they were out in the jungle, men allowed their beards to grow out. On Nik, the short, prickly shadow made his face look even more rugged. She met his mouth, cherishing it with her lips, wanting to give something back to him, knowing the pressure he was under. She wanted to whisper, "*I love you*", but the words stuck in her throat as she broke away from the kiss. His eyes had darkened and she sensed his urgent need for her. Fire ignited in her lower body and her breasts tightened beneath his intent inspection. There was a predatory look in his eyes, one that sent heated signals throughout her. She knew that look. Knew what it meant. And her lips parted.

Nik groaned. "Come, if we don't leave soon, I am going to take you here and now…"

"Let's go," she urged softly, pushing him out the doorway, giving him a teasing look. Following Nik out of the hut, she settled her cap back onto her head. He caught her hand, keeping her close, cutting his stride as he took her down the center of the village.

When Daria had first arrived, it had been an active village with dogs, kids and mothers out and about. The men had been sitting by their huts, smoking or cleaning their hunting gear, readying themselves to go out into the jungle to hunt wild pig. Now, it was practically a ghost town. The cooking pots hung with no one in attendance. The dogs had disappeared along with the children and women. Her heart squeezed over the terror that this team had brought down upon these otherwise happy, hardworking people. They had welcomed her with open arms. Now, it was eerily quiet and she felt the palpable tension surround her.

Daria tried to brace herself to meet her relative. Nervously, she tugged at her neckerchief, wanting to make sure it was in place to hide her birthmark. It was. Up ahead, she saw Pavlovich talking with Korsak. The drug lord's guards were nowhere to be seen and neither was the rest of the team. They were probably in their huts, resting up, drinking water and grabbing some food from their rucks. She took a deep breath as Nik slowed their approach to the pair.

When Pavlovich raised his head, his eyes narrowing upon Daria, she felt her stomach twist and tighten. It shocked her how much they had in common, from their gold-brown eyes to their black hair and same general shape of their faces. Her heart felt as if someone were ripping it open. Daria didn't have his mouth, which was thin, or that jutting chin that spoke clearly of his pitbull demeanor. His eyes were not wide-set like hers were, either. There was only the slightest slant to his eyes, unlike the definitive tilt of her own. He lifted his chin, surveying her, and she felt like a prize horse beneath his inspection. Worse, as Nik halted in front of them to introduce her, she felt a coldness wrapping around her. His eyes, although her color, were flat. Lifeless. As if he had no soul. A frisson of fear jagged through Daria as she forced herself to give them both a weak smile.

"Don Pavlovich, please meet Daria McClusky. She's an orchid botanist, down here to do research and write a book about them."

Rolan smiled warmly and offered his hand. "This is quite a nice surprise, Ms. McClusky. It's an honor to meet you," and she shook his hand.

Daria nodded. "Thank you, Don Pavlovich." She looked up toward Nik. "I don't know who was more surprised, me or Nik. I hadn't expected to see him for goodness-knows how long. He told me that your team was hunting for minerals, and he wasn't sure when he'd get back to Aguas Calientes."

"Hmmm, rightly so," Rolan murmured, giving Korsak an amused look. "Well, we must take advantage of your beautiful presence. I'm sure my team boss can find room to invite you to dinner with us tonight."

Daria shook her head. "I'm sorry, but I've got a touch of something, maybe food poisoning, and I'd like to just rest in my hut. If you don't mind?"

Rolan frowned. "Are you leaving, then?"

"No," Daria said. "I'm hoping by morning I feel better. And I'll be leaving after breakfast with my new orchids. I'll be heading back to Aguas Calientes with them. Once there, I will create botanical drawings of each of them."

"Well," Rolan said smoothly, "perhaps when I return there, I will look you up?" And then he stared over at Nik. "Merely a social courtesy, of course."

Daria slipped her hand into Nik's. "Of course. I'm open for lunch if I happen to be in town."

Pavlovich arched an eyebrow. A silence spun out before he finally gave a nod. "I hope you feel better. You do know that Morozov is a medic?"

"Yes. I've already asked him for something to help my symptoms." Daria gestured down the village toward their hut. "Now that we're done with introductions, I'm going back to lay down. If you'll excuse me?"

Nik released her hand and watched her walk away. Turning, he saw Pavlovich watching Daria closely and he wanted to step over and tell the Don that she wasn't to be pursued by him. But Nik said nothing. It had become clear to him that the new mafia leader wanted to understand the pattern of this team, the stops, and get to know the Indians and meet the chief of every village. Pavlovich was initiating a very different campaign to the one Korsak had been running. He always sat at dinner with each chief and their family, and through his own interpretation skills, promised them he was bringing them food, aid and more medicine. Korsak had sat through those dinners grim and unresponsive, but Nik had felt the rage vibrating through the black ops soldier. His days of raping were over, it appeared. Nik almost liked Pavlovich because of that alone, but he couldn't say anything to anyone.

"Go and be with your lady," Rolan said equitably. "You're very lucky to have snagged her, Morozov."

"I think so, too," he told the Don. He turned to Korsak and said, "I'm going to hold a clinic later after she's bedded down and resting. Is that all right with you?"

"I don't care," Korsak muttered. "Do what you want."

Pavlovich smiled a little, appearing thoughtful. "You've done some good work here in the last five years with the villagers, Morozov. I saw the little children around you earlier when we first came into the village. That's always a good sign. The team bringing good will to the village is always a plus. Makes them want to help us even more."

"I always have candy on me," Nik said, grinning. "They know it, too."

"I like your style of getting the villagers to trust you. I believe in winning hearts and minds because they'll work for us, not against us. These people need medicine and you're here doing just that. You've held a clinic in every other village we were at, and I can see how the people love and respect you." And then he grimaced. "At least they don't run away from you, Morozov. They run toward you." He frowned, looking pointedly over at Korsak.

"Have you noticed, Korsak? Everyone is hiding when your team comes into a village? Even the dogs go running away. They won't even bark at you. The inhabitants have done this at every village we have come to. They're afraid of your team, with the exception of Morozov, here. When I return to Aguas Calientes, I'm going to create a protocol for you and your team to follow that is very different from the way you've been dealing in the past with these Indians. We need not only their goodwill, but I want their hearts bent on collecting the cocoa leaves and making cocaine from them for us. Give them more food, health and medical services. Kindness, not threats."

Korsak lifted his upper lip and said, "You'll make them lazy, Don Pavlovich."

"What do you think, Morozov? Is he right?"

The last thing Nik wanted to do is get between these two men. "I know all the people of the villages could use a dentist out here. An eye doctor, too. If you could pay for someone to come from Cusco, meet us at the villages, and come in once a month to help, that would go a long way toward getting the Quechua to appreciate your generosity. They are a hardworking people, and giving them back their health would be a very positive step."

Nik wasn't about to speak up and damn Korsak. He wasn't so sure the angry Russian wouldn't take out his pistol and put a bullet in his head even though Pavlovich was standing right there next to him. Better to be diplomatic. But he saw something in the mafia leader's expression, a gleam in his eyes that told Nik the man was onto Korsak's violent, abusive ways with the villagers. If nothing else, if the tense, distrustful environment between the teams and villages changed under Pavlovich's reign, that would come as a huge relief to Nik. No more little girls or young women would be raped by these predatory bastards. That was a miracle Nik had never expected, and his opinion of the mafia leader grew greatly as a result.

CHAPTER 18

Daria was walking down the center of the village toward their hut, when shots suddenly rang out through the air. She gasped, automatically crouching. She had no weapons on her! She turned in Nik's direction, terror in her expression. He was running toward her, his face hard.

Nik cursed, gripping her arm, yanking her toward the hut.

Screams of women and children filled the air.

Curses in Russian exploded along with AK-47 fire as Korsak's team rallied against the attack, firing back down the path leading into the village.

"Diego Valdez's men!" Nik yelled, shoving Daria into the hut. He lunged for the weapons beside his medical ruck.

Daria let out an 'ooooff' as she hit the dirt floor. She heard bullets tearing through their hut, whizzing barely above her head. "Give me my pistol!" she yelled, holding out her hand.

Nik crouched low, AK-47 in his right hand, jerking open the ruck, tossing her the Glock.

"It's loaded, bullet in the chamber. Stay here!" he yelled, twisting around, leaving the hut and disappearing.

Coolness flowed through Daria. She was a sniper in full control of her emotions as she took the safety off the Glock and rolled back onto her stomach. She heard shouts, screams and terror among the villagers. Breathing hard, she scrambled forward on her stomach toward the door. More bullets ripped through the hut, the dried reeds that made up its walls exploding, creating clouds of dust, making it hard for her to see. She had no Kevlar vest on to protect her. She elbow-crawled out through the doorway, and headed toward the corner of the hut to try and get a bead on the rival drug lord's soldiers.

How many of them were there? Daria had no answer, not familiar with the two Latin drug lords who were actively fighting this Russian intrusion into their cocaine territory. She had no idea how large a force was attacking the village. Her mind narrowed and focused as she saw at least thirty men in jungle cammo, armed with AK-47s, pouring into the clearing, firing wildly and indiscriminately. That was too bad for them she thought, her mouth flexing, her eyes slits as she placed both hands on the Glock and began to pick her targets.

Daria knew the ex-Spetsnaz black ops soldiers would be as lethal as she was. They never sprayed and prayed. They picked a target and fired in brief, concentrated bursts. She heard the deep chatter of AK-47s behind her, knowing it was the Russians returning fire. They were out in the open, vulnerable, with nowhere to hide. Thatched huts provided absolutely no protection at all. In a small corner of her mind, she was grateful Nik had his Kevlar vest on. It wasn't a Level 4, only a Level 2, but it would give him protection. It was better than nothing. She didn't see Pavlovich wearing one at all, although his two guards did. How she wished she had hers on right now!

The Latin soldiers were all dressed differently from one another. There was no single, focused plan of attack as they ran helter-skelter through the village. The air was alive with the singing and humming of bullets being fired all around her. Her mind worked like a trap snapping shut, her full focus only on the nearest man, who'd spotted her on her belly near the hut, racing toward her, firing at her.

She heard screams behind her. *Men. Russians?* Daria didn't know and wasn't going to risk turning to find out. God, don't let it be Nik! A tiny part of her slow-beating heart cringed. *Please, don't die! Don't die! I just found you, Nik!* Sweat ran down her face, stinging her eyes and she continued to slow fire, her hand bucking savagely from the massive kick of the powerful Glock. It was a pistol that took humans down with one shot, which is why so many operators used the weapon. She had one herself, but it was back in Virginia, in the Shield armory locker.

All other sounds were blotted out. Daria winced as a bullet exploded in front of her, six inches from her face. She closed her eyes, dirt flying around her. That was close! Mouth set tight; she opened her eyes. They were blurry from the dust in them. Making a frustrated sound, she jerked her hand up, wiping them quickly, before returning it to grip the butt of the pistol.

More bullets peppered her position.

She felt a sting and then numbness in her upper right arm, ignoring it. Firing, the roar of the Glock blowing her hearing, she saw her attacker and fired back. In one shot, he was down and out of the fight. Daria realized she was at the point of the spear. Her and Nik's hut was the nearest to where the jungle path opened out into the village behind her. She saw more and more soldiers begin to spot her and send a hail of fire into her position.

She heard Russian boots thudding up behind her. And then, the soldiers landed on their bellies on either side of her, slow-firing their AK-47's, giving her support. Daria didn't look to see who they were. Rather, she remained concentrated on slowing down the hoard of Latin soldiers trying to overrun her position. The man who fell next to her grunted. She was peripherally aware of his AK-47 flying out of his hands, a bullet taking him out. Jerking a look, she saw it was Korsak. Blood was streaming from his chest. He lay gasping, his arms flailing. Next to him was Brudin, who was firing back. Next to him was Nik. They were all wounded, some more so than others, herself included.

Glancing quickly at her right arm, Daria saw blood was running down it and dripping off into the soil. Ignoring it, feeling no pain, Daria knew no nerves had been cut or her fingers wouldn't be working so well as she gripped down on the Glock and kept firing it. She heard movement to her right, but did not look. She sensed that Nik had gotten up and raced past her for the medical ruck. She knew he was going to try and save Korsak's life. The bleeding Russian leader was now gasping like a fish out of water beside her. There was nothing she could do to help him. If she and Brudin didn't continue to fire, the force closing in on their position would overrun and kill all of them. There wasn't a choice. Her hand bucked again and again.

Daria sensed Nik drop back down beside her and crouch over Korsak. She saw around a dozen of Valdez's soldiers suddenly halt as orders roared out in Spanish from somewhere out of sight beyond the curve in the path that led into the village. Suddenly, the men turned on their heels and ran, sprinting for cover, ducking and weaving every which way from rounds still snapping around them, before disappearing around the bend.

"They're gone!" Brudin snarled, getting to his feet, glaring down the empty path. "Yellow, cowardly bastards!"

Daria stood and turned, seeing the carnage left behind in the wake of the firefight. At her feet, Nik worked frantically to stop the bleeding from Korsak's chest. It was a sucking chest wound through the man's lung, and she knew it could kill him. Nik placed a square patch of adhesive foil over the bullet wound and Korsak stopped gasping as much. Her heart beat was slow and steady. There, fallen in the midst of the barren land between the village and the jungle, lay Rolan Pavlovich and his two guards. None of them moved where they lay crumpled in a heap. Each had been riddled through and through. A lump formed in her throat. She saw Duboff laying on his side near another hut, wounded but alive. Kravec lay unmoving nearby, dead.

"Nik? Pavlovich is down," she managed in a torn whisper.

"They're dead," he said in low, guttural tone, focused on Korsak. "I'm sorry..."

"Are you sure?" she demanded, starting to run toward them, Glock still in hand.

Daria didn't wait to hear Nik's grunted rejoinder. She was aware of villagers cautiously peeking out of their huts, their eyes all wide with terror and locked on that bend in the path. Would the drug soldiers come back around it and attack the village again? She didn't know. Tucking the Glock into the waist of her jeans, she leaned down over the mafia boss. His body was twisted and he lay on his back, his eyes open and unseeing. He wore no protective vest, the red blossoms of four bullet holes stitched across his chest and stomach. Swallowing hard, Daria knelt down, and pressed her trembling fingers against the exposed column of his neck. Flashes of her own past overrode her eyes and she shut them, feeling no pulse on Pavlovich's neck. She winced, reopened her eyes, and saw the half-moon birthmark on the side of it.

He was dead, just as Nik had said.

Tears trailing down her dirty cheeks, she went over to the two security guards. Both had died of head wounds. Someone in that drug team had been either a lucky or damned good shot.

Next, she went over to Duboff who was slowly sitting up, gripping his arm, blood leaking out between his fingers. He stared darkly up at her, but said nothing. Daria saw the question in his eyes as she approached him. Who was she really? How did a botanist know how to shoot that well?

"Morozov will be here when he can," she told him.

Duboff nodded, his gaze following her as she picked up the two AK-47s from Pavlovich's dead guards and slung them over her shoulders. She went into the hut and dug through the men's packs, grabbing a heavy leather bag of AK-47 magazines out of one of them. They might need these fully-loaded magazines, should Valdez's group decide to come back and finish them all off. Glancing warily at the still empty path, she didn't know what to expect from Valdez's soldiers. Would they regroup and then attack again? Lifting her head, she saw Nik and Brudin working as a team over Korsak. She wasn't sure if the Russian would make it or not.

Walking quickly back over, she positioned herself near them, keeping her focus and attention on the path. "Duboff has an arm wound. He's okay but needs your help when you can give it to him."

Nik nodded. "In a minute. Kravec?"

"Dead. So are the two guards with Pavlovich."

Nik nodded, working quickly, rummaging around in his medical ruck.

"Will they come back? Do you know?" she asked Nik in a low voice.

"They might," he grunted. "Brudin, get the sat phone. Make a call to that Russian helo in Aguas Calientes. Get it up here right now. If we don't get Korsak to the Cusco hospital within the next two hours, he's going to die."

Brudin, for once, didn't argue with him and got up, jogging quickly back toward his hut.

"Nik?"

"Yes?"

She heard the hard, clipped tone in his voice. Her gaze moved slowly around the path's opening in the jungle wall, looking for any movement that could mean a second attack from Valdez's men. "What are we going to do now?"

"Get the hell out of here as soon as possible. Korsak is stable for now."

"What's Valdez's MO? What is he likely to do next?"

Snorting, Nik growled, "We've taken out twelve of his men. This is the heaviest pitched battle we've had with them in five years. I don't think he wants to waste his soldiers against us again. He's probably gone, running back down that path to a fork that can lead either up to the Highlands or further down another jungle trail."

"He won't attack again?"

"No. Highly unlikely."

The men scattered motionless across the ground in front of them did not move. Daria knew that when black ops soldiers got into a battle, they went for head or center-mass shots and they did not miss. And when they fired, it was to kill, not maim or wound. She quickly and thoroughly perused each of the soldiers lying like broken rag dolls between them and the jungle wall. Not one of them moved. She would bet they were all dead, but didn't want to take that risk. She rose slowly to her feet, taking an AK-47 with her along with the tucked-in Glock.

"Where are you going?" Nik demanded, suddenly reaching out, grabbing her wrist, stopping her.

Daria looked down at Nik. His face was a hard mask, his blue eyes so pale they almost had no color. "Checking the bodies. I don't want one of them to rise up and shoot one of us in the back later."

He released her. Quickly, he jerked the vest off himself, handing it to her.

"Put it on?"

Grateful, she nodded, set her weapons down and slipped into the overly-large vest. It hung on her much roomier than she was used to, but she was glad to have it all the same. Daria saw so much in Nik's eyes, but he said nothing else, returning to sliding an IV into Korsak's arm. She felt his anguish and worry for her. No one was left unwounded. Nik's face was dirty, bloody, and she also saw blood on his left forearm where he'd taken a grazing bullet. As Brudin had limped away, she'd seen blood spreading slowly down his left calf, staining through his cammos. Her gaze fell to Korsak, now unconscious. Picking up the weapons, keeping an eye on the path, silence settled around her.

Daria was vaguely aware of the sobbing of some women far behind her as she checked every dead soldier thoroughly and carefully, removing weapons and any identification she could find on them as she went. It was grisly work, but it had to be done. Daria could still feel the high from the adrenaline that had punched her system into high gear. Somewhere down the road, she knew she'd crash from it. But not right now.

After making sure all twelve men were dead, she walked silently toward the path. Taking the AK-47 off her shoulder, she held it at the ready, its selector on semi-auto. She saw the muddy imprints of many boots down the path as she warily followed it around the bend, not knowing what to expect. The silence was as heavy as the humidity that drenched her body, dampening her clothes, making them stick to her. Above her, she heard the plop, plop, plop of water condensing at the highest peaks of the jungle canopy and slowly dripping downward from one leaf to another.

Wanting to make sure Valdez and his men weren't coming back, Daria followed the path for more than half a mile until the point where it forked. She saw a lot of muddy boot imprints leading downward, toward the Machu Picchu area. By the time she'd turned back a mile further down the boot-printed trail and returned to the village, lot of the natives had begun to slowly come out of their huts. They had to be scared out of their minds. Daria wondered if any of them were wounded. She saw Brudin kneeling by the unconscious Korsak, the butt of his AK-47 planted on his thigh, his scowl on her.

"They've left," she told Brudin.

He eyed her, distrust in his expression. Daria could see him silently questioning who the hell she really was. She carried her own AK-47 planted against her hip, muzzle up. The position told Brudin a whole lot, and he looked confused by her. To carry a rifle in that position meant she expected trouble. Only a black ops soldier would know that. And she was supposed to be a botanist. Daria wasn't going to fill in the missing pieces for him anytime soon. Her gaze dropped to Korsak.

"How he is doing?" she demanded of Brudin.

"Stable. Morozov just checked him." Brudin hitched a thumb behind his shoulder. "He's taking care of Duboff right now."

"What about the rest of the villagers?" she demanded, lifting her chin, her gaze moving across the people standing shaken by the attack.

"I don't know," he grunted. "I don't care."

Daria nodded, seeing Nik working over Duboff, creating a sling for his wounded arm. She was more worried about the villagers and headed toward the chief's house. Placing the AK-47 in the chest harness she'd picked up from one of the dead security guards, Daria safed it and pointed the muzzle downward, meaning she didn't expect an attack. The terror in the eyes of the Indians tore at her as she walked through their folds. The children hid behind their mothers' skirts, eyes huge and afraid. The men were grim. The women were badly shaken, some of them still sobbing. She quickly found Chief Vega. He had his arms around his two young sons. Speaking to him in Spanish, she asked him if there were casualties.

He shook his head.

That was a miracle in itself, Daria thought, trying to manage a smile for the children who clung to her, their thin arms grasping at her hips and legs. She grazed her hand across their shining black hair and murmured to them that everything was going to be all right. It wasn't. But the children needed that calming support. None of the Indians looked at all well. Daria understood their fear as never before. There were two major South American factions warring for the cocaine in Peru's Highlands. Two drug lords: Valdez from La Paz, Bolivia, and his nemeses, Marco Suero from Lima, Peru, had ruled this region long before the Russians had intruded in on their territory five years earlier. Both were billionaires. Both had raised mercenary armies to take over the cocaine trade in this region. Until the Russian invasion had come along. And, according to her brief from Jack Driscoll, these villages were always being captured or recaptured. Either by the Latin drug lords or, in this case, Korsak and his Russian team. Now, the tables had been turned once again.

Daria held the six children who clung to her within her arms. She understood the grip of utter fear that these Indians lived with daily. They had chewed coca leaves before climbs up into the Highlands for centuries. To stop the altitude sickness that always came with such high elevation. But, now that cocaine was a thing, their whole world had been turned upside down into an ongoing nightmare that had no end. As Daria lifted her chin, her gaze fixed on Nik helping Duboff stand and make it over to where Korsak and Brudin were recuperating, she felt deeply for the village's endless plight. How any of them had escaped being killed by the massive wave of bullets fired into the area by Valdez's men, she didn't know. One thing for sure, Valdez's soldiers were intent on killing everyone on the Russian team.

She wondered where Killmer and his men were hiding. Having no idea, and understanding they did not want to reveal themselves to this Russian team, Daria assumed that they had probably faded away into the embrace of the jungle, never seen, never detected. Mace and his team were probably just as surprised by the attack as they had been. Daria didn't know the full history of the various drug lords' war with each other. She squeezed the children's shoulders, murmuring words of comfort, placed a kiss on each of their heads and urged them to go back to their parents. Turning, she apologized to the chief and his wife Elisa, asking if they would bury the dead. The chief said they would. Daria thanked them and left.

As she walked by Pavlovich, his skin now graying, her heart tugged in her chest. Tears burned in her eyes. Halting, Daria stared down at the man, eyes focused again on the quarter-moon birthmark on the side of his neck. She felt numb inside, not grief-stricken. And maybe, she supposed, that is the way it should be. Taking out her cell phone, she took a picture of his face, and then one of the birthmark. This was a part of her family history whether she wanted it to be or not. A heaviness entered her chest and she tucked the phone away, slowly walking over toward Nik and the remnants of his team.

Brudin looked up at her, his eyes feral. "Who are you?" he growled in Russian.

Nik, having just sat Duboff down, lifted his head, his gaze pinned on her.

"Just a botanist," Daria replied coolly, stepping out in front of the little band. She studied the path, never dropping her guard. Valdez could always change his mind and come back.

"Like hell you are," Brudin snarled.

Nik got up from Duboff's side, stepped over, and knelt down by Korsak. He pulled the stethoscope from around his neck and listened to the man's heart and lungs in turn.

Daria ignored the shaken Brudin, saying nothing. Her hands were at her sides, but the Glock was in her waistband, and the AK-47 hung from her chest harness, each ready to use if necessary.

Nik looked at his watch. "That helo should arrive in another fifteen minutes. Let's get the wounded to the tree line over there," and he pointed toward it. "The helo has enough room to land there, just outside the village."

Daria watched Brudin get up. He limped, his mouth tight, eyes blazing with rage as he and Nik carried Korsak to the impromptu LZ. They came back and Brudin hauled Duboff upright, helping his teammate to his feet.

Nik stood, hands on hips, his gaze on Brudin and Duboff in the distance. Turning, he looked over at Daria. "You've got a graze on your arm," he said, his fingers gently moving around the bloody area. "Let me take care of you now?"

His touch was calming. Daria nodded. "Triage! Stat!" and she gave him a cutting, lopsided smile.

"Yes," he murmured, helping her sit down next to his ruck. He donned a new pair of latex gloves, producing a bottle of sterile water and a large, clean white gauze pad, quickly cleaning the area around the wound with them. Daria sat positioning herself so that she could keep one eye on the path and the other on the Russians.

She absorbed Nik's nearness, his quiet, calming strength as he cleansed the wound. It stung and she grimaced, but didn't flinch away from his ministrations. "What now?" she asked him in a low voice.

"I'm going to get Korsak to the Cusco hospital. They'll take him in for surgery," he said grimly.

"Will he live?"

"I hope so. It's going to be close."

"If he does?" and she lifted her head, studying his blood-speckled face, his features dirty and sweaty.

"Then," he rasped, quickly patching up the graze and placing a waterproof bandage around her arm, "we have to move quickly. I need you, once we get to the hospital, to peel off and make a call on your sat phone to Jack. This is our chance to snatch Korsak right out of that hospital, if he makes it through surgery. A US Nightstalker medevac helo that I know is based down in Lima could get him out of here and into CIA hands. We could get him to the States. Peru allows the US to have a few military aircraft within their sovereign territory. I know there's a medevac on standby down there because of the Special Forces teams in this area. I'm sure Jack can get the CIA to release it to us to fly Korsak out of here and back stateside."

Daria saw the grim determination in Nik's features and replied, "If he lives, and we can get him out of here, Dan and you will have political asylum." She saw his gaze falter for a moment, saw the wash of emotions clearly in his eyes, his game face slipping. They'd been through so much, and Daria recognized the reaction for what it was: adrenaline crash. It exhausted a person suddenly, without warning. It allowed all the withheld emotions to vomit up like a volcano through them and release. It totaled them physically, mentally and emotionally, and only a good night's sleep would help them recover their previous strength the next day.

"Yes." He released her arm. "Do you want a sling?"

Shaking her head, she said, "No, I want my hands free and available." Her voice lowered. "Brudin's suspicious."

"I know he is," Nik agreed wearily, repacking his ruck and closing it. He stood, pulling it over his shoulders. He held his hand out down to her. Daria took it and he pulled her to her feet.

"What do you think he'll do?" she asked.

"I don't know. He's the wild card." Nik gave her a concerned look. "We maintain our cover."

She smiled a little, sliding her arm around his waist for a moment. All Daria wanted to do was move into his arms and feel safe. None of that was possible right now. "Well, one thing he does know," she said with a chuckle as they began to walk toward the treeline.

"What's that?"

"That I'm on your side. I wasn't firing at the Russian team," and she gave him an enigmatic look, grinning.

Nik gave her a tired grin in return. "Yes, he'll figure that much out. But whatever you do? Once we land at the Cusco hospital? Get away from all of us. Go make that call. I'll meet you in the ER unit downstairs, afterward. Brudin is going to have to have surgery on that leg of his. He's probably gotten one of the bones fractured and that means they'll keep him in the hospital."

"You and I can leave the hospital," Daria agreed.

"Duboff will be staying in the hospital as well." Nik studied her briefly. "We can use the Russian apartment that Korsak leased. No one else will be there but us. We can talk and make further plans there." His mouth flattened, his eyes growing anxious. "Korsak *has* to survive."

Daria wanted to hold Nik in that moment, to give him assurance, but she could do neither. "He'll live. He has you as his medic. You're the best," and she meant those words as never before. Now that she'd seen Nik operate under combat conditions, she knew how able he still was to help save lives. This knowledge did nothing but make her love him even more. She was starting to climb down off her adrenaline high, too, her emotions raw and more on tap.

"God," he muttered, shaking his head, "I hope so. Everything… *everything* hangs on Korsak living…"

Daria felt sorry for Nik, saw the angst in his stormy blue eyes, heard the thick emotions in his lowered voice. How badly she wanted to hold him. Give him a sense of safety he'd never known ever since Dan had been wounded. She found his hand, dirty and bloody as it was, and gave it a quick, firm squeeze.

"Look, let's just take this an hour at a time," she counseled him, holding his exhausted gaze. "Together. I'm here for you, Nik."

He gave her a warm, intense look. "You are so very brave, *moya kotya*. Today, you showed your jaguar side. I watched you in combat. It's not something I ever want to see again because I feared for your life." He reached out, grazing her cheek briefly. "We have so much to talk with one another about after things calm down and get sorted out."

Swallowing hard, Daria felt her fierce love for Nik suddenly rise and flood her chest, making her heart pound with yearning only for him. "I was worried for you, not myself."

He snorted and gave a rueful shake of his head. "You really are a sniper at heart."

Daria couldn't say anything else as they walked within earshot of the Russian team. In the distance, she could hear the thick chopping noise of a helicopter coming their way. Soon, they would be out of here, flying Korsak and the rest of the wounded team back to Cusco. She stood near Nik while Brudin studied her beneath his drawn brow, his eyes hard with distrust. She was glad she had weapons on her, although, right now, she didn't think Brudin was going to do much of anything. Korsak was his friend and he'd been with him for two years, so his main focus was on him, not her. Still, Daria did not trust the Russian bastard at all. There were equal measures of malevolence, censure and suspicion in the man's eyes, all aimed at herself and Nik.

Glad that she had the sat phone the Russian team didn't know about, Daria was going to make sure that she was the first one off that Russian helicopter once it landed. If Brudin thought he could capture or accost her for his own brand of interrogation, even given his leg wound, she wasn't going to allow him the opportunity. She would leave her weapons on board the helo. To walk even a single step with them on civilized Peruvian soil would be foolhardy. The *policia* would descend upon her and throw her in prison, permanently. She knew the Russians would also leave their weapons behind once they landed in Cusco. That gave her an opportunity to escape Brudin once and for all. If she never saw his pig-like face again, it would be too soon. All Daria wanted was to see Korsak live through all of this.

Stealing a quick glance over at Nik, who monitored Korsak, kneeling at his side, she saw the set of his mouth. His expression was one of worry. What if Korsak didn't make it? What then, for Nik?

CHAPTER 19

NIK SAT TENSELY in the lobby of the surgical ward. Exhaustion gripped him, but his heart, his soul, was focused on Korsak who was presently in there under the knife. He heard a noise and looked up. Daria was there; her face unreadable. She was as dirty, bloodied and as grim looking as him. She carried her ruck over her shoulder. The tiredness in her gold-brown eyes tore at him. He could have lost her out there today. It had been so close…

She sat down near him, placing her ruck on the floor. "Anything yet?" she asked him quietly.

"No… nothing… too soon. It's going to take hours. I just don't want him to dump and his heart stop."

She pushed tendrils of hair back off her face, grimacing from the grit she felt beneath her fingertips. "What about Brudin and Kravec?"

"Both in surgery, too. I found out from the surgery nurse that Brudin has a fractured tibia in his lower leg. Kravec has a torn artery. Both should be short surgeries and they'll live, no problem." His mouth flattened and he slowly rubbed his sweaty, dirty face.

"Why don't you go back to the safe house and get cleaned up then?" Daria suggested quietly, laying her hand on his shoulder. "I'll stand watch here for you."

He pulled in a deep breath and his hands fell to his thighs. "First, tell me what your sat phone call yielded. Did you talk to Jack?"

"Yes. He patched through a call to the CIA and I talked to all of them at once. They're just as shaken up by Valdez attacking out of nowhere as we were."

"They shouldn't be," he said grimly, scowling. "It's always been a chess game between the Russians and those two Latin drug lords. It's just this time that Valdez caught us off guard. That's never happened before. The more I think about it, the more I feel that he's been planning this for a while. He never knows where we're going next, either. Wrong place, right time for him and his soldiers to take us on."

Daria nodded, moving her hand gently across his tight shoulders. "I managed to get a hold of Kilmer and his men, too."

"Bet they were as surprised as we were."

"Yes. They backed off. But, because they have silencers on their weapons, they were shooting in from back behind the tree line on our behalf."

Nik nodded. "I thought they might. They just needed to stay out of sight."

"Right. And they're all okay, no injuries."

He studied her as he placed his elbows on his opened thighs. "Has anything changed with the CIA regarding Korsak?"

"They want him alive, Nik. I pinned them down on their promise to you and Dan, to bring you into the country, giving both of you political asylum. Provided Korsak was delivered alive to them. They're initiating a C-130 Air Force flight as soon as we know if Korsak is going to survive. It will take them six hours to reach Lima, Peru. They'll authorize a Nightstalker medevac Black Hawk down there to fly up here to Cusco during the daylight hours and pick up Korsak as soon as he can be moved. If that all goes according to plan, once they have him on US soil, then you and I are going to take a flight down to Lima on a commercial jet and go home." Daria gave him a searching look, her hand coming to rest on his broken shoulder. "Home."

Shaking his head, Nik muttered darkly, "So much could go wrong, Daria. I could be stuck down here if Korsak dies on the surgery table."

"I know," she said softly, seeking and holding his worried gaze. Moving her hand across his shoulder she added, "It's a waiting game. It's not doing you any good to stay here. Go get cleaned up? Come back, and then I'll go over to the apartment and do the same."

Stiffly, he rose and offered his hand to her. "Come here," he said thickly.

Daria rose just as stiffly, her joints starting to lock up on her. She stepped into the circle of his open arms.

Nik groaned as she fitted herself against him, her head resting on his shoulder, her strong arms enclosing his waist. His future dangled on the scales of the precarious balance he'd worked years for to build. Korsak was on a surgery table fighting for his life. He nuzzled Daria's neck, inhaling her scent, kissing her softly here and there. "How are you doing? Having a relative gunned down in front of you?" He felt her quiver and knew that it had to be tearing her up inside. Daria had certainly not envisioned a drug lord for a relative.

"I'm numb right now," she muffled against his neck. "Exhausted, like you. It's going to take me... weeks... months... years... to sort out Pavlovich and the fact that we're on the same family tree."

He held her tightly, his chin resting against her mussed, dusty hair. "I know... I know, *moya kotya*. But I'm here for you. All right?" and he eased her away from him just enough to study her darkened gold eyes swimming with tears.

Daria wasn't numb. She was struggling with so much internally and she knew this wasn't the place or time to let it all out. She needed to cry.

Nik wanted to be the one who held her and soothed her while she found her way through all this unexpected shock and grief. He knew she wouldn't cry now. He'd seen her in action during the recent firefight and knew she was capable of brutally crushing her emotions in order to meet the end objective. In this case, he understood she was being brave for *him*. He was walking the edge of the sword. His whole life was up for grabs. And Nik had no idea on which side of the blade he was going to land. He saw all of his internal turmoil understood in, underlying, the expression in her eyes as she searched his own.

"Thank you for being here," Daria whispered, leaning upward, her mouth finding his.

The moment her lips slid across his, inducing warmth, chasing away the icy fear in his gut, Nik groaned, and his mouth crushed down on hers. He wanted to impart so much in that kiss with Daria. She could have died out there today. That destabilized him in equal part, as Dan not having yet received the medical help he deserved. Daria had stolen his heart quietly, gently, and now the fierce love he felt for her blossomed throughout him. Her mouth opened eagerly beneath his, alive, denying the death they'd both dodged today. Her very breath affirmed life. That special spicy scent that was simply her infused him with hope against the brutal reality that dogged his heels. And, when Daria moved her hips against his, the fire that had lain in barely smoldering coals within him, flared to life in his lower body. Loving Daria was like getting an IV infusing him with life against his death sentence here in Peru. He was so grateful she was in his life. There was so much to tell her, to share with Daria, but this wasn't the time or place to do it.

Reluctantly, he parted from her mouth, staring down into her exhausted eyes. "The apartment is nearby," he rasped, sliding his fingers across her dusty cheek. "I'll be back as soon as possible…"

THE CHANGE IN Nik upon his return was like night and day to Daria. He was clean and shaven, his hair combed, and was wearing a set of ivory chinos, and a red polo shirt that showed off his well-sprung chest. He looked even better to her as she penetrated his garments with her sniper's gaze, missing nothing. Standing, she met him at the door.

"No change. No one's come out to say anything about Korsak. They just brought out Brudin and he's in recovery right now. The nurse said he was doing fine, but he will be kept here for two days under observation."

Nik halted, cupping her jaw, placing a light kiss on her brow. "And Kravec?"

"Already out and in recovery, too. He's going to be here for three days before they release him."

"Good," he murmured, his gaze centered on her. "All good news."

"Yeah," she muttered, taking his hand, kissing and releasing it. "I asked about Korsak, but the surgery nurse said they were still working on him."

"She's not going to tell you anything," Nik murmured. He picked up her ruck, settling it on her shoulders. Handing her a piece of paper, he said, "This is the safe house. The digital combination for the front door and the apartment are here."

"Okay," she said, "I'll be back as soon as possible." Daria wanted to remain in contact with Nik, but knew she couldn't. The light burning in his blue eyes, the care, the love he held for her, was clearly there despite his fatigue. And it *was* love and Daria knew it. She gripped his fingers, squeezing them. "I'll be back…"

She found the three-story ivory stucco apartment building four blocks from the hospital. It was early evening, quitting time in Cusco, and the streets were jammed with cars trying to get home. Square plazas, all busy with foot traffic, intermingled the streets throughout the ancient pre-Inca city. Daria worried over the potential spies Valdez could have in Cusco. Did they know about the Russian's safe house in the city? She wasn't about to drop her guard. She missed her firearms, and wished she still had them on her. The knife in her ruck was her only defense should they find her and try to capture or kill her. Daria's senses were on full sniper alert, taking nothing or anyone for granted.

She worried over Nik at the hospital. If Valdez and his men had tracked him there, they could go after him, too. There was no safe ground right now. Her mind gyrated back and forth between her mafia relative's recent demise and the outcome of Nik's dilemma with Korsak, balanced as it was on the thin blade of a scalpel, and his brother Dan's future, bound by fate to the skill of that scalpel-wielding surgeon. How badly she ached for Nik to come to the US. She wanted him in Alexandria, Virginia, with her. She loved him. Her heart felt squeezed by an invisible fist, twisted, and the pain was almost too much for her to bear. Somehow, she had to stuff all her escaping emotions into a box and slam the lid shut. As she crossed a busy street, the smell of gasoline exhaust in the air, the sun sending orange shafts through the metropolis of buildings as it slanted in the west, Daria forced herself to remain alert.

She had just changed into some dry, clean clothes, a set of jeans, a pink-capped tee, when her sat phone rang. Hurrying to her ruck on the kitchen table, she punched the button, seeing that the call was from Jack Driscoll.

"We just got word Korsak is going to make it," he told her.

Jagged relief plunged through Daria. "Thank, God," she whispered, her hands tightening around the sat phone. She sat down in a chair. "How did you find out?"

"Got an undercover mole in the hospital," was all he said. "Nik will be told shortly by the surgery nurse."

Grinning, she said, "What next?"

"The CIA is initiating that C-130 to fly down two days from now. In the meantime, we want you and Nik to play guard dog for Korsak. We don't trust Valdez at all. We're sure he and the other drug lord, Suero, have spies in Cusco. You're going to have to stand guard in shifts. I've already contacted the *policia* and they are going to provide protection as well, but frankly? They aren't someone I'd trust with my grandmother, much less with someone like Korsak in the mix. There's too much graft and corruption in the ranks and I wouldn't be surprised if Valdez and Suero had their own moles inside the police department."

"I agree," she said grimly. "What about the CIA giving Nik and Dan political asylum? Have you heard anything on that front, Jack?"

"Yeah, the State Department is moving on it right now. When I know, I'll call you."

"What if Korsak suddenly dies?"

"I talked to a woman at the State Department who's tasked with bringing Dan out of Ukraine to the US. I asked her the same question. She said she has a green light on this, that Dan is going to be on a US flight out of Kyiv, Ukraine tonight, Virginia time, regardless if Korsak dies in transit or not."

She swallowed; her voice suddenly emotional. "Seriously? They're going to give Nik and Dan what they want even if Korsak suddenly goes belly-up?"

"Yes. The woman said that Nik has been exemplary in his position as a mole. He's gotten Kilmer and his men a lot of valuable intel over the past two years. It's a go, Daria. And," he chuckled a little, "given your reaction, I think there's a little something between you and this medic?"

She placed her hand over her eyes, shutting them, pushing back tears of joy. "Yes… just a little."

"You know," Jack said, irony in his tone, "Alex said it would happen."

"What would happen?"

"That you'd fall in love with Nik. He said it was inevitable. That Nik is the kind of man any woman in her right mind would fall for."

She managed a choked laugh, wiping tears from her eyes. "He's extraordinary, Jack. One of a kind."

"Well, if he's Alex's stature, then I want to speak to him about offering him a job with us."

She frowned. "He's really exhausted, Jack. This undercover work has torn him apart. It's been five years of unrelenting pressure and hell on him. I mean, I don't know what he'll do or say to you about a job offer. Please don't push him right away on that angle? He needs serious decompression first."

"Well, I kinda thought, given the circumstances, he could come home with you, live with you at your place and rest up. And, when he feels like it, if he's interested in Shield Security, we might talk. I could use a Peru analyst in our planning section. He'd do well there."

Daria knew Nik had his eyes set on getting his paramedic license once in the US. "We'll see," was all she'd say.

"Listen, I'll be in touch as things fall into place. Don't let down your guard. Valdez and Suero have spies in that city. The *policia* in Cusco have been sent approvals by our State Department, asking that you and Nik be fully armed while you provide security for Korsak. They've given their permission and the Assistant Chief of Police will give you the identification and approval by the President of Peru to open carry while you are there in this country."

"That is such good news. I was worried about that. I'm going over right now, as soon as we click off, to meet with Nik."

"Yes, tell him everything. Are you okay?"

"I'm fine. Don't worry, I'll stay on top of things. And we'll work out an around-the-clock guard schedule regarding Korsak. We're not leaving the *policia* to guard him. No way."

A CIA REPRESENTATIVE, Jeffrey Luminos, was already in the mix when Daria walked into the surgery lobby. She saw the Peruvian case officer speaking with Nik. It made her smile a little to herself as Nik sensed her presence, stopped the conversation, and and walked over to her.

"Korsak is going to make it," he told her, gripping her hand, smiling with relief.

"I know," and she quickly explained some of Jack's call to him. To say that Nik looked ten years younger was an understatement. Before, his eyes had been a turgid blue, shadowed and filled with anxiety. Now, they glistened with undeniable joy and Daria smiled with him. The tension he always carried dissolved away, his shoulders thrown back and proud once more. The weight this man had carried on his shoulders was something no one else could ever imagine. But Daria knew it.

"Luminos," Nik said, turning toward the case officer, "is paving the way for us. He's already spoken to hospital officials. The Assistant Police Chief was here earlier and handed us our identification badges, papers, and approval to open carry. We're going to be granted a pistol each on our person while we stand guard over Korsak's room, so we're in good stead with the country's laws."

"Wonderful," Daria said, shaking the case officer's hand as she continued to look aside at Nik. "How are you doing?"

Nik grinned tiredly. "Right now, I feel numb inside, Daria. I'm afraid this isn't real. That I'm imagining all of it."

"You've been dreaming of this moment for the last five years," she offered him gently, with a sympathetic look. There were shadows beneath his eyes, and his skin stretched tautly across his high cheekbones, telling her of the toll this had taken.

"And now that it's here," and he shrugged, "it doesn't really seem possible, Kitten." He leaned down, kissing her cheek. "Only you feel real to me."

"It will slowly sink into you, Nik. You need time to decompress. Come on, introduce me to this case officer? I need to be brought up to speed."

Daria listened intently to the forty-year-old Peruvian CIA contact. He actually turned out to be an American citizen, born in the USA, and had been tagged to work in Peru, his parents' home country. Luminos was sharp, disciplined and organized. They sat huddled together at one end of the lobby waiting room, speaking in English in quiet tones. Luminos was going to continue on and coordinate everything further, now that their open carry approval was official. He'd already slipped them pistols, a Glock 18 each, which they both hid down the back of their waistbands, along with three magazines filled with bullets which they stowed away in their rucks. Daria already felt safer just having the pistol on her. He gave them his cell phone number. Right now, he wanted them to use the CIA safe house in the city. Like her, Luminos didn't trust the Russian safe house, thinking it could already be compromised by Valdez or Suero's local spies. He gave them a key card and intel on the other safe house, telling them to go there to live, sleep, clean up and eat.

A nurse came into the lobby, calling for Nik. He excused himself and rose, walking over to the petite Peruvian nurse in her white uniform.

Daria turned to Luminos. "Does Korsak know what's going to happen to him yet?"

"No, but I'll be the one who lets him know. Right now, he's coming out from under anesthesia and is in recovery. I'm going down there right now to remain with him. I want you two to decide who's standing watch first. I don't want you conversing with Korsak. You're to stay outside his room at all times. I'll be the one to answer his questions."

"Will he even know we're there?"

"Not if I can help it. I've got the hospital staff up on that floor already brought up to speed. They know he's a political prisoner of the USA, but that's all. And that you and Nik are the USA security guards at Korsak's door. The *policia* will also be sending men."

"What if the Cusco *policia* are moles? What if Suero or Valdez has bought them off?" She saw the man's face grow tight.

"It's up to you two to always be on guard when they send over an officer to stand guard with you. I couldn't get the *policia* to back down on this. The police chief knows what is going on. Him, I trust. But I don't trust the men under him. Too much graft and corruption."

Daria grimaced. "A way of life in Central and South America, I'm afraid."

"Yes," he grunted, getting up. He smoothed his dark blue pinstripe jacket with his hand. "Here comes Nik. Fill him in? I need to get down to see Korsak."

Daria nodded, watching Luminos stride out of the waiting room like he owned the place. Clearly, he was a case officer with a lot of power at his disposal. She was grateful the CIA had sent someone like him to coordinate everything. Right now, all she wanted to do was get the hell out of Dodge. As long as they were in Peru, Suero or Valdez could reach out and tag them. Worse, infiltrate the hospital and kill Korsak. She held Nik's gaze as he walked over and sat down next to her.

"What did the nurse want?"

"Just to bring me up to speed," he murmured. "Korsak's coming out of recovery in about twenty minutes. His vitals are stable, thank God."

She reached out, sliding her fingers down his bare arm. His muscles responded beneath her fingertips and she wanted to just hold Nik, give him a safe place for once. "He's tough."

"He's Spetsnaz," Nik agreed quietly, opening his fingers, entangling them with hers. "You look beautiful, did you know that?" Her hair was dried and covering her shoulders like a cape. "I wish... I wish we were anywhere but here right now."

"Makes two of us," she agreed, watching the entrance out of habit.

"Listen," he said, holding her gaze, "when this is over? When Korsak is safely taken to the US? What are your plans, Daria? I need to know."

She warmed beneath his intense, burning look. "When you're finished with the State Department, I'd like you to drive to Alexandria, Virginia. I want you to stay with me, Nik. At my home." Her heart beat a little harder in her chest. "Would you?" Never had Daria wanted anything more. She added, "Alex and Lauren live nearby. About five miles away from me. I know Alex is dying to see you again. Hug you. Make lots of good, hearty Ukrainian food to put all that lost weight back on you," and she smiled a little, seeing hope come to his eyes.

For five years, Nik had been starved emotionally and spiritually. Daria knew the toll that could take on a person. She'd been out on ops for three to six months, alone in a rugged desert, without the things in her life she needed to sustain her soul. She understood better than anyone that Nik was running on empty emotionally. His soul was dying a little at a time. She wanted to be like life-giving water and sustain Nik on every level, bringing him back to the world of the living. Back to a normal existence.

"I'd like that very much," he told her, his voice thick with feeling.

Daria didn't want to talk about Jack's job offer. She knew Nik wanted desperately to get into the medical field. It was where his heart and soul lay. "It would give you a chance to decompress. Alex is like a big brother to you. I think between him and Lauren, eating good Ukrainian food and having a real home, you'll recover more quickly."

He lifted his hand, sliding his finger across the slope of her cheek. "All I want, Daria, is you. Everything else is less important to me. I do love Alex like a brother. We have saved one another's lives many times over the years down here. But my heart is focused on us. On you. I know we haven't had the time to properly get to know one another. I have so many questions, so many conversations I want to have with you, Daria."

She closed her eyes, resting her cheek in his opened palm, her heart squeezing with so much love for this man that she couldn't speak for a moment. She felt his mouth on her other cheek, grazing her flesh, making her breasts ache for his knowing touch, her lower body flaring to life, remembering the ecstasy he'd given her already. And would again. Opening her eyes, she lifted her cheek from his palm and held his narrowed, heated gaze. "Yes, I want the same thing. We'll sort things out over time, Nik. Dan will be flown to the U.S, to Colorado Springs. That's where that neurosurgeon and his technical team are located. We're going to be busy and your focus will be on him, where it needs to be, after he arrives. He's never been to the U.S, and Dan's going to need a personal support team. You and Alex. Good friends."

"That's all true," he murmured, holding her gaze, "I was told by Luminos earlier that the State Department has already put things in motion to bring Dan to Colorado. Until then, I will be decompressing with you at your home. I'm coming home to you, Daria. We *WILL* spend quality time together, Kitten, that's a promise. I will devote my time and love to Dan, but you are equally important to me, to my heart..."

The words, *I love you*, nearly tore from her lips. Daria saw the road ahead of them, saw the responsibilities once more, heaped upon Nik's shoulders as he cared for his brother daily once he arrived in Colorado. "We'll find the time."

He caressed her hair, smoothing some strands into place, "Oh," he promised her huskily, "no matter what I do during the day, at night? I am in your bed, holding you, loving you, Kitten. And I will hold you afterward and we will talk."

"And laugh," Daria reminded him, her lips hitching upward. "The danger will be gone, Nik. We'll be safe, finally. It's going to be a whole new, wonderful world for you and I."

CHAPTER 20

Upon the couple's landing at Reagan International Airport, the CIA immediately took Nik away to question him. Daria had been pulled aside and driven to her home outside of Alexandria, Virginia, by another CIA agent. Nik went through three days of long hours giving the CIA the intel they wanted from him. He'd been isolated at a posh D.C. hotel, although he'd had daily connection with Daria by ZOOM on his laptop. Afterward, he'd rented a car and had driven up to Daria's place.

He parked the rental outside her two-story cabin hidden out in the woods and she met him at the gate of its white picket fence. The strong scent of dried pine needles entered his flaring nostrils as he allowed her to tug on his hand as she pulled the gate open, beckoning, pulling him down the path and into her home. She was wearing a pair of white shorts and a red midriff, sleeveless top that outlined her breasts. Her black hair swung long and shining, making him hunger for her as never before. Even better, she was barefoot! Truly, she looked the wild female jaguar.

Even though his gaze was centered on her, as a black ops soldier he automatically began to absorb his surroundings. There was a profusion of red poppies, yellow Black-Eyed Susan's and purple Cone Flowers ranged along the length inside the picket fence, their heads waving slowly in the lazy, humid mid-summer breeze. The cabin stood towering over them, its pine logs shining a dull gold in the sunlight. The grass was neatly cut and embraced three sides of the home. He liked the porch that wrapped around it, spotting two rocking chairs on the deck. Nik wondered if Daria sat out there sometimes to watch the sun come up in the east. He'd like to be beside her and share it with her if she did.

"Are you tired?" Daria asked, releasing his hand and closing the screen door behind him.

"Part of me is. Other parts aren't," and he saw her give him a wicked look, her gaze drifting downward. Yes, he had an erection. He'd dreamed of being here with her. *Coming home.*

"I can see that," Daria murmured, giving him a mischievous look. "Are you thirsty?"

He allowed his black ruck to slide off his shoulder and drop on the butterscotch leather couch and followed her into the L-shaped kitchen. "I am." *For you,* but he didn't say it.

"A beer?"

Nik shook his head. "No, water is fine," he said, following her to the kitchen sink, his eyes never leaving her shapely legs. Only when Daria turned and he saw the angry, puckered scars of the knife wounds on her left thigh, did some of his ardor dissolve. She had suffered greatly, in so many ways, just as he had.

As she pulled a glass from the cupboard, he looked around. The cabin was an open-concept layout, the kitchen and living room large and flowing into one another. He liked the sparseness of the area, neat and clean. There was a butterscotch-color leather couch and two overstuffed burnt-sienna-colored chairs with a large crimson and gold cedar coffee table the centerpiece between the whole ensemble. In another corner was a rocking chair with a quilted pillow on its seat. The red brick fireplace against the northern side of the cabin completed it. There was homey warmth to this place. He could feel it and he started realizing they were safe. Really safe. No interruptions by Brudin. No staying on guard twenty-four hours a day. Nik felt as if he were a snake shedding the heavy, armored skin he'd had to wear for so long. The lamps on the end tables were antique, Eighteenth Century. He liked that Daria had created rooms that reflected her taste, not mimicked out of some must-have home interior magazine. It was a hodgepodge of furniture, but most importantly, it was inviting and a metaphor-like cradle to his exhausted spirit that fed him in the best of ways. He liked that she had picked some of the wildflowers from around her fence and placed them into a bright red glass vase on the round, oak table that sat at one end of the kitchen area.

"Your home is as beautiful as you are," he murmured.

"Thanks. It has taken me nearly three years to get it decorated." She glanced at him and said, "Not that I'm a designer. I wanted furniture that reflected me when I can get some downtime between missions."

"I can see that. I like it," and he met her gaze, feeling his entire body go from tiredness to anticipation. Nik saw her wanting him, felt it in his core, and had never wanted anything more than Daria.

"I love rocking chairs, as you can see," and she placed the glass beneath the spigot.

"You are a woman who is always in motion," he teased, "either in your mind or physically speaking."

"You're right, I am," Daria assured him, handing the glass of water to him.

She rested her hips against the counter, studying him as he drank thirstily, his Adam's apple bobbing repeatedly.

Wiping his mouth, Nik set the glass on the swirled red, brown and gold granite counter. The cupboards were made of cherry wood, darker than the pine logs, a reddish hint tinging the beautifully crafted wood. He reached out, sliding his fingers through her hair, "It's done, Daria. I'm officially here in the U.S. Dan will arrive a week from now. He already has his medical team in place and the State Department is going to handle everything for him."

She nodded, giving him a caring look as she leaned into his fingers exploring through her hair, her scalp leaping with pleasure. "You've got to be relieved." She moved away from the counter and into his arms, resting her hands against his chest. "Korsak is talking?"

"Yes, to both questions. The CIA is very pleased. He's angling for Witness Protection, asking to stay in America and getting a new name. He knows the Russian mafia will try and find him and hunt him down if he doesn't. They may, anyway. I don't really care if that monster lives or dies."

She moved her fingers across the expanse of the gray t-shirt he wore. To an outsider, Nik would probably look like a young man in his late twenties or early thirties, and might be mistaken for a fitness consultant. She saw his thick biceps move beneath the material of his sleeves and she wanted so badly to touch his body, absorb him, and capture him deep within her. It had been nearly five days since parting from the Lima airport in Peru that they'd been in physical contact with one another.

She lifted her gaze, seeing the joy banked up in his eyes. The changes in Nik were stunning. The stress around his eyes and mouth were gone. His face was relaxed as never before and it made him look so much younger. He was finally free of a five year past he'd carried like a millstone around his neck. She slid her fingers slowly across the material of his shirt, feeling his muscles tense beneath her grazing, exploring touch.

"The people at the State Department have been very forthcoming," he told her, hope in his deep voice as he slid his fingers through her loose hair, enjoying the sensation of its cool silkiness against them. "Dan will be flown to the USA. There had been a last-minute red tape issue, and it has taken longer than either of us wanted. They are going to call me and let me know specifics when everything is in place. The team in Colorado is alerted and expecting him. And, because this ongoing brain sync takes months, the State Department has leased him an apartment nearby. He will be kept busy to a degree, but they said he would have a lot of free time to do what he wants to do, within the limits of the TBI issues. I will fly out to be with him for a week or two, and then come home to you. I want to make sure he's doing all right and that he knows we're close and will help in any way we can as he recovers."

She smiled a little. "That's wonderful. And yes, we'll be there to support him, for sure. You look so much younger right now, Nik. I've got to think it's because that green hell marathon is over?"

He dragged in a deep breath, resting against the counter, allowing her to lean up against him, their hips meeting, melting hotly against one another. He moved thick strands of hair across her proud shoulders. "Yes." And then he gave her a wry look. "I haven't looked at myself lately in any mirrors, Kitten. My mind... heart... were on getting through the mass of paperwork, red tape, interviews, and making sure Dan would be allowed into this country, and," he leaned down, taking her mouth gently, his lips barely against hers, "dreaming of the day that I would be right here with you in my arms, touching you, kissing you...," and he nudged her lips open more, feeling them bloom hotly beneath his with barely constrained eagerness. He could feel Daria trying to control herself for his sake. She wanted to give him time to come down from all the demands on his time, the intense briefings that would last hours at a time. The truth was, he needed to be here, with her. He needed to hear her voice, feel her tender touch, absorb the joy shining in her wide, flawless gold eyes for him alone.

Her mouth opened like the petals of a fragrant orchid beneath his coaxing. Her hair swirled around his face, her arms locking behind his neck as she pressed herself wantonly against him, her hips sensuous, sliding teasingly against him. Nik groaned, taking her mouth with primal hunger, his senses exploding as he tasted her and smelled that spicy female scent of hers that drove him crazy.

Tearing his mouth from hers, breathing unsteadily, Nik picked her up into his arms in one smooth, unbroken motion. "Guide me to your bedroom," he growled thickly, already carrying her across the living room toward the hall. Society and niceties be damned. He wanted his woman more than he wanted oxygen to breath. Daria gave him a sultry smile filled with promise, her arms settling around his shoulders, relaxing fully in his embrace.

"Second door on the left, and the door is already open," she said, her voice wispy. "Welcome home, Nik. That is OUR bedroom from now on."

Nik's whole world centered on Daria. He barely noticed the heavy gold brocade drapes open at the large window, the outside air flowing in between their flutterings, giving the room a woodsy scent. He could smell it on her skin and hair as well. Taking her over to the king-sized bed of red and gold cedar, he deposited her on the dark green bedspread, watching how her hair haloed out around her head and across the pillow.

"I need you," he rasped, unbuckling his belt, unsnapping his jeans, his gaze locked on hers.

"I need you more." She nodded and sat up, pulling her red tee off, revealing that she wore no bra.

Heat shot through his throbbing lower body as he watched her small, beautiful breasts revealed. He smiled.

"I like that you don't wear a bra." Nik divested himself of his boots, jeans, and boxer shorts. He saw Daria stare appreciatively at his erection. Her eyes were heavy-lidden, filled with arousal, lips parting as if she could hardly wait to savor him.

"I hate bras," she muttered, laying down, lifting her legs and pulling off her shorts.

As he hauled the gray t-shirt off his head, his eyes widened considerably. "You're not even wearing… panties…" and he chuckled, shaking his head. "Don't tell me you wore neither down in Peru?" He rolled on a condom.

Daria gave him a playful pout and knelt in the center of the bed. "I did only because I had to. From now on? You'll just have to keep my secret that I don't wear a bra or panties, generally speaking."

He felt his erection throb in celebration of that reply as he joined her on the bed, matching her wicked grin. "I was right after all," he said thickly, laying down and bringing her beside him. "You are more wild jaguar than human. I like that."

"And you," Daria whispered, dragging her nipples through the hair across his chest, pushing her hips against his erection, "are more jaguar than man. I've always known that about you," she whispered, framing his cheek with her hand, looking deep into his eyes, suddenly serious. "We never got the time to really know one another, Nik. Starting right now, that changes."

"Alex texted me. He wants to meet me today, but I told him that sometime tomorrow would do, instead." He skimmed her flank, running his fingers across her hip, bringing his strength to bear, silently asking her to nestle hotly against him.

Daria whispered back, "He and Lauren are coming over for dinner tomorrow night at seven. We have the rest of this day and all of tonight, Nik, with no interruptions. Let's make the most of it…"

He gave her a feral smile, drowning in her half-closed eyes. "You aren't leaving this bed," he growled. Her lips lifted, amusement in her eyes as she smoothed her hand across his chest, appreciation in her gaze.

"Check that one. I'm starving for you and I want you now. I'm more than ready…"

In some ways, Nik felt as if he were in an unfolding vision he'd dreamed so many times while away from Daria. They'd spent hours on Zoom, talking and learning so much about one another when he had to work with the CIA, but in his dreams at night? She was in his arms and he was exploring her just as he was doing right now, his lips caressing her tight nipples, slipping his hand around that curved flesh, hearing a sharp intake of her breath, feeling her press urgently against his hips, wanting him, wanting the pleasure she knew he would give her.

The languid warmth of the afternoon and the semi-darkness of the bedroom surrounded him along with her aphrodisiac-like scent, combined with the subtle woodland fragrances drifting through the nearby opened window. Nik moved his hand downward across her rounded belly, felt her tense as his fingers moved across those black curls, sliding downward, easing her open, testing her, seeing if she was ready. And she was, his fingers coated with her slickness, the scent touching his nostrils, making him groan with animal need. As he stroked her folds and entrance, she quivered in his arms, soft sounds emitting from her throat, letting him know she liked what he was doing. He was going to do so much more. Capturing the nipple, he suckled her strongly, easing a finger into her entrance. Daria tensed, her hips thrusting upward, wanting more of his lavish, teasing touch. He felt that swollen bud awash with her thick fluids and knew without a doubt that she was more than ready.

He became lost, wrapped within her scent, the soft curves of her body, as he focused on her. More than anything, Nik wanted Daria to come first. He knew that a month without having her would make it incredibly tough to control himself as completely as he might want. Her body was damp, twisting and turning as he eased a second finger within her, sliding deeper, finding that second spot within her that was so connected with that bud at her entrance. She gave a sharpened cry, her back arching upward, her fingers digging into his shoulder as he teased that inner flesh of hers, feeling her begin to constrict around him. Taking his lips to her other nipple, lightly rasping his teeth against it, she suddenly cried out, her entire body bucking against him. He smiled, continuing to stroke that sweet spot within her, feeling her entire tunnel contract tightly around his fingers. Her cries were hoarse, her fingers opening and closing frantically against his shoulder as the orgasm burst through her like an overflowing dam.

Daria pressed her face against the column of Nik's strong neck, sobbing, clinging to him as he continued to milk her sensitive body, trusting him. His heart swelled with love for her as he felt the convulsions seizing around his fingers over and over again. His chest flooded with such joy that he thought he might truly die from happiness. The sweet, gasping sounds tearing out from between her lips was music, bathing his heart and his soul. This woman utterly trusted him. Without question. She had already put her life on the line for him, protecting him in that firefight. There was never any question in Nik's mind that Daria didn't love him just as fiercely as he loved her. And, this afternoon, he was going to show her just how much he did. She was a living feast, a beautiful banquet before him, sweet, ripe, and ready to be eaten, savored and worshipped by him.

DARIA FLOATED BETWEEN heaven and unknown, colorful galaxies around her that she saw behind the lids of her closed eyes. Her body was glowing and satiated. Nik held her in his arms, his long, hard body curving protectively around hers, holding her in the aftermath of their second round of lovemaking. The clock read four p.m. Sex with Nik was mind blowing for her. She had never had a lover as skilled as he was. And he was more than welcoming of her wild woman ways and needs, smiling, urging her on to pleasure herself with his body. To say they were sensual and earthy together was an understatement. Her body hummed with a level of satisfaction it had never known.

His skin was still damp as he lay with her in his arms, his long, hairy leg across hers, holding her flush against his hips. Daria could feel him becoming harder, longer, her belly resting against his erection. And she smiled, sliding her fingers against his powerful neck and broad shoulders in the aftermath. Nik was still breathing raggedly, his heart pounding beneath her palm. His hand moved in a caressing gesture across her shoulder and down her long spine, memorizing her. She nuzzled against his neck and jaw, placing soft kisses along it, hearing a low growl of satisfaction in his chest that reverberated through her. Everything about this man was pure, unadulterated pleasure. And they'd only just begun to explore the sexual landscape with one another. Daria was glad he was remaining here, with her, to rest, to decide what he wanted to do with the rest of his life.

Nik eased her onto her back. Daria gazed up at him. His hair, although military short, was mussed and she smiled, sliding her fingers through those strands, taming them back into place. She saw the stormy look in his eyes, knowing Nik was aroused once more. So was she as his fingers slid through her wet, slick folds, gently teasing her entrance once more. "Who's more hungry?" she asked, her voice husky, her hand stilling against his cheek, watching that predatory look come to his eyes as he felt how wet she had become once more.

"Mating heat between two jaguars," he growled, stroking that bud once more. "Did you know they mate for life?"

"Mmmm... whatever we have between us... I like it... don't stop, Nik..."

NIK SLOWLY AWOKE, aware of Daria in his arms, her body against his. What time was it? He barely lifted his head, looking at the clock on the dresser opposite the bed where they lay tangled against one another. It was nine p.m. They had fallen asleep in one another's arms. Delicious, stolen hours with each other. His body was utterly sated and he greedily absorbed Daria against him, her breasts pressed against his chest, her arm languid and relaxed across his torso, her one leg crossed over his. She was sleeping deeply and he lay there cherishing this moment with her as the full moon sent shafts of light around the edges and the opening of the curtains at the window.

Nik inhaled her sexual fragrance, the scent of her skin, and felt the cool silk of her hair against his neck and shoulder. He loved this woman with his life. They'd been through so much in such a short, concentrated amount of time. There was no question she loved him even though neither had spoken the words to one another... yet. Nik felt he knew Daria well enough to understand why she hadn't. They'd known each other less than three months. Both of them were mature and knew the value of waiting. As he lightly grazed her shoulder, feeling the cool velvet of her flesh beneath his fingertips, he was more than content to wait. They had silently shown one another through their love making that they did, indeed, cherish one another. Daria had already given him her heart, her body and her beautiful, fiery Russian and Mongol soul.

The joy that filtered through his heart were feelings he had never thought possible. This woman had walked into his life a stranger, on a mission. A contact. And she'd sat down in that church next to him and he'd felt his whole life altering in those brief minutes she'd spent with him. He was still amazed and stunned by that singular event. Nik had never thought that he'd ever meet a woman that he would feel like this about. Daria consumed his soul, fed his starving heart, sent him spinning into unparalleled happiness with her just being herself. He knew this was love. *Real love.* Unquantifiable, unmeasurable because their hearts would have the time now to leisurely explore one another fully and completely. His hand curled protectively around her shoulder as he felt his way through all of the bright, glowing feelings now quietly consuming him.

Daria stirred, made a happy sound in her throat, stretching languidly against him, nuzzling him. He opened his eyes, staring up at the darkened white plaster ceiling, enjoying her awakening beside him. A smile drifted across his mouth as he felt her hand move languidly across his chest and ribs, as if silently delighting in touching him with such intimacy. Slowly, he propped himself up on his elbow, watching her awaken, her eyes barely open, their gold depths drowsy and cloudy. His mouth stretched in welcome as he lifted his hand, easing the curtain of hair away that had fallen across her face so he could see her expression fully. She was like a mysterious, beautiful orchid whose petals were shyly opening before him. Nik once more felt like he was in some incredible dream that he never wanted to end.

"When I first met you, *moya kotya*," he began in a low, dark tone, "you shook my world apart. I didn't know what to think about you. All I could do when you sat down next to me in church, was feel emotions I never knew I had until you awakened them with your nearness." He saw her eyes widen a little, a bit more of awareness in them as he spoke in Ukrainian to her. His voice was gravely with remnants of sleep. "For whatever reason, you trusted me from the beginning. I could feel it, Daria," and he brushed his thumb across her pink cheek, savoring her growing more and more aware of them here together, the sleep slowly dissolving from the depths of those glorious jaguar-gold eyes of hers. "I felt like a man starving in a desert until you came and fed me the richness of your love, from your heart. You fed me in ways that I'm going to share with you from now on. I want to show you in small and large ways how much you mean to me, Daria. I never realized just how starved and dying I was until you entered my life. That five-year nightmare of being with that drug team, had taken me down."

She sighed softly and caught his hand, taking it and nestling it between her breasts, studying him in the lulling silence. "You carried your brother on your shoulders for those five years, darling. It was one of the first things I realized about you, the many loads you wore on these broad shoulders of yours. I know you don't see yourself, Nik, your strength, your heart and love for Dan. You were more than willing to sacrifice yourself for him because you loved him. I know he didn't ask that of you. You willingly gave it to him because he is your brother. It says something so incredible about you, my warrior, that it leaves me breathless just thinking about what you've accomplished." Daria brought his hand to her hip, released it and slid her fingers through his hair, watching his eyes change, grow darker with arousal, with wanting her again.

"You were worth pursuing, Nik. And I didn't go down to Peru with any thought of a relationship with you. It just happened." Daria caressed his cheek, the stubble making her fingertips tingle. "You walked into my life, and I'm forever grateful…"

He took her hand, placing a wet kiss in her palm. "I'm not the only one carrying wounds, Kitten. You have your own, and I want to help to heal them as you're healing mine."

She relaxed in Nik's arms, content to be devoured by his warm, loving gaze that embraced her in the quiet of their bedroom. Somewhere outside the opened window, Daria heard an owl in the darkness, hooting, a counterpoint perhaps to their deep, searching and offered heart thoughts they were sharing with one another. Nothing was more important to Daria than this.

Nik was vulnerable with her, open, without ego or defense. Her soul hungered for such honest talk, bathing her with the intimacy that had done nothing but grow stronger and deeper with every minute spent with this man. Her warrior. Her wounded soldier. Her heart. The deepest scars Nik carried were mostly invisible, the ones that really counted. And Daria could see them.

"We're both wounded and shattered in different ways," she quietly agreed, stroking his jaw, allowing her fingers to trail down his neck to its nape. "We have all the time in the world now, Nik. I don't want you anywhere but living here with me. We've earned the time to get to know one another fully, without danger surrounding us."

"I agree," he growled, kissing her parting lips, her nose and then her brow. "But what do you want, my beautiful jaguar mate?"

She frowned and then shook her head. "My life changed when I met you, Nik. I didn't know it was going to at the time, but I see that now."

"Your leg?" and he reached down, caressing the puckered wounds gently. "You still have healing to do. You shouldn't be going out on another mission, Daria."

"I hear you and I don't disagree." She slowly eased out of his embrace and sat up, crossing her legs, remaining in physical contact with him. "You've shown me things I've never had before, Nik and I want... need the time... to digest all of them. I want to appreciate all of you, in every way. I don't want to be running off around the world on another mission right now."

Her brows fell and she said, "I'm twenty-nine years old. My body has taken a lot of physical stress and punishment as a sniper over the years. Meeting you has made me realize what I want out of my life. Every time I think of having to leave you here and take off on an op, my heart crumples in my chest, Nik. It cries. I want to cry." Daria gave him a pleading look. "Maybe I'm in love for the first time in my life and I never knew what love was until I met you?"

His heart leapt from her softly spoken words. Giving her an adoring look, he rasped, "I didn't know what love was until I met you, my sweet jaguar woman. I really didn't."

Daria reached out, stroking his torso, feeling each rib beneath her fingertips. "I think we're both asking for time alone and at home with one another?"

"Yes, and frankly? I'm glad you won't go out on another mission, Daria." Nik gazed into her half-closed eyes. "Perhaps we have earned the right to have a life with one another, instead? Happiness has eluded both of us. Perhaps it's our turn to have it now? With one another?" And he caressed her lower lip with his thumb, watching her gold eyes grow dark with need of him once again. To be wanted, to be loved were two things he never thought he'd ever have in this lifetime. His had been a life of sacrifice, not largesse.

She caught his hand, slowly opening it with her fingers, kissing his calloused palm, her gaze never leaving his as she did so. Lifting her lips away, folding his large hand between her own two smaller ones, she whispered, "I love you Nik. I did from the beginning. I tried to tell myself I was crazy. That it couldn't be so. How could I fall in love with a stranger I didn't know? And yet, as I sat next to you in church, there was such a rich wealth of feelings exploding from my heart toward you that it left me breathless, my mind blown by what was going on between us. I had no idea if you felt anything like I was feeling, but the emotions, the sensations, literally swept through me, dragging me along and I couldn't fight it." Daria gave him a rueful look. "The truth? I didn't want to fight it, Nik. I didn't know what it was at first, but I wanted to find out. I was sexually drawn to you, no question. But there was so much, much more and we were in a pressure cooker where it was impossible to explore what we had."

"I felt the same way, *moya kotya*," and Nik shook his head, giving her a look of wonder. "What I want to do now that I'm here? I want to explore the universities and colleges in Virginia, and find the best paramedic program they have available. Once I accomplish that, I'm going to go for a PA, physician's assistant. I can have my own office; patients and I will be content. I know I'm a good combat medic, but now, I want to turn my skills toward a peaceful landscape. I will always want to help people, stop their suffering, and ease their pain. It's who I am."

She whispered Nik's name, rising to her knees and sliding her arms around his shoulders, holding him tightly against herself. "That is the man I fell in love with," she whispered brokenly against his ear. "Don't ever change, Nik. You are healing me, too, whether you know it or not."

He rasped Daria's name, taking and easing her on top of him as he laid down on his back. He felt her softness, her body giving here and there against his, felt the heat explode where their hips met and fused naturally with one another. Daria gripped him with her woman's strength, her brow against his jaw, clinging to him in the best of ways, as if trying to absorb him fully into herself. It was a stunning, beautiful feeling and he savored it, his hand slowly moving up and down her strong, capable back. He could feel how tight and firm her body was beneath his exploring fingers. He absorbed her warm, moist breath against his neck and chest, celebrating how well they fit one another, like lost pieces that had finally been found, fitted back together and come home to one another.

"We," he told her huskily against her hair, "are going to have a beautiful, blossoming life with one another, my woman. We'll have ups and downs, I'm sure. But we'll have one another and that is more than most people are ever blessed to have in a lifetime."

CHAPTER 21

THE FOLLOWING EVENING, Daria felt tears stinging her eyes as she stood back beside Lauren Parker-Kazak as Alex surged through the opened door and bear-hugged his dear friend, Nik. She quickly wiped the tears from her eyes as Lauren drew a few steps closer, smiling.

"This is a meeting that's been a long time coming," Lauren told Daria, sliding her arm around her shoulders.

Daria hugged her sniper instructor friend. "Nik was so excited about seeing Alex once more," and she watched the two men in the hall. They were speaking in Ukrainian, their voices thick with emotion. Alex Kazak had worked for three years with Nik in the same Russian drug team in Peru. Alex was the size of a massive Ukrainian bear, six foot three inches tall, heavily muscled, with black hair and hazel eyes. In comparison, Nik was six foot tall and a lot leaner. Ropy-muscled. When Alex threw his arms around his boyhood friend, the medic just about disappeared within his thick, tree-branch arms. They slapped each other heartily on the back, repeatedly hugging one another.

Daria saw tears streaming down Alex's face. Nik's expression was hidden to her. She could only see his heaving back, indicating a similar reaction. Tears leaked from her own eyes. Lauren gave her a soft look, wiping tears away, too.

The sum of emotions pouring out of them all was palpable. And wonderful. Daria absorbed the ecstatic happiness that embraced all. Even more important was that the two men could cry in one another's arms. The deep sobs filled the hall. Her heart clenched as she watched the two men embrace, each head bowed against the other, their shoulders shaking. Seeing hardened soldiers become emotional through their mutual trust in one another, allowing that awful backlog of grief and horror pour out, enriched Daria's soul. Daria didn't know many American soldiers or Marines who would display such in front of anyone. But these two friends, who had shared so much anguish and danger together – and survived it, could and did. They were real men in her eyes. Real men cried. It was such an important part of their healing individually, and for each other. They'd seen too much. Things they'd never forget. Daria and, she was sure, Lauren knew just getting to offload the emotions, even though the images of horror would never be gone, was a huge, healing step in each of their lives.

There were no dry eyes in the hall, or in the living room and Daria ached to hold Nik as she heard the animal-like sobs ripping out of him. Alex held him, patted him on the back, his face ravaged with pain, tears for his closest friend glistening in runnels unashamedly down his cheeks. Daria hoped that someday she could hold Nik when he was hurting like this. The bond he had with Alex was special and she understood that and felt so glad that he was here for his partner of so many years.

Nik had endured two more years of hell than Alex had. Daria knew the concern Alex had always held about Nik being on the front lines as a CIA mole, always worried he'd be found out by Korsak, and then slowly tortured to death. She'd seen the distress in Alex's eyes often and knew intuitively he was thinking about his friend who was laying his life on the line for his injured brother every day, without rest.

Finally, the men broke apart, gave each other silly grins as they wiped the last of the tears from their faces.

"Welcome home, brother," Alex rumbled, gripping Nik's shoulder and giving it a good shake. "It is about time."

Nik gave him a strained smile, gripping Alex's meaty shoulder back. "Yes, more than due time. I'm just glad it's over." He turned toward Daria and Lauren. His gaze centered on the woman he loved. Seeing her face wet, her eyes dark with emotion, he released Alex's shoulder and walked over to her, taking her gently into his arms, kissing her hair, holding her against him. He saw Lauren move around him and walk over to her husband, comforting him as well.

"It's all right," Nik rasped against Daria's hair. "This is a happy meeting. Tears of joy. Okay?" and he eased her back to hold her glistening gaze that held so much love for him in its depths. He saw her wet lips part, the lower one trembling slightly, as she raised her hand to cup his cheek.

"We're crying for both of you," she whispered unsteadily, trying to smile, but failing. "It's wonderful to see men being able to hold one another let it go, and cry."

His mouth stretched ruefully. "We are brothers in spirit, *moya kotya*. Alex has saved my life so many times…"

"And you have saved my sorry ass, too," Alex growled, his arm around Lauren as he moved, bringing her with him to stand before the other couple.

Nik nodded; his expression serious. "It's over, Alex. That's all I care about. Dan will be coming to the US in about six days. He'll be free. And he's already scheduled for that brain scan technique."

Clapping him on the back, Alex said, "Come, it is time to celebrate. I have been cooking for two days straight, wanting to give you a good, hearty meal that will make you think of our farm life in Ukraine." He looked over at Lauren, his face growing tender with love for his wife. "Shall we begin to bring in the banquet?"

Lauren grinned. "Yeah, let's haul in that food. I'm hungry."

"Let me help?" Daria asked, her arm around Nik's waist.

"No, no," Alex said, waving his hand at them. "All you need do is set the table for four people. Lauren and I have this."

Daria gave Nik a warm look. He looked ravaged and relieved on the surface of his expression, but so many other emotions surfaced from beneath it. "We can do that." She tugged at his waist. "Come on," she coaxed gently, giving him a tender smile. Daria didn't feel like eating, and she was sure Nik probably wanted to wait, but he would put himself out for his beloved friend, Alex Kazak. The closeness of their bond was beautiful to behold, and Daria was so glad that Nik had Alex to talk to. No one could understand the pressure, the terror and suffering he'd gone through more than Alex. They'd shared them those unrelenting hellish years together. She was grateful that life had given each of them another chance after a time of such danger. A time where the knife-edged balance of life-and-death had swirled relentlessly around them daily.

Daria watched Nik begin to recover throughout their evening meal. The laughter, the spattering of Ukrainian mixed with English, the jokes and stories that Alex and Nik told, had them all laughing. Lauren didn't understand Ukrainian, so they would stop and translate for her when needed. The meal they ate was huge but, to Daria's surprise, she was hungrier than she had thought at first. Nik seemed to recover fully, eager to sup the Borscht soup. Alex knew Nik's tastes and had been in the kitchen preparing these courses for him for days. Lauren helped as a sous chef while Alex, who was a true chef at heart, had made this wonderful meal of Beef Stroganoff, potato salad and yeast-risen rolls that they were all eagerly consuming.

Lauren and Daria removed the dishes afterward. Alex had made a dessert of honey Babka, a sweet, moist apple cake with a cream cheese topping. Lauren placed it on the table. Daria made them thick, strong Ukrainian coffee. Once they were all seated back at the table, cups full, everyone settled in to taste the luscious dessert.

"So?" Alex said in English to Nik, "Will you meet Dan in Colorado Springs, when they fly him in from Ukraine?"

"Yes, I will."

"I'm going too," Daria said, holding his gaze.

"I wouldn't want it any other way," Nik told her, giving her a warm look.

"The CIA will want to debrief him at some point?" Alex asked.

"After his initial round of brain syncing. Whenever the red tape gets worked through."

"The CIA will be happy to speak with him at length."

"I know," Nik sighed. "I'm working with the State Department to defer that to another time, giving him time to recuperate. His TBI affected his speech and thought patterns, and the CIA realizes that until, or even *if* this, cutting-edge technique works, they aren't going to have much communication between them," Nik said, spooning the dessert into his mouth.

Alex raised his eyebrows. "What shape is Dan in, Nik?"

"He's mobile and he has no problem walking. It's his speech center in his brain that was affected. When he speaks, he'll hesitate mid-sentence and it might take him thirty seconds to finish it. At least his speech is coherent, it has a beginning, middle and end. I talked with one of the technicians this morning and he felt Dan had a chance at nearly full recovery."

"I remember," Alex said, "that Dan was Spetsnaz like you. A combat medic."

"Yes, he was, Alex. And he was a super soldier. He's earned all kinds of medals for bravery. He had a reputation in the ranks as one of the best medics. He used his field surgeon skills continuously, and he saved so many lives."

Lauren asked, "Do you think if this technique is successful that Dan will want to go back into the military in some capacity? Or does he want to remain a civilian?"

Shrugging, Nik said, "I don't know. I don't know much of what is really in his heart and mind. I'm hoping he will want to remain in medicine in some capacity, but we'll see."

"Well," Alex said, smiling a little over at Nik, "you will find out soon enough. Once he finishes the brain sync sessions, will you get him back here to Virginia? What is your plan?"

Nik looked across the table at Daria. "We've talked it over, and Daria is all right with Dan taking up residence in the spare bedroom of her house. At least, short-termed. I'm sure Dan will need some adjustment time and we want to give it to him. The CIA is willing to lease him an apartment on a short-term basis close by where they'll debrief him. I'm not sure where the best place for him is right now. I feel he'll need some downtime just to get his life together and get used to American ways of living. Daria and I felt we could give him family support and stability if he stayed with us. Good food, love, care and guidance."

"Sounds like a solid plan," Alex agreed. He grinned. "And we should plan on all of you coming over for dinner at least once a week for some good, solid Ukrainian food."

Daria smiled, her heart singing with so many good emotions. She could see that the stormy look in Nik's gaze was dissolving. His eyes were red-rimmed and she knew how much that crying had taken out of him. In another way, it was healing because he was starting to discharge that five-year backlog of trauma, getting all that darkness out of himself. All she wanted to do right now was hold her brave warrior who had paid such a terrible price for his brother. Dan, she was sure, would never know the extent of Nik's efforts. She was also sure Nik would never speak of them to him either, not wanting his brother to feel any guilt over his sacrifices.

"Are you okay with Dan being here?" Lauren asked her.

Daria cleaned her plate and placed it aside with the fork. "Yes. I think Dan will use the house and us as kind of a launch pad. Nik is in touch with the neurologist who is going to perform the brain syncing sessions with Dan. He's asking where the best place is here in Virginia, for where his long-term recovery should be located, because Dan is going to need that kind of support at first."

"Good to know this," Alex agreed, giving Nik a look of pride. "Ukraine families stick together like glue."

"Come here," Nik rasped, pulling Daria into his arms after they had showered together. He gathered her into his arms, pulling up the sheet to their waists as they lay naked against one another. He kissed her mussed hair, still damp here and there. Alex and Lauren had left two hours earlier, near nine p.m., giving them time to themselves. He heard Daria sigh softly, her lips pressed against his neck, brow resting against his jaw as he lay down on his back.

"What a day," Daria whispered, moving her hand across his hard, contoured torso until her palm rested over his heart. "How are you doing?"

His mouth quirked as he stared up at the darkened ceiling. Only the glow of a small night light in the hall flowed weakly through their opened door. "I feel ravaged inside, like someone has clawed my guts apart."

Her arm around his torso tightened. "That's what I thought."

"Couldn't be helped, Kitten. I knew meeting Alex was going to bring up a lot of old, stored emotions."

"I'm glad you two could cry with one another. That was so important. It is healing for both of you."

"Maybe, as combat medics, we understood it was healing to cry out our pain and terror." He moved his fingers across her upper arm, still wrapped up as he was in those feelings from the past. "Too many soldiers learn to cry alone, where no one can hear them."

"Having Alex is healing for both of you, going forward, Nik. Maybe people from Ukraine are a lot smarter than their Russian counterparts?"

"Yes," he said in a hushed tone, kissing her temple, "but having you at my side is more important."

"I want to hold you when you want to cry, Nik."

His heart twinged and he slowly rolled onto his side, holding her shimmering, dark gaze. "You will, I promise," he choked. "But I want to be here to hold you, too, Daria. You have much stored from that night in Afghanistan when you were wounded." He trailed his finger across her brow, pushing strands of hair aside. Looking deeply into her wounded eyes, he added thickly, "I love you. You must know that by now. I know time must mature our relationship with one another, but as I sat there at the table earlier and saw how much grief you held, I didn't want one more day to go by without letting you know how I feel about you." He kissed her brow, inhaling her scent, allowing it to stir his lower body to vibrant life once again. He couldn't be around Daria and not want to make slow, delicious love to his wild, natural woman. He saw tears glimmer in her eyes as he spoke those words to her. Felt a surge of powerful emotions radiate from her to him.

"I love you, too, Nik," Daria whispered, her voice low and unsteady, searching his gaze. She touched his lower lip with her fingers briefly, mustering a faint smile. "Like you, I was going to wait, too. But this evening, when Alex held you so tightly, the love between you so strong and unbreakable, I just knew that I couldn't keep it from you any longer, either."

"We're so much alike, Kitten," and he leaned over, caressing her lips. Nik felt her response, her arms wrapping around his neck, drawing him down upon her. The streak of fire where her nipples brushed his chest, her mouth opening eagerly to his, her scent unraveling him, told him of her love for him in unspoken ways. Nik languished against her lips, tasting her fully, deeply, their tongues moving against one another, heightening the throb in his erection now pressing insistently against her belly. Never had he loved as he loved this woman who bravely opened her heart fully to him. Daria made no demands upon him, was content to be given what he could, and asked for nothing more. Slowly, kissing each corner of her mouth, he eased away from her, drowning in her starlit gaze that caressed him. "You are my life, my heart and soul, Daria. Never question that."

She nodded, tenderly stroking his cheek. "There's so much hope in front of us, Nik. A lifetime filled with happiness, good things instead of so much suffering. The past is behind you now."

He laid down on his back, urging her up against his side once more. She laid her head on his chest and contentment flowed powerfully through him. "I'm mulling over what we talked about at the table tonight. When Alex suggested instead of me going for a paramedic's license, to get serious and take the years to become a P.A., a physician's assistant. That is one rung below a medical doctor here in the USA. If I could pass and get that license, then I could bring in a far better income than as a paramedic."

She smoothed her hand across his chest, the heavy thud of his heart beneath her palm. "It's a good idea. Alex has studied the US medical system, Nik. He knows just how skilled you are. And I think he's right that you're already far beyond the paramedic level right now."

"We are taught combat field surgery, Kitten. We are both very highly trained. Most medical doctors cannot perform battlefield surgery and have their patient survive."

"How do you feel about working under a doctor's direction once you get your PA's license?"

Shrugging, he said, "I think I would like that a lot. I love children, always have. I was thinking of perhaps applying to a woman doctor who is a pediatrician, and seeing if she needed a PA's help. I know that possibility is at least two years away, but it is the direction I would like to take." Nik rolled his head to the right, catching a glimpse of her gaze up at him. "I have five-hundred thousand dollars in a Bermuda bank account. Three-hundred thousand of it is for Dan's recovery. I have two-hundred thousand left. I know I can support us with that, plus pay my university costs to become a PA."

"I'm bringing in good money, also, Nik."

He frowned, looking deep into her half-closed eyes as she continued to stroke his flesh with her fingertips. His skin skittered and tightened with pleasure wherever her fingers drifted across his chest. "We need to talk about you."

Daria eased away from him, her head coming to rest on his upper arm, fingers still on his torso. "My full recovery, by any chance?"

"Yes, that first," he murmured, propping himself up on his elbow, the palm of his free hand ranging slowly up and down the curves of her torso, hip and thigh. "I want you to get a different doctor. I want to be part of hearing what he or she will say about those four wounds. I want to continue to massage that area nightly."

"I can do that," she said. "When I go to see Jack tomorrow, I have a lot to discuss with him, Nik." Daria's brow moved downward for a moment as she considered her next words. "I talked to Lauren. I asked her how she liked running the sniper school at Shield Security, instead of being out on ops. She said she was ready to stop being a sniper, that she loved Alex, and she wanted to be home to have a life with him." She searched his rugged features, his eyes narrowing as she spoke. "I've made a decision, Nik. I'm going in to tell my boss, Gage, that I'm no longer available for missions."

"Thank God," he uttered, caressing her cheek. "I was going to talk to you about that, Daria."

"I'm already there," she assured him quietly. "You made me realize how much trauma I have over that op when Melissa was murdered. I need time and I need some therapy help. I'll work with our shrink at Shield because she's a trusted person, a woman, and I think I'll be able to open up to her a lot more than to a man." And then she said, "With the exception of you, Beloved. I feel like you will hold me when I start falling apart from all the emotions that I'm still holding inside myself over that busted op."

Nik's voice grew low with emotion. "I will *ALWAYS* hold you, Daria. You can come to me as a safe harbor in your life at any moment of any day. I will always protect you, my Kitten."

"I know that." She sighed. "I'm hoping that Jack will be okay with my decision. Lauren said she needs two more sniper teachers because the sniper course has become so popular that she must hire other field-experienced people to help her with the growing program. Foreign countries who are democratic, are sending their people over to get this training. I'm hoping Jack will let me make a lateral move over to Lauren's school and then I can teach what I know, be safe, and come home every night to you." Daria reached up, lightly touching his full lower lip. "I love you, Nik. I don't want to be torn apart from you. I want my life bound daily with yours."

"Sweet words, my Kitten," he said, nodding and remaining somber. "We've earned this time together, you and I." He picked up a few strands of her dark, shining hair.

"I want to continue my therapy," she agreed, her voice scratchy. "I've got a lot to work through. If Jack will approve my lateral move, and I believe he will, then I'll have your love to hold me on bad days after I get done with an hour's worth of therapy. I can come home, talk with you, cry, and if need be, you'll hold me." Daria gave him a searching look, seeking his approval.

"I'll do so much more than that," Nik promised her, his voice ragged with raw feelings and understanding. "I will listen closely. And if you want to scream, I will listen to those cries from your wounded soul, *moya kotya*. And I'll always be there to hold you. No matter what." He kissed her forehead, his lips lingering against her temple, and then trailing down the slope of her cheek. "But I worry," he admitted, lifting his head, holding her tender gaze. "I worry that if Dan stays with us and you are feeling raw, that it will work against you."

"I don't know," Daria admitted. "We don't know what shape Dan is in emotionally, either, so it's a big unknown. A question mark for all of us right now."

"My protectiveness is extended to you first, Daria. I want to give you a place where you can heal, not be upset by the intrusion of my brother." He kissed her lips. "I want you to feel safe when you come home because I know how vulnerable you will be feeling, my Kitten."

"But he needs a place to feel safe too, Nik. Remember, he's coming to a foreign country he doesn't know anything about except what he's heard. He doesn't speak good English and that makes communication hard for him. I really think we need to give him our home, our hearts, for a little while until he at least gets his feet under himself."

"We'll see," Nik murmured. "You are my first priority in my life. If that is a better plan, then we will go that direction. I just want to protect you, give you this home that you love so much, to be a place of healing and safety for you… for me."

Daria made a soft sound in her throat as she leaned into Nik, claiming his mouth. As she finished the kiss, she whispered, "We have so much to look forward to."

"Then," he grated, his lips near her ear, "at some point, my woman, you and I will talk of marriage because it is on my mind and in my heart. When the time is right? I will come to you with a set of rings, Daria. All you need to do is tell me when and I will ask for your hand, your heart…"

She nuzzled him, her lips resting against his, feeling his love flow through her like warm honey, wrapping sweetly around her heart, flowing downward, enclosing her aching lower body that wanted him so badly right now. "We're going to live together, explore one another, Nik. We've got the time, and finally our dreams have collided with one another. And yes, I will let you know. I need to get through some serious healing first, and then I know I'll be ready to look forward with you. Until then, I need to clean up and work through my past."

"I know you do, and I'm here to support you every step of the way," Nik promised, taking her mouth gently, absorbing her into his soul and his yearning heart that opened with her love for him.

THE END

Don't miss Lindsay McKenna's next Shadow Team series novel,
Hostile Territory.

Available from Lindsay McKenna and Blue Turtle Publishing and wherever you buy eBooks.

Excerpt from Hostile Territory

MACE KILLMER REMAINED hidden just inside the Highlands tree line waiting for the Night Stalker Black Hawk helo bearing his new sniper, to arrive. *New year, new sniper.* They were in the dry season of Peru and even at eleven thousand feet, it was cold an hour before sunset. A hundred yards either side of his position were his other two special forces sergeants, M4's with bullets in their chambers, watching and keeping an eye out for Volkov and his band of killers. They had run hard through the jungle, climbing from seven thousand feet to the present elevation, keeping the local Russian team at a distance. Volkov had no idea they were in the area, stalking them, and Killmer wanted to keep it that way. Still, he was uneasy with the ex-Spetsnaz Russian who was known as The Butcher. The Russian team had five ex-Spetsnaz soldier in it. His team only had three.

It was always a cat-and-mouse game that Killmer had to play with these Russian mafia drug teams. A radio call came in and he pressed the mic once, letting the pilot know he was in position at the correct GPS in order to land. His gray gaze swept out in the open area. To his right sat La Paloma, a village, a mile away. He saw the men slowly moving around in that village, getting ready to end the day's work. Thin wisps of smoke rose from tripods with kettles beneath them, the thatched hut village surrounding the food area. The smoke from the fires spiraled into the air, moving down toward the lower altitude far below them.

He heard the thunking of the blades of the Black Hawk. Lifting his spotter scope, he saw the dark green, unmarked Black Hawk, climbing up the face of the Highlands. The altitude they flew in made it tough on the machine. Restless, he stood up, remaining hidden for the most part, behind the wide trunk of a hundred foot tree towering above him. The light was getting better. He and his men had cleared the landing area of any loose rocks and twigs so they wouldn't be swooped up by the blades as the Hawk landed.

His CIA handler, Tad Jorgensen, had spoken highly of the sniper from Shield Security, that was coming in to assist them in finding and killing Volkov. He snorted. The last damned sniper sent down to them was a woman. Lauren Parker had promptly gotten herself kidnapped by Petrov, which threw their entire team into chaos. Instead of going after Petrov, they now needed to search and find her before Petrov killed her. Luckily, the managed to locate and rescue her and Nik Morozov, who helped her escape. Rubbing his stubbled jaw, Killmer scowled heavily. He'd told his handler he wanted no more women snipers. He didn't give a damn how good they were. One was fucking enough for a lifetime.

The Black Hawk became more and more sharpened and crisp looking the closer it go to where they were located. Mace called his men, letting them know the Hawk was landing. The sniper on board had orders to clear the helo and head directly into the tree line. There was no way Mace and his men were going to stroll out in the open. Not with Russian mafia teams around. And they knew without any doubt, that the Army Special Forces teams were on the ground, in their back yard and hunting their asses. They were very watchful, more so than usual.

Mace slipped his M4 off his shoulder, snapping off the safety, holding it tensely, his gaze ranging widely. He wanted no surprises when this Hawk landed. He needed that damned sniper alive and hungry for a kill. He watched the Hawk lower quickly, the Night Stalker pilots bringing the bird in fast. They were most vulnerable at take-off and landing, so it was going to be a swift egress. He'd been told by his handler that S. Chastain was a Marine Corps trained sniper. That was good. They were the best trained in the world. Bar none. He might be Army, but he would at least acknowledged the Marine Corps did SOME things right. And well.

The gusts of out flow wind as the Black Hawk's nose came up, sent ninety-mile an hour gusts in all directions. Mace told the helo to land. The copilot acknowledged his order and he saw the nose level out, the tricycle wheels touching the earth. Huge clouds of dust rose around the bird. Mace crouched, rifle in place, watching to the right and left, like his men were doing. They were responsible to keep that Black Hawk and the pilots safe.

The noise was deafening, the whine of the engines on top of the helicopter familiar to Mace. He couldn't see the bird land because it was swallowed up in the thick, roiling dust that was lifting twenty to thirty feet skyward into the sky. The puncturing of the blades buffeted his body and he leaned into the side of a tree for balance, so it wouldn't send him ass end over tea kettle. It had happened more than once.

The copilot notified him that the passenger has egressed and they were now lifting off. Mace rogered the radio transmission. The Black Hawk went straight up like an arrow shot out of a bow. It banked and then slid down over the side of the harsh, rugged cliff face where they had come from. Mace took a breath of relief, standing to his full height, watching the clouds of dirt intently. Any moment, that sniper would appear out of the dust.

His gray eyes narrowed as he saw someone with a rifle in one hand and a heavy ruck on their back, trotting out of the billowing dust. He saw the long legs, the cammos the sniper wore, his face and shoulders hidden by the roiling clouds. He was pleased the dude was humping his gear without a problem, heading straight for where Mace was standing. As the figure got clear of most of the dust, Mace's black brows dove downward. *WTF?* His eyes stung and watered from the dust being sent like a storm into the tree line. Wiping his watering eyes, he blinked several times. He HAD to be seeing things!

Mace's mouth dropped open. He promptly snapped it shut, rage tunneling through him. The figure materializing out of the dust was a woman! He clearly saw her face, those long black braids she wore down the front of her cammie jacket. She was tall and medium boned, her shoulders wide and capable. She was carrying her ruck which he knew easily weighed around sixty pounds. She was in good shape.

Mace didn't want to stare at her face, but he did. It was oval, a golden color and she had high cheekbones, her face wide, brow broad. He swore she was Native American because the black hair framed those fearless looking green eyes that reminded him of the swamp oaks where he grew up in North Carolina. And damned if his lower body didn't take off like it had smelled a woman in heat! Damn it! Grimly, he moved out and just in front of the tree so she could spot him. And spot him she did, making a quick, trotting correction toward him.

Mace didn't want to be influenced by the fact he thought she was a damned hot looking woman. She couldn't be more than in her late twenties. It was her wide green eyes, framed by thick black lashes, that grabbed his immediate attention. Big black pupils surrounded by that rich green color, a thin black ring around her iris. The look of an eagle. She didn't miss a thing, Mace saw, as she aimed herself at a steady trot right up to where he was standing.

He saw the calm look in her face and he couldn't tell what the hell she was thinking as they silently sized one another up. She moved her XP sniper rifle, enclosed in a rain proof sheath to her left hand. Thrusting out her right hand toward him, he heard her say, "I'm Chastain. Sergeant Killmer?"

Mace stared down at her offered hand. She had long, tapered fingers. A graceful woman's hand. He quickly saw a number of old, white scars across the pack of her hand. A part of him wanted to grip her hand and feel her flesh, feel her feminine fingers. Another part reared back in anger. He refused to take her hand, glaring down at her. Mace saw her full lips purse, her eyes hardening as she dropped her hand.

"I'm Killmer. Shield was supposed to send a man," he snarled. "What the hell happened?"

"They decided a man couldn't handle this assignment, Sergeant. So they sent a woman instead."

He reared back at her droll reply, her gaze unwavering and never leaving his, challenging him. Mace would have respected her if she'd been a man. Never mind that he could see the soft fullness of her breasts even beneath that thick cammie jacket she wore. Chastain was tall. Maybe five ten or five eleven. And she sure as hell wasn't afraid of HIM, her face giving nothing away except the fact she was pissed off at his poor manners.

"This is a mistake," he growled. He called in his men, ordering them to meet them. They had to make tracks or they could run into Volkov and his blood thirsty team.

"Sure is," she said in a growl that matched his own. "Let's get this show on the road. I want Volkov sooner, not later." And then she added acidly, "So I can get the hell away from the likes of you as soon as possible."

Mace almost laughed. Almost. Well, he could see she was nothing like Lauren Parker insofar as personality went. "What'd you do, Sugar? Drink a quart of vinegar this morning for breakfast?"

Her fine nostrils quivered and her eyes went narrow as she considered his gruff reply. "I don't like bullies, Sergeant." She jammed her index finger down at the damp floor of the jungle. "Let's settle this right now because I don't want to spend one more minute in this team energy of yours with your attitude. I'M NOT YOUR ENEMY. Volkov is. So get your head screwed on straight about this op and stop this sniping at me because I'm sure as hell not taking it from anyone. Especially you."

Available from Lindsay McKenna

Blue Turtle Publishing

SHADOW TEAM SERIES
Last Stand
Collateral Damage
No Quarter
Unforgettable

NON-SERIES BOOKS
Down Range (Reprint)
Dangerous Prey (Reprint)
Love Me Before Dawn (Reprint)
Point of Departure (Reprint)
Touch the Heavens (Reprint)

WOMEN OF GLORY SERIES
No Quarter Given (Reprint)
The Gauntlet (Reprint)
Under Fire (Reprint)

LOVE & GLORY SERIES
A Question of Honor, Book 1 (Reprint)
No Surrender, Book 2 (Reprint)
Return of a Hero, Book 3 (Reprint)
Dawn of Valor, Book 4 (Reprint)

LOVE & DANGER SERIES
Morgan's Son, Book 5 (Reprint)
Morgan's Wife, Book 6 (Reprint)
Morgan's Rescue, Book 7 (Reprint)
Morgan's Marriage, Book 8 (Reprint)

WARRIORS FOR THE LIGHT
Unforgiven, Book 1 (Reprint)
Dark Truth, Book 2 (Reprint)
The Quest, Book 3 (Reprint)
Reunion, Book 4 (Reprint)
The Adversary, Book 5 (Reprint)
Guardian, Book 6 (Reprint)

DELOS

Last Chance, prologue novella to Nowhere to Hide
Nowhere to Hide, Book 1
Tangled Pursuit, Book 2
Forged in Fire, Book 3
Broken Dreams, Book 4
Blind Sided, BN2
Secret Dream, B1B novella, epilogue to Nowhere to Hide
Hold On, Book 5
Hold Me, 5B1, sequel to Hold On
Unbound Pursuit, 2B1 novella, epilogue to Tangled Pursuit
Secrets, 2B2 novella, sequel to Unbound Pursuit, 2B1
Snowflake's Gift, Book 6
Never Enough, 3B1, novella, sequel to Forged in Fire
Dream of Me, 4B1, novella, sequel to Broken Dreams
Trapped, Book 7
Taking a Chance 7B1, novella, sequel to Trapped
The Hidden Heart, 7B2, novella, sequel to Taking A Chance
Boxcar Christmas, Book 8
Sanctuary, Book 9
Dangerous, Book 10
Redemption, 10B1, novella, sequel to Dangerous

Kensington

SILVER CREEK SERIES

Silver Creek Fire
Courage Under Fire

WIND RIVER VALLEY SERIES

Wind River Wrangler
Wind River Rancher
Wind River Cowboy
Christmas with my Cowboy
Wrangler's Challenge
Lone Rider
Wind River Lawman
Kassie's Cowboy
Home to Wind River
Western Weddings: Wind River Wedding
Wind River Protector
Wind River Undercover

Everything Lindsay McKenna

My website is dedicated to all my series. There are articles on characters, my publishing schedule, and information about each book written by me. You can also learn more about my newsletter, which covers my upcoming books, publishing schedule, giveaways, exclusive cover peeks and more.

lindsaymckenna.com

Made in United States
Troutdale, OR
01/21/2024